WINTER

D0169772

FRANKIE ROSE

Cover design by Frankie Rose
Formatting by Max Effect

"Never regret thy fall,

O Icarus of the fearless flight

For the greatest tragedy of them all

Is never to feel the burning light."

-OSCAR WILDE

PLEASE BE AWARE that the original version of this book was published under the pen name Nikita Rae back in December, 2013.

There are **SIGNIFICANT DIFFERENCES** between this book and the original, namely that a number of chapters have been removed, and others have been added from Luke's perspective.

THE ENDING is very different, too, in that there is no cliffhanger. I can't say any more without ruining the ending for those who haven't read the story…

If you have **ALREADY READ** Winter and intend to buy book two, Summer, when it is released, it would be **ADVISABLE TO RE-READ** this version in advance. Some points may not make sense in the second instalment of the story otherwise.

Best,

Frankie

ONE

CEILIDH

THE NAMES of the men my father killed are a mantra, a twisted beat to accompany the throb of my heart and every single step I take through life. *Sam O'Brady. Jefferson Kyle. Adam Bright. Sam O'Brady. Jefferson Kyle. Adam Bright.*

When I breathe in, it's Sam. When I breathe out, it's Jefferson, or Jeff, depending on how well you knew him. Adam exists somewhere in the space between breaths, the stretched-out moments when I forget to breathe at all. I knew Adam. He was Maggie's father, the basketball coach at Breakwater High. His brother was the town's mayor, so everyone had known his face.

I had this dream that once I escaped the confines of Breakwater, things would change for me, things wouldn't be as hard, but I haven't taken any chances. My family name is synonymous with pain and murder no matter where I seem to go, and that's why I've abandoned it. That's why, when I left my past behind in small town Wyoming to come to college, I became

Avery Patterson.

"Avery! Hey, Avery! Wait up!" Morgan Kepler jogs after me down the corridor as I exit my English class. She either recognizes me by my bright blonde hair, or because I'm clutching my file to my chest, keeping my head down like always. I give her a smile as I hurry out of the School of International and Public Affairs, one of the most infamous landmarks of Columbia University. Morgan, for some reason, has befriended me. She's wild and outspoken in a way I never have been. Maybe I would have turned out like her if my father hadn't shot three men dead when I was fourteen years old. But then again, who knows who I could have been.

Morgan smells like mint gum and Issey Miyake. She flashes me a bright smile when she pitches up at my side, nudging me with her shoulder. "Are you coming to the ceilidh tonight?" The word—sounds like "Kaylee"—is foreign to me.

"The *what* now?"

She twists her dark auburn hair around her index finger and grins. "Irish for party, apparently. The girls from Upsilon are dressing up as sexy leprechauns. Bitches."

I groan, hiding behind my folder. "No way, Kepler." Sexy leprechauns, my ass. And Greek girls? I'm not spending my evening hanging out with a bunch of Xanax-popping, neurotic bitches. Especially when it's a Thursday and last time I checked, classes aren't done 'til Friday. "I'm not partying tonight. I have midterms next week."

"So do I," Morgan laughs. "But that doesn't mean I can't give myself one night off." She lets go of her own hair to tug at mine. I find myself wishing I'd given in to the insane urge I'd had to chop it all off a few nights back. If it were an inch long instead of curling loosely well past my shoulders, she would have nothing to grab hold of. Most importantly, guys wouldn't stare at me whenever I passed them in the corridor, making assumptions based on my appearance. Blonde equals easy. Blonde equals stupid. The majority of girls at Columbia with hair my color get it out of a bottle and are known for being all party. I've considered going brunette.

I slap Morgan's hand away, giving her a tight smile. "I'm no good at cramming. I have to work harder than you to score a good grade. At this rate I'm gonna be a massive failure and no one will hire me. I'm gonna have to come live with you for the rest of my life. You'll be forever wishing you'd let me alone so I could concentrate."

"Pssshhh." She tips her head back, moaning. "Please! We're going to be living together after college, anyway. And besides, you're never gonna be home. You're going to be some hotshot journo that gets invited to all the celeb parties, out all night harassing the A-list elite for the inside track on their failing marriages and boob jobs."

Morgan has entirely the wrong idea about why I want to become a journalist. The very last thing I have in mind is reporting on the society and celebrity columns. "Yeah. Real funny."

"Avery!" Morgan hooks her arm through mine and pulls me off my path toward the Low Memorial Library, instead guiding me off campus, towards Morningside Heights, where we both live. "You have to start enjoying yourself." She gives me the look she reserves only for me, the one that says I'm losing myself again. I told Morgan about my dad by mistake; she is the only person at Columbia University who knows. We got so drunk one night that I threw up into a trashcan on Broadway and blabbed the whole story—the shock of being told my dad had committed suicide after he'd killed three other members of the Breakwater community, that I'd been a social pariah since that day, and had been kicked and punched and bullied through the last four years of high school.

I barely knew Morgan at the time. I was seriously lucky that she was a loyal friend from the outset. I almost killed myself creating this new persona; I don't know what I would have done if I couldn't be someone new here. Avery Patterson's an ordinary girl from Idaho. Her extended family didn't disown her because of her father's transgressions, and her own mother certainly didn't dump her on her father's best friend's doorstep so she could forget all about her old life to become a coldblooded prosecutor in the city.

Morgan draws her eyebrows together, arching over piercing gray eyes. "You *know* we have to go," she says.

I groan again. "But why?"

"Because I'm a redhead. I look killer in green. And you need to get laid."

I thump her arm as she pulls me through the entrance of our building on 125th Street, guiding me up the first flight of stairs. "That's the very last thing I need. I don't have—"

"If you say you don't have time for sex, I am literally going to scream!" A group of girls on their way down the stairs stop talking to shoot us both dirty looks.

"You're making people think I'm a complete whore, Morgan."

"So what? You'd find life a whole lot more fun if you were a bit more 'free' with your attention."

I don't justify that with a response. She opens the door to her apartment and I head straight for her room, throwing myself down onto her bed. My shared apartment is another three floors up, so we usually hang out at her place between classes because it means less cardio. Unfortunately, we weren't lucky enough to score each other as roommates in the housing lottery and no one was brave enough to trade off the books.

"You haven't been on a single date since the start of college. You realize that's what your freshman year is for, right? Meeting guys? Everyone knows this." Morgan begins hunting for clothes. She's one of those people that appears tidy and organized on the surface but in reality is all over the place. That certainly explains the row of empty hangers and the towering pile of scrunched-up satin and lace in her closet. And under her bed. I like how carefree Morgan is, but sometimes her messiness makes me nervous. My apartment? My apartment is spotless—

4

something my roommate Leslie has been good enough to maintain.

"I thought freshman year was about figuring out what you wanted to major in. Laying the groundwork for achieving a solid degree," I tell Morgan. She ignores me, throwing random items of green material at me.

"Yeah, but you've already done both of those things. Oh!" Her head appears around her closet door. "You know, I can find someone to take you if you like?"

"Jeez, Morgan, I'm not going!"

"Yes, you are. Hey, is your mom still paying you a ridiculously huge allowance each month to make up for the fact that she's a bitch?"

My shoulders slump. Dear Lord, the girl is so transparent. This isn't the first time she's used my mother's American Express to buy herself a new outfit. "We are *not* going shopping right now."

AS USUAL, through diabolical and nefarious means, Morgan gets what she wants. Later that night I find myself pressed up against a horny leprechaun-ette and a shirtless guy with a painted green torso. Whether that's an Irish thing or not I don't know, but he certainly smells of whiskey. When their make out session develops into heavy petting, I decide enough is enough. Morgan is talking to Tate by the kegs, laughing behind her hand the way she does when she's flirting. She thinks her smile is bad because her lower teeth are slightly crooked. She should be thanking her lucky stars she wasn't forced through the nightmarish dentistry ordeals I was as a kid, just to satisfy her mother's vain pursuit of possessing the "perfect" child. Yeah, that's right—*possessing.* Like I was an inanimate object or something.

Morgan and Tate have had an on-off thing for the past six months, and watching them skirt around each other, pretending to be only vaguely interested, is getting really boring.

"I'm leaving," I announce when I manage to shove my way through the crowd towards them. Morgan drops her hand from her mouth and scowls at me.

"No way, we just got here!"

"It's one thirty. We've been here three hours, and I'm sick of random douchebags with green face paint grinding on me and calling me *darlin'*. No one can pull off a decent Irish accent when they're wasted."

"There are a couple of Irish people here. I bet they can," Tate interjects.

I hitch an eyebrow. "Regardless of any genuine, bona fide Irish people in attendance at this party, it's still time to go home."

Morgan jabs me with her index finger, not hard enough to hurt but hard enough to tell me I'm ruining her chances of screwing Tate. "You're a complete buzzkill, young lady."

"Don't worry, you can stay. I'm all right to walk back on my own."

"No way. Didn't you read the college orientation and safety handbook? No walking alone at night." Morgan shoots Tate an apologetic look. "Maybe we could catch up tomorrow night instead?"

"Sure. We could rent a movie. Night, ladies." He turns and disappears into the press of bodies leaping up and down to the sounds of "Jump Around" by House Of Pain. Morgan pokes her tongue out at me.

"I could strangle you sometimes." She grins as she says this, though. Bitch is fickle. She'll have forgiven me before we reach our building. We don't get that far, though. Halfway down the steps leading from the frat house, a police car pulls up on the sidewalk, the red and blues rotating, throwing tall shadows across the street. The girls in tiny green mini skirts and high heels smoking outside scatter when the siren buzzes, squealing like morons.

6

"Shit!" Morgan wrings her jacket in her hands. "Can we get by without them talking to us?"

"Don't freak out. It's probably just a noise complaint."

"No, Ave. I don't wanna get caught up with these guys tonight."

Morgan doesn't exactly have a healthy respect for the law, but there's no reason she should be so worried about a three-second telling off. "Don't freak out, it's gonna be fine."

I immediately regret my words. That happens way too frequently these days. When the doors of the police car open and the two officers step out, my stomach falls through the floor. "Oh, *shit!*"

"What? *What?*" Morgan clenches the top of my arm, fingernails digging into my skin. She looks absolutely terrified.

"Nothing, it's just ..."

Luke Reid.

Luke Reid is what. I haven't seen him in his uniform in almost four years, but not much has changed. He still looks smoking hot in it. Luke was the all-star hero of Breakwater High. Girls dropped at his feet like swooning maidens in distress in the hope that he would catch them as they fell. I'd been dazed by Luke in the same way most fourteen-year-olds are dazed by god-like seniors. People had actually mourned when he'd graduated, students and teachers alike. He'd passed on a full ride to college courtesy of a football scholarship to join the police force. He kept in touch with me after he left for one reason and one reason only. A reason I don't want to think about right now. A reason I've tried to forget all about in the three months since I moved to New York City and successfully managed to avoid his ass.

His black hair is shorter than usual but still a little longer than a cop's probably should be. Same deep brown eyes, though. Same strong jaw line. Shock registers on his face when he catches sight of me. He pauses for a second as he walks around the car, taking a moment to rein in the surprise of me tripping down a set of frat house steps in one of Morgan's impossibly short tube dresses. I cringe at the look on his face. He doesn't seem too impressed.

"Iris?"

My whole body shrinks away from that name. I glance at Morgan and see the surprise in her eyes. I told her my real name, but she's never heard anyone use it. "Iris?" she hisses. "Does this guy know you?"

"I'll explain later," I whisper. I take a deep breath and face Luke, trying to pretend I'm sober. That doesn't work, of course. My breath smells like Bud Light and the plastic cup of warm whiskey I found on the sticky kitchen counter an hour ago. "Hey." I give him a weak smile. "Been a while."

"Yeah…" He looks quickly from me to Morgan and back again, clearly trying to piece everything together in his head. I feel strangely sorry for him. Ironic, right? Of the two of us, I'm the pathetic one in our odd relationship. Luke sends me a twisted smile. "I went back to Break a couple of months ago. Stopped by Brandon's but he said your mom had shipped you up here to college. I did a search but I couldn't find you registered anywhere."

My cheeks redden. It never occurred to me that he'd actually look for me when he couldn't find me. People move on with their lives all the time. They move away from home. They get new jobs and they run from their shitty pasts. Even regular people do that. I kind of figured he'd shrug his shoulders and move on. Maybe be glad of the fact that he wouldn't need to feel quite so responsible for me anymore. Instead, he searched the police database to find out which school I was attending? Does the police database even contain that kind of information? I don't know what to think about that. I shiver and pull myself closer to Morgan. She is as stiff as a board, staring straight at Luke. I nod, biting my lip.

"Yeah, you wouldn't have. I changed my name. I didn't want … I didn't …"

"I understand," he says, saving me from saying it. Loud shouts and cheers leak out onto the street as the doors fly open and three girls teeter down the steps behind us. They immediately freeze, their hyena-like laughter paused as soon as they land eyes on Luke and his partner. At first I think it's because they're cops, but the tallest one, a brunette with smoky, dark, fuck-me eye make-up squeals and rushes forward, placing a well-manicured hand over her ample cleavage. "Oh my god, you're Luke Reid, aren't you?"

Luke looks seriously uncomfortable. Like he just got caught with his pants down in a big way. His partner rolls his eyes. "Here we go again."

Luke clears his throat. "I'm on duty, ladies. Have you been drinking tonight?"

The smile drops from the brunette's face. Her two blonde friends grab her by either arm and start guiding her down the stairs. "No! No way, officer. We were just leaving," one chuckles nervously. From the look on the brunette's face she might just be willing to get busted drinking underage if it means she gets to stay and talk for another minute. She's walking backwards, mouth open, as her drunk buddies drag her away.

I can't help it. I have to ask. My black heart is inquisitive. "What the hell was *that*?"

Luke rubs a hand across his jaw, looking away. "I've played a couple of times in a few bars. Sometimes people recognize me."

Luke's always played guitar, not that I ever really got to hear him. When we were at school, it was enough for most of us lovesick teenagers to sit and observe him and his friends from a distance. He always seemed pretty shy about playing, anyway. Always did it somewhere far from lunch crowds. And now he's apparently playing in bars? "What, like in a band?"

Luke's partner answers before he can even open his mouth. "Yeah. Reid's quite the celebrity. We got us some One Direction shit right here."

9

Luke bites down on his jaw, his embarrassment suddenly gone. In fact, he looks seriously pissed off. "Can you just shut the hell up? Go inside and scare some teenagers, will you? Fuck."

His partner shrugs, completely unaffected. "Whatever you say, man." He stomps up the steps, one hand on the hilt of his night stick like he's planning on making use of it any second now. Cheering blares out into the night again as he lets himself inside. Luke rubs at the back of his neck, staring at my feet.

"So, uh, you're tearing up the place, huh? We've had five phone calls about loud music and disturbance at this address."

I look back at the house, seeing all the drunk people, painted green, laughing and swigging back beer inside. It doesn't look great that I'm stumbling out of the building, especially since those girls a moment ago weren't the only ones not old enough to be drinking. "We were just leaving, too, actually."

"Uhuh." Luke stares at me for a moment, his dark eyebrows twitching like he wants to frown. "Why don't you guys wait until we're done here? This'll only take a second. I'd really like to talk to you, Iri—" He breaks off, and I catch the look in his eye. Hurt? Definitely conflicted. He doesn't know what to call me.

"Avery," I say quietly.

"Avery." He nods. "It's nice. I'll get used to it."

I send him a faintly apologetic smile and clear my throat. "We're in a rush to get home. I have to be up real early. Could we catch up another time?"

The radio over Luke's breast pocket squeals, making Morgan jump out of her skin. Static fills the air for a second before Luke leans down and speaks into it.

"Unit 23 responding to noise complaint. Copy." He looks torn as he allows another couple of girls to skitter off down the street. From inside the house, the sound of smashing glass and then a riotous cheer makes him frown harder. "I really have to sort this out. Can I call you tomorrow?"

Morgan's fingernails dig into my arm. What the hell is her

problem? "Tomorrow's fine. I have to study for my midterms, but yeah …"

"Okay, tomorrow. Write down your number." He hands me his notebook—it has his police number and an embossed golden badge on the front. I flip it open, looking up to find him watching me as I quickly scribble down my cell phone number. I give it back and he purses his lips. "Thanks."

We pass on the steps as Morgan and I descend and he goes up, and I see that look in his eye that always makes me dread our catch-ups. It's pity. I hate being looked at like that. As Morgan and I make our way back towards campus, I wish I'd thought faster. I wish I'd been sober or smart enough to write down the wrong number.

TWO

ROSITO'S

MORGAN MAKES me run the next morning. Running and I aren't even vaguely acquainted let alone best friends; it takes a few strongly worded threats and the promise of chocolate waffles to get me out the door at six a.m. It's bitterly cold, the morning air determined to freeze my lungs from the inside out. We last all of twenty minutes before the temperature gets the better of us and we head to Jacquie's Breakfast Diner.

"You realize," I say, sliding into the booth opposite Morgan, "ordering pancakes with a ton of maple syrup is going to make your ass fatter?"

"Fuck you."

"Fuck you right back."

The woman in the booth opposite us glares, not that Morgan notices. "So, we going to put it off much longer?"

I squint at her, trying to ascertain whether there's any point in pretending I don't know what she's talking about. It's not every morning she shows up on my doorstep demanding exercise. This is all subterfuge, and I know what she's after. Her jaw is set, which means I am shit outta luck. Luke. She wants to know about Luke. "He's just a guy I used to know back home," I tell her.

"And?"

"And nothing."

"Don't give me that, *Iris*," Morgan quips. "There's a whole well of gossip here and you've been holding out on me."

My face blanches at her use of my real name. I haven't had to hear it in months. Even my mom calls me Avery now. It's as though, if she can pretend I'm someone else and not Maxwell Breslin's daughter, she, in turn, can pretend she was married to some other guy named Patterson and not a cold-blooded murderer.

I look down and see that my hands have clenched tight and I'm ruining the waffle house's laminated menu. Morgan sees. She screws her face up into a fairly good impersonation of remorse. "Fuck. Sorry, Ave. I'm not too smart sometimes."

"It's okay. I just … I'm not her anymore." I make myself sick sometimes. I think I'm getting stronger and then I end up saying something like that, something that makes me sound weak as fuck, and I think about killing myself. Not because I'm sad and tired of feeling like this, which I am, but because I'm pissed off and exhausted with feeling like this. But killing myself is just about as weak as it gets, I figure.

"I know," Morgan says. "I won't do that again, I promise."

I shoot her a guilty smile, but a part of me fizzes a little inside. I occasionally think that, even though she's been a great friend to me, Morgan *likes* to say the wrong thing sometimes. Like it makes her feel better about herself or more powerful or something. "Thanks."

The waitress comes and takes our order; we both get the same thing—Belgian waffles with chocolate sauce. By the time our coffee arrives, Morgan is over her mild/pretend embarrassment of upsetting me and back in Spanish Inquisition mode.

"So, how do you know him?" The salacious glint in her eye tells me she's hoping for a hot hook-up story. Boy, is she going to be disappointed.

"He went to my school. He was a cop in my home town for a few years before he moved out here."

"Uhuh …" She nods, taking a sip of her coffee, never taking her eyes off me.

"That's it."

"That's it?"

"Yeah."

She looks around the room like she can't believe what she's hearing.

"You knew that guy back in Hicksville and you didn't claim him immediately? What's wrong with you, girl? You do realize he's fucking beautiful, don't you?"

I blow out a long breath and drop my head against the table. "Yes, I know how hot he is. He was also twenty when he left town and I was sixteen. Plus he has a girlfriend: Casey Fisher. They dated the whole way through high school. Moved out here together and everything. So …"

"None of that should have been a problem."

I just stare at her. If the tables were turned and I was saying drastically inappropriate things, Morgan would be rolling her eyes right now. My mother forbade that particular trait when I was younger, though. I haven't been able to do it ever since, despite how much I may want to. "Well, it would have been pretty difficult. And illegal. And besides, I was a mess. My dad …"

A horrified expression develops on Morgan's face. "Fuck. This guy didn't … was he on the force when your dad, when he …"

Killed three men. People always have trouble spitting that one out. I focus out of the window, trying to shut out the memory of Luke Reid on my doorstep, telling my mom that my dad was dead. My cheeks have flushed red; this is another one of those moments where I think Morgan might be saying the wrong thing on purpose. I can't call her out on it, though. She'll think I'm crazy. Instead, I tell her, "He and his partner were the first officers on the scene. He'd only been on the job four days. Nothing like that had ever really happened in Break before. He puked in my mom's rose bushes."

"Man, I'm sorry, dude. I'm hopeless sometimes. There just seemed to be something there between you, so I thought …"

"There *is* something there. Luke's always felt sorry for me. I suppose being the one to find my dad and the others imprinted itself onto his brain and now he can't shake it. We used to meet up whenever he was back in town. Mostly we'd grab a coffee and he'd just talk at me." Our conversation stops when the waitress arrives with our food. I stare intensely down at my waffles, wishing I'd ordered something different. I keep on meaning to become a black-coffee-and-bagel New York City person, and I keep on forgetting. I push the plate away, and I go back to staring out the window.

Sam O'Brady. Jefferson Kyle. Adam Bright. Sam O'Brady. Jefferson Kyle. Adam Bright.

"That other cop said he was in a band, right? I wonder where they play. Hey, if you want me to answer your phone later, I can ask him if you don't wanna seem too eager?" She clearly didn't just hear a word I said—that for the past five years I have associated Luke Reid with finding out my dad was dead. The girl has selective hearing. I shoot daggers at her and she shrinks back into her seat. "Or I can tell him you have avian bird flu and you can never see him again. It's no problem. I am a master of deception."

I allow myself a small laugh and kick her under the table. Maybe a little harder than I need to. "It's all right. I can handle it."

But I honestly don't know if I can. Having Luke in my life here is like bringing a piece of Breakwater into the relatively safe, happy world I've built for myself at Columbia. It could ruin everything. When I speak to him later, I know what I am going to do. I'm going to tell him the truth. He'll have to understand that I want to put my past behind me. Surely no one in the world could begrudge me that.

LAST CLASS of the day is Media Law and Ethics, one of my favorite subjects, but I bolt out of the building as soon as Professor Lang excuses us. Usually I hang back to catch him after class. He doesn't seem to mind that I have an exhaustive list of questions that always needs answering. I'm the annoying bastard in the front row who won't shut up. Today, though, all I want to do is get back to my place and check my phone to see if Luke has called. I need to get this over with. The calm that I've found in being utterly inconspicuous here is going to be ruined until I tell him I don't want to meet with him anymore. That I don't want to see him ever again.

I take the low steps outside my building at a jog and race up the four flights of stairs to my apartment, hoping Leslie won't be there. My housemate wears too much perfume. She also spends a lot of time studying in the library, especially after class, so there's a possibility that I'm going to have some privacy. When I burst through the door, my heart sinks in my chest. Leslie sits on the sofa with her headphones in, tapping her bare foot on the worn leather as she types on her laptop. She glances up at me, cropped brunette hair all over the place as usual, and gives me a half smile, pulling out one of the earphones. She's an active listener, the kind of person to smile and nod regardless of what's being said to her. It drives me a little crazy, though not as crazy as Morgan, who's just not listening at all most of the time.

Leslie smiles as soon as she sees me. "Good run this morning?"

So I wasn't the only person Morgan woke up banging on the

apartment door at five thirty this morning. I pull a sour face and throw my bag on the table. "Sorry about that. She's incredibly pushy sometimes."

Leslie shrugs a shoulder. "S'okay. I got up right after you left and squeezed some study in. Everything worked out for the best."

Leslie is a New Yorker through and through. Her parents are internet business gurus who set up a dot-com company back in the early nineties. They sold up about five years ago and have been comfortably living off the interest of their amassed fortune ever since. Leslie's studying business in the hope that one day she'll have a fortune of her own, but in the meantime she's okay with accepting the healthy amounts of cash her mom and dad throw at her. She's like me in some ways; her bank account is always full but her parents barely know who she is. At least she *has* two parents. And one of them isn't Max Breslin.

I kick off my sneakers and flop back onto the sofa, reaching for my cell on the coffee table where I'd left it earlier before classes started. I normally take it with me, but I knew I'd be looking at it every five minutes if I had it on me today. I didn't need that kind of distraction.

My heart speeds up as I hit the start button. Nothing. No texts. No missed calls. *Nothing.* I blow out the breath I've been holding and toss my phone back onto my pillow.

"Expecting a call?" Leslie asks.

I stare up at the ceiling. There are sticky marks dotted all over it where glow-in-the-dark stars were tacked to it when we moved in. I knew I was going to get along with Leslie the moment she suggested we pull them down. "Dreading one, more like," I mutter.

She *hmm*s like she knows all about that, but she doesn't ask questions. I set myself up at my desk, placing my phone beside the keyboard so I can answer it straight away if Luke does call. He probably knew I had classes all day and he's waiting until this evening. That thought makes my stomach roll. I spend half an hour trying to type up the vague notes I scribbled in class but they are less than useless. I give up in the end. I type in my email account details and decide to clear out my inbox instead. Two new messages wait for me.

The first is from Amanda St. French. My mom. She filed the paperwork to go back to her maiden name before they'd even finished shoveling the soil into my dad's yawning grave. She didn't go to the funeral. It was just Brandon and I. The priest banged on for twenty minutes about the grievous sins committed by people in this life and how we needed to beg for repentance if we were ever to be accepted into heaven. That had scared the crap out of me when I was younger. My dad hadn't been religious, and I was haunted for years by the idea that he was burning up in hell because he hadn't had the opportunity to repent. After that, I spent a long time angry, hoping that he really was burning in hell because of what he'd done. Because he'd ruined my life. Now ... now I don't know what I think anymore.

The subject bar on Mom's email is blank as usual. Her message will be the same script she sends me at the beginning of each month, detailing that she's deposited my allowance in my account. She always manages to make it sound like I'm not grateful—not grateful that she is paying my way at college. Not grateful that she finally helped me escape Breakwater once and for all, when she was the person who abandoned me there in the first place.

Aviary,

Find attached a copy of the remit for your allowance. Remember to keep hold of these for your records. I have increased the amount this month in light of the approaching holidays. You might like to do something with your friends at Christmas. I am headed to Hawaii with my sister. She has had some troubles with her new husband and wants to go snorkeling to take her mind off things. I assume you will be headed back to Brandon's for Thanksgiving?

Hope you are well,
Amanda.

Aviary? I choke back a dry laugh. She can't even spell my new name. That error could be forgiven by the fact that it's new and she is still learning to use it, but the other things, the other hurtful aspects of the email, make my blood boil. The whole thing's stilted robot speak—my mother hasn't used a contraction a day in her life—that makes it sound like she's communicating with a complete stranger, not an actual person she pushed out of her vagina. And she's heading to Hawaii with her sister for Christmas? Oh, I wasn't under any illusion that I'd be spending Christmas with my mother despite the fact that we live in the same city now. No, I am more stunned by the way she said *my sister* instead of your Aunt Clare. And going to Brandon's for Thanksgiving? The real pièce de résistance is her sign-off, though. *Amanda.* At least she used to admit to being my mother. Now it appears her sister is no longer my aunt and she is going to be Amanda from here on out. Tears prick at my eyes as I stare at the screen, refusing to blink until the text starts swimming. I don't cry very often, but when I do it's my mother who makes me.

I clear my throat and screw my eyes shut for a moment. When I open them, I hit the delete button. I am stronger than this now. I can't let her affect me anymore. The next email is from Brandon. I open it wearily, and my temper spikes. Mom blind-copied Brandon into the email she'd sent me, obviously her way of letting him know that I was being foisted off on him for yet another holiday.

Brandon had been my dad's best friend since elementary school. They'd played football together through college and they'd fallen in love with and married sisters. Brandon's wife, Mom's younger sister Melanie, died from cancer when I was two, and Mom hasn't been able to handle Brandon ever since.

She says he reminds her of Aunt Mel, so she keeps him at a distance. Apparently it's a repeating pattern of hers, neatly bundling together all the things she wishes she could forget.

Hi Avery,

Looks like your mom's going to be busy this holiday. Want to come and join me in my non-celebrations? You know how I don't go in for that sort of thing anymore, but it would be great to see you. We can burn some pumpkin pie and smoke some crack just like the good old days. Let me know if you need anything, kid. I'm only on the other end of a telephone.

Love Brandon

I've never smoked crack, let alone with my Uncle Brandon, but he has a wicked case of dad humor. He's convinced the college monitors our emails. He thinks it's funny to set off some red flags every now and then. I have no idea if the college does monitor our emails, or if smoking crack would actually even be a red flag, but it still makes me smile. I don't smile very often, but when I do it's Brandon who makes me. I miss him. Not enough to ever head back to Breakwater, of course. I am never going back there again.

I'm shutting down my computer, promising myself that I'll reply to Brandon tomorrow, when the door knocks. Morgan's too lazy to walk up to my apartment, so any visitors we get are usually for Leslie. My roommate's headphones block out the interruption, though, so it's left to me to answer. I'm really not expecting the person on the other side of the door.

"Luke? What are you doing here?"

Luke's out of uniform and wearing a plain black t-shirt and faded-out jeans. His look still carries a little of the skater style he used to rep in high school, although there's a rocky, harder edge to him now. It's always a surprise to see him in his casual clothes. Right now I'm surprised to see him period. He shoves

20

his hands in his pockets, drawing my attention to the fact that he's gotten some fresh ink. Black swirling lines peek out from below his shirtsleeves. Nowhere near low enough to ever be visible in his uniform but still low enough for me to see them when he hunches his shoulders.

"Sorry. I should have called but I got this feeling yesterday that you were gonna blow me off, and—"

Leslie yanks the door open wider behind me, tugging her headphones out of her ears. "Hi!" she says, her voice all easy breezy. "Are you a friend of Avery's?"

Luke smiles back cautiously—a rueful expression. "Yeah, I'm a friend of *Avery's.*"

This is only the second time he's ever said my name. It sounds strained coming out of his mouth. I stare at him, trying to figure out what the hell he is doing here. What he is doing *inside my apartment building.*

"Are you going to invite your friend in, Avery?" Leslie asks. I can hear the suggestion in her voice: *I can leave if you need me to.* I sigh and give Luke a look I hope isn't too difficult to read. Morgan always says I'm pretty transparent with my emotions, so there's a good chance he'll be able to tell I am seriously pissed.

"No. We're going out for coffee." I head into my room to collect my jacket and my purse and when I return to the living room, Leslie is still standing by the doorway, twirling her short hair around her finger. It's embarrassing to watch her devour him with her eyes. I'm used to it, though. Unlike Luke, who, despite how often this must happen to him, never seems to get over the embarrassment factor of being the cause of such predatory looks in women.

I storm past him into the hallway and set off walking without checking to see if he's following me. After all the times I've met with him and all the weirdly awkward conversations we've shared, I still don't know him well enough to be openly mad at him. He must sense the fact that I need some space because it isn't until we get to the exit of the building that he says anything.

"Hey, I'm sorry, okay? I know I've messed up here. Avery? Hey, Avery!" He grabs hold of my arm and spins me around. I'm grinding my jaw together to keep from saying anything I'll regret later. "Listen, this … I wouldn't usually do this, but I wanted to talk to you. There's something you should know. I wanted to tell you when I went back to Break in September but you were already gone. It's important."

I stand there with my jacket still in my hand, contemplating putting it on so I can stop shivering, but I'm too hyper-aware of him staring at me to move. I huff out a deep breath and stare at my shoes. Luke's hand brushes mine for a second as he takes my jacket and leans forward so he can put it over my shoulders.

"It's November, Avery," he whispers. "You're gonna get hypothermia."

I shrug it off so I can thread my arms into it properly. "Okay. So you want to tell me something? You should probably do that so I can get back to studying. I have those midterms I told you about last night, remember?"

"Can we go grab some food? I came straight over after I finished my shift. I'm starving."

I fold my arms across my chest and glare at him. "How did you even know which was my apartment?"

"How do you think? I slipped some chick in the hall a fifty and she told me."

This would be another great time for an eye roll. "Great. Now people are gonna think I have random guys coming up here at all hours."

"Avery, c'mon." Smoke billows on his breath when he speaks. He shoves his hands into his pockets again, tensing his shoulders against the cold. Having just told me off about not wearing my jacket, it is kind of ironic that he doesn't have one.

I shake my head and scowl. "Where's your car?"

"In the ProPark." He nods his head up the street and starts walking slowly, making sure I'm following. I ball up my fists in my pockets, contemplating just turning around and going back inside. I don't though. I trail after him, seething the whole way.

LUKE PARKS up outside Rosito's and jogs around his '67 Ford Fastback to open my door before I have a chance to do it for myself. The journey over to the restaurant was quiet. Too quiet. I don't know what he wants to talk to me about but he was on edge and that put *me* on edge. I mean, what can he possibly think is so important? There are only a few topics of conversation that we can really share, and all of them lead back to Breakwater. I sure as fuck don't want to talk about that place, but Luke looks determined. He always was stubborn. He hasn't changed much since high school, really. Sure, he's perhaps a tiny bit taller and he's definitely filled out, but the twenty-three-year-old version of him looks pretty similar to the eighteen-year-old version.

I step out of the car, giving him a begrudging smile of thanks as I dodge past him to jog for the restaurant door. Luke doesn't hang around either. We both sigh a little when I pull open the pasta house door and a blast of hot air hits us in a wall of heat. At least I don't have to add freezing cold to my list of reasons to be uncomfortable.

A waitress with orthopedic shoes and a name tag that says, *Welcome! I'm Rosie!* shows us to a table, grinning in an inane way that says she's probably been doing the job for many years and she doesn't even realize she's smiling anymore. She supplies us with some menus and a wine list and leaves us to it.

"You gonna eat?" Luke asks, flipping open his menu.

"I guess." I scan the menu and pick out a duck and squash ravioli dish that sounds good and then go about picking my nails under the table. Luke slides my menu away and places it with his at the edge of the table to signal that we've decided. I glance up at him, waiting for him to say something. It's annoying when he doesn't; he's dragged me here, after all. If we have to sit through an awkward dinner before he gets to the point, my nerves are going to end up irreparably damaged. We have to talk about something. It's all too tempting to just sit here and appreciate how amazingly long his eyelashes look against his skin as he scans the room. Dark, like charcoal smudges. I shake my head. I don't want to think about things like eyelashes or biceps or perfectly straight teeth and smiles that make my stomach feel quivery. I'm not the kind of person who gets to think about shit like that.

"So …" I do my best to make my voice light. "Are you still with Casey?"

Luke's mouth twists up at the corner. He drums his fingers against the starched white tablecloth. "Not for over a year now."

My eyebrows shoot up. I told Morgan he had a girlfriend just to get her off my back, not doubting that he and Casey would still be together. Theirs was one of those rock-solid high-school-sweetheart-type affairs. Saccharine sweet. Luke and I haven't ever really talked about relationships before. If he and Casey broke up over a year ago, that means he was single the last time we met for coffee back in Break. Why would he mention that, though? He never tells me about his life. He just wants to know about mine.

"Oh. I'm sorry," I say, because it seems like the appropriate thing to say.

He shrugs. "Don't be. I'm not. It was mutual." He picks up the saltshaker and sets about twisting it around in his hands. "What about you? You still dating … what was his name?"

"Justin. And no. That relationship lasted all of five minutes. He found out about my dad and, well … you know how it is."

Luke chews on his lip. "People are just jerks, Iris. There are good ones out there, though."

He doesn't realize he's forgotten my new name. I shift uncomfortably in my seat, about to remind him, also about to laugh bitterly at the possibility there's a guy alive willing to date me after the crazy shit that's gone down in my family, but before I can do any of that Rosie returns with a small notepad in hand. Luke orders Bolognese—why do guys always do that when they order pasta? Always with the Bolognese—and a beer. I order my ravioli and smirk when I tack a beer on at the end, too. Luke doesn't bat a single one of those long black eyelashes at my order. Neither does Rosie. She set us up with cutlery and disappears without any chitchat, which makes her the very best waitress in the world. Our beers arrive and I take a long pull at the bottle before setting it down and squaring off at Luke. "You get why I'm mad, right?"

He replaces the saltshaker with his beer, which he rolls between his hands, fiercely studying the bottle. "Yeah, I'm not entirely oblivious. I know I'm probably the very last person you want to see. I keep cropping up in your life. I get that you want to move on. I've been pretty selfish over the past few years, continually rehashing everything with you, but I've been dealing with my own ..." he looks up at the ceiling, blows out a long breath, "bad memories, I guess. After tonight, I can totally understand if you never want to see me again. But there's something you need to know, and the news should come now and from a friendly face so you have time to prepare."

My stomach twists. None of this sounds good. Luke's face doesn't exactly look friendly, either; it looks crumpled and concerned. I hate it. I really fucking hate it. "Just tell me."

"Don't you want to eat first?"

If he waits one more second to explain what's going on, the hot ball of pent-up fear and paranoia in my chest is going to explode and all that will remain of me will be the crater left in the bench where I am sitting. "Please, jus—" I close my eyes and try to remember who I am now. *Avery Patterson. Avery Patterson. I. Am. In. Control.*

"Have you heard of the Wyoming Ripper?" Luke asks abruptly.

"No. Should I have?"

His brown eyes stare straight at me, making me twitch. His eyebrows pull together. "No, I guess not. You were young back then. People probably tried to keep news like that off your radar."

I grip hold of my beer and take another swig, never taking my eyes off him. He's building up to something, and I have a really bad feeling about it.

"The Wyoming Ripper was the name the media gave to a serial killer who murdered a string of teenaged girls in Wyoming about five years ago. They were," he flinches, picking at the label on his bottle, "they were pretty brutal murders, Iris." He immediately realizes his mistake this time and clenches his jaw. "Sorry. *Avery.* I *will* remember, I swear. Anyway, the murders stopped suddenly. There was never any other trace of the perpetrator. A lot of people on the force thought perhaps he'd died or something." Luke swallows. "Colby Bright's written a book claiming that your dad was the Wyoming Ripper. That the reason there were no more murders back then was because your dad killed himself. It's coming out in a couple of months. I thought you ought to know. The press … the media, well, they're gonna dig it all up again."

The beer bottle shakes in my hand. I set it down on the table and stare at the beveled rim of the glass. My mind stops working but my body seems to kick itself into overdrive. This is an all-too-familiar sensation. I start to tremble, every part of me vibrating like the very molecules I'm constructed out of are pulling in opposite directions, wanting to escape.

"Avery?"

I look up at Luke and open my mouth to speak. I'm breathing far too quickly. It feels like the oxygen I'm drawing inside my chest is carrying a thousand razor blades down my windpipe with it. *"Colby Bright?* Adam Bright's brother?" I whisper, my voice incredulous.

"Yeah. He's running for mayor again. It's purely a publicity stunt. They'll never be able to prove it was your dad who killed all those girls."

"Publicity?" I'm repeating random words now, but I can't for the life of me form a proper thought. I stand up and the room tilts on a drunken angle. "Excuse me."

Luke gets up when I leave the table, his hand pressing lightly on the base of my spine as I hurry toward the ladies' room. I shove back the swing door and rush into a stall before I throw up everywhere, getting most of it on the bathroom floor. The second time my stomach heaves I do better, hitting the bowl for the most part. This used to happen to me all the time, but not so much recently. It's only now, sitting on the floor of a chemical-smelling bathroom with regurgitated pancakes splattered all over my Chucks that I realize how long it's been since. I fall back and slump against the stall door, staring at the grainy pattern on the opposite wall. It takes ten minutes for the cold to seep up through the tiled floor and into my bones. I get to my feet and rinse out my mouth, doing my best to fix up my mascara where it's run. When I leave the bathroom, Luke is waiting for me, leaning up against the wall. He looks troubled.

"You want me to take you home?"

I walk numbly back to our table and sit down. "Yeah, but … I think I just need a minute. Can we wait a sec?"

"Sure." He sits back down in his seat and starts cracking his knuckles. "I'm sorry. I've been trying to think of a way to tell you but—"

"Do you think he did it?"

Luke goes still. "No. No, of course not. I knew your dad. He was …"

Loving? Kind? Always smiling? A complete joker?

I bite back the bile in my throat and snatch up my beer. The bottle's empty in three mouthfuls. "I need something stronger."

"I don't know if that's such a good idea."

At this point Rosie arrives with our food and my stomach clenches. She goes to set our plates down but Luke sighs and

27

holds up his hand. "Any chance we can get that to go?"

If Rosie's bothered or even cares that we're being difficult, she does a damn good job of hiding it. "Not a problem, kids."

She disappears with our food and returns a minute later with two plastic containers. Luke pays and we leave. Outside, he pauses at the passenger side of his Fastback. "If I take you home right now, what are you going to do?"

I grip my hands around my arms, too hollow to shiver or even react to the bitter weather. There's an arctic locker inside me, way colder than anything New York in November has to offer. "I'm going to call Morgan and she's going to hook me up with a bottle of Jack," I tell him, knowing that she will. She's my best friend, after all, and she has a stash of alcohol that would shame a liquor store. Her dependence on alcohol is almost at a level with mine. Only difference is I never buy any, especially when I know I can just drink all of hers.

Luke huffs. "If I take you to a bar and get you a shot, do you promise you'll go home and go to bed?"

I level my gaze with his and register the worried look on his face. "No."

He sags against the car and rakes his hands through his hair. "Okay. You're coming with me."

"Luke, no! I'll be fine, I—"

"You're a goddamned beautiful girl, Avery. I'm not letting you loose in New York City where any frat jerk could take advantage of you." He opens the car door and ushers me inside, and I comply without a fuss. I choose to ignore the fact that he just called me beautiful. I'm far too screwed up to feel weird about that right now. I have no idea where Luke's taking me but if it isn't towards a bottle of something seriously strong, I'm leaving. Half an hour later, we pull up outside a three-story brick building in Wiltshire. It looks like it was probably a factory of some sort once upon a time, but now it's apartments. Luke lets us in and leads me toward an elevator in the lobby, but I shake my head. I am already having trouble breathing. The last thing I need is an enclosed space. He seems to understand and we take the stairs up all three flights. There's only one door up here besides the scuffed metal ones giving entry to the elevator. Luke pulls a set of keys from the pocket of his jeans and opens the door.

The apartment is open plan and huge. I'm too empty to really look around, but I do notice a lot of black furniture and more than one guitar leaning up against the walls. Luke guides me to a breakfast bar, where he gathers up pencils, pens, and a stack of sheet music into a messy pile, clearing the countertop. He sits me down on a cushioned stool, then proceeds to rifle through his cupboards. After a second he produces two rocks glasses and sets them down on the counter.

"What's your poison?"

I look at the glasses and then look up at him. "You realize I'm going to be a mess," I say. I do get messy when I drink. It's the only way I cope some days.

"I know." He pulls a pack of cigarettes out of a drawer in the breakfast bar and ignites the gas ring on the cook top so he can stoop down and light it. "But if you need to be a mess, I'd rather you were a mess here where I can keep an eye on you. It's just me, Avery. I'm not going to judge you. I'll never judge you."

He hands me the cigarette and I take it even though I don't smoke. It burns as I pull on it and my head starts to spin again. I hand it back, fighting the urge to repeat my vomiting act from earlier.

"No?" he asks.

"No."

"Okay." He flicks on the extractor fan and smokes the cigarette in silence before running it under the tap and tossing the stub in the bin. When he comes back to the counter, he has an unopened bottle of whiskey in his hand. He pours us both a shot and does his—I watch his throat work as he swallows—but I hold mine in my hand, staring at the counter for a long moment before I put the glass to my lips and knock it back.

The burn of the alcohol is a lot better than that of the cigarette. "How many were there?" I ask. Luke remains silent while he refills our glasses. When he hands my glass back, I drink its contents immediately.

"Fifteen," he says quietly. "All between the ages of thirteen and seventeen."

Fifteen young girls. Five years ago, someone killed fifteen young girls and now Colby Bright is about to tell the world the man responsible was my father. Chalk that up with Colby's brother Adam, Sam and Jeff, and Maxwell Breslin is a few weeks shy of being declared a serial killer. I bite the inside of my cheek and force myself not to cry. I manage it, but it's a hollow victory. I may have fooled myself into believing that I am stronger than I was back in Break, but the truth is that I'm just as brittle. Prone to breaking, myself. By the time I reach over and collect up the whiskey bottle, I may not be crying but the fragile shell that was Avery Patterson has shattered into a thousand pieces.

THREE

HANGOVER

MOVEMENT WAKES me.

"Hey." Luke sits down on the edge of a large bed. A large bed that isn't mine. He holds out a glass of water and a pack of Tylenol, but when I don't take them he sets both items down on a small table beside the bed. I frown and prop myself up on one elbow, trying to figure out why the room is spinning.

"Where…?" I manage. I wake up in strange places sometimes. *Where* is often my first question.

"My place. I gotta go to work but I wanted to let you sleep until the very last minute. I have just enough time to take you home if we leave now. Can you manage it?"

He isn't in his uniform. "You aren't even ready," I groan, hiding my face underneath the pillow.

"I don't wear my uniform while I'm going to and from work. People might see me and follow me home or something. Cops get lynched that way." He tugs on the pillow, freeing it from my embarrassingly pathetic grip. "You can stay and sleep some more if you like. You can just lock up when you leave."

I think about it. I think about falling back to sleep in this big, comfy bed, and it is tempting. But the idea of having to try and make my way across New York City via public transport with the biggest hangover I've ever had is enough to counterbalance that. I should be better at this, being hung over, but the truth is hangovers kill me. They seem to get worse with every year I get older.

"Give me a minute. I'll be fine."

"All right. I don't mean to be a dick but you'll need to hurry. I can't be late."

I crack an eyelid and survey Luke head to toe. He's wearing a light gray hoodie that's a size too big for him over another plain black t-shirt. The jeans are faded out again, frayed around the pockets. He really can pull off a scruffy look. He slips out of the room and I sit bolt upright in bed, holding my palm to my temple when my head begins to pound. I'm freezing cold. I knock back the Tylenol and get up, realizing I'm still fully dressed, and pull on my shoes—which I find only by tripping over them at the bottom of the bed. Very uncoordinated. I suppose a half bottle of whiskey will do that to a person. Luke is waiting by the door with a big sweatshirt in his hand when I come out of the room. He doesn't look half as bad as I feel.

"How much did you drink last night?" I croak.

He puffs out his cheeks and shakes his head. "As much as you."

"You look completely fine."

"Well, I feel like shit if it's any consolation."

I hurry to him and take the sweatshirt out of his hand, slipping it over my head, grateful for the warmth. I catch sight of a welter of rumpled blankets on the black leather sofa where he must have slept. "That actually does make me feel a little better."

He exhales in a tired way and smiles. "Well, they do say misery loves company."

I AM miserable all day, but thankfully I don't have to deal with any company. Luke drops me home—another silent car journey—and when I get back to the apartment Leslie is already gone. I tumble back into bed, knowing there's no way I'm making class today. I haven't missed a single class since the semester began, and now I've ruined that perfect record because ... I don't want to think why. Fucking Colby Bright. Asshole.

When I wake up six hours later, Leslie's standing over my bed pulling a pretty disgusted face. "It stinks like a brewery in here. Why does our whole apartment stink like a brewery?"

I groan and pull the covers up over my head. She drags them off me despite my feeble attempts to cling onto them and points to the door.

"Shower. Right now."

She opens the windows as I gather up my towel and wash bag. My bedroom's freezing cold by the time I come back freshly scrubbed. Admittedly, I do feel a whole lot better now that it doesn't taste like something crawled into my mouth and died while I slept.

"Your phone rang," Leslie says, pointing at my cell. It lays on top of my bed, where it appears Leslie has stripped my sheets and replaced them with some of my fresh bedding.

"That bad, huh?"

She smirks at me and slams the window closed. "Worse."

I have four missed calls from Morgan. For some reason I'd expected to hear from Luke, but there's nothing. I text Morgan and tell her I'm too ill to meet her for coffee. She replies almost immediately:

Morgan: I know some guy paid Melissa Collins fifty bucks to find out which apartment was yours. You'd better call me right now! I need details.

I turn my phone off and hide it back under my pillow.

The rest of the night is spent wondering how much I've missed in my classes. I eventually get around to replying to Brandon's email. I don't really know where to begin at first. I start out determined not to mention what Luke told me about the Wyoming Ripper and Colby Bright's accusations, but that resolve lasts all of five seconds.

Hey, Uncle B.

Thanks for the offer but I don't think I can face coming back there just yet. Maybe you could come to the city? We could rent an apartment and go ice-skating or something. I know you hate it here, but it would be better than sitting back at the house moping. I'll even watch the game with you!

So, I need you to confirm something for me. I met up with Luke Reid last night, and he told me what's been going on back in Break. Is it true? Does everyone think Dad killed all those girls? I know there's no real way to know what happened with those men that day, but he would never have attacked teen-aged girls. They were the same age as me! There's just no way. Please tell me no one's listening to Mayor Bright.

Love you,
Avery.

I should make more of an effort to reassure Brandon; I know he worries about me. I should tell him how much I'm enjoying college and about the new friends I've made, but I don't have the energy. The nightmare from four and a half years ago is still replaying in even the brightest aspects of my life, and I'm never going to escape it. I go to sleep with my heart pounding in my chest, unable to escape the feeling that something terrible is looming on the horizon, about to ruin everything I've worked so hard to build for myself.

As I fall asleep, I realize I never gave Luke my *I-never-want-to-see-you-again* speech.

FOUR

NOAH

"**NOAHS ON** exchange. This isn't high school. I understand that I can hardly punish you for your actions at college, Ms. Patterson. Everything's down to you. But I can suggest that you could make up for your pajama day by helping our visitor adjust to life at Columbia. It isn't easy joining a subject midsemester. He's going to need all the help he can get." Professor Lang is sterner than I've ever seen him before. Actually, I've only ever seen him at ease and happy as we talk about class topics. Obviously he is a different person when you get on his bad side. Now I get what everyone is complaining about all the time. "Aren't you going to spin me some yarn about unexpected kidnappings or retrograde amnesia, Miss Patterson?"

I kick at the table leg of his desk and curve my shoulders, trying to shrink away from the fact that I can't even be bothered to make up an excuse for my non-attendance. I did this all through high school. Sullen and unresponsive is my go-to, never seemed to fail me. Having a psycho-killer father buys you some leniency, it turns out. People are always handling you with kid gloves like you might just up and explode one day. Not so in college. It appears I need actual words to excuse myself this time.

"I was hung over."

Silence.

I slowly raise my eyes up from the floor and face him, holding my breath. I don't know what I was expecting—that maybe he'd find my honesty charming and send me on my merry way with a neatly typed-up sheet of notes. Not so much. He looks disappointed, which is about the very worst thing he could be right now. I hug my file tighter to my chest and go back to looking at the floor.

"Are you serious about this course, Miss Patterson?"

"Yes. I've dropped the ball this week but I swear it was a one off."

"You *have* dropped the ball, and at the very point when you should be concentrating the most. You know these midterms are pivotal if you want to gain entry into our journalism program, yes?"

"I do."

"And I know that's the career you've chosen for yourself. I really thought you were committed to building something for yourself here, Avery. Was I wrong?"

I feel like utter crap. I'm twelve years old again and Dad has just caught me lifting a twenty from his wallet. It's a rare event these days, me wanting to please someone. I find myself resenting Lang for producing such a needy response from me. "You weren't wrong, Professor Lang. I *will* catch up on the information I missed and I will do well on my exams. I have to." *I have nothing else left.*

Professor Lang pushes off from leaning against his desk and paces over to the window. He folds his arms across his chest and sighs. "Why do you want to be a journalist? What is it that appeals to you so greatly about this particular career path?"

I really don't feel like getting into this with him, but just like with the hangover confession I'm still too delicate to summon up the energy to lie. It appears two-day hangovers are going to be in full effect from here on in. "Something happened to a friend of mine when I was younger and the press ... they were like vultures. They printed all these lies and made her family's life hell. I want to become a journalist so there will be at least one person out there telling the truth. To set the record straight."

Professor Lang's shoulders stiffen. "And that's why you enjoy my class so much. I tell you, there aren't many people too concerned in the law or the ethics behind news reporting these days. Everyone's too preoccupied with finding the next big story to worry about whether it might be true or not." He turns away from the window and walks to his office door. "I commend your drive, Miss Patterson, I really do. But you should know ... there's a big difference between a determination to be successful at something, even if it is for the right reasons, and wanting to change something that happened in the past. You won't get any justice for your friend or her family by pursuing this goal. You're a smart girl. You realize that, don't you?"

I swallow the tight lump in my throat and walk out of the door he holds open for me, fighting back the urge to tell him I'm not stupid. I already know there's nothing I can do to change my past. "I'm sorry, Professor Lang. I won't let it happen again."

He peers over his glasses at me, the lenses scuffed from where he habitually puts them down the wrong way. "I know you won't. You're too stubborn for that."

NOAH RICHARDS doesn't sound like an Irish name. He doesn't look Irish either: no ginger hair, not a single freckle in sight. Slightly wavy locks of dark brown hair poke out from beneath a beanie pulled down tight over his ears. Light gray eyes and a wicked smile. He looks cramped folded up into his desk, so he's probably quite tall. I recognize two other guys from class talking animatedly with him, sitting on top of their desks as I unwillingly trudge over toward them. Noah stops talking when he sees me heading over and the others quickly follow his gaze. I know how guys look at me sometimes, but I can usually avoid acknowledging it. It makes me feel like a little girl when they watch me like that. It's as though I regress back to an eight-year-old and it feels seriously inappropriate for a guy to fantasize about me. Because they do. Fantasize, that is. My tits are bigger than most women's. I have a cupid's bow mouth that some drunk guy on the subway told me was perfect for blow jobs. The rest of me is skin stretched over bone and muscle, and none of it seems to matter. Mostly, guys watch me in the hallways and I can keep my head down and pretend I don't notice. It's much harder to ignore when I have to approach them and talk to them directly, however.

Noah sits up straighter as I arrive, tugging on his beanie. I look at the other two guys, wondering if they're going to continue sitting there when it's obvious I want to talk to Noah. Yes, apparently they are.

"Uh…" I swallow, doing my best to meet Noah's eyes. "You're the exchange student, right?"

"Yeah, ah am." His accent isn't what I was expecting. It isn't strong or over-pronounced, just a faint lilt. He flashes me a wicked reprobate smile but his eyes seem kind. He isn't picking me apart like the other two are. "Ah'm Noah. This is Freddie and Kyle. They're the lucky bastards putting me up this semester."

I know who they are. I saw them at the party the other night with Morgan. The guy on the left, Freddie, was the make-out guy I kept getting shoved up against. "Right. You're in the same frat as Tate," I say. "The ceilidh." The whole Irish party thing makes more sense now. They must have held it in Noah's honor.

Noah's eyes shine a little and his smile grows wider. "Good pronunciation." He holds out his hand. "And you are?"

"Avery. I'm Avery Patterson." He gives me a firm hand-shake—nice, considering most guys think they'll crush your bones if they squeeze too hard. Dad always warned me never to trust a guy with a limp handshake. If he were around, he would have approved of Noah's.

"Nice to meet you, Avery."

"Likewise." *Get to the point, Avery. Get to the point.* "I ... Professor Lang said you might need some company. I just want-ed to offer my services."

Freddie and Kyle both start snickering openly. I realize too late what I've said could sound dirty, especially if you are a mo-ronic nineteen-year-old guy. Jackholes.

"Don't you guys have somewhere else to be?" *I* have some-where else to be—anywhere but here—but then again I have some ground to regain with a certain professor, who I know is watching me speak to the new kid. Freddie and Kyle look at me in that surprised way that people do when they poke an injured animal with a stick and it turns around and bites them. They still haven't left, though. Noah is looking at the professor when I turn back to him, chewing the cap of his biro. His eyes narrow. "This is a punishment, ain't it?"

"No. Maybe. I mean, I know what it's like to not know any-one—"

"Ha!" Kyle reaches over and slaps Noah's arm. "Are you kidding? This guy already *knows* half the female populous of Columbia." He makes a point of gazing off into space. "Man, what I wouldn't give for an Irish accent."

"Shut your mouth, Kyle," Noah laughs. It's a joking com-mand but Kyle obeys all the same. "I've not had any problems settling in, thanks, Avery Patterson, but if you want to study or hang out sometime, I'm all in."

Both Kyle and Freddie manage not to laugh this time, but I

can tell it's killing them. I really didn't expect Noah to say that. I'd expected him to brush me off and make a joke out of my awkward offer as soon as my back was turned. He seems completely genuine.

"Okay, well, great." I give him my best *"I'm normal, I swear"* smile and take my leave. Well, that was unexpected. No laughing as I leave and take my seat. Or none that I can hear, anyway. As class commences, I allow myself to look over once to see if they're whispering behind their hands. Kyle and Freddie are studiously taking notes. Noah is frowning out of the window, still chewing on his pen cap.

FIVE
SMELLS LIKE SEX

THREE WEEKS pass and I don't hear from Luke. I make up the slack in school and do well in my midterms, despite being permanently distracted and on edge. Brandon is joining me for Thanksgiving, which is surprising since he hardly ever leaves the town where he grew up. I've booked us an apartment on the Upper East Side so we'll have a proper kitchen to cook with instead of living out of hotel rooms. It cost a fortune but Mom really wasn't kidding when she said she'd increased my allowance. The difference is more than enough to cover the accommodation and everything we will eat and drink while he's in town. Only three more days and I'll get to leave college and relax.

"Gonna miss ya, kid," Morgan tells me as we walk back from class. Snow covers the ground now, coating everything in a four-inch layer of grimy slush. At first I thought it would be bad business walking outside with snow on the ground, but so far I've been wrong. It turns out people are too cool for snowball fights at Columbia University. I like that. Makes me feel like I'm actually surrounded by adults.

I tuck my arm through Morgan's and dip my chin into my scarf, trying to warm the air I breathe in through the wooly material so it won't burn my lungs quite so badly. "I'm gonna miss you, too. You sure you don't want to join me and Brandon? We're probably just going to drink beer, eat crap and watch bad movies."

Morgan pulls a face, stomping in the snow. "You have *no* idea how much I would love that. My mom's a freakin' holiday nut, though. She'd lose her shit if I didn't come home." Home for Morgan is a nine-hour drive away in Charlestown, West Virginia. New York is the farthest her mom allowed her to move out of state. Apparently not far enough for Morgan.

"You could always catch the red eye instead of driving. That would save time and you could have a couple of days after Thanksgiving in the city with me after Brand leaves. He's got to be back at work."

Morgan lets us into our building and kicks off the snow from her boots in the lobby. The floor is filthy and streaked with grubby track marks. A "WET FLOOR" sign lays on its side in front of the elevator. It'll probably be stolen by some frat jerk before the day's out.

"I'd love that, Ave. Let me see if I can swing it with the folks. I kinda feel bad for Dad trapped there by himself sometimes."

We drop by Morgan's apartment but her roommate has a friend over and the noise is ridiculous, so we go up the extra flights of stairs to my apartment and make ourselves comfortable. Leslie is in the library studying but she's left a small package and a note on the kitchen counter.

"Holy crap, is that hot chocolate? Please tell me that's hot chocolate," Morgan chatters, throwing herself back onto the sofa. I read the note.

Step one: Drink me.

43

Step two: Prevent freezing of lady parts.
Step three: Save world.

L xoxoxo

It's a shame Morgan and I don't get to share an apartment, but I really did luck out with Leslie. Aside from the hordes of people who are always stopping by to see her when she's in, she's always really thoughtful. More than I deserve. I swipe Morgan's booted feet off the upholstery and crack open the tin of hot chocolate.

"Get your filthy footwear off the furniture, Kepler. I take it you want some of this, then?"

"If it's no trouble." She smiles sweetly. Butter wouldn't melt. "And I'm also gonna need something warm to wear, unless you're okay with me climbing in your bed."

"Don't even think about it. Just because I don't have any guys in mind doesn't mean I want you to be the first person other than myself to rub up on those sheets."

Morgan looks offended for all of three seconds, until I go to my room and rummage around in my drawers to find a sweatshirt for her. I toss her the very first thing I lay my hands on and go about making us some drinks, warming some milk on the stove.

"What *is* this?" Morgan holds up the huge sweatshirt in front of me, and I suddenly realize what I've given her: the sweatshirt Luke loaned me post freak out almost a month ago. She slips it on over her head so I see the big block capitals on the front—NYPD. "Fuck, this smells good, Avery. Why does this shirt smell like sex?"

An instant fire burns at my cheeks. I'm not a virgin, but I'm also not very comfortable talking about sex. Possibly because my only experiences with men have been awkward and thus far rather unpleasant. "It does *not* smell like sex."

"Oh yeah, it does. Or it smells like a guy I most definitely would kill to have sex with. This is that cop dude's, isn't it?"

"Wow. Excellent powers of observation there, Sherlock. What gave it away? Could it be the huge New York Police Department logo emblazoned across your chest?" I stalk over to her and tug at the sweatshirt sleeve. "Take it off. I'll find you something else."

"No way!" She bunches up the front of the sweater and holds it to her face, inhaling deeply. "This is the best thing that's happened to me all day. How the hell do you have this?"

I've kind of avoided telling Morgan about the night at Luke's apartment. I don't like purposely keeping things from her, but telling her about that night means filling her in on Colby Bright's book about my dad. And that's not something I am ready to do just yet.

"He loaned it to me ages ago. I just haven't had a chance to give it back."

Morgan eyes me suspiciously. "And you say there's nothing going on with you and this guy?"

"No. There is nothing going on with me and that guy." I turn away from her so I can tend to our drinks, stirring furiously.

"In that case, I think you should return this sweater to our lovely peace keeper immediately, and I think you should let me come with you. It's a crime to let a hottie like that go to waste. Get it? A crime?" She laughs an ugly laugh at her own lame joke and I pretend I haven't heard her. I hand over her mug and plunk myself down on my swivel chair, staring at the liquid inside my cup.

"Don't ignore me, Patterson. I'm serious. I want a shot at that guy if you're not taking one."

"He's got a girlfriend, I told you." I'm training my face into a blank mask now that I know I am flat-out lying to her. She's ridiculously hot. Guys go crazy for her rich auburn hair coloring, too. There's no reason why Luke wouldn't want to hook up with her, and the last thing I need is him running around my building. I try picturing what I'd say to him if I bumped into him in the hallways after he'd paid her a visit. The idea of it makes me shudder.

"What about Tate, anyway?" I ask. "I thought things were good with you guys?"

Morgan purses her lips and scowls. "I haven't heard from him in five days. I fell asleep with him on Sunday night. I think he's still mad at me."

"Why would he be mad at you for falling asleep? You crash there all the time."

A faint smile ticks at the corner of her mouth. She raises an eyebrow and gives me a scandalous look. Realization dawns. "Oh, you fell asleep *with* him. While you were …?"

"Yep. Apparently it was the height of rudeness, especially since he was pulling out all of his best moves at the time."

"Oh god, Morgan," I laugh, trying to suppress the laughter itching at the back of my throat. "You are probably the only person I know who could fall asleep during sex."

"I've done it before," she announces. "I'm probably going to do it again. It was his own fault, anyway. He was taking way too long down there."

She says this as I'm taking a swig of my drink, and I come close to spraying hot chocolate all over the living room wall. We laugh like the evil bitches we are, only regaining our composure when my cell phone starts ringing. Morgan wipes her eyes and leans over to collect it off the coffee table, tossing it to me.

Unknown number.

I frown at the screen—*one heartbeat. Two. Three*—until Morgan throws a cushion at me. "Answer it, woman. An unanswered call is a missed opportunity."

Usually the opportunities I'm presented with over the phone are ones I'm all too happy to miss. Morgan doesn't understand why I never answer calls from unknown numbers. Back in high school it was one of my fellow classmate's favorite pastimes to prank me and scream "murder spawn" down the phone before hanging up. Just another thing I don't want to have to explain. Better to just answer the phone this once and get it over with.

"Hello?"

"Avery Patterson?" The voice throws me, instantly familiar and not at the same time.

"Yeah?"

"It's Noah Richards. I got your number from your friend—what is it, Maria?"

I feel my ears pull back. I turn and stare at the girl feigning nonchalance to my right. "No, I think you mean *Morgan*." The woman in question smiles innocently, studying her flawless nail polish.

"Yeah, that's it, Morgan. I've seen you two hangin' around. I was wondering if your services were still on offer?"

I can literally hear the smirk in his voice, but he doesn't sound like he's being a jerk. I sigh, whacking Morgan on the shin with my balled-up fist. "What's up? Have Freddie and Kyle moved out of state?"

Noah laughs. "Nah, but they are going back home for the holidays. I'm spending Thanksgiving with a bunch of friends in the city. Everyone's leaving at the end of the holiday weekend. That means I'll be a poor lonely foreigner in the big smoke with no one to hang out with. I heard you were gonna be around. Any chance you might like to catch a movie or something? Purely in the interests of keeping me out of trouble, you understand."

I frantically try to think of something, *anything* that will mean I don't have to go to a movie with Columbia's hottest, most popular exchange student. I come up blank. Morgan shimmies forward so she's literally on the edge of her seat when she sees I'm hesitating, pulling a warning face. She clenches her fist at me, threatening physical violence if I don't say yes. She obviously knows why he is calling. I flip her off and spin around on my office chair.

"Sure, Noah. That sounds great. I've got family with me for a couple of days but I'm free after that. You can just shoot me a text and we'll work something out."

"Grand!"

He hangs up and I drop my cell onto the coffee table, doing my best not to launch myself at Morgan.

"Who was that?" she asks breezily, and I can't do it anymore. I pounce onto the sofa and proceed to thwack her mercilessly with one of the cushions.

"You know damn well who that was, you witch!"

"Aggghhh! Stop, stop, okay, okay! I admit it. Stop!" she squeals. I sink back and let the cushion drop. "I'm sorry, Avery. He just asked so nicely, and that accent...I couldn't help it!"

"Whatever." I nail her one last time with the cushion and let out a long sigh. "And I'm serious—take that sweatshirt off. I don't want you funking it up with your out-of-control pheromones. I don't intend on having to wash it before I return it."

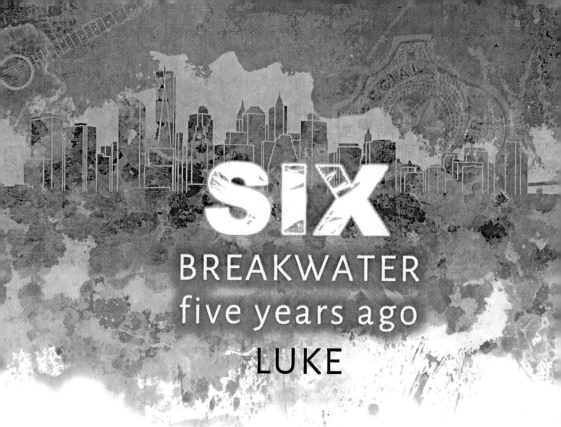

SIX

BREAKWATER
five years ago
LUKE

THE CRUISER pulls up alongside the curb. I can't turn and look at the house yet. Chloe's unbuckling her seatbelt, clearing her throat with a grim look on her face, but I can't move. My hand's still resting on my Glock, like there's still action to be taken, something to be done about the horrific things I've witnessed. Some way to prevent it.

Every time I blink, I can still see the bodies strewn every which way on the ground. Every time I close my eyes, I can still see Max, twitching on the bare concrete, choking on his own blood. God, I can't fucking breathe.

"You'll shoot your dick off with that thing if you're not careful," Chloe says softly. She kills the engine. We sit in silence for a moment, her staring at me, me staring at the dash. "It's only been a couple of days, Luke. I know it might not seem like it now, but there will come a time when this sort of thing doesn't faze you anymore. It's just harder this time. Harder 'cause you knew the guy."

I close my eyes, wondering if I've made a massive mistake. Maybe I shouldn't have become a cop. Maybe I should have gone to college like everyone expected me to. Taken that scholarship and become a fucking business major or something. I let go of my holster, flexing my hands open and closed so that my knuckles turn white. "I'm okay. I'll be okay."

Chloe smiles at me sadly. "I know you will, kid. Come on. Let's get this over with."

The world feels like it's closing in on me when I step out of the car, though. I face the house, and the first thing I see is the kid's face at the window. Max's daughter, Iris. Only fourteen years old, for fuck's sake. She looks like a fucking ghost.

"Thought she was supposed to be catatonic," Chloe says, head tilted up at the window. Iris doesn't register my partner, though. She stares straight at me, and I know I can't do this. I can't fucking do this. I slump back against the hood of the cruiser, shaking my head. "They haven't fixed up the window yet," Chloe observes. When we came here five days ago to tell what remained of the Breslin family that Max was dead, Iris had thrown a chair through the huge pane of glass in the downstairs living room. It's still boarded over, ugly chipboard stained and mottled with damp. The sound of Iris screaming still rings in my ears, even now.

"This is too much," I say. I hear the words coming out of my mouth, knowing they're true. Max was more than a friend to me. He took care of me. He watched over me when no one else could. How am I supposed to look his fourteen-year-old daughter in the eye and keep my shit together?

"It's all right," Chloe says, placing her hand on my arm. "Sit this one out. I only need to confirm a few details with his wife, anyway. Just stay here, okay?"

She goes inside the house, and I feel fucking pathetic. I turn my back on Max's house. For the first time since we found him in that warehouse, I let myself cry. I'm nearly twenty fucking years old. I'm a trained police officer. I shouldn't be fucking in tears on the lawn of one of my victims, and yet here I am, tears streaking down my face. This is the very worst second of the very worst day of the very worst week of my life.

My breath catches in my throat as I feel something on my arm—another hand, comforting me. And there she is—the girl I wanted to avoid, fourteen-year-old Iris. So much for not being able to face her. It doesn't look like I have much choice now. She's colorless, like a ghost, washed out in her white pajamas. Her skin is utterly bleached of color. That mass of blonde hair— so, so pale, spun gold—doesn't help matters either. She looks like she's on death's door. "Why are you crying?" she whispers. Her voice cracks, like she hasn't used it in days. According to the papers, she hasn't. The media have been laying it on thick, saying she's in some sort of coma.

I don't trust myself to speak at first. Instead, I look out over the endless trees that stretch on forever between the Breslin's property and the town of Breakwater, reflecting on the fact that this is the first time I've properly met Iris. That strikes me as wrong somehow. Max loved her so much. I'd always wanted to meet her. It just never seemed appropriate approaching her in school. She was always surrounded by friends, joined at the hip with that Maggie Bright girl. I was older. It wouldn't have been right. People would have talked.

Iris lays her head on my shoulder, and I can feel her start to shake. She's crying. My own tears stop immediately. I'm locked frozen, suddenly unsure what the hell I'm supposed to do. "Please," she sobs. "Tell me why you're sad." She begs me, as though knowing why I'm hurting will stem her own pain.

"You really want to know?" I carefully wrap my arm around her; it seems like the right thing to do.

She looks up at me, eyes filled with tears, grief all over her face, and I'm filled with an abrupt and overwhelming need to take this away from her. To make it all go away.

I tell her what her dad was to me. I tell her what he did for me.

She cries into my jacket, and I carry her upstairs to her bed, and the whole time her mother doesn't look at her once.

SEVEN
SUPER EIGHT

"SURPRISE!"

Brandon shows up on the doorstep of the ridiculously large apartment I've rented with a huge red ribbon looped around his head, complete with a messy bow tied on top. Grinning at me with his arms spread wide, he waits expectantly for me to tumble into his embrace. He still thinks I'm twelve and I'm gonna laugh at that shit. And I do laugh, but only because it makes him happy. Brandon is the only man on the face of the planet who I'll pretend anything for. I love the quirky bastard. I let him scoop me up into a hug, squeezing him back until he pretends to wheeze and choke.

"What's wrong with you, kid? You tryin' to crush an old man to death?"

Where Morgan and I have an arrangement not to fish for compliments, I've never managed to convince Brandon to follow suit. He's incorrigible. I wave him into the apartment, helping carry his bags inside. "You're forty-six, Brand. You're hardly old. It's not like you're about to fall down dead."

He drops his bag on the kitchen floor and sweeps his hands back through his thick brown hair. "You see that shit?" He jabs a finger at the top of his head. "That's a receding hairline. I'm losing more hair in a day that I can possibly hope to regrow. I've calculated that if it continues to fall out at this rate, I'll have a comb-over by this time next year."

He doesn't have a receding hairline at all. He knows it. He's just being a fool. I shove the other bag I've carried in for him into his chest and tut. "Come on, then, old man."

I show him the three other spare rooms and he throws his stuff into the one opposite mine before immediately cracking open a beer. "It smells great in here, Ave. What have you been up to?"

"The usual." I take his beer can from him and put it back in the fridge. "It's not even eleven. You'll be asleep before the food's ready and I'm not listening to you snore while I try and eat."

Brandon tramps into the living area of the apartment and sinks down onto the sofa, sulking. "You're turning into your mother, you know that?"

That has to be the most offensive insult anyone could possibly give me. "Fine! Screw you, buddy. You can drink all the beer you want and fall asleep. I don't care. I'll watch *Charlie St. Cloud* and polish off some wine. I'd much prefer that over being abused by you!"

Brandon pulls a face and kicks his feet up onto the glass coffee table. "No way. No Efron in this apartment. I won't stand for it."

Brandon thinks Zac Efron is genetically modified in some way. The last time I tried to watch that movie he chucked a fit. I smile and throw myself down next to him, knocking his feet off the rented furniture as I do.

"What's new with you then, old man?" I don't really want to know the daily happenings of his life in Breakwater, but since my dad died he's really stepped up. Taken care of me. I feel bad that he's back there on his own most of the time. He's a little rough around the edges, and in a town like Breakwater that doesn't earn you any friends.

"I'm gonna tell you something now," he says, "and you're not gonna believe it for one second."

I sit patiently waiting for him to spill his secret. Ten seconds tick by but he just sits there, smirking at me. "Well, come on then! What?"

"I," he says, grinning while he pulls a pack of smokes out of his pocket, "went on a date." His eyebrows waggle comically as he flicks a cigarette into his mouth.

"What? You old dog! Who with?" Brandon didn't go on a single date the entire time I lived with him. He probably hadn't been on one before then, either. Maybe not since my Aunt Mel died. I finally realize what Brandon is about to do as he leans forward to light his cigarette—I snatch it out of his mouth.

"*You* didn't hire this place. When you're responsible for the deposit, *then* you can smoke indoors. There's a balcony. Now tell me who you went on a date with."

He groans and tips his head back against the sofa. "I took Monica Simpson out to that fancy Thai place you like, and she was bor-ring." He stretches out the word so it sounds like two, and I bite back a bark of laughter.

"Monica Simpson? Candice Simpson's mom?"

"The very same."

"The one with…" I gesture with hands towards my chest. Monica is a petite woman but she has a huge chest that nearly all the men in Breakwater have fantasized about getting their hands on. She'd already suffered through two breast reduction surgeries by the time I left high school.

"Exactly."

I can't keep the laughter in this time. "Why on earth did you ask her out? I mean, she seems like a nice enough woman, but …"

"I didn't ask her out. *She* asked *me*."

That makes it even funnier. I guess I am too used to him after all the years I spent growing up with him, but Brandon would probably still be considered a good-looking guy by some people. Older people. Much, much older people. I laugh hard enough that I snort.

"Hey! I hope you're not finding it funny that a woman asked me out. These are modern times, y'know. It's completely normal for the broad to ask the guy. Maybe you should keep that in mind, huh?"

I give his arm a light punch and rest my head against his shoulder. "I'll be sure to remember."

"Don't get too comfy, kid. I didn't get that smoke out the packet to look cool. I fully intend on lighting it. On the balcony!" he adds before I can object. "Plus I have something for you."

"A gift?" I sit up straight and grab hold of his arm. "Since when do we do gifts at Thanksgiving?"

"It's an early Christmas present. I thought it might be nice to give you something now for having me up here and cooking and everything."

I eye him suspiciously. "Will we be opening presents together on Christmas, too?"

"Yes," he laughs. "I swear. I'll come back to the city if that'll make you happy. We could even rent this ritzy palace again. Now, do you want your present or not?"

"Of course I do."

Brandon hurries to his room and comes back thirty seconds later with a large box in his hands. It's wrapped in *Transformers* gift paper.

"Aw, *Transformers*. You shouldn't have." He hands it over and I do the whole *shake-it-to-see-if-you-can-tell-what-it-is* bit. "You didn't steal this from under some poor kid's Christmas tree did you?"

"Scout's honor."

I tear off the paper and stare down at the box in my lap. It's a video camera, the kind I'd always wanted when I was a kid. A Super Eight. I'd forgotten about my dream of someday becoming a movie director, but Brandon clearly hasn't. He collects up the shredded *Transformers* paper and scrunches it in his hands.

"I figured you could, y'know, practice filming yourself for when you're a TV reporter or something."

I look up at him, stunned. "This probably cost a fortune. A working Super Eight? They're almost impossible to get ahold of now."

"Yeah, well, I'd love to pretend I spent big but I'd be lying. It's been sitting in the attic for years. I used to screw around with this old thing before you were even born. Your dad, too. He used to bribe me with beer so I'd let him borrow it."

There are so few things that link me back to my dead father these days. The knowledge that he used to film with the camera sitting in the box before me has my eyes welling. I reach inside and lift it out, surprised by how heavy it is. It looks like a speed gun traffic cops use—a small lens, a boxy square, black metal housing and a grip handle. I point it at Brandon, closing one eye as I aim, and he smiles a sad smile.

"Your aunt used to film our games with that bad boy. I'll show you how to use it later. But first ..." Brandon holds up his cigarette and grins, a little of his melancholia drifting away. "I must smoke."

EIGHT

IT'S A DATE

THANKSGIVING DAY is over in the blink of an eye, and Brandon has to leave pretty much immediately. The joys of being a business owner. I spend most of the next day tinkering with my new Super Eight in the living room of the apartment, the ceiling to floor windows displaying New York City's dramatic skyline—a jigsaw puzzle of concrete teeth bared against a winter sky. Brandon showed me how to use the camera, or at least the bare bones of how it would point and shoot *if* I didn't mess with any of the buttons. As soon as he leaves I do just that, tinkering with all the settings, trying to figure the thing out. There are still two days before I have to return to college and I fully intend on keeping busy during that time, getting to grips with my new toy. It isn't like I've forgotten Noah's request to go see a movie, but I still get a nervous rush when I see his name flashing up on my cell on Friday night.

"Hey, Avery Patterson. How was your Thanksgiving? You been living off turkey sandwiches or what?"

Ironic, since this is indeed the case. "If I never see another slice of turkey, I will be one happy girl. What about you, Noah Richards? Have you overeaten and drunk too much in keeping with our most cherished American holiday?"

"Whoa, whoa, whoa. Did you just give me the full name treatment?" Noah stifles a laugh on the other end of the phone. "I guess I deserve that after using yours, but *I* look like a Noah Richards. You don't look like an Avery Patterson. I'm relying heavily on positive affirmation, saying your name every time I speak to you, just to make sure I don't call you something else."

Resentment flares up in my chest. It's not a pretty feeling. I've worked damn hard to make sure people think of me as plain, boring old Avery Patterson, and to have Noah come out with something so flippant as *you don't look like an Avery Patterson* has my cheeks instantly flushing. Does he know something? How could he, though? I mean, the only four people in the whole world who know about my name change are Morgan, Brandon, Luke and my mother. No way any of them are spilling the beans. "What do you mean by that?" I ask.

There's a short silence on the other end of the phone before Noah chuckles quietly. "Sorry. I didn't mean that you weren't...*memorable*. You're exactly the opposite. It's just...sometimes a person just doesn't look like they fit into their own skin. Like if they were only called Sam instead of Harvey they'd be more themselves. I don't know. Like you, for instance. You look like an Evie or a Charlotte. It's all that blonde hair and your button nose. Should I stop talking now?"

Sometimes a person doesn't fit into their own skin. Noah can't know how right he is. From the age of fourteen, I never really did feel like I fit into my body. I never thought I was who I was meant to be. I've been trying for years to convince myself as well as other people that the mask I wear is in fact my true face when the truth is ... I don't even have a true face. The person I was meant to be died all those years ago when I found out the man I worshipped was a murderer. Noah doesn't know all of that, though. He's just trying to be cute. "It's okay. I can assure you, though, my name is Avery. Boring, plain old Avery." He may have his positive affirmations, but I have my own brand of mind control. If I say it enough, if I tell him I'm a nobody and believe it, maybe he'll actually believe it. Sometimes these things are a work in progress, though.

"I think you might be underselling yourself there, sweetheart. You strike me as very interesting indeed," Noah says. "Either way, I wasn't calling to offend you. I was calling to see if you'd be interested in letting me take you to the R-rated movie I saw reviewed in *Gore Fest Magazine.*"

I slump back in my chair, feeling words hovering at the back of my throat. I don't know what the words are yet; they're taking a long time to form. This really is starting to sound like a date. "I don't know. That sounds rather bloody. I'm usually more of a comedy kind of girl. What score did *Gore Fest Magazine* give this film?"

Noah pulls in a long breath that makes it sound like he's smoking. "Five out of five decapitated heads." I can hear car horns blaring on the other end of the phone and then Noah starts swearing profusely. "Jeez, what is it with you bloody New Yorkers trying to kill everyone when they try and cross a road?"

"Did you use the crosswalk?"

"No."

"That's your problem, then. Jaywalkers get crushed under the wheels of America's industry. Its industry, in this case, being a monstrous fleet of yellow-and-black taxi cabs." I can picture that. Hundreds of cabs for as far as the eye can see, barely an inch between bumpers, mowing people down without a second thought, and all in the name of getting this client to his meeting on time. Getting this model to her photo shoot before all the coffee's gone. Such bullshit.

"Yep. Just another thing that I love about the US, y'know. The citizens of the most powerful country in the world can't cross a road safely without being designated a specific area to do so. Can't you people be trusted to look both ways and just cross a bloody road like everyone else?"

The image of Noah standing on a street corner anywhere in New York and saying something like that out loud is hilarious; he's probably going to get lynched if he breathes another word. I prop myself up by my elbows on the kitchen counter and consider my options: go out with the seemingly nice, hot guy from class, or stay in the apartment alone, reading an instruction manual. The age-worn Super Eight manual is actually really interesting, but still…

"You there, Avery Patterson? You wanna come watch a bunch of people get hacked to pieces with me or what?"

Delightful imagery. I've never been one for blood and guts but maybe this is exactly what I need—a little hammer horror to put my life into context. "All right, Noah Richards. I could be persuaded."

"Great. Get your ass down to the Beekman Theater on 2nd. I'll grab our tickets and some popcorn. You like chocolate?"

I smile despite myself. "I like chocolate." This might actually be fun, and listening to Noah speak in that accent of his really is quite something. "Hey, Noah," I say, reaching for my jacket. "What's the movie called?"

"Way Out of Wyoming. About some psycho killer who murdered a bunch of girls. Apparently it's based on a true story. We can go and see something else if you like, though? The new Adam Sandler movie looks good if you're into comedy. Do you have any preferences?"

My hand tightens around the phone. *Sam O'Brady. Jefferson Kyle. Adam Bright. Sam O'Brady. Jefferson Kyle. Adam Bright. Sam O'Brady. Jefferson Kyle. Adam Bright. Sam O'Brady. Jefferson Kyle. Adam Bright.*

"Avery?"

"Uh…sorry, Noah, I…" My throat is so dry I can't swallow. "What did you say?"

"I asked if you had any preferences? Adam Sandler?"

I fix my eyes on the digital clock on the oven, forcing oxygen in and out of my body. "No, I don't care really. Just pick whatever. But not that one. Not the Wyoming one."

Noah completely misses the way my voice cracks. He chuckles and says, "Man, girls are such pussies" and then he hangs up the phone.

I don't leave the apartment right away. I head from the kitchen into the lounge where I've set up my laptop and sit down in front of it, activating the Wi-Fi on my cell phone. Once my laptop recognizes the Wi-Fi hotspot, I head straight to YouTube and type in "Way Out Of Wyoming Trailer". The comments at the top of the page are bad. They all refer to how fucked up the movie is. How it made someone's mom, sister, girlfriend puke. Loud rock music starts up and the trailer finally loads. For the next minute and thirty seconds I stare at the screen and watch without blinking once.

"When teenage girls started going missing across Wyoming, police officials never suspected they were dealing with a serial killer. There was no motive. No profile. No pattern. And for the killer's victims, no hope of escape."

Scenes of young girls being chased through woods strobe on the screen, accompanied by the breathless, frantic sounds of someone running for their life. At the end of the trailer, an image of a masked man brandishing a rusty machete flashes up, and a high-pitched scream rips over the brash guitar music, ending the clip on a dramatic note. I slam the laptop closed and slump back, chewing on my thumbnail, trying to figure out a way to stop my stomach from rolling. They've made a movie out of it. *A motherfucking movie.* Everyone in the whole country is going to be talking about it, especially since it looks like one of the most gruesome things I've ever seen. That means they'll be talking about my dad, too, if anyone catches sight of Mayor Bright's book. And they will. Because that's just my luck.

NOAH WASN'T kidding when he said he'd grab us some snacks. I rock up just in time to catch the box of Milk Duds he's trying to balance on top of the biggest bucket of popcorn ever.

"Whoa, nice catch!"

"Thanks." I manage a smile and stuff the box into my pocket.

"Hey, I saw that!" Noah shakes his head, grinning. "I don't know...been acquaintances for all of five minutes and she's already stealing my confectionery."

My smile grows a fraction bigger. I silently hope he'll think the redness of my cheeks has a lot to do with the biting cold outside instead of suspecting I had to fight tears the whole walk over through the Upper East Side. Noah's cheeks are a little rosy, themselves; he probably isn't going to notice. He's wearing another beanie—I don't think I've ever seen him without one. He's gone for a smarter version of his casual dress: a thin black sweater over a button down shirt, and stone washed jeans. The sweater looks really soft; I imagine how it would feel against my skin.

Noah cracks a smirk. "I got us tickets. You okay? You look a little dazed."

I'm not dazed. I'm sick to my stomach from watching that trailer, and now it looks as though I'm staring at the sweater choice of the guy I'm on a maybe date with, wondering how it would feel if I rubbed my cheek against it. "Sorry. I just space out sometimes. Shall we go in?" *What if the movie directors caught wind of Mayor Bright's accusations while they were planning the film? Did they use my dad's name in it? Do they call the Wyoming Ripper Maxwell Breslin in the newest box office hit?* These questions run into each other, back-to-back worry as Noah leads us into the movie theater. Morgan's always going on dates with guys to the movies. She gives me the gossip on each one as soon as she gets back to her apartment, filling me in on whether she's likely to be seeing them again. A lot of that—the seeing-them-again part—rides on which seats the guy picks out for them. Too close to the front and he's too interested in the film. Too close to the back and all he wants is to stick his tongue down her throat. There are apparently varying degrees of nerd or perve as you get closer to the middle of the theater, and Morgan's given me the rundown, row by row.

Noah picks out a couple of seats three quarters of the way back from the screen—not exactly far enough from the back row to suggest he wasn't thinking about sitting there, but still a respectable distance from the hook-up spots. If he were on a date with my best friend instead of me, Noah would probably have already scored himself a second one. He lets me in first and then sits down, offering me the popcorn. "You wanna steal this, too, seeing as you've already confiscated my Milk Duds?"

"I thought they were *our* Milk Duds?"

Noah's face changes a little, shadowed in the dim light of the theater. "I like the sound of that," he says quietly.

I frown. "Like the sound of what?"

"Doesn't matter," he smirks, shaking the popcorn under my nose until I take some. "What are you doing for Christmas, Miss Patterson? Heading back to … where are you from?"

"Idaho," I lie.

"Idaho …" Noah narrows his eyes as he gazes off into the distance. "I know nothing about Idaho."

Neither do I, so please don't fucking ask me about it. I shove a handful of popcorn into my mouth and shrug. When I've finished slowly chewing, the curtains have parted and the screen flickers into life. "Whereabouts in Ireland are you from?" I whisper.

His gray eyes glint in the dark. He leans closer so I can hear him. "Belfast, but I spent a lot of time in London when I was a kid."

"Oh. I didn't think the Irish liked the English very much?"

A slow smile curls at the corner of his mouth. "Some of us don't. Some of us don't care anymore. Me ma sent me there back towards the end of the nineties to get an education. She didn't want me growing up around all those guns."

As a child who grew up around guns, it seems strange to me that some parents would want to shield their children from them. The irony of that thought hits me as I'm having it. My father always taught me that his gun was not a toy. That I wasn't to touch it. He'd had a license for his handgun. The one the police had found, clip emptied, next to his body in that warehouse back in Breakwater. "Is there still a lot of gun crime in Ireland?" I ask, shivering my way out of that thought.

Noah nearly blows Coke out of his nose. He coughs so violently, the lady with the soccer mom haircut in front of us turns to give us an irritated look.

"Oh, calm yourself, woman, it's the adverts!" he snaps, rolling his eyes. Then, to me, "Did you just ask me if there's a lot of gun crime in Ireland?"

I blush under the incredulous stare he's giving me. "Yeah? I thought things were peaceful there now." I get the impression I should be feeling pretty stupid.

"Oh, boy." He takes a deep breath. "Yes, there's a fair bit o' gun crime, especially where I'm from in Northern Ireland. Not as much now as there used to be, though. I guess, in your defense, we're not making the news every night anymore. There was a lot of conflict when I was growing up. The Loyalists and the Republicans, the Protestants and the Catholics ... everyone had a finger on a trigger in one way or another. My family thought I was better off out of it."

"And you ... what are you?"

Noah's eyes narrow again. "What do you mean?"

"Are you a Loyalist or a Republican?"

"Do I have to be either?"

I tip my head to one side, studying him. "Most people are something when they grow up in an environment like that."

Take me, for example. There are people out there whose family members have done really shitty things. They handle the vile acts committed by their blood in one of three ways. Option one: they deny any possibility that their beloved son/brother/ husband/wife, etc. could ever have been responsible for such terrible crimes. Option two: they pretend the unhinged perpetrator they thought they knew so well simply never existed. (That's how other friends and family members end up with broken jawbones—*don't you talk to me about him! Don't you ever even say his fucking name to me!*) Then there's option three: they accept what's happened and they run from it. They become a different person themselves, to create distance as a coping mechanism. Is the coping mechanism because they hate what their loved one did? Maybe. But mostly it's to ease the associated guilt of the atrocity, because they feel like they're being judged. If they were related to the murderer, surely they had something to do with the whole thing, right? I'm number three. My therapist back in Breakwater didn't need to tell me that.

"I try not to involve myself in things that don't concern me," Noah says lightly, but there's a guarded look in his eye. "Me mother and father are Catholic, though you won't find me frequenting the house of God on the weekends."

I don't get a chance to ask him anything else. The movie starts. After a warning glance from the woman in front of us, we settle into silence to watch the film. Noah laughs long and hard through the next hour and a half, and I manage a few splutters of my own, even through everything else crowding my mind. We've polished off half the popcorn and the Milk Duds by the time the credits roll, but my stomach feels oddly hollow. Noah dumps the trash on the way out, and we blink as we emerge into the lit foyer. The place is buzzing with people queuing for tickets to the late night showing.

"These guys all get to see the murder flick. You owe me," Noah complains, grabbing the sleeve of my jacket so he can guide me through the sea of people, chattering and jostling each other to get ahead in line. The cold is startling when he tugs me outside. It's snowing again, this time much heavier than the flurries the city has experienced over the previous weeks.

The traffic on 2nd is bad as usual, the cab drivers leaning on their horns despite the fact it never gets them anywhere any quicker.

The curled ends of Noah's hair catch flakes of snow as they descend. The rest land on his beanie, melting almost instantly. He becomes suddenly shy, shoving his hands into his jeans pockets. "So, I'm aware I touted this as a movie-only deal, but I was wondering if maybe you wanted to up the ante and grab some food as well? I know a place close by where they have good live music."

My stomach growls right on cue, betraying me. It'd probably be smart to head back to the apartment, but I can't exactly tell him I don't want to eat after that embarrassing rumble. I glance up and down the street, seeing what Noah must see—that we're surrounded by normal people. People who probably haven't heard a thing about some new movie. They're just out for dinner, enjoying the holidays together. I'm suddenly incredibly jealous of them with their simple, uncomplicated lives. I look back at Noah to find him wearing a hopeful expression.

"Come on," he says, smiling, "No turkey, I promise."

"No turkey, huh? That *is* a big promise." I sigh. "You know what? All right. Let's grab some food."

Noah doesn't do much to hide how pleased he is. He offers me his arm. I hesitate a second before linking my own through it. This is very new ground for me. I'm not sure how to act. The guys I've been on dates with before were Breakwater guys, and Breakwater dates were more perfunctory trips out in public before the male in question tried to get into my pants. Tried and mostly failed.

There's a small smile playing over Noah's lips as we make our way down 2nd Avenue. I catch him look at me out the corner of his eye. We walk one block over and cross onto 1st, where Noah directs me to the doors of a bar aptly named O'Flanagan's. "You're kidding, right?"

He's wearing the biggest shit-eating grin ever. "Hey, I'm Irish, okay? I get homesick." He guides me inside and we're met with applause and whoops from at least a hundred people, all pressed up tight against each other like sardines. Their backs are to us, watching someone in the far corner strumming an instrument by the bar. Goodness knows what all the fuss is about but the place smells amazing. My stomach growls again, making Noah chuckle. "Sit here, darlin'. I'll grab us some bar menus." He points me over to the only empty booth in the place. I shuck off my jacket and scarf, rubbing my hands together to try and warm them.

"Last song! Let's grab some water for our parched musician," a voice announces over the speaker system. A series of moans and boos are chanted by the crowd.

"Screw the water, get him a beer!" a woman yells.

Another woman catcalls, "Tequila body shots!"

Whoever is up there is causing quite a stir. Noah and I pick out what we want to eat. He gives me money for his food and heads to the bathroom, while I head to the bar to place our order. I'm getting my own cash out when I hear a familiar voice behind me.

"I'll get that, Claire. Put it on my tab." Luke Reid, standing right next to me, tips a bottle of water to his lips, sweat beading on his forehead. My knees buckle like someone just took a sledge hammer to them. His dark hair is damp and messy, ruffled in that *I don't give a fuck* style only a few guys can pull off convincingly.

"Luke?"

He screws his mouth up to one side, raising his eyebrows. How the hell does he make that rued look so ... so ...

"Hey, Beautiful." He sets the bottle down on the bar and frowns at Claire, the bartender—she's scowling at me. "What's wrong?" he asks.

"Nothing wrong, Luke. It's just that she's ordered two meals and some beers."

He blinks at her like she's just said something in Swedish. "So?"

"Okay," she answers, shrugging. "I thought you might have thought she was on her own or something, is all."

Luke smiles down at me, nudging me with his shoulder. "She thinks I'm trying to hit on you."

"You don't have to pay for our food, Luke." This is getting more awkward by the second.

"I know I don't. I want to, though. That so bad?"

I stuff the money I'm holding in my hand directly into my pocket, color burning at my cheeks. "Um, thank you. I didn't know you played here." I feel the need to clarify that, just to make sure he knows I'm not stalking him. That's the last thing I need.

"Yeah. I sometimes play here before a night shift starts. Amps me up. The twelve-hour shifts can drain you sometimes." He nods over to Noah, who's returned from the bathroom and is sitting behind us. "You on a date?"

"No. No, of course not." *Of course not?* What am I, some kind of virginal fucking nun? I can be on a date if I want to be. I pull my shoulders back, standing a little straighter. "Well, kind of. It might be. I'm not really sure."

Luke, still staring at Noah, frowns. His expression is a dark one. "Haven't defined the relationship, huh?"

"No, it's not a relationship. We don't have … I mean, it's not …" I hate that I've turned into this person, this girl who can't speak properly. It's terrible. Luke bends the guitar pick in his hand so hard the green plastic turns white. He tosses it onto the bar.

"Okay, well good luck with it, whatever it is. I gotta go. I have one last song to play."

"Sure."

He tips his head to one side and half closes his eyes, staring at me intently. "You know I'm always here, right? If you need anything, all you gotta do is holler, Ave. Especially if you need anyone's kneecaps breaking." He shoots Noah a pointed glance when he says that. I haven't told him people call me Ave now. It just falls out of his mouth like it's obvious. He backs away, taking four steps before he turns around and disappears back into the crowd. The people part for him like he's freaking Jeff Buckley reincarnated or something.

"Who was that?" Noah stands behind me, propping himself up against the bar by one elbow. He's smiling, but his forehead is furrowed.

"Just a friend," I tell him.

Claire walks back behind the bar, shooting daggers at me as the crowd erupts into cheers and whistles. From this position, I can just about see the top half of Luke's upper body as he climbs onto what must be a small stage in the corner. He places a guitar strap over his head and sits down—I'm assuming there's a stool there.

"What are the chances, huh? You know the guy who plays here," Noah says, leaning close so he can speak directly into my ear. His breath skims across my neck, hot, and I have to fight the urge to take a step back. It's not that it isn't nice. It is … but, I don't know. Something's stopping me from enjoying his proximity as much as I might have done twenty minutes ago. I'm not stupid enough to pretend I don't know what that something is. Or *who*. I just refuse to admit it.

"Thanks for being so welcoming tonight," Luke says softly into the mic. His voice is somber, and a hush falls over the sea of people between the bar and the stage. People whisper to each other, as though it's imperative they hear every last word out of his mouth. "I only have one more song to play tonight. It's not one of mine, it's a classic. This song means a great deal to me, so I hope you enjoy it."

Luke strums a few chords out on his guitar, staring down at

the frets, even though I'm a hundred percent positive he doesn't need to look to find exactly where each of his fingertips should be. It takes a moment before I recognize the slow progression of the chords he strums out. When his foot starts tapping out a familiar rhythm against the stage my throat begins to close up. It's "Blackbird." "Blackbird" by the Beatles. The only song my father knew how to play—his favorite. Luke's brows pull together and upwards as he starts to sing, and my stomach lurches. Oh god. His voice is beautiful. Rough and perfect and full of emotion. He sings like it's his heart that's on the floor right now, not mine. The words—about fixing broken things, broken hearts and broken wings, learning to fly—each one of them punches through me until I feel like I can't breathe.

"Can we ... do you mind if we sit down again?"

Noah nods and gives me his trademark smile, guiding me back to the booth. It's a short song so I only have to struggle through two more minutes of "Blackbird" before it's finally over and the screaming college girls are doing what they do best again: screaming.

"He's good," Noah says, slugging back some of his beer. The words themselves are complimentary but his tone doesn't necessarily marry up with them.

"Yeah. He is." And he really is. But why ... *why* did he have to play *that* song?

"Encore! Encore!" The body shot girls have clearly had at least one more round of tequila. They don't seem keen to let Luke off the stage without another song.

Noah laughs, watching the scene play out with bemusement. "What is this, fricken' Madison Square Garden or something?"

I risk a look behind me and Luke is holding up his hands, doing his best to navigate his way off the stage without offending anybody. Doesn't look like he's going to be successful, however. The girls bar his way, high-heeled feet tapping with expectation. Luke drops his hands, resignation settling in on his face. He sits back down on his stool. "All right, all right. One more song. Make it a cover, though. You guys decide."

"What can you play?" someone shouts close by.

Luke smiles, his teeth flashing in a genuine smile. "Anything you got."

"'Radioactive'!" the same guy calls.

"Yeah, 'Radioactive'!"

"'Radioactive'!"

Luke just nods his head. This time he doesn't look down at his guitar. He lets his eyes roam over the bustling bodies in front of him as he starts to slam out a bluesy, raspy version of the popular Imagine Dragons song. This performance is so different to the one I just witnessed. "Blackbird" was filled with tangible pain, while this is playful and electric. I get goose bumps when he mimics the part where Dan Reynolds sings, *"breathing in the chemicals."*

"Food's here," Noah says, drawing my attention back to the booth. Wow. I've been staring at Luke and completely ignoring the guy who brought me here.

"Shit, sorry. I've just never seen him sing before," I apologize, as Claire drops our burgers off at the table. She doesn't spare either of us a glance. She's too busy ogling Luke.

"You known him long?" Noah asks, picking up his burger.

"We grew up together," I say. "He's older, though, we never really hung out or anything."

"Hmmm. Another Idaho local in the big bad city."

"Huh?" I'm inches away from blowing my cover completely when I begin to ask him what he means. I remember just in time. I'm from Idaho now, which means Luke now has to be from Idaho, too. Man, this is getting complicated. We eat our food as the whole bar sings along to the chorus of the song. When it's done, people disperse and talk in groups, ordering more drinks and food from the bar. I feel the intense pressure of Luke's gaze as he packs up his guitar and walks silently out of O'Flanagan's. He doesn't even say goodbye.

The awkward moment between Noah and I passes as soon as we leave the bar, and he insists on walking me back to the apartment. He doesn't hang around for an invitation inside; he just leans forward and carefully tucks a strand of hair gently behind my ear.

"You know," he says, "if I didn't like you, now would be the time that I tried to kiss you."

"What?" Part of me wants to laugh. Laughter is such a foreign thing to me these days that I never really know whether it's the appropriate reaction, though. Noah has a perfectly serious look trained on his face, and I don't really want to offend him. Even after the burger mix-up, I think there's still potential here.

"Oh yeah, that's right," he says. "I'd be all over that if I didn't like you. Kissing, lip biting, hands everywhere, the works." He wiggles his fingers at me and winks. Definitely joking now. The laughter I finally allow myself now feels like it might be a beat too late.

"That makes absolutely no sense."

"It totally does," he disagrees. "If I didn't think you looked like some kind a' angel with all that blonde hair and your ridiculously cute nose, I'd definitely be trying to sleep with you right now. But as it stands, my hands and my lips are going to behave themselves tonight. I want more than one shot at giving them what they want."

I tuck my chin into my jacket, knowing he'll still be able to figure out that I'm grinning by the way my eyes are crinkled at the corners. "That's the second time you've said that."

"What?"

"That you think my nose is cute."

Noah tips his head back and laughs, attracting the attention of a couple walking by on the street. They smile at us when they pass, and Noah holds his hand out. "Wait up a second, can I ask you guys a question? Don't you just think this girl has the cutest nose? I've told her *twice* now but I think we need an outside opinion."

The man and woman, both rugged up in thick coats, laugh. "It's cute, all right," the woman agrees.

"See?" Noah thanks the couple by giving them a low bow, which is ridiculous and cute at the same time, and they go on their way, their boots crunching in the snow. Noah takes a step toward me and suddenly there's no more space between us.

"Whoa. I thought you weren't going to kiss me," I say, panic rising up in my throat.

Noah purses his lips, staring down at me for a second. He really is tall. I freeze when he reaches up and gently brushes my hair back again, this time with both hands. His fingertips graze my jaw on either side when he lets them fall. "I'm not." He touches his index finger to the tip of my nose and smiles, backing away. "Might do soon, though."

"If I let you." This, right here, is one arrogant son of a gun.

A dangerous smile spreads across Noah's face. "If you let me."

I pace up the steps and open the door to the apartment building, and the whole time Noah backs away down the street, watching me with that same mischievous look on his face. I'm single, and so is Noah, which means I am allowed to enjoy him flirting with me, teasing me with the promise of future kisses to come. So then why does it feel so wrong? I know exactly why, and it sucks. I head inside with Luke's greeting from earlier ringing in my ears:

Hey, Beautiful.

NINE
CONTRACT

LUKE

WYOMING'S JUST as cold as New York, but when I walk out of O'Flanagan's my body still locks up. The frigid night air stabs at my lungs. I hover in the entranceway, letting the air bite at my insides, fighting an unwinnable battle. Unwinnable, because I never know the right thing to do where *she* is concerned. Was it weird that I didn't say goodbye? Should I go back inside and say it now?

You are not *walking back in there now just to say goodbye. Fucking idiot.* What the hell is wrong with me, anyway? I try not to think about her, but just like always she's there, at the forefront of my mind, demanding attention. And now she's started showing up where I am, too, when I'm trying to stay the hell away from her.

Iris Breslin.

There are a thousand and one places she could have gone with her date tonight, but no. She had to walk into the one bar where I was playing? What does that say? I spent weeks trying to hunt her down when I found out she's moved to New York, gave myself a serious fucking headache over it when I couldn't track her down, and now here she is. First, I run into her at the frat party call out, and now here she is at O'Flanagan's. Sure, I went looking for her in between those two events, but whatever. That was for a good reason. Now, it's as though the universe is trying to throw us together.

I hike the strap of my guitar case higher onto my shoulder and step out into the crowds. I can't go back and talk to her. It would look weird, and besides, I have a shift to get to. Law enforcement isn't really a job you can be late for. Not without earning yourself a chewing out from the higher ups, and those are really unpleasant.

I have to catch the subway to reach my precinct. The walk to the subway station is freaking cold, but my mind is distracted from the bitterness of the weather by thoughts of Iris with that guy. That motherfucking guy. He looked like a complete asshole.

My cell phone rings halfway between the bar and the subway station. I snatch it from my jeans pocket, a cowboy on the quick draw, glad of something to do other than walk and think. Walking and talking is much better.

"This is Reid."

"This is Cole. What up, asshole? Since when do you answer your phone like you're in *CSI New York*?"

"There is no *CSI New York*, anymore," I reply. "It got cancelled. And I answer my phone like that because the only people who call me on this number is work."

"And me. I call you on this number."

"Unfortunately." Cole Rexford, bass player of D.M.F and all-round wise-guy shrugs on the other end of the phone—I *know* he does. I can practically hear it. Cole could be a professional shrugger.

"Are you coming over to my place in the morning? We need

to talk to you," he says.

"*We* need to talk to you? Who's we?"

"Me and the other guys. I had a phone call this afternoon. They were here at the time."

"Just tell me." I don't like the sound of ominous phone calls. Especially ones that apparently involve D.M.F as a band.

"Better if we all sit down and iron this one out, Luke." I can hear the hesitation in Cole's voice. He knows. If this is what I think it is, he *knows* what I'm going to say.

"Just spit it out. I'm not driving around the city all night, wondering what the hell I'm gonna be walking into when I knock on your door, Rexford."

Cole sighs. "All right, fine. But just so you know, I don't want to hear you say a word right now. I want you to think long and hard about what this could mean for you and for the rest of us."

"All right."

"I'm fucking serious, man. You have to think about it."

"I just said all right. Spit it out!"

"MVP have offered us a deal. I know you said not to send in that demo, but shit, man. Our new stuff is on fire. You can't deny that."

Most Valuable Player Records, MVP if you're anyone who has to say their name more than once, is the biggest recording studio in America. And I *did* specifically tell Cole not to send in a demo of our music because they are also based on the west coast, in L.A. of all places. "No way MVP would ever offer us a deal without seeing us play. They would have contacted us, come down and watched a gig before that," I say. I have this shitty, sinking feeling before I finish speaking, though. I hope my suspicions are not correct. I really hope they're not, because if they are, that means Cole and the guys have done something far worse than just sending in a CD without me knowing about it.

On the other end of the phone, Cole keeps his silence.

"Tell me you did not speak to them without telling me. And tell me you did not fucking let someone come down and watch us play without warning me first, Cole."

"It's not like it would have made any difference, man. You played like a fucking hero that night. They loved you!"

So he did it. He did fuck me over. "I can't—" I glance around, making sure no one's listening to me. I'm surrounded by a thousand people walking the streets of New York, but it can't be helped. "I can't fucking believe you did that, Cole. Of all the shitty, underhanded things you could have done—"

"Luke! You may have this idea in your head that you're not meant to be a musician full time, but let me tell you something, okay? Anyone who's ever heard you play disagrees with you. And, hey, you may be happy working long shifts for absolutely no thanks from the New York Police Department but I'm not exactly content in my work as a bank teller. And do you really think Pete and Gus are gonna be satisfied with being laborers for the rest of their lives? We've worked hard for this, man. We *do* want it. It's all we want."

I freeze, hunching my shoulders, stooping over the phone as people shove past me. "Then you guys go and get it, Cole. I'm not stopping any of you from chasing down your dreams. I don't wanna be that guy. I'm *not* that fucking guy."

Cole makes a choking sound. "Oh, but that's the beautiful part of this whole situation, isn't it? We would go out there and chase down our dreams, man, but that isn't what MVP are looking for. See, they might not want *us* without *you*."

The line goes dead.

"AIM FOR his legs. Take him out, Reid, Jesus Christ!"

Some of the things you see as a cop—man, I never thought people could be so messed up. I launch myself at the guy running down the street—no shoes, no pants, dick swinging free—

and tackle him, taking him to the ground. The homeless guy, I think he's homeless, at least, hits the sidewalk with a bone-jarring crunch. I think I've broken something at first, but then I realize it's the fully loaded ice pipe we were originally trying to arrest him for possession of, before the guy started racking up subsequent offences: resisting arrest, assault, indecent exposure and public urination to name just a few.

"You fuck—you fucking bastard!" the guy wails. It's a mournful wail. "That was my last—last hit," he chokes out. Through his scruffy beard and a couple of weeks' worth of dirt, he looks like he's about to cry, and I'm hit with a wash of guilt low in my gut. Fucked, I know. Meth is highly addictive. It ruins people's lives, probably ruined this guy's life, and yet I feel bad that I've deprived him of the only thing he cared about.

The symmetry of the situation hits me, then. I find myself wondering whether I'm really sorry I crushed this guy's drugs into the snow, or am I simply feeling bad because of the guys? They want a record deal so bad, and lying in the trampled snow, my face only inches away from some belligerent guy's naked ass, uniform soaked, shoes covered in piss, I'm beginning to think I might actually be crazy not to want one, too.

"Get him up. Get some cuffs on him," Tamlinski heaves out. He bends over, hands braced against his knees, and spits into the snow. "Fuck me." The old guy managed to nail my partner right in the balls before he took off down the street, hence the assault charge. He's as white as a sheet.

I scramble to my knees, producing my cuffs, all the while kneeling lightly on the old guy's back, waiting for him to try and make a break for it. Now that his hit is gone, though, the fight seems to have left him entirely.

I secure the handcuffs around his wrists and help him to his feet. "Give me your jacket," I say to Tamlinski.

"Why do you want my jacket?"

"Guy's naked from the waist down, asshole."

Tamlinski shakes his head. "I'm ain't having his junk rubbing up against my jacket. You give him your fucking jacket!"

"Tamlinski, I already have urine soaking the bottom of my pants. It's inside my goddamn shoes. *Now hand it over*." I hold out my hand, waiting. My partner gives me a murderous look as he slips his NYPD bomber jacket from his arms.

"I swear to god, if he pisses on that—"

The homeless guy sways next to me, grinning. He's missing most of his teeth. "I don't need to go no more. I already went."

"Don't I know it." I wrap Tamlinski's jacket around his body, and the three of us make our way back to the cruiser, a hundred feet up the road.

Back at the station, Tamlinski throws his jacket into the locker room trashcan. My pants swiftly follow suit. I rinse out my boots and hold them under the hand dryer, swearing to myself under my breath. No one asks me what I'm doing. Being thrown up on/pissed on/ shit on is a common occurrence around these parts.

It takes us a clear hour to book the homeless guy, get changed and back out onto the streets. Tamlinski insists that I drive us to the very limit of our patrol to an all-night diner on the pretence of grabbing us *the best bagels in New York*—every single diner in New York sells the best bagels—but I know the truth. I give him shit for it when he clambers back into the cruiser.

"You asked her out yet?"

"Asked who out?" he frowns, thrusting a brown paper bag stained with grease at me.

"Her." I point to the curvy blonde-haired girl behind the counter that Tamlinski's been flirting with for the past thirteen minutes. She sees me pointing and mistakes my gesture for a wave. She waves back, grinning like an enthusiastic schoolgirl.

Tamlinski smacks my arm down. "Don't fucking point at her, man. I'm trying to play it cool."

I'm helpless against the grin that spreads on my face. "You are *not* playing it cool." I shake my head. "Not even a little bit."

"Fuck you, man. You're just jealous. Where's your girl, huh? In the whole eighteen months we been partnered, we ain't never done a drive by on any hot piece of ass that *you* like. Your balls have probably shrunk to the size of chickpeas."

"Chickpeas?" I throw the cruiser into gear.

"Deny it. When was the last time you got laid, Reid?"

I grin, but the truth is that he's right. It's been a long time since I got laid. A really long time. Two years ago to be exact. Casey and I, we were good when we were just kids and nothing mattered. We slept with each other only a couple of weeks into our relationship, and then we kept on screwing each other for years. The sex never seemed to matter, until one morning, after we'd just moved to the city together, Casey climbed on top of me and I looked at her, *really* looked at her, and suddenly it *did* matter. I realised I didn't love her.

We stopped having sex that day. It took her a full twelve months before she left. Maybe I should have broken up with her instead of waiting for her to be the one to go. But I just kept thinking ... give it more time. Maybe you'll fall back in love with her. Maybe it'll start to mean something again. It was fucking stupid of me, really. Such a waste of time. I realized too late that I never loved her in the first place. It never did mean anything. She was just the hottest girl in my year, and I was just a selfish teenaged prick.

My smile dulls as we drive on into the night. "We can't drive by on the girl I like, Tamlinski. The girl I like lives in another precinct. And *I* respect the boundary lines." The precinct boundaries aren't my only problem, either. There are other boundaries to consider, too.

The rest of the shift passes. Eventually. I don't go to Cole's place. I'm too tired and too pissed off to talk to him rationally about the contract. It'll have to wait for another time. I'm exhausted as I climb the stairs back up to my apartment. I open up the front door and I strip off my t-shirt, shedding clothes as I head straight for the fridge and a cold beer. I don't see the shape of her at first. All I see is *intruder*, and all I think is *gun*. I'm charging forward, readying to take the fucker down, when I hear her voice.

"Jesus, Lucas. Stop! It's me. *It's me!*"

My hands curl into fists. I should have known better than to even think about her. This happens with a startling frequency, after all. Speak of the devil and the fucker will appear.

"Fuck, Casey. What the hell are you doing in my apartment?"

She gives me that full-lipped pout of hers that used to drive me crazy. Back when I didn't know or care what a manipulative bitch she was. "Oh, baby. *Your* apartment?" She stalks toward me, her heels clicking against the hardwood. She places her palm against my chest, leaning in, close enough that I can smell the perfume she always used to wear in high school because she knew I liked it. "Not too long ago, this place was *our* apartment, wasn't it? Our living room. Our kitchen. Our bathroom." She raises one eyebrow, looking me in the eye. "*Our bedroom?*"

TEN

BETRAYAL OF
THE FLESH

THE DARKNESS is almost perfect, which is why every single one of my senses seems to be compensating. My sense of smell, my hearing, taste — everything is heightened. And there's my skin, of course. Every square inch of me is lit up like a Christmas tree. My breathing twines with the breathing of another, someone else sharing my bed with me. The syncopated harmonics of our inhalations and exhalations combine with the delicious rustling of skin on skin—our bodies wrapping around one another.

I don't think about who I'm with, where I am. The only things that matters are his hands on me, his mouth on mine, the growing need that exists between us.

"Avery." The voice is familiar, I know it, have known it all my life. But I've never heard it in this context before. Never heard it breathing my name like it's a plea for help, like I am the only person capable of saving him.

"Luke, oh my god..." I can't think straight. There is something about this situation, something strange, but I'm too wrapped up in him, wrapped up in my sheets, in the way my heart is hammering in my chest to do anything about it. I don't want to do anything about it. "I need you. I need you so bad." Strong, capable hands rove over my body, cupping my breasts, leaving a trail of fire down my belly, and hesitating between my legs. I want him to touch me there. I want him to touch me there so badly. I curve my body into him, unembarrassed by my need.

"Avery, what do you want? What do you want me to do to you?"

I want everything. I want him to consume me, to own me, to light me on fire. "Touch me," I whisper. "Make me come. Make me come all over your fingers." There's something inside me, something possessing me. I would never normally say those words, never know how to ask for what I want. But right now, I'm happy to direct his hands, his mouth, his entire body to exactly where I need it. Strong arms wrap around me, lifting me up from the bed. My naked skin slides like silk across Luke's, and then he is underneath me. I can feel him rock solid between my legs, his hard-on pressing insistently against my pussy. I lower my body weight fractionally, enjoying the way his body tenses at the contact. He wants me, I can feel it. He pushes me back gently so that I'm sitting upright, straddling him, and then his hands find their way to my hips. His right hand grazes my skin, sending shivers of pleasure exploding through my nerve endings. And then his fingers ... his fingers head south, searching out the very center of me. It doesn't take long for him to find what he is looking for.

"Slowly," I murmur. I grind into his hand, feeling liberated and whole and incredibly brave. Luke's hips press up beneath me, applying the most amazing pressure against my clit, all the while his fingers stroking in small circles against the swollen bundle of nerve endings that seem to be controlling my brain.

"Is that good, Beautiful?"

"So good. So good," I pant.

"You want me to fuck you?"

I really do want Luke to fuck me. But I need him to make me a promise first. "On one condition," I moan.

"Anything. Anything you need."

I take hold of Luke's hand, guiding his fingers as they move on me. I hear his sharp intake of breath, his moan of pleasure. "I need you to swear you're going to fuck me as hard as you can. I want you to promise you won't stop until we both come together, until you make me scream your name. Think you can do that?"

Luke's laughter is strained, labored. A little surprised. "I can do that. I can do that, no problem."

"Then do it. Make me scream." I dig my fingernails into his chest and he groans, hissing in a combination of pain and pleasure. The next thing I know he's pushing my body back and sliding me forwards, his hands on my hips again, pulling me down onto him. Having him inside me is like nothing else I've ever felt before—he stretches me, thrusting deep inside me, and suddenly it's not dark any more. Fireworks light up my head, sucker punching me, and Luke makes good on his word. He fucks me hard. He fucks me until I'm screaming his name.

"Luke!"

I sit bolt upright in bed, adrenalin laying siege to my heart.

What the fuck? No, seriously, *what the actual fuck*?

What the hell was I just dreaming? The answer to that question is ricocheting around my head like a goddamn pinball. Breathing way too hard, I find myself pressing my thighs together, fighting the sensation that I was on the brink of something very amazing only two seconds ago. "No. Fucking. Way." There is no way I can handle dreams like that. Not with Luke Reid. I just can't allow it happen. I let my head fall forward, catching my breath. My sheets are a mess, completely wrapped around me and drenched with sweat. Perfect.

I fling them off, climbing out of bed and scrubbing my hands over my face, trying to rid myself of the sensation that I was having the best sex of my life a moment ago.

And with a guy I really shouldn't be thinking about, to boot.

ELEVEN
SURPRISE, SURPRISE

"SO YOU didn't even get kissed last night?"

"Nope." Well, Noah didn't kiss me, anyway. And dream lays don't count. I crunch down on a carrot, knowing how much it annoys Morgan when I eat on the phone. "Noah said something about wanting to have the opportunity to do it more than once."

"You know what that means, don't you?" Morgan sounds a little strained. She's nursing the hangover from hell courtesy of a night in with her parents. Apparently, the only way to handle such an event is to get roaring drunk on expensive tequila.

"No, what does it mean?"

"It means he's a player. He must be okay with *kissing* some girls just once, if you catch my drift."

"Could mean that," I concede.

"And that's okay with you?"

I think about how complicated everything is for me right now; do I really need the potential for something serious with a guy on top of all that? The answer is a resounding Hell No. I'm definitely not ready to think about emotions and feelings and all that other complicated stuff. That might require me to analyze the foray my subconscious took into Porno Land last night. "Yeah, I think I'm okay with that. I mean, he's an exchange student, for crying out loud. He'll be going back to Ireland at some point. Plus I won't have to explain anything about before, if we're just having some fun."

Morgan makes a choking sound down the phone. "Excuse me? Did I just hear you say, 'having some fun'? I think all the hard liquor I drank last night has my ears on the fritz."

Morgan Kepler, queen of hyperbole. I pop the rest of the carrot into my mouth and chomp down extra hard. "I'm not that straight-laced, Morgan. At least, I don't think I am."

"Trust me. You are."

"I resent that."

"I resent being accused of many things, but that, unfortunately, my dear, doesn't make them untrue."

"All right, well, maybe I don't want to be straight-laced anymore, then. Maybe I just want someone to take my mind off things. That's what Noah did for me last night—he made me forget for five minutes. That felt really good." Until we hit O'Flanagan's, of course. I've left that whole section of the night out of my story. I don't feel like explaining Luke and his incredible voice, or the fact that he sang "Blackbird." Morgan will only pick every single second apart and that will confuse things even further. And right now, some clarity would be great, given how muddy the water has gotten.

"I'm happy for you, Avery. You need some light entertainment in your life. And I'm sure that lovely Irish boy knows at least a hundred different ways to keep you lightly entertained."

I let out a loud sigh. There's a chance she's right. Of course, there's also a chance I'm sticking with Noah because anything else is far, *far* too complicated. "When are you coming back to campus?"

"Late tonight. You wanna grab a coffee at lunch tomorrow?"

"Sure." I hang up, the beginnings of a headache pressing in on my temples. I did my best to sound interested in Noah on the phone, but I'm going to have to work a little harder to convince myself. Maybe it's time to put Lucas Reid out of my head once and for all. If I'm honest with myself, he's been on my mind a lot since that night outside Tate's frat house, during waking hours as well as in my dreams. I shouldn't be letting myself. I should just stop. Allowing him to occupy space in my brain is sure to be just another road leading to pain and misery for me. For starters, Luke knows all the hideous details of my past. He *found* my dad, for fuck's sake. We've been meeting up since I was a kid so he can make sure I am okay. So he can try and find some sort of closure to the whole affair. Undoubtedly, he still sees me as the snot-nosed kid who kicked and screamed and smashed her living room window when she found out her father was dead. Those are the reasons why Luke will never feel anything for me beyond pity and perhaps a protective sense of duty.

There are other reasons, too. Normal ones. He's older, he's lived in the city on his own for years, and I'm just starting out at college. I know he's incredibly good looking, even if I pretend that doesn't affect me—it totally does—and that means he can probably have any girl he wants. On top of everything, I desperately don't want to feel anything for him because every time I look at him, I see his face on the day he came to our front door. I witness the horror of what he saw, the guilt of what he had to tell us. I see Breakwater and everything I want to leave behind. I need the man out of my life for good.

TINSEL WRAPS around the banisters in the stairwell in Luke's apartment, red and blue. Weird. It's a little early for Christmas decorations, and usually most places are decked out in red and green, anyway. Maybe *everyone* who lives in this building is a cop. I hike all the way up to the top floor and stoop down to leave the NYPD sweatshirt I've bundled inside a Macy's bag deposited in front of Luke's door. Luke's is the only apartment up here so the chances of someone else finding it before he returns from work are practically non-existent. I'm about to turn and walk back down the stairs when the apartment door opens and Casey Fisher steps out wrapped in a black and gray hound's-tooth trench coat. I freeze, completely stunned by the fact that Luke is back so early from his supposed twelve-hour shift, and that his ex-girlfriend is coming out of his apartment.

"*Iris Breslin?*" Casey sputters. She straightens and looks me up and down, the way people do when they're mortified and intrigued at the same time. She's cut her long black hair since high school but she still has a look of Snow White about her: bruised, pouty red lips, incredibly pale—that sort of thing. She's the type of person to stay out of the sun so her skin won't age. Much thinner that she used to be, she has a rake-thin New York chic working for her.

"Who are you—" Luke appears in the doorway behind Casey, shirtless, his dark hair all over the place. The tattoos that were playing peekaboo below his shirtsleeves the other day are much more extensive than I'd originally guessed. I would check them out if I weren't locked to the spot by the horrified look in his eyes. There's panic there, too. "… talking to?" he finishes.

Casey turns back to look at him, arching a perfectly sculpted eyebrow. "I see you're still fascinated by the macabre."

"Casey, don't," he growls, low in his throat. The sound sends vibrations through me like an earthquake. He stares at me, his eyes never wavering. I open my mouth to say something, but does anything come out? No, of course not. A handful of things rush through my head, none of them good. I could point out that I have a reason to be here. It would be simple enough to grab the Macy's bag and point inside, but then Casey will know Luke loaned his sweatshirt to me, and I don't want her thinking …

God, what don't I want her thinking? I stare wide-eyed at Luke for another second before my legs seem to make up their own minds and I turn and bolt down the stairs. I'm halfway down when the very worst thing happens. After all the times Luke has gotten my new name wrong, he picks now to get it right.

"Avery, wait! Avery!"

I choke out a sob and run.

TWELVE

HOOK, LINE & SINKER

THE LIBRARY is the warmest place on campus, which means it's packed. After a full morning of classes, I met Morgan here to study but so far not much studying has been done. At least, not on her part. She's been making out with Tate for the better part of forty minutes and the librarian looks ready to cause someone bodily harm. I'm in a terrible mood anyway, so it's probably a good thing I'm being ignored. That is, until …

"I'm going to pretend I'm not mortally wounded that you haven't texted me since our non-date." Noah slides into the seat beside me, hat pulled down over his ears, grinning mercilessly. I drop my pen into the crease of my book and try to produce a smile from somewhere—hard to do since my nerves are still shot from my run in with Casey Fisher. And Luke. Half naked, mussed, sexy as hell Luke. Urgh. It's not Noah's fault, though. None of this is.

"Sorry. Aren't you supposed to text me? Isn't that the way it's done anymore?"

Noah shakes his head, still flashing me a full row of pearly whites. "The metro male is no long the pursuer, but the pursued. I'm gonna need you to apologize."

"Apologize?"

"For giving me two sleepless nights in a row. It's fairly unkind, torturing a man so."

"Noah Richards!" Tate declares, slapping the study table. He and Morgan have finally come up for air, and my best friend looks positively devilish. I don't need her observing any interaction I have with Noah; she'll only interfere, which never ends well. Tate reaches over and bumps fists with Noah.

"You got those books, man?" he asks.

Noah nods, heaving his messenger bag up onto the table. "Just came by to drop them off for you. And also I wanted to stalk Avery Patterson over here, seeing as she's making me do all the work." He produces two textbooks the size of small telephone directories from his bag and slides them across the table. Morgan places a manicured hand on top of them and eyes the two of us.

"She's making you do all the work, huh? That's *rude*, Avery."

Oh boy. Here we go.

"That's what I thought," Noah laughs. "Unless ..." He turns to look at me. "I've got completely the wrong idea, haven't I? I've been walking around for two days thinking you fell for my pathetic attempts to seduce you, and now I'm here embarrassing myself because you're not interested."

"Oh, she's interested, honey," Morgan purrs. I want to slap her but she's freaking crazy in a fight. I'd only lose. It's better keeping her on side, so I just shoot her a foul look. The look she sends back is completely oblivious—*you can thank me later.*

"So you *did* fall for my pathetic attempts at seduction, then?"

I squirm, trying to avoid the toe of Morgan's Steve Madden boot under the table as she does her best to bruise my shins. I'll hear about this for weeks if I don't play along. "Of course I did. Hook, line, and sinker."

Noah's bravado doesn't slip; he's a consummate professional when it comes to flirtation. However, I do notice a flicker of relief in his eyes. Tate, who's been rifling in his wallet, tosses Noah a wad of cash across the table. "Thanks, dude. Would have had to pay a fortune to buy these new."

"No worries, I don't need 'em anymore."

"What are you doing today?"

Noah bumps me with his shoulder, grinning. "Got reading to do later. But right now? Right now I'm taking Avery Patterson for lunch."

WE GRAB lunch at the very first diner we come across off campus; we're too cold to be picky, and the smell of fresh coffee draws us in off the street. Margo's is packed to the rafters, filled with college students who've had the same idea as us. A small, bird-like woman is pinballing from table to table refreshing people's coffee mugs. The windows run with condensation, and every time the door jangles open and a new customer enters the people inside groan and holler for them to close the door.

Noah and I find a vacant booth and I order a coffee and some pumpkin soup. Noah orders a burger and an espresso. When the waitress leaves he leans across the table and smiles at me. I was wrong before: he does have freckles, they are just so faint they're barely visible, scattered lightly across the bridge of his nose. He stares at me without a scrap of shame.

"What?" Nerves are getting the better of me. I'm not used to someone studying me so intensely.

"Oh, nothing. I was just wondering what you were doing for Christmas break?"

I remember Brandon's promise to come back to the city.

Mental note: *must contact the owner of the apartment to see if it will be free.* "Not much. Just hanging out with my uncle again. What about you?"

"I'm going to be on placement."

"Over the break?" Our coffee arrives. I free-pour an unhealthy amount of sugar into the bitter black liquid. Noah raises an eyebrow but doesn't say anything about my sweet tooth.

"Yeah, my uni back in London would only let me stay two semesters if I completed my placement alongside my time here. Means I have to sacrifice baby Jesus' birthday party, but that's okay. I've never been one for Christmas."

"Huh. You've clearly never done Christmas in New York." I stir my coffee until I'm sure I'm not going to get a mouthful of un-dissolved sugar, and then take a deep draught. "So where are you completing your placement?"

Noah opens his mouth and lets out a laugh that sounds a little nervous. "Uh ... Africa."

"*What?* I thought you were interning at a paper or something! Africa? Why?"

"I figured before I came here that since I was gaining an international education I might as well make it really interesting. I organized to go and work for a not-for-profit agency in Sierra Leone, reporting on the conflict."

"But ..." *that's dangerous*, I want to say. Then again, from what he said about his childhood, Noah's used to finding himself in dangerous places. I raise my eyebrows and hold my coffee mug out to him. He chinks it with his own. "Kudos to you for doing something important instead of slinging caffeine at the *New York Times*."

He laughs. "They wouldn't have me. Heard I made bad coffee."

Our food arrives and we make small talk, Noah occasionally tapping me with his foot under the table, trying to keep his face straight while he pretends he hasn't done anything. I somehow manage to ad-lib my responses to the questions he asks me about my family, sticking to the truth as much as I can: my mother lives in New York too, but we don't get on; my uncle raised me the past four years; my passion for journalism comes from hard lessons learned in the past; my father is dead.

He tells me about his family back in Ireland, about being an only child, the pressure he was under to join the family business before he had a massive blow-up with his dad and left home for a while. Our stories couldn't be more different. It seems his parents are overly involved in every aspect of his life, or at least they try to be. My own mother doesn't want anything to do with me anymore.

The cold is somehow worse when we leave Margo's, maybe because the soup has warmed me and loosened the tension in my bones. Noah chuckles as I shiver, wrapping my arms around my body and stamping my feet in the snow.

"Here," he says, pulling me closer. He rubs his hands up and down my arms furiously, and I laugh as he jostles my body. The sound of my own laughter sobers me up pretty quickly—seems like it doesn't even belong to me. When Noah considers me thoroughly warmed, he stops and looks down at me, his eyes searching my face. For a moment I think he's going to lean down and kiss me, and from the wry look on his face Noah knows it. His eyes sparkle when he says, "Not yet, Avery," and pulls me back toward campus.

THIRTEEN

YOU WILL NOT BE SAVED

LUKE

"**THE RIFF** just doesn't sound right. And Pete? Pete, are you paying attention, man?" Cole's on the warpath today. Pete's bearing the brunt of our bassist's wrath, but I'm not exactly immune. My head's not in the game. I'm too busy cringing internally over Casey leaving my apartment just as Avery showed up. I mean, what are the fucking chances? I'm pretty sure she was crying when she ran down those stairs.

"Luke, start from the top, huh? And make sure you don't drop the last chord on the chorus. You're sounding like shit today." Cole still hasn't forgiven me for not signing that damn contract with MVP. For not going around to his place to discuss the matter after work. And I still haven't forgiven him for sending the demo CD behind my back in the first place. Makes for a very spiky dynamic as we practice our newest song, "Into The Deep." I wrote it in the space of a couple of hours, drunk, after Avery passed out in my bed. That was the night I told her about Mayor Bright's book. Seems like a long time ago now. The song's about forgiveness and shame. There's a pinch of guilt thrown in there, too, but I try not to write about that anymore. Max never liked me writing about guilt. Seems like it's my go-to emotion when I'm spilling things out onto paper, though. Hard to move past.

We start from the beginning of the song, me coming in first, then Pete on the drums, then Cole on bass. Gus is last, his rhythm guitar providing the final element of depth needed to round out the melody. At this stage we're just nailing down the music. It's how we do things—get the nuts and bolts down first and then add in the lyrics later, when our hands can work without thinking through the progressions of the song. The other guys do it this way to accommodate me, especially since I'm the only one singing most of the time, but it's the only way I know how. It's how Max taught me.

My fingers move over the frets of my Les Paul—a custom I bought with my first paycheck back in Break. Black lacquer, with silver, swirling etchings all over the body. It's a thing of beauty. My pride and joy. After all the years of playing with it, the guitar's like an extension of my body. A fifth limb. I know exactly where my fingers need to be at any one time. I find that very comforting.

By the time the song's done, I've committed the whole thing to memory. I could feel it settling in my bones as I played, ce-menting itself inside me. I won't ever need to look at the written music again.

"Better. That was much better," Cole says. He scrubs his hands over his shaved head, his tattoos out and on display de-spite the fact that it's fucking freezing in his apartment. The guy insists on living in an old warehouse down on the docklands, simply because the acoustics are great for our practices and he has no neighbors to piss off. The ceilings are high, though. Makes for very chilly winters. "I guess we can run through some of the other tracks now. Make sure everything's tight before we start playing gigs again. Luke, you've made sure you're not working the twenty-sixth, right?"

"I'm off," I confirm.

"Great."

That's all I get from him. *Great.* Sighing, I slip the guitar strap over my head. I lean her against the wall, and then I head outside, searching for the pack of cigarettes that I've taken to carrying around with me. I don't want to smoke. I don't like it. I do it very infrequently. Inhaling on a cigarette seems to be the only thing that can clear my head these days, though. Plus, it gives me a moment away from the tension inside Cole's place.

The world outside is gripped in frost. There are countless track marks leading up to Cole's front door, created back when a light layer of snow fell and now frozen into the shapes of compounded, icy boot prints. Slippery as fuck. Pillars of fog and smoke rise from the surrounding buildings, some of them still housing industrial works. Some of them converted into expensive apartments.

A homeless guy sits on the low wall of the shipping company opposite. His name's Reggie. We pick him up sometimes for loitering. Move him along. He's infamous across the whole of New York City for the sandwich boards he usually wears— always some doom and gloom slogan scrawled across the front. The sandwich board's missing today, though. Instead, there's a sodden piece of cardboard propped up against the wall beside him. On it, in thick black letters: You Will Not Be Saved.

"Don't I know it, buddy," I murmur under my breath. The cigarette smoke burns at my lungs, the air too cold, but I hold it long and deep in my chest anyway. Back inside the warehouse, Pete starts drumming, loops and rhythms in no particular order. Just an excuse to hit something hard. I find myself wondering what Avery's doing. Always, what is Avery doing?

My cell phone starts to ring. I recognize the area code right away. A Wyoming number. Not my mom, though. I answer, tossing my smoke into the frozen ice and grinding it under the heel of my boot just in case it is Mom and she can hear me smoking. "This is Reid."

"Luke, Chloe Mathers. How you doing?" I break into a smile. Chloe Mathers was my very first partner. She was like a big sister to me, took me under her wing when I first joined the police force.

"I'm great," I tell her. After all, it would be really self-indulgent to tell her the truth. "What's going on? Everything okay?" Chloe was the one who told me about Colby Bright's awful book idea. She'd texted me to let me know. It's been such a long time since I've actually heard her voice.

"Yeah, just thought I'd call, see how you were getting on. How's New York?"

"Cold." I laugh. "How's Breakwater?"

"Same. Saw your sister yesterday at the hospital. Had to drop off a drunk with a head wound at the emergency room. Emma was the nurse who came to treat him. She's all grown up, Luke. Hard to believe. I still remember you two when you were kids, tearing up the neighborhood, causing all kinds of chaos."

I haven't seen Emma since she graduated from college. Hearing from someone who knows her, who's seen her recently, is like a weight lifting from my shoulders. "I know, right? Had any exciting cases recently?" We ask each other this whenever we do get a chance to catch up. It's a nosy-cop thing. Of course, my cases are usually more interesting than Chloe's. Breakwater's not exactly a hub of organized crime.

"Actually that's partly why I'm calling. They're talking about re-opening the case, Luke."

I don't need to ask which case she's talking about. The murders of Adam Bright, Sam O'Brady and Jefferson Kyle, along with Max Breslin's subsequent suicide, have been *the* case in Breakwater ever since it all happened. "Why? Why would they do that?" Something's brewing on the horizon; I can sense it. And it's not something good. Avery's only just getting over the news of Bright's fucking book. Now this?

"I don't know," Chloe says. "The higher ups aren't exactly

forthcoming with any information. They just asked the officers who worked on the case at the time to go through their notes, make sure they didn't miss anything. Maybe they're trying to actually find something that'll link Breslin to the Ripper killings after all."

This isn't good news. Bright's book is making some outrageous claims, yes, but if the police are actually looking into it … god knows what that means. "So you're doing it? You're going back through the files?"

"I am. And I wondered if you would, too."

"Chloe, I don't know. I'm not a member of Break PD anymore. Did the captain ask you to talk to me?"

"No, he didn't. I asked him if I should involve you and he said no."

"Then I'd say it's a pretty good idea if I stay the hell out of it, wouldn't you?"

"You *did* work on the case, Luke. And you have the sharpest eyes I know. Maybe after all this time, you'll notice something you didn't pick up on before."

"I don't know, Chloe." There's a banging on the window behind me—Gus pulls a face when I turn around, flipping me off.

"Come on, man. We got work to do!" he calls through the glass.

"Are you still in touch with Iris?" Chloe asks.

"Yeah. She goes by Avery now, though."

"Have you told her? About what her dad said when we found him?"

The blood chills in my veins. "No. That information was classified when the case was closed."

Chloe breathes deeply on the other end of the phone. She's quiet for a moment, thinking. "That's good, I think. For now. It'll all come out soon enough, you realize? Especially if they're going to be digging everything up again."

"I know." And I know it's going to destroy Avery.

"Then don't you think, if we're being asked to go over the files again, looking for connections to tie Max into the Ripper killings, that it would be good to have someone out there, going through them to prove his innocence?"

When she puts it like that, I can hardly argue. I press my fingertips into my forehead; this is going to get complicated really quickly. "Okay, fine. You can send the file through. But not to the station. You'll have to email it to me."

"I had the same thought."

"LUKE! Come on, man!" Cole appears at the window this time, a plectrum gripped between his teeth.

"I gotta go, Chloe. I'll speak to you soon, though."

"Okay, I'm sending this stuff through now. If you find anything, get in touch right away."

We hang up, and I head back inside the warehouse, my stomach turning over and over like a washing machine.

"There he is." Gus grins at me, his blond hair falling free of its topknot. "You talking to a girl, man?"

"No. It was a work call. Sorry, I had to take it." Cole doesn't say anything, but I can tell he wants to. Yet again I'm putting my career as a police officer in front of the band. I suddenly feel like shit. "I'm sorry, guys. Look." I hold up my phone, making a show of switching it off. "You've got me. One hundred percent."

The remainder of our practice session is easier, less tense. Cole thumps me on the arm when we nail one of our harder, more complex songs first time round. We hang out for an hour or so after, drinking a few beers, and it's like before all of this madness with MVP. It's chilled. It's good.

When I get home, I check my email and Chloe has made good on her word. The entire Breslin murder file has been scanned and emailed through to my personal account. I start opening attachments, my mouth feeling as though it's lined with sandpaper. The information is so familiar. The photos and still frames: all pictures I have seen before, seared into my mind.

On top of the Breslin file, Chloe's also sent through the file for the Ripper killings. I open the first image, adrenalin pulsing through me as I take in the four symbols I never thought I'd see again. I never *wanted* to see again.

It hits me hard in the gut: if we didn't link these symbols to Avery's dad back in the day, why do the cops think they can be linked to him now? It seems strange. As I'm printing off the image of the symbols, it occurs to me that there might be one person who might know something about them, might be able to connect them with Max Breslin. But the very last thing I want to do is drag Avery into this all over again.

I may not want to, but I already know as I start printing off more of the files that it's going to happen.

FOURTEEN

ICARUS

WHEN I arrive back at the apartment, there's a note from Leslie on the kitchen counter, along with a bright orange envelope. I read Leslie's note first, my body locking up as I scan the paper.

> Roomie,
>
> That guy from last month came by to see you. He looked tired as hell. I'd still date him, though. Maybe you could tell him that if you see him again. I need an older guy in my life! Anyway, he practically begged me to give you this. He made me promise not to read it, said something about mail fraud being a federal offence (who is this guy???)
>
> Anyway, I'm staying in the city tonight with my sister but I'll be back tomorrow. If anyone comes by the apartment for me, tell them they can

reach me on my cell. See you soon,

Leslie xoxo

I know what's inside Luke's letter. It's an apology for Casey and for letting her in on my new identity. I don't think I can face reading that right now. I slide the envelope into the drawer of my nightstand and make myself some dinner, trying not to let myself sink into a black mood. I'm almost too cowardly to check my phone when it buzzes much later, worrying that it might be Luke. It's not, though. It's Morgan.

Morgan: Where are you? Come party with me!

I'm about to take a shower before bed. It's way too late to be going partying with Morgan. The woman doesn't seem to have any sense of timing.

Me: Are you lit, Morgan Kepler?

Morgan: Like a house on fire!

I laugh, but then turn my phone off. She'll be texting me all night otherwise. It's when I'm brushing my teeth that I realize I'm being pathetic and I should just read Luke's damn note. I get into bed at eleven thirty and retrieve the letter from my nightstand. When I open it, I'm a little taken aback. It's not an apology. Not even close. It's a single white piece of paper with four symbols drawn onto it.

Any of these symbols mean anything to you?

I immediately recognize one of them. The one that looks like a number eight on its side is fairly common. It's the symbol for eternity. I scan over the other markings, trying to think back. Are any of them familiar? I can't be sure. I don't think so. I flip over the piece of paper to see if Luke has explained anything on the reverse, but it's blank. I sit up in bed and stare at the symbols for another five long minutes. Why is Luke asking about them? And why is he not explaining himself? The endlessly curious part of me wants, no, *needs* to know.

Is that why he did it? To make me call? I shove the thought aside and slip the envelope back into the drawer. After a few minutes spent arguing internally with myself, I take out my cell phone and bring up Luke's number. I refuse to call. No, after the other morning outside his apartment, the vile look on Casey's face, the horror on his? I can't bear the thought of hearing his voice. I go with a text message instead.

Me: Why?

I hit send before I can chicken out and tuck my cell under my pillow, trying to put it all out of my head. It buzzes a couple of minutes later.

Luke:It's important.

Me: That's not an answer.

Luke:It's related to the Wyoming Ripper. I still have a friend back at Break PD. They asked me to help them out. I'm looking into a couple of things.

I have no idea what Luke is doing snooping into the Wyoming Ripper case, but it can only mean one thing: trouble.

Me:You have the file? Can you get it?

I wait, wide awake, for at least half an hour before I get a reply.

> **Luke**: I'm at work right now. I finish at 8 a.m. I'll call you then.

I don't bother replying. What's the point? He's going to call regardless, and I really want to know if he has that file. There has to be evidence in there that my dad is innocent. There certainly isn't going to be any evidence to prove his guilt, of that much I'm certain. If Luke has it … if he has that file, I *am* going to see it. I am going to tear it apart until I find a way to prove my father didn't kill all those girls.

"What are you up to, Monster?" I'm eight years old, diving in our indoor swimming pool for the seashells my father has tossed into the shallow end for me.

"I'm a mermaid, Daddy!"

"Of course you are, Monster."

I growl at him, baring my teeth, half of which are missing.

"You're getting ferociouser and ferociouser every day, my little mermaid monster." He laughs and lobs one of the shells I've collected back to the bottom of the pool. I growl even louder, throwing in a stern frown and a downturned mouth for good measure.

"Miss Wilmott says ferociouser isn't a word, Papa."

Dad's brow creases, and he bends down to pull off the Italian leather shoes my mother bought him. "She did, did she?"

"Uh-huh."

"Well you just tell her that it exists in Dr. Evil's dictionary, okay? She won't be able to argue with that."

"Okay, Papa. She taught us about a Greek moth today."

My dad laughs out loud—a hearty belly laugh, even though

he doesn't have the paunch to back it up. "Do you mean myth?"

I nod solemnly. "It was about a boy whose papa made him some wings out of feathers and wax so he could fly out of prison. He went too high up in the sky, though, and they melted off."

"Ah, I know that story. That's one of my favorites. Do you remember his name?"

"Icarus, Daddy! His name was Icarus!"

FIFTEEN
OVERDOSE

LUKE

A TWELVE-HOUR shift can seem like it will never end. That's how I'm feeling when the call comes through. One minute I'm thinking about what I'm going to say to Avery, what I'm going to ask her, and then the next my badge number is blaring out of the radio on my appointment vest.

"Officer Reid, please report over to ninetieth. Your presence is being requested by a drug overdose victim. Ambulance is en route."

Tamlinski, in the driver's seat, gives me an accusatory look. "Who you know over in Williamsburg?" he asks. That's the area ninetieth serves—East Williamsburg and parts of Brooklyn.

"No one. I don't know anyone over there." I speak into my radio, my head spinning. "Why me, dispatch?"

"Victim is one Morgan Kepler. Says she won't speak to anyone but you. Victim is violent. A danger to herself and officers on scene." The dispatch operator drops her professional tone. "Kid sounds like one crazy bitch, Reid. They want your ass over there to calm her down before she ends up giving herself a heart attack."

Morgan Kepler? The name's familiar but I can't place it. Tamlinski's already turning the cruiser around. "All right, copy. We're on our way."

Tamlinski gives me shit the whole way across the city, asking me if this Morgan girl is the piece of ass I've been hiding from him. I come close to punching him in the side of the head. There are police cruisers and an ambulance already at the scene when we arrive. The residents of the walk-up are all standing out in the hallways, eyes wide, hands covering mouths, as me and Tamlinski take the stairs at a run.

As soon as I see Morgan Kepler, I remember who she is. She was the girl with Avery the night we were called out to that noise complaint. The redhead. She's screaming at the top of her lungs, her face a brilliant shade of crimson, when we reach the apartment where she's collapsed. She stops when she sees me.

"You. You're here," she says.

"Hello, Morgan. What's going on, huh?"

"I don't …" She looks around, as though she's seeing her surroundings for the first time. She looks suspiciously at the EMT trying to take her vitals.

"I don't know why I'm here," she says. "Where's Tate?"

"Who's Tate?" one of the officers on scene asks me. "She was screaming for him first, before she started screaming for you."

"I have no idea who Tate is."

"But you know who *she* is, right?" He gives me a disapproving look. Cops aren't meant to hang around with drug abusers. Especially not crazy ones.

"Vaguely. She's a friend of a friend."

"Oh, Avery!" Morgan seems to come to, her eyes bloodshot and round, fixed straight on me again. "I need Avery, Luke. Can you get her for me? Can you get her?"

"Yeah, I can get her."

"We need to keep her still, Officer. Can you keep talking to her?" a female EMT asks me. She has a scratch on her face, underneath her left eye; I get the feeling Morgan might be responsible.

"Yeah, sure."

The EMT tries to strap an oxygen mask to Morgan's face. She lashes out, screaming again. "Morgan? Hey, Morgan? Can you remember Avery's cell number? I can call her for you if you like?"

"You ... you have her number," she wheezes. The eyes roll a little, showing too much white. "You're in love with her."

"What? Did she tell you that?" I can't help it. The question jumps out of my mouth before I can stop myself.

"No. But I know her. And I saw ... the way you looked at her. It's true. You love her, right?"

"Yeah, I guess so."

"You need to call her for me, okay? You need to tell her not to call my parents. Stop. STOP!" She kicks out, aiming for the EMT who's now trying to check her arms for track marks, but she lands a solid hit on me instead. From my crouched position at Morgan's feet, I fall back, landing on my ass, nearly knocking Tamlinski over, too.

Morgan's arms and legs start shaking violently. She's seizing. "Okay, we're gonna need some room now. She's going into shock," the other male EMT says. I scramble backward out of the way, watching on as they work on the girl. By the time they've got her loaded up on a stretcher and they're hurrying her down the stairs, it's pretty obvious things aren't looking good.

Tamlinski turns to me, the insensitive bastard grinning like a fiend. "So. I take it we're off to see *Avery* now, huh?"

SIXTEEN
MIDNIGHT RUN

AT FIRST I think the thumping is loud bass music coming from a car out on the street, but the rhythm is off. It's more of a hammering sound. I roll onto my side, trying to block it out but it's no use; it just keeps coming. After another ten seconds I realize someone is actually shouting my name. My eyes snap open—*Shit! Shit! Shit! Shit!* I scramble out of bed so I can rush to get the front door, nearly face-planting when my ankle snags in the bed sheets. The living room is freezing and pitch black.

"Avery! Avery, open up. It's Luke."

I falter, my hand on the doorknob. What the hell's going on? He said he'd call when his shift ended, not try and knock my door down at 3.45 in the morning. I yank the door open in the huge, threadbare t-shirt I use to sleep in, immediately noticing the woman from 6B standing in the hallway leaning against the wall, her hair at angles. Luke looks grim when his eyes meet mine. He's in full uniform and his partner, the same stocky, short guy with the Brooklyn accent I saw him with at the Irish party, stands beside him. Why would he bring his partner here to talk to me? I frown and try to chase away the remnants of sleep from my head. Luke clears his throat.

"Sorry to wake you, Ave. We need to talk to you."

"Couldn't this have waited until the morning?" I hiss, wrapping my arms around my body. "You said you were going to *call*. And you didn't tell me whether or not you have the—"

"This isn't a social call." The tone in Luke's voice is clear: *this has nothing to do with your dad*. His deep brown eyes are wide, unblinking, like he's focusing really hard. I take a second to actually look at him properly, to take in the way he holds himself and the way he's staring at me. This is exactly how he looked when he turned up on our doorstep five years ago. A sudden stab of panic rises up in my throat, making me choke.

"Oh god, what is it?" My hand flies to my mouth. "Is it Uncle Brandon? Is it Mom?"

Luke shakes his head and gestures past me. "Is it okay if we come in for a second?"

"Just tell me!" The wall of calm I've been trying to keep in place comes crashing down. "Tell me right now!"

He places his hand gently on my shoulder and pushes me into the apartment, walking in after me. His partner follows, pulling the door closed behind him.

"Luke, what's going on? Please, just tell me. If it's Brandon, you can tell me. Whatever it is, I'm fine, I can take it. Please, Luke—"

"Stop, okay. Take a breath, Beautiful." He guides me through the apartment, peering through doorways until he comes to my bedroom. He sits me down on my bed, then positions himself by the window. "It's not your mom or Brandon. It's that girl, the one I saw you with coming out of that frat party—Morgan."

"Morgan?" Every part of me goes still. I'm dizzy from lack of oxygen before I take another breath. "Is she dead?" I whisper.

"No, she was taken to hospital. Looks like she's overdosed

on something. She was asking for you before she passed out. The doctors have her in an induced coma while they try and clear the drugs out of her system. She's pretty sick, Ave."

A strangled sob fills the room—a weird, alien sound that couldn't possibly have come from inside me. I cover my mouth with my hands and suddenly I can't see. My room, Luke, every-thing—it's all consumed by the tears flooding my eyes.

"I have to go. Can you take me to the hospital? I need to go right now. Her parents, they live in Charlestown. They need to be told. It's going to be hours before they can get here. She needs someone with her, Luke. She needs ..." I'm incoherent before I know it, trying to form words but only managing more sobs. Luke picks me up from the bed and pulls me into his arms, and then I'm crying into his police vest while he strokes his hand over the back of my head, whispering things into my hair. I'm too numb to hear what he's saying; I just cling onto him until I feel like I can handle standing on my own.

"What kind of drugs do they think it is?" I mumble, while trying to formulate what I'll need to take with me to the hospital.

"It's looking like ecstasy at the moment but it's too early to tell. Do you know who she might have gotten pills from?"

"No, no way! I don't know anyone like that. Morgan would never take anything willingly. She must have been spiked."

I'm pulling a sweatshirt over my head when he asks, "When was the last time you heard from her?"

"Uh ... I guess about six, six thirty or so. She was ... she was already drunk. She wanted me to meet with her at Tate's place to party. Is that where they found her?"

Luke's radio starts to chatter but he ignores it, and for some bizarre reason I find myself marveling at how damn tall he seems in his uniform. "No. The ambulance picked her up from an address in Williamsburg. She was with a bunch of guys from King's College."

"But that's in Manhattan."

"I know. They were at a party. No one seemed to know who had thrown it. None of them had ever met Morgan before tonight."

That makes even less sense. I feel sick. Morgan was slipped drugs at a party where she knew no one? What the hell was she doing out there in Williamsburg with a bunch of complete strangers? And where the hell had Tate and Noah been? Luke averts his eyes when I pull a pair of jeans up my naked legs. I tug my boots on angrily and get my coat.

"I'm going to kill whoever did this to her."

"Let's just make sure she's okay first, yeah?"

Luke and his partner, Officer Tamlinski, drive me down to Woodhull hospital in north Brooklyn, where Morgan was taken by the ambulance. I do my best to keep myself in one piece; Morgan will be pissed at me if I collapse into a useless wreck, and I can't handle Luke seeing me like that, anyway. It's bad enough that he feels sorry for me because of everything else. I won't add this to the list.

The city traffic is much lighter at four in the morning but it still isn't great. Being in a cop car definitely helps move things along, especially when Tamlinski hits the lights and sirens to get us through the most congested areas. The cab drivers are still jerks, though, and there are plenty of people on the streets. I hunker down in the back of the cruiser, pulling my coat up around my ears, and I wrack my brain, trying to figure out how Morgan has landed herself in an induced coma. Fuck, I'm going to wring that girl's neck when she wakes up.

"Okay back there?" Tamlinski asks as we pull into the hospital parking lot.

"Yeah, I'm freakin' stellar, thanks. My best friend's possibly dying and half of Columbia just saw me get carted off in the back of a police cruiser."

Luke doesn't say anything, just continues staring out of the windshield with a clenched jaw. Tamlinski sucks his teeth and mutters something under his breath. As soon as he parks up, I unclip my seatbelt and am trying to open the door when I realize there's no handle. Luke gets out and opens the door for me, offering me a tense smile.

"We prefer it if the people we arrest don't tuck and roll."

"Uhuh." I climb out and start to head inside, but he catches me by my elbow.

"This didn't go down in our precinct. I'm not technically supposed to stay with you, but I will. I'll show you where Morgan is, and—"

"No! Luke, it's fine. Don't get yourself into trouble on my account."

His jaw sets as he slams the cruiser's door closed behind me. "I'm not leaving you alone, Avery."

"Luke! I don't … I don't *need* you to stay, okay!"

"I'm not leaving you alone."

I glance up at the hospital, light pouring out of every window, staff loitering around the side so they can smoke out of sight of the lung cancer patients, and I feel myself wilt a little. The thought of sitting in a waiting room on my own for who knows how long isn't appealing at all. But what choice do I have? "Okay, fine, I'll call someone."

"Someone?"

"Yeah, *someone*. Morgan's boyfriend, Tate, or maybe I'll call *my* boyfriend."

Luke's eyes frost over. He voice is positively arctic when he asks, "That guy from the bar?"

"Yeah, the guy from the bar." And then, "No!" I hide my face in my hands, trying to get a grip. This is ridiculous. Now I'm lying to him? "Not the guy from the bar. I'm not really seeing him, but—"

"It's okay. You just focus on your friend right now." Luke's eyes have defrosted, although he still looks seriously pissed when I lower my hands. "Are you going to be all right?"

I bite the inside of my cheek, feeling tears prick my eyes. "I think I got it."

"All right Well, call me if you need me."

Luke remains behind in the dark, his eyes burning holes into my back as I stomp across the parking lot. I don't look back when I reach the entrance; I just pause to wait for the automatic doors to open, and then rush inside. The nurses' station is deserted when I get there, which is typical. I wait ten minutes before someone shows up, and when the stout nurse does arrive, she's hostile, to say the least. I ask her where I can find Morgan Kepler and she stabs her finger at the floor.

"Follow the blue line to the ICU. There'll be another nurses' station there. You're not going to be able to see your friend until she's stable, though. I'd have stayed home and gotten some sleep if I were you."

I almost snap that if she were me and had stayed home, she would have been a royally shitty friend, but I manage a tight smile and set off following the thick blue band on the floor. I trace it to an elevator, where it disappears. Does that mean I'm supposed to get on the elevator? There's a blue sticker next to the button for the fifth floor. I get on and ride it up to five. When the doors roll back, the line on the floor picks up again. I pull my coat around myself, trying to avoid the hollow gazes of the people sitting in chairs along the hallway, until I locate the nurses' station. An older nurse with smudged mascara and a weary expression tells me that the angry nurse downstairs was right—there's no chance I can see Morgan until she's out of the woods. She directs me to take a seat with the other folks in the hallway and promises she'll come find me if there is any news.

I collapse on a plastic fold-down chair and stare at my sneakers, immediately in need of someone else to be here with me. The fear rolling off the others, all sitting in silence, is palpable. They're in the same boat as me, waiting to find out if someone they love is about to die. Car crash. Assault. House fire. There are a hundred and one different ways a person can end up in a place like this. I don't want to think about any of them.

I need Leslie. Maybe Tate and Noah, depending on what they have to say for themselves. My hand goes to my pocket, searching for my cell, and I almost choke when I realize I left in such a panic that I forgot to bring it. My purse and all my cash, too. I'm stranded way across New York City with no money and no cell phone and no hope of having either one any time soon. There isn't much I can do about it, so I sit back and stare at the wall, trying not to contemplate what will happen if Morgan dies. I don't want the first time I meet her parents to be when they find out she's dead. Sleep takes me after a while, but it's an awkward, restless sleep thanks to the uncomfortable chair. The nurse comes and finds me at six a.m. to tell me nothing has changed. The next time I come to, I find Luke sitting next to me. He's in his regular clothes: a dark hoodie pulled up over his head, ratty jeans and beaten-up DCs. He doesn't notice I'm awake for a minute. I watch him tapping away on his cell phone, gently frowning. He looks tired, but he still came. Gratitude washes through me. I was hideous to him and he still showed up.

My voice cracks when I speak, broken from sleep. "Hey."

He starts and almost drops his phone, giving me a half smile. "Hey, yourself."

"Sorry about earlier." I drag my hands back through my hair—god, what must I look like?—and sit forward, stretching out stiff joints. Luke stoops down and collects a takeaway coffee cup, which he then hands to me.

"It's okay. You were polite compared to some of the crap I usually get, trust me. Drink this. It should still be warm."

I take a swig and smile a little when I taste how sweet it is; Luke has watched me empty sachet after sachet of sugar into my drinks during our many coffee catch-ups back in Break. It's nice that he remembered. "Thanks, Luke. Thanks for being here."

He nods, scratches at the back of his neck. His eyes have that soulful look to them that always makes me think he needs

118

protecting from the world. I have no idea why, when he's the one protecting everyone else for a living, but that's what I've always thought.

"Just finished?" I whisper.

"No, it's nearly ten."

"What?" I can't believe I managed to pass out for so long. "Has the nurse been by again?"

Luke nods, leaning back in his chair so his shoulder touches mine. "Yeah. No change. They're going to try waking her up soon, though."

I draw in a shaky breath and clench my fists. "Do you see this happen to many people?"

"A few," he sighs, taking a sip of his own coffee.

"And what usually happens? Do they ... do most of them make it?"

Luke dips his head into his hood, staring at his hands. "Some of them do."

Some of them. I blow out a strangled breath and bury my face into my hands. "This can't be happening. This *seriously* can't be happening." Luke doesn't lie and tell me everything is going to be okay, because there's a real chance it isn't going to be okay. Lies aren't going to change that. He places his hand on my back, and the physical contact loans me enough strength to pull myself together. When I uncover my face, he leaves his hand there and I don't say anything because I need him right then. "So are you going to tell me about those symbols?" I murmur, chewing on my thumbnail.

"They were left on the bodies of the murder victims," he says in a hushed voice. "There were only three symbols for a long time. Toward the end, the fourth one appeared. That information was never released to the public. I wanted to see if they were familiar to you. Killers are usually looking for recognition when they start out murdering. If your dad—" I suck in a breath. Luke pauses, but only for a second. "If your dad was responsible, he probably would have had these drawn out somewhere."

"Why? Why would he ... wouldn't the killer have hidden it so he wouldn't get caught?"

Luke twists the drawstring from his hood through his fingers, tapping his foot against the scuffed linoleum floor. "No, not really. Serial killers usually want to get caught. Typically they're proud of their handiwork. They want to claim responsibility in the end."

"Proud?" I can't breathe. My dad would never have been proud of intentionally hurting anyone, let alone *murdering* them.

"I know, it's sick. But these people usually are. Sick, I mean."

That's a given. A caustic remark is on the tip of my tongue, but when I turn to look at Luke, the nurse from before is walking down the corridor. A pair of glasses perch on the end of her nose now, and the rings under her eyes are even more pronounced. The statue-like people around us realize she is approaching at the same time, and everyone turns to face her. It's like watching a time lapse of flowers opening to the sun as fifteen or so hopeful faces gravitate towards her. She walks past them, crushing them each in turn as she makes her way over to me and Luke.

"Morgan's awake," she says bluntly, her shoes squeaking as she pulls up in front of us. Those are the most amazing two words I've ever heard in my life. A tidal wave of relief crashes over me. I slump forward, drawing in a ragged breath. Luke's hand finds mine. "You still won't be able to see her for another couple of hours until we've got her stats leveled out a bit, but she's going to be fine. No sign of brain trauma, no internal damage. She's one lucky girl. We're going to need to discuss rehab for Miss Kepler once she's feeling up to it, but—"

"Rehab?" The nurse is stoic when I meet her gaze. She's obviously had to tell people this before. "Morgan doesn't need rehab. Her drink was spiked."

120

"It's standard procedure for us to ask some questions when OD patients come in, kid. And from her responses and the notes we have on file for her, Morgan requires medical attention."

"What? No way! I'm her friend. I'd know if she were doing drugs."

The nurse plants her hands on her hips. She gives Luke the kind of look that suggests she'd like a little help. "I can't discuss the content of Miss Kepler's interview with you, but I will say this: drug users hide their addictions well. They get good at concealing things, and they get good at lying. You should talk to your friend, Miss Patterson." She stalks away and vanishes through a set of double doors at the far end of the corridor, and I watch her back the whole way until she's gone.

"Morgan doesn't need rehab," I say, clenching my fists.

Luke doesn't look at me. He swigs his coffee and sighs. I'm on the verge of repeating myself when the elevator doors *ding* open and a man and a woman with panicked expressions burst into the corridor. I know in an instant they're Morgan's parents; the woman's auburn hair is a dead giveaway. Luke starts to stand but I hold my hand out. I definitely don't want to be the one to tell them about their daughter, but they deserve to hear the news from someone who knows her. I can at least do that.

SEVENTEEN
ADDICT

TURNS OUT I don't know Morgan as well as I'd thought. Her parents aren't shocked when I tell them she OD'd, and they don't believe for a second that her drink was spiked. Morgan has landed herself in hospital twice before through drugs. TWICE. She's struggled with cocaine and pills since her senior year, and her mom and dad packed her off to Seabrook House in New Jersey for three months. They only let her come away to college this far out of state because she maintains regular appointments with her doctors there, and they apparently know what kind of behavior to watch out for.

Well, her doctors can't have been doing their job. And I haven't been the only one keeping secrets. The difference is Morgan knows all of mine, or most of them anyway, and I've trusted her. She hasn't trusted me.

Luke drives me back to Columbia after Mr. and Mrs. Kepler start shouting at the already harassed nurse in the ICU; there's no way I wanted to go in and see Morgan while her parents were there and her mom was crying so hard. I'll go back later during visiting hours. Mad isn't even close to describing how angry I am at Morgan, but she still needs a friend right now. When she's out of hospital and capable of standing on her own two feet, that's when I'll tear her a new one.

"I'd offer to go grab you some breakfast," Luke says as he unclips his seatbelt, "but I had a hell of a shift and I'm gonna pass out any second now. Can you come by my apartment when you're done? I'm sure there's some things you'd like to look at."

I swivel in my seat. "So you've got it? You've really got the Wyoming Ripper file?"

Luke gives me a small nod. "A copy of it, obviously. My old partner, Chloe, she scanned everything and emailed it through for me. I ... I could get into some serious fucking trouble if I showed it to you, Avery. So could she."

"You've *got* to show me, Luke. I have to know. I have to—"

"Okay, okay," he says, placing a hand on my knee. "I figured as much, but you can never, *never* tell anyone, all right? I don't wanna get ass raped by all the people I've put in prison because you let this slip."

"I would never. I swear." Luke seems content, if a little uneasy with my promise. Reality suddenly hits me—the file that could condemn my father as a serial killer is within Luke's possession. Can I do it? Can I really open up that file and rifle through it? I guess I don't really have a choice. "I won't be able to come by until later. Is that okay?"

Luke reaches across and unfastens my seatbelt, his knee pressing up against mine. I shift uncomfortably and stare at him. He seems engrossed by the way I've gripped my hands tight in my lap. His forehead creases a little when he looks up at me. "No problem. I'm off for the next three days so it doesn't matter what time. Call me, though. I don't want you traveling across the city after dark, Beautiful. I'd prefer to come and get you if it's late."

"WHAT THE hell were you thinking, Morgan?" Her skin is even paler than usual, her eyes are bloodshot. She's so weak she can barely sit up without help. Even then it seems like a lot of work.

"It's not like I did this on purpose," she croaks.

"Didn't you?" Mrs. Kepler stuffs her used tissue up the sleeve of her cardigan. Why people do that I can never work out. It's so gross. "People are beginning to wonder if this was a cry for help, Morgan. The doctors have already explained that to us. Addicts use these events as a way of getting attention."

"I don't need help, Mom!"

"Oh, yes you do, young lady. And you're going to get it. You're going back to Seabrook. My daughter is not going to end up dead in some seedy—"

"I can't go back to Seabrook. I have school." Morgan clenches her jaw muscles, glaring at her mother.

"And what use is school to a dead person, Morgan Marie? If you're dead, then it won't matter whether you graduated college or not. You're only a freshman. You can go back to Columbia next year when you're fit and healthy."

Morgan looks distraught. I want to comfort her but that would feel weird with her mom staring at me like I'm intruding on a private family moment. I probably *am* intruding on a private family moment. I twist the leather strap of my purse nervously and make to get up.

"Don't leave, Ave, please. Mom, can you give us a little while to talk?"

Mrs. Kepler's severe expression deepens. "I'm not letting you out of my sight, kiddo. Who knows what you'll get up to while I'm gone. If this is the only way you'll—"

"*Mom!*"

"No, Morgan. I'm sorry. You can't be trusted."

Morgan's face turns bright red, something I've never seen before. She bunches up her bed sheet in her fists and squeezes, her whole body locked tight. "Mom. Get the fuck out of my room right now. I want to talk to my friend. You can come back in when she leaves."

Mrs. Kepler flinches back. Her lower lip wobbles like she might burst into tears. I feel sorry for the poor woman; she must be worried out of her mind. She gets to her feet and slings her woolen trench coat over her arm, trying to appear unflustered. Her eyes are wet with tears when she looks at me. "I want to thank you for waiting here all of last night, Avery, but I also want you to know that I don't trust you. I don't trust any of Morgan's friends, seeing as it's likely one of you gave her that dirty pill. In the future I won't be leaving Morgan's side. If you want to come and visit her again, I'm going to have to ask that you don't bring a bag with you into the room."

She swings around and slams the door behind her as she storms out, blowing over a get-well-soon card that must have come from someone on campus. My jaw hangs open. Morgan's mom just accused me of potentially supplying her drug-addicted daughter with pills. Laughter threatens to bubble up in my throat. *Me.* A drug dealer. The very idea is ridiculous.

Morgan cringes and falls back against her pillows. "I'm sorry. That was—"

"Totally okay," I tell her. "She's worried about you."

"She's always blowing things out of proportion."

I give a hard laugh and get up out of my chair so I can sit on her bed. It's all I can do not to grab hold of her and shake her hard. "She's not blowing anything out of proportion. You nearly died. Are you gonna tell me what the hell you were doing at that party and why you were *taking drugs*?" Her eyes drop to the bed, avoiding mine. She looks like a naughty five-year-old who's being scolded for no reason. The whole *woe is me* act ain't gonna fly. "Seriously, Morgan. Tell me, because I am shit outta clues as to why you'd do something like this. How many did you even take?"

She looks at me finally, her eyes swimming. "I know you're not going to believe me, Avery, but I only took one pill, I swear. I've been clean for months and months. I took one a couple of weeks back and it was fine, so I thought I could do it again. I have no idea how I got to that party. I just remember being there and Tate getting really sick and then … I wake up here with a tube down my throat." A single, fat tear rolls down her cheek. She brushes it away angrily. "My mom's never going to let me go back to school now. Never in a million years. I had a coke problem and she thinks I'm back on the slippery slope because I took one single pill. This is so messed up."

"It really is," I agreed. "Wait, you took a pill a couple of weeks ago? When? Where?" I've been with Morgan at the last few parties she's attended. I'm wracking my brain, trying to figure it all out, when …

"Oh, god, Morgan. *The Irish party*? That's why you freaked when you saw the cops?"

Morgan slumps back against her pillow, staring up at the ceiling. "I'm sorry, okay. I thought it would be all right, and it was. Nothing bad happened. I didn't wake up the next day desperate for coke or anything. I felt great, remember? We went running. It's no big deal."

"No big deal? Shit, Morgan, if it wasn't Luke, if it had been some other cop who wanted to search you, what would he have found?" I'm met with a tense silence that speaks for itself. "Great. That's just fucking great. And now here we are with you in hospital. I can't believe you don't remember anything. Jeez, Morgan, anything could have happened to you!"

"Yeah, well, it didn't. I've already been poked and prodded at. I've suffered through the indignity of a rape kit, and I was thoroughly un-interfered with. Tate took care of me. I just hope *he's* okay. He was so sick when I saw him last. He was puking his guts up. He hasn't been by yet; he must be terrified of bumping into my parents. Will you tell him to come anyway? I *have* to see him. This is all getting completely out of hand." Morgan drops her head into her hands and starts crying. Instead of hysteria, it's the exhausted weeping of someone who ran out of tears hours ago.

"I'll find him. I'll tell him," I say. "Can you just swear … please swear to me that you're never going to touch anything like that again. Please?"

She shifts in the bed and falls into my arms. "I promise, Avery. No buzz is worth all of this."

The nurse comes in then, with Mrs. Kepler hot on her heels, and I make my excuses and leave, wondering if Morgan is going to keep her promise. Doubting she will.

Luke's Fastback pulls up outside the hospital at eight-thirty, forty minutes after I call him to come get me. The heat and the music are cranked up high when I get in. Luke hits the volume control so that the indie tune he was listening to is a muted buzz in the background. The past few times I've seen him he's been clean shaven, but now the dark shadow of stubble is already marking his jaw. His hood is pulled up again, hiding most of his face. He opens my door for me and drives us back to his place without saying much. He asks after Morgan and smiles briefly when I tell him her mom accused me of being a drug dealer, but then we fall into an easy kind of silence. He hums along to the music and waits patiently when the traffic is particularly bad. I watch him out the corner of my eye, trying to figure out why it's so easy to sit in silence with him. I can't think of anyone else I've ever been able to do that with. Not even Morgan or Leslie. There always has to be something going on, something to chatter or laugh about. Luke just seems content to … *be*.

When we pull up outside his place, he jumps out and grabs the door for me like he usually does. The only difference is that this time I thank him properly. I'm trying. I'm trying really hard not to be a bitch, but this defense mechanism I've worked up over the past five years is a hard one to shake. It's kept me safe.

Made me feel untouchable. And now, when I want to lower my guard a little, I'm finding it's the hardest thing to do. Luke gives me a broad smile and gestures me into the building.

"Did you eat at the hospital? I was going to order some Chinese," he says at the top of the stairs, producing keys from his pocket and rattling them as he opens his front door. I push the memory of Casey Fisher's evil smile out of my head and shrug. "I didn't eat. I could go for Chinese."

That seems to please him. He orders a whole bunch of stuff he assures me is good while I properly inspect his apartment. The last time I was here was after he told me about Mayor Bright's book and I drank myself into oblivion. I hadn't been in the most observant frame of mind back then, but now I'm feeling particularly nosy.

The place is open plan, the epitome of bachelor pad. A huge flatscreen TV is mounted on the wall, the other side of which a bookcase is filled with DVDs. His books are all on the floor—seems a little backwards to me—but what he's done with them is pretty cool. The row of books presses from one side of the apartment to the other, the height undulating in waves as they grow taller or shorter. I pace along, checking out what kind of stuff he reads. There's a bit of everything there: Stephen King, Neil Gaiman, Dickens, even a few poets. To round things out there's a huge stack of comics at the very end. *Spiderman.* Luke doesn't strike me as the type of twenty-three-year-old that reads *Spiderman.*

"You like Stan Lee?" His hot breath grazes the back of my neck, and I nearly jump out of my clothes. My heart feels like it's seizing in my chest. Guy can really sneak up on a person. He pushes back his hood when I turn around and pulls his sweatshirt up over his head, revealing a simple, plain black t-shirt underneath. He has a lot of those—all ridiculously tight across his shoulders, his arms, his chest. Hell, they're tight everywhere. His jeans are slung a little low off his hips; it isn't a style I'm usually into, but they aren't as low as some guys wear them; he makes them look unbelievably sexy. I scowl and slip by him, angry with myself for even admitting that.

"Not got a clue who Stan Lee is, I'm afraid."

Luke pulls a mock-horrified expression and follows me into his kitchen. "He only created some of the most amazing comics ever. The man's a genius."

"Then why are you keeping his masterpieces on the floor?"

A slow smirk tugs at Luke's lips. He really needs to stop doing that. He steps forward into the kitchen so I have to back up to give him room. I panic for a second when he reaches out—I think he's going to touch my face—but he leans toward the fridge and plucks a postcard out from underneath a magnet. He hands it over and raises an eyebrow. The card is plain black apart from some block white lettering:

Floor: the world's biggest shelf.

I roll my eyes and clip it back to the fridge. "You kept that just so you could use it in this situation, right? I bet you get to reference it all the time."

"All the time," he murmurs. There's a playful glint in his eye that I've never had directed at me before. It makes my skin prickle. I back out of the kitchen and sit down at the breakfast bar in the same spot I occupied when I polished off half his whiskey supply. "Want a beer?" he asks, his head disappearing into the fridge.

"Sure, thanks." He produces a Bud Light and sets it down in front of me, and then starts rifling in his cupboards for plates and cutlery. "Aren't you having one?" I ask.

"Uh, no. I'll have to drive you home later. It's kinda frowned upon for cops to get DUIs."

"I can get a cab, it's fine. I'm not drinking on my own." I hold out the beer and shake my head. Drinking alone is bad enough. Doing it in front of a guy you're liable to spill your guts to? So not a great idea. He shrugs and gets another bottle out of his fridge for himself. He leans back against the black marble counter—all the furniture seems to be black in this place—and twists the top off, looking at me. I follow suit and take a swig, aware that he's still staring.

"What?"

"Are you sure you want to do this, Avery? I mean, there are some pretty horrific things in this file. Have you seen a dead body before?"

I swallow back more beer and set the bottle down on the counter, picking at the label. "No, I haven't. I don't really *want* to see one either, but …"

Luke stuffs his free hand into his pocket and studies me. He's trying to assess whether I can handle whatever is in the file or not, and from the torn look on his face he doesn't think I can.

"You can't hold out on me, Luke. I need to be ready for this nightmare when Colby Bright releases his book. It's all lies. I have to be able to prove that."

"Okay. Fine. But you're going to freak the fuck out. Be prepared for that, too."

He disappears down the long corridor to the right of the kitchen and when he comes back he's taken his shoes off and there's a bulging manila file in his hand. A split red elastic band holds it all together. He drops it onto the breakfast bar in front of me and goes back to leaning. The file is so huge, I can't even pick it up with one hand.

"Your old partner sent this over for you?"

"Yeah."

"You must be good friends."

"We are, kind of. She doesn't have much family. Her sister died when she was a kid. Parents are both long gone. I think I'm the closest thing she's got to a living relative."

That's sweet. And so like Luke to be that for someone. I eye the file, frowning. "Have you already looked through this?"

He shakes his head. "Not all of it. Just the evidence relating to the first few killings. I wanted to wait for you." I place my hand on top of the file, but Luke places his own over it before I can open it. "Remember, you can't tell anyone about this.

Ever."

I nod. "Secrecy, good. Prison sex bad."

"Yeah, prison sex *really* fucking bad."

I give him a reassuring look—*I won't let you down.* He reads me loud and clear. Removes his hand. What the hell have I ever done to earn his trust? I sure as hell don't feel like I deserve it. And am I really strong enough to do this? It's one thing watching a horror movie or reading about something in the news. It's another matter altogether being faced with the gory, clinical details of murder—to see the actual pictures and read the statements of the victims' families. The stack of paper underneath my hand feels like it's burning a hole into my skin. For a moment I consider pushing it away and telling Luke to forget it. But then I think of Dad. I fill my lungs with oxygen, grasping at my resolve.

"Come on, then. Let's do this."

EIGHTEEN

DEVIL'S IN THE DETAILS

THERE ARE four categories on the front page of the file, each with subheadings: Immolation, Decapitation, Poisoning, and Drowning. Under each are names. Some have more names under them than others. For instance, decapitation has seven under it, while poisoning has only two. I scan over the names, all female, testing to see if I recognize them from somewhere. Maybe they were on the news. Maybe I even knew some of them. The names are just names, though. No faces materialize when I turn them over in my head. Just girls who went missing one day and wound up murdered. I swallow, knowing instinctively that Luke is watching me. I flip the page over and look up at him.

"What does immolation mean?" I try to keep my voice nonchalant. Luke leans closer across the bench.

"It means to be burned to death."

"On fire?" Luke nods slowly, and I think maybe I'll throw up. I swallow. Hard. "So all these girls died in one of four different ways?"

"Yeah. Which is part of the reason why it was so hard for the police department to catch the guy. He wasn't like a regular serial killer. Usually they have a pattern, like I was saying before. There's a reason why they kill the people they kill. It's useful to figure out their pattern and build a profile from that. You can make predictions based on that profile—how they're going to behave in the future. It's worked a hundred times before when we've tried to catch a killer. It was different this time, though. None of the psychologists on staff could figure this guy out. Couldn't figure out how the symbols tied any of the victims together, either. The only obvious clue was the way they died, but that didn't give us anything."

My pulse feels oddly present everywhere, pumping in my lips, feet, fingertips. It's hard to focus when my body is itching to push away from the counter and get as far away from the file as possible. "What do you mean? How was the way they died an obvious clue?"

"Sorry, I'm not explaining myself very well. The four ways of dying and the four symbols tied in together. See." He flips forward a couple of pages and plucks up a sheet of paper, which turns out to be a copy of a photograph in startling Technicolor. A close-up of a hand, palm upwards, laying on what looks like wet grass. Blood mottles the pale skin over the wrist. Where the fingers are curled inwards, the nails are shored up with grimy crescents of dirt and blood. In the center of the palm is the first symbol I'd recognized, the sideways figure eight, burned into the skin. The flesh is puckered and angry. I suck in a sharp breath through my mouth. Not through my nose. I swear I'll be able to smell the story this picture is telling me if I breathe through my nose—burning, coppery, and pungent. Luke turns over the photocopy and points to the scrawled text on the back.

Janie Peterson, March 15th

Decapitation. Found 3 miles outside Rock Springs off the I80

"They figured out the correlation between this symbol and decapitation pretty quick. Seemed like the most popular way for this guy to kill. Nearly half the victims went out that way. It always seemed like there was a struggle beforehand. Most of the officers who worked the case, still working the case, thought the killer let the girls go before he tracked them down."

"Why? Why would he do that?"

Luke finishes his beer and puts the bottle in the sink. He gets another two out of the fridge and sets one down in front of me. "Sometimes they like the chase," he says awkwardly. "There was no real way for these girls to escape. He took them out to abandoned areas a couple of miles from the road. It was probably enough to give them a fleeting hope of escape. In truth, they didn't stand a chance."

Bile rises at the back of my throat, making my mouth sweat. My mind takes me back to the trailer for *Way Out Of Wyoming*. The ragged, terrified breathing of the girl who had been running for her life. I don't need to see the movie to know the poor girl doesn't make it. My hand shakes as I twist the top off my second beer, closing my eyes as the cold liquid snakes its way down my throat.

"Easy. We don't want a repeat of last time," Luke says softly. "If this is too hard for you, I can keep looking and give you the updates if I find anything." He's trapped with that look of worry again. I shake my head. There's no motivation like the thought of having my father's name cleared to keep pushing me forward.

"I can't," I murmur, quickly draining half my beer. "This is important. I'm probably gonna have nightmares for the rest of my life but I can't give up. My dad would never give up on me." Luke's laugh startles me. It's short and sharp and perhaps a little derisive. I bristle, rocking back on the stool. "What was that for?"

Luke's eyes sharpen when he looks at me. "What's *what* for?"

"Laughing like that. I can't do this with you if you think I'm crazy. My dad was a good man, Luke. I've spent the past five years defending him to everyone but you. I don't have the energy to start now. I didn't think I needed to." I'm about five seconds from boosting out of my seat and fleeing the apartment. Luke must be able to see it in my eyes.

"I wasn't being a jerk, Avery. I was laughing because of how ridiculous this whole thing is. I guess I'm bitter. You don't have to defend Max to me. I know he was a good man. He wasn't just my science teacher in high school, y'know. He was my friend. He was the only one who helped me when I needed it."

"What?" I can't picture that—my dad helping Luke. He's been gone for so long that I've forgotten who he was to the outside world. Every memory that I covet of my father relates to what he meant to *me*. The Max Breslin that was a teacher at my school, a volunteer at the local fire station, that mentored young boys in the Breakwater community on his weekends, has been practically forgotten. I hang my head, wrapping my arms around my body, making myself small. If Luke says Dad helped him, that can mean only one thing. "My dad mentored you?" I ask quietly.

"Yeah."

I can't look at Luke. He sounds angry. I want to know why, but I can't ask. The only boys Dad mentored in Breakwater were from broken homes, young men who had suffered in the foster care system, the victims of various forms of abuse and neglect. Luke comes from a good home. His mom and sister are sweet; I've known them my whole life. His father and mine were members of the same shooting club, for crying out loud. I still remember them going out hunting together on the weekends before Clive Reid was killed—shot by a misfiring rifle when I was just eight. Luke would have been eleven or twelve at the time. If my dad was mentoring Luke, then it was probably because of that—the grief he must have suffered from his own father's death. And that's probably a wound Luke doesn't want re-opening. I respect that, know exactly what that's like. I down the rest of my beer and keep my eyes off him, not sure how to act. Focusing on the file is probably the best thing I can do, even if makes me want to throw up.

"Rock Springs has to be seventy miles away from Breakwater," I muse, staring down at the photocopied image. The copying process has captured the many fingerprints that rim the picture. It looks like a lot of people have handled the original, probably pored over it, trying to work out what it means. Luke remains silent for a minute. His voice is strained when he speaks.

"Doesn't matter. Killers like this aren't afraid to travel with their work." He collects up my empty beer bottles and discards them in the sink with his, and then rifles in the counter draw, rattling loudly. I know what he's looking for.

"Since when did you start smoking, anyway?"

He has the pack in his hand when he turns around. His expression is stormy. "I don't normally. Casey started a couple of years back. I used to have the occasional one when we were out at a club or something. Since we broke up I've probably smoked about ten cigarettes, total. This pack's over a year old."

That probably explains why he doesn't even have a lighter. He ignites his gas cooker and hunches over it so his t-shirt hikes up, exposing his lower back. His cigarette's burning when he turns around. I avert my eyes, worried at how intensely I was staring at that small strip of bare skin. Luke still looks stressed.

My bad temper and I are the reasons for the uneasy tension radiating off him. "I'm sorry for snapping at you," I tell him, finally manning up enough to meet his eyes. He shrugs and takes a drag off his smoke, his jaw muscles ticking.

"It's okay. You have every reason to be defensive. I'm guessing your dad never mentioned he knew me."

I shake my head. "Dad never said anything about the people he mentored. He told me when I was little that it was confidential. That promising to keep a secret was sometimes the only way you *could* help someone."

"I loved that about him, Avery. I trusted him. He was kind to me. I was jealous of you for so long."

My hands still on my beer bottle. "What? Why?"

"I don't know. I guess there were days …" He clears his throat and looks past me out of the window to the city beyond, the lights and the traffic and the masses. "There were days when I wished he was my dad, too."

Luke's never said anything like this to me before. He's never even given me a hint that he knew my dad beyond being in his class at school and finding his dead body. A hard lump forms in my throat. I can't pick apart my churning emotions long enough to work out how I feel: sad for him; curious; hurt because of that pained look in his eye. The anger I feel is a little confusing; it takes me a second to work out why it's even present. Luke clearly shared a bond with my father, something strong enough to still devastate him five years after his death. A bond strong enough to make him leap to my dad's defense even after everything that's being said about him. This revelation makes things a little clearer now. Luke actually shares a little of my story—the humiliation and the pain of people slandering someone important to you—and some sick part of me doesn't want to share it.

"I need another beer," I tell him. Instead of asking him to pass me one, I get up and fetch it myself. His eyes follow me around the breakfast bar and into the fridge, burning into the side of my cheek. The pressure of his gaze is unbearable—has my heart pounding in my chest. I glance at him out of the corner of my eye to find him poised awkwardly, frozen absolutely still. He doesn't blink.

"D'you want another one?" I ask, trying to keep my voice steady.

"Thanks," he whispers. He takes the bottle out of my hand. We both flinch when our fingers touch. I don't like the electricity that comes with that contact. It makes my head spin in an unwelcome way. The smoke from Luke's cigarette fills my head; I've somehow gotten really close to him. I frown, reaching past him, and the expression on Luke's face flickers. I hit the extractor fan button on the oven. The fan whirs into life, and the abrupt, harsh sound sucks the tension out of the air. Luke gives me a wry smile, taking one last drag on his half-smoked cigarette before backing away to run the butt under the tap before he throws it away. I return to my seat, fighting the color threatening to rise in my cheeks. I know it, I could see it in his eyes when I leaned over him: he wanted to kiss me. And the worrying thing is that, if he'd have tried to do it, I wouldn't have stopped him. The dreams, the constant thoughts of him … I'm not completely obvious to what my body wants. What my heart wants. Thankfully, my head seems to be in control most of the time.

Luke is all business when he turns back around. The conflicted look has disappeared. "So this is probably really unlikely, but did your dad keep a journal?"

"No, not that I know of."

"Do you think your mom would have kept it if he had?"

A scathing laugh escapes my lips. "I have no idea. I doubt it. She got removers to come and pack up her stuff when she moved here so she wouldn't even have to go through his things. I'm pretty sure everything he owned was left in the house."

"Wait, she still owns the house in Break?"

I shoot him a wary glance. "*I* own it now."

"*What?*"

I slug back more beer. I know where this is headed, and I don't like it. What the hell can I do about it now, though? "I inherited it when I turned eighteen. Mom expected me to sell it. She was pretty pissed when I told her I wanted to keep it." That argument had the final nail in the coffin of our dead relationship. I can still remember the disgusted look on her face when she told me I was sick and needed help if I wanted to cling onto a mausoleum where "that kind of evil" had lived. I know Luke is staring at me again, like he expects me to say something else. I don't.

"We should go search for a diary, then. I can't *believe* the place has been sitting there empty all this time," he mutters.

"Well, it is out of the way from town. You'd never notice it's been permanently empty all these years. It's not like you'd ever drive past it on your way somewhere." I'd always loved how secluded our family home was, how far away from the world I'd felt living there with just my family and crazy old Mrs. Harlow next door. Mrs. Harlow died a year after I'd moved in with Brandon. Now my uncle is the only person who ever goes up there. He makes sure the place is secure and in good repair. Keeps the heating running on low in winter to avoid damp. I used to drive up there when I was feeling particularly crushed by the kids bullying me at school; I'd think about setting it on fire, razing it to the ground, but I'd never had the nerve. "I'm not going back there, Luke. I can't."

"But it—" The intercom buzzes loudly, cutting him off. He sighs. "Food's here." He stares at me a moment longer, then his eyes snap to the door, like he's had to force himself to look away. He brings the Chinese into the kitchen and dishes up in silence. When he gathers the photo and some other papers that have fallen loose from the file, neatly tucking everything away so we can eat, I'm secretly glad. He doesn't bring up going back to the house again until we are halfway through our meal.

"You know, if he did keep a journal or a work diary or something we might be able to disprove Colby Bright's theory. He could have alibis back in Breakwater the days those girls were killed."

Alibis. That sounds like such a guilty term to use, but he's right. Am I being utterly unreasonable refusing to go back there? It certainly might look that way to Luke, but the truth is I'm terrified. I'm *limbs-locked-up,-I-can't-fucking-breathe* terrified by the thought of stepping through the entranceway of that house. "Maybe … maybe you could collect the keys from Brandon and go up there next time you're home?"

Luke looks uncertain. "I wouldn't know where to look for anything, Avery."

"Brandon could help you." I'm being such a coward. I know it, but courage has been a little thin on the ground of late.

"Maybe," Luke compromises. I can see the doubt in his eyes, though. We finish up our food and I wash the dishes while Luke pretends not to watch me. In turn, I pretend not to notice, rinsing out our beer bottles and shoving them in the recycling.

"Are you still getting a cab back to Columbia?" he asks when I'm done. I glance up at the clock on his wall—almost midnight.

"Yeah, I'd better call one now."

"Wouldn't your boyfriend come get you?" he asks, leaning forward onto the counter. My shoulders tense, hearing the odd note in his voice.

"If he had a car he might. Like I said, he's not … I'm not really sure if he's my boyfriend. We're just hanging out." Telling Luke that Noah and I are "just hanging out" probably makes me sound slutty. Great. Now he'll think I'm sleeping around. "Not that we're … not that I … we're not—"

Luke smiles and brushes a hand back through his hair, disturbing it into that ruffled, just-fucked look. "It's okay, Avery. It's good that you're with someone. You should be happy."

I give him a painfully small smile, bile burning at the back of my throat. "You, too. I know she probably hates me because of my dad, but I'm still glad you're working stuff out with Casey. You were together for so long. I suppose it's natural that you'd want to give things another go."

A fleeting frown flashes across his face. "Casey and I aren't together, Avery. She was here to pick up some of her things. Oh

140

…" Realization dawns on his face. "*Oh,* it probably looked really bad that I was all …" He doesn't say it, but I think it: *half naked, hair all over the place, looking sexy as hell.* He rolls his eyes, the sound coming out of his mouth more like choking than actual laughter. "No, I found her in here when I got back from work. I was about to take a shower when she stepped out of the shadows. I thought she was robbing the place or something. She told me she came by to look for one of her mother's rings. We had a massive fight about her just letting herself in, and then you showed up. Probably the worst timing ever."

A knot of tension eases in my stomach; I feel like I'm floating three feet off the ground. "Yeah, she looked like she was going to attack me."

"She thought … she asked me if I was seeing you," Luke says. He focuses on the countertop, staring firmly at the swirls in the cool, graphite marble.

"Ha! Wow, she must think you're crazy."

"Why d'you say that?"

"Well, there's the obvious. What did she say? That's right: '*I see you're still intrigued by the macabre.*' I'm a walking freak show to people like her. And then there's the fact that you're old."

"I'm not old!"

"Sorry, no, of course you're not. You read *Spiderman* comics, after all. I meant to say you're older than me."

"By three and a half years." I glance up to find him glaring at me. Another stormy, intense look I've never seen him wear before. "Three and half years is nothing once you leave high school, Beautiful." For the first time, his nickname makes my skin flush. It's the tone of his voice—low and serious and soft.

"I guess." I feel awkward, pinned by the way he's looking at me. I pull on my jacket and start backing over to the door. "Thanks for dinner, Luke. And thanks for …" I'm not sure if I'm supposed to thank him for sharing the gruesome pictures and information, but he has taken a risk in showing me. I feel like I should thank him for trusting me. He stalks across the room and puts his hand on the front door, holding it closed.

"You're not leaving this apartment, Avery. It's way too late. You didn't call a cab."

I laugh, trying to pull his hand away. "This is New York, Luke. There are thousands of cabs out there. I'll flag one down in seconds."

His hand doesn't budge. "This *is* New York, Avery. There are thousands of *psychos* out there. You'll be mugged in seconds, more like."

"You have a warped view of the populace. Comes with the job," I tell him. He really has to, doesn't he? Working as a cop surely must jade even the most optimistic of people. Luke just crooks me a savagely sexy smile and leans his head against the door, still not letting me out.

"You can stay here. Sleep in my bed. I'll take the couch again, I really don't mind."

"Luke."

"*Avery.*"

I know he wants to say Iris and that makes my ears burn hotly. He's too close. I shuffle back an inch and he turns so his back is pressed against the door. He crosses his arms across his chest, highlighting how corded and muscular they are. I look down at my feet and try to think of something to say that will distract me from the inappropriate thoughts flooding my head.

"I'll only stay if you take me to the hospital in the morning."

"I can do that," he whispers.

So he makes himself up a bed on the sofa, and for the second time I fall asleep in Luke Reid's bed. This time, however, I'm sober enough to smell him on his sheets. Clear-headed enough to acknowledge he is lying twenty feet away on the other side of a door, and weak enough to admit to my traitorous body-wide ache because of the fact.

NINETEEN

EASIER

"WHY ARE my sheets on the floor?" Luke hands me a plate of toast. He's buttered the slices all the way to the edges as if he somehow knows I won't eat them otherwise. I shrug sheepishly and accept the plate.

"I was too hot?"

"You're crazy. It was freezing last night. I woke up three times 'cause my hands and feet had gone numb."

My hands and feet didn't fare that well either, but I couldn't deal with having his bedclothes on top of me. It felt like *he* was on top of me, and I was scared by how that made me feel. I crunch down on a piece of toast and chug the coffee he's made for me—extra sweet again.

"I'm gonna grab a quick shower, then I'll drop you off at the hospital, okay?"

"Sure thing."

"If you want a shower, too, you're more than welcome to join me," he says, winking. I choke on my mouthful of coffee, the scalding hot liquid shooting up the back of my nose. Luke bursts out laughing. "That's what I thought." He slings a huge white towel over his shoulder and vanishes down the hallway, leaving me struggling for oxygen. *That's what I thought?* He expected me to spray my drink everywhere? Did he think I was reacting out of horror or embarrassment? Because, holy hell, my reaction was embarrassing. I wipe the back of my hand over my mouth, still staring after him.

I don't get it. Luke seems like the perfect gentleman ninety-nine point nine percent of the time, and then he goes and says something like that. It doesn't seem like him at all. But then, how well do I really know him? I know the sad, *I used to wish your dad was my dad* side of him. But there's more, I know that. He has a steady, quiet confidence to him sometimes. I think an entirely different person might be right there, hiding beneath the deeply thoughtful looks and the pensive silence, waiting to sneak up on me and destroy me. A small part of me wants to storm down the hallway and rip the bathroom door open so I can give him a piece of my mind for teasing me. And another, worryingly large part of me wants to storm down the hallway and rip the bathroom door open so I can strip naked and make him screw me in the shower.

I hear the water running, and my skin breaks out in goose bumps. *Stop thinking about that! Stop thinking about that, dammit!* I've got to take my mind off Naked Luke, dripping wet, running his hands over his soaped-up, ridiculously toned body. How my body would feel slipping and sliding against his as he pushed inside me again and again, the scorching hot water raining down on our writhing bodies. What the hell is wrong with me?

I can't be thinking about that. I just can't. I inch over to the low sideboard and stroke my fingers across the file that still sits there. The instant I make contact with it, it feels as though I've been doused with a bucket of cold water. Well, at least the tactic worked. My heart rate trebles when I find myself opening the file up at random. I've opened up in a safe place. Barely legible text, scrawled in blue and red and black biro, marks page after page after page. I flick through them, not focusing on the paper for too long in case I read something I don't want to see. Stupid, really, considering I want to pick this apart until I find something to clear Dad, and I'm too nervous to even read the reports. I'm about a quarter way through the file when a photo slips out of the papers and floats down to the floor. The face of a pale young girl stares up at me from the polished hardwood flooring, about fifteen years old. Her blonde hair is so colorless it's almost silver. Other than the bleached whiteness of her skin and the fragile purple tinge to her lips, she doesn't particularly look dead. Her blue eyes are open, staring; the accusing glare behind them makes me shiver. I suppose she looks a little like me when I was her age. More than a little like me, in fact.

"Already playing detective?" Luke, only inches behind me, makes me jump so hard I nearly drop my coffee.

"Geez, are you trying to … kill me?" My brain momentarily shuts down when I see he is only wearing a towel and water is beaded across his naked chest and down his arms. I'm right back to my fantasy from the shower. The tattoos I've been catching glimpses of are pretty extensive: tribal black ink that traces across the tops of his shoulders and down his arms a short ways, stark and contrasting against the faint golden tan of his skin. Over his right pec, the letters D.M.F are scrawled in swooping cursive.

I snap my eyes to his face so I have to stop staring, and Luke gives me a slight smile. He stoops to pick up the photo, displaying that the tattoos continue onto his back, too—arching, tribal wings that sweep across his shoulder blades in broad, powerful black lines. The ink really compliments his body, mirrors the way his muscles shift under his skin when he moves. He straightens, holding the towel around his waist, and hands over the photo.

"Here." The smile on his face has grown, like he knows exactly what I'm thinking. If he does, he's apparently not going to oblige my fantasy by losing the towel, flinging me over his shoulder, carrying me to his bedroom, and punishing me really hard.

"Thanks." I snatch the photo back and study it intensely. The fierce clenching of my jaw probably counters the hot blush on my face, but still … I'm reacting like a thirteen-year-old who's never seen a shirtless guy before.

"What's the D.M.F stand for?" I ask, pretending to be unfazed. But holy shit, am I fazed.

"S'the band's name," he tells me. "The guys thought it'd be amusing to tease people with initials and never tell them what they stand for."

"And what *do* they stand for?"

Luke cocks an eyebrow, his smile ruinous now. "I'd literally wash up on the banks of the Hudson with no teeth or fingerprints if I told you that."

"Well, damn. That's rather dramatic."

"You've never met my bandmates."

I need to keep talking. If I stop, I'll just end up standing here with my mouth hanging open. I hold up the photo that fell out of the file. "Do you know who this girl is?"

Luke sweeps his wet hair out of his eyes and glances at the blonde girl staring lifelessly out of the picture. "No. Like I said, I was waiting for you before I looked at everything." He carefully places his hand over mine and turns the image over, leaning closer to read the writing on the back.

Loreli Whitman August 6th
Poisoning. Shore of Jackson Lake,
Grand Teton National Park.

Poisoning. That explains why there's no blood in the picture. No signs of a fight. I step away from Luke and slot the picture back in the file. "Only two girls were poisoned, right? What was it? What did the killer use?"

"Strychnine. It's a convulsant. Both girls asphyxiated. These were the two last killings before they stopped altogether. They were also the only ones with the fourth symbol on their palms." Luke leafs through the file until he finds a picture of the symbols and points out the one the poison victims were branded with. It's the circular one from the piece of paper Luke sent me the other day—the one with two smaller circles inside.

"My contact in Wyoming PD says these girls were different to the others. Their deaths weren't as violent. Well, in comparison, of course. Asphyxiation's still a horrible way to die."

I take a sip of my coffee and sit myself down on the leather sofa, trying not to picture how that would feel. Luke carries on talking. "She said it was almost like they'd been treated reverently. Their hair had been brushed out and their finger and toenails had been painted. They were wearing dresses their parents had never seen before. It was like he'd decided to dress those two up like dolls."

"That's totally sick. But why was it so strange?"

"Because …" He cups his hand to the back of his neck and grimaces. "The other deaths were so different. Violent and cruel. They weren't treated with any kindness. They were defiled in most cases. Some worse than others."

My chest tightens. *Defiled*. Such an awful word. Conjures images of a violent sexual abuse that doesn't even bear thinking about. I rub my eyes with the backs of my hands. I've considered asking about that—whether the girls were raped— but I haven't had the nerve. I keep linking these brutal acts with the allegations being made by Colby Bright—that my dad is behind all of this—and it's too much to take. "I think I'm going to be sick."

"Sorry, Ave. I know this is hard. I shouldn't have involved you. I'll do most of the digging myself from here on in. I'll let you know if I come across anything noteworthy, okay?"

I try to steel my nerves, try to form words to tell him that it doesn't matter and I can do it, but I really can't. Can't form the words, and can't face the details, either. Maybe it would be better to let him do the legwork. But my dad … that would feel like I'd failed him. Let him down. "Luke?"

"Yeah?" He looks at me, eyes filled with an intensity that makes my breathing sharp. I force myself not to look away.

"Does this not bother you anymore? If I just keep going, will it get easier?"

Luke's expression falls flat. "No. It never gets easier."

Noah: Hey, where are you? Turns out Tate's not been home since the party. The cops are looking for him.

Noah's text comes as we're headed over to Woodhull Hospital. Luke's eyes flicker to my cell phone. I'd better respond or it will seem weird.

Me: Shit. On my way to the hospital right now. I'll have to tell Morgan.

Noah: Meet you there . . .

"That the non-boyfriend boyfriend?" Luke asks.

"Yeah. He said Tate, the guy Morgan was with at that party, still hasn't come home. Morgan asked me to find him for her. She's going to flip out when I tell her that not only have I not found him, but no one else has seen him in two days, either. Do you … do you know anything about him?"

He shakes his head. "Wasn't my precinct. I could ask a few questions, though."

"Him being missing for so long, that doesn't sound good,

does it?"

Luke gives me a tight-lipped smile. More of a grimace. "No. No it does not."

When we arrive at the hospital, Luke gets out of the car and walks me to the building, but then pauses at the sliding glass doors. The whole world is covered in a layer of frosted glass today, stark and cold, and Luke is the only vibrant thing in it. His cheeks have reddened from the short walk across the lot. His green scarf stands out against the muted blues and variances of white and gray.

"You want me to come in with you?" he asks, bouncing on the balls of his feet to keep warm. I don't really know what to say. Luke and Noah in the same place? That makes me feel all kinds of wrong. But I do want him to stay. Probably more than I should. I open my mouth to speak but wait a second too long; Luke's easy smile doesn't disappear entirely so much as dim. He starts walking backwards, burying his hands in the pockets of his leather jacket. "Because if you've got people coming to meet you, that means I can go home and work through that file. If you don't need me."

If you don't need me. I bite down on the inside of my cheek. "Thanks, Luke. Thanks for running me around and for dinner last night and, well, everything, I guess."

He pulls his hood up, still backing away. "That's what friends are for, right?"

Something impetuous makes me speak before I can stop myself. "Are we? Are we friends, Luke?"

He pauses, blowing out spirals of smoke on the cold morning air. "Of course we are, Beautiful." He gives me a small smile and then he is gone.

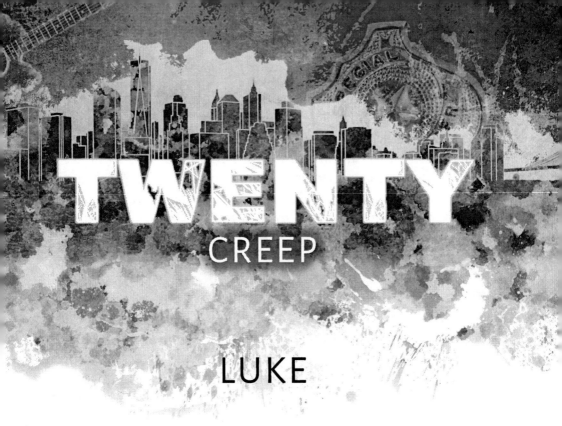

TWENTY

CREEP

LUKE

I REPLAY her asking me that question as I drive away. *Are we? Are we friends, Luke?* Each time I hear her voice in my head, I feel sick. Of course we're friends; she knows we are. She knows, deep down, we're more than that, but she's denying it. I understand why. I get it, I always have. To Avery, I represent so much pain and heartache. But to me, she's something else. I think I've given up hoping that one day she'll wake up and I won't be *Luke, the cop who worked on my father's suicide/murder case* anymore. I might be *Luke, who makes everything feel better*, or *Luke, the guy I fell in love with despite everything*.

I should never have asked her if that text was from her boyfriend. Every time I think about the guy she was with at O'Flanagan's, I want to punch a fucking wall. And I've been in fights with walls before. I never win.

It really sucked that she hesitated when I asked if she wanted me to stay with her at the hospital. Like, really sucked. I could see that she'd changed her mind by the time I was walking away, but it was too late then. I'd committed to leaving, and neither one of us needed the situation being made any more awkward. So I'd left. And she'd gone inside to meet that Noah guy—I can't believe I actually bought them dinner that time. What the hell is wrong with me?—and I never got to check in on Morgan.

I haven't seen the girl since the walk-up in Williamsburg, where she clung hold of me like I was the only thing anchoring her to reality. When I get back to the apartment, fully intending to go through Max's file with a fine-tooth comb, I find Cole sitting on my doorstep, his guitar case propped up against the wall next to him. The guy smirks at my surprised expression, knowing exactly what I'm thinking without me having to say it.

"If I'd have called," he says, "you would have told me you were busy."

"I am kinda busy," I tell him. I open the door to the apartment, leaving it open behind me so he can follow me inside. "What's up, Cole?"

Dark hair, dark eyes, lots of tatts. The guy works out just as much as I do, as well. When people meet us for the first time, they often mistake us for brothers. And Cole *is* a brother to me. I love him like he's my blood. We fight like we're blood, too. He throws himself down on my couch and busies himself with getting his guitar out of its case. "I came to have a much-needed conversation with you, man. I need you to take a look at what MVP have sent through for us."

I can see it now—the stack of papers underneath Cole's guitar, as thick as a telephone directory.

"They sent through a contract?"

"Just something for you to consider." Cole starts plucking at his guitar—"Highway to Hell" by ACDC. I grin at him, because that was the first song we ever played together, when we ran into each other at an open mic night two years ago.

"I don't have time to read through all of that, Cole."

"Then how about I paraphrase it for you? They're offering us a year's contract. You know what that means?"

"What does that mean?"

"That means you can take a sabbatical from work for twelve months and see how you like this whole rock star thing. And don't tell me you can't," he says, pointing a finger at me. "I researched that shit. You can take a whole year and still go back to your job at the same pay grade, same lowly rank of officer, if you really want to. We put out one album with them and if we hate it, we can all go our separate ways."

"Where's the sense in that? Me wasting a year if I'm only going to go back to the cops?"

"Because, *asshole*, MVP will have realized we're awesome with or without you by then. And you'll have realized that you can't live without this shit in your life, as well. So we all win. We can extend our contract and then move onto world domination."

"And what if I don't *want* to take a year off from work?"

Cole shoots daggers at me. "They've offered us complete retention of our artistic rights. They've given us a *six-month* window at Paramount. Most first timers get a few weeks and if they haven't created a masterpiece they're kicked out on their asses. And not only that, but they've said we can pick and choose who we want to work with. Our choice of producer. Our choice of guest artists, if we want them. No one else gets this deal, Luke. No one but us. And all you have to do is give us one year of your life. You owe me a year, man. Come on."

If he were shouting and hollering at me, it would be easy to get mad and kick his ass out. But he's not. He's one hundred percent cool, calm, and collected. He really wants this—I can feel it radiating off him like electricity. And I do owe him a year. I don't break very often, but when I do it's always been him I've turned to. He's scraped me off the floor when it's counted. I take off my jacket and throw it on the couch, sitting down beside him. He passes me his regular acoustic guitar.

There aren't many people Cole Rexford would trust with his baby. I run my fingers up and down the strings, playing the opening to "Creep" by Radiohead. Cole starts laughing.

"I take it you think my tactics are underhanded?" he asks.

"Oh, no." I shake my head, pouting. "I think you're Mary Fucking Teresa." I keep on playing, humming the melody.

"They said you can write everything. No outside interference," Cole tells me. "And imagine the fucking women, Reid. Jesus. You've been stuffed away up here in your tower like motherfucking Rapunzel, afraid to let her hair down for too long. You need to get some tail."

This is not the first time I've heard this from Cole. He's convinced that if I start thinking with my dick, serving my community will no longer matter to me. I'll be more like him. And Cole Rexford is definitely more interested in fucking the community than serving it. He has no clue what it means to be in love with another human being. I replace the line *I wish I was special* that Thom Yorke usually sings with, "I don't wanna fuck tail," swiftly followed by, "you're such a creep. You're a weirdo."

Cole exhales sharply, throwing his feet up on my coffee table. "Is this about her again? That girl, Iris?" I may or may not have told him about her after a gig one night, when some drunk chick with fake tits was trying to stick her hand down the front of my jeans. I never told him she changed her name, though. Probably better that way.

"This isn't about Iris. This is about what I think I should be doing with my life, Cole. I want to help people."

He looks at me sideways, one brown eye narrowing into a slit. "You want to stop the bad shit from happening, then. Because of what happened to you when you were a kid."

I just close my eyes, my fingers now aimlessly picking out chords I like the sound of.

"But you can't stop it. You have to know that, right? People do awful shit to each other every day of the week. You're not some fucking superhero from one of your comics, dude. Bad stuff will still happen in this city, regardless of whether you're a cop or you're the guy singing on the radio."

I just smile. I smile because he doesn't get it. "I know that, Cole."

"Then will you promise me? And no fucking around this time, okay? Promise me you're gonna think about it. One year, Luke. One year of your life. That's all I'm asking."

I nod my head in time to the rhythm I'm plucking out, eyes still closed, thinking. "All right, man. All right. I promise I'll think about it."

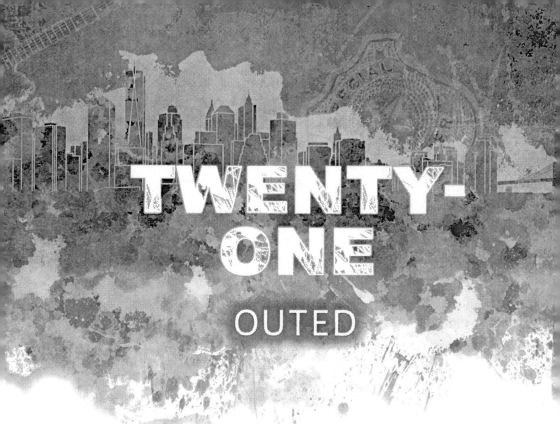

TWENTY-ONE

OUTED

MORGAN TAKES the news of Tate's disappearance pretty badly—there are a lot of tears and swearing. Her mom lets me take her home—unexpected—but only after she's signed a contract. A contract Mr. and Mrs. Kepler have actually had notarized by a lawyer, stating that she'll attend counseling and rehabilitation sessions at Seabrook House without fail. If she misses one appointment, she'll no longer be allowed to stay in school, and she'll have to go back to full-time rehab.

I sit in between Noah and Morgan on the cab ride back to Columbia, and the three of us remain utterly silent. I feel sick. I should be worrying about wherever the hell Tate is, but I'm not. I'm worrying about Noah's hand on my leg and how much I wish it was Luke's. We arrive back at Columbia in time for me to drop her at her apartment before I leave for class, promising to come by as soon as I'm done. In truth I'm seconds away from skipping; it would mean spending more time with Morgan and making sure she's okay, and it would also mean avoiding Noah.

And I want to avoid Noah like I want to avoid the plague. It feels shitty, but I can't help it. My mind keeps going back to the moment outside Woodhull hospital where Luke asked me if I wanted him to stay, and I paused. I should have told him to stay. I should have told him I *did* need him, because I do. It makes no sense that I should feel that way. It will undoubtedly only end up with me getting hurt, but there's no denying it any longer.

Skipping Media Law and Ethics isn't an option, though—not after Professor Lang's disappointed speech last time. Noah walks with me, hands thankfully to himself now. I'm almost glad when we arrive late—the auditorium is packed, which means we can't even sit together. Our seats are about as far apart as they could be, in fact. As soon as the class commences, I'm relieved I made myself come. Lang's in a fiery mood today.

"The news is no longer folded sheets of paper that we buy should we happen to remember on our way to work. It's alerts on our phones, pop-ups on our computer screens, interruptions to our favorite television shows. Global events are instantly reported mere seconds after occurring. With everything so immediate, so push of a button, so in our faces, we need to ask ourselves, how have the roles of journalists evolved in the wider world? What are their duties? Their responsibilities?"

I can't help but feel like Professor Lang's gaze lingers on me a little too long. My suspicions are confirmed when he removes his glasses and polishes the lenses on his untucked shirt. "Perhaps you have some thoughts on this matter, Miss Patterson?"

Curse him. He's never called on me before. This is entirely because of what I said to him in his office the other week. All eyes are on me—a sensation instantly unpleasant and confronting. "I … I personally feel that there's an onus on journalists to be truthful in their reporting. The truth has to be the most important thing, right?"

"You're asking me, or you're telling me?"

Fuck. I do *not* need this today. "I'm telling you."

Lang frowns, returning his glasses to the bridge of his nose. "Okay. So if we work to that principle—that the truth is the most important factor here—how does a journalist know fact from fiction when they're required to report on something so quickly? Before someone else can jump in with both feet and beat them to the punch?"

"I don't know. I guess that's where fact checkers come in."

"Fact checkers?"

"Yes."

"This isn't the seventies, Miss Patterson. Anyone with a smart phone and enough common sense to ask questions can do so freely. You request a fact checker at the *New York Times* and you'd be fired on the spot. Your job as a journalist is to be able to quickly and efficiently check the veracity of your information in person. If you need a week to comfortably confirm your sources before going to print or, indeed, to air, then you should perhaps go to the *New Yorker* and become a fact checker yourself."

The class titters at Lang's remark. Why the hell am I being torn a new one? So far I've been invisible in this class, and I've liked it that way. But worse than being the center of attention right now, Lang is challenging me to defend my decisions. Decisions I'm sure he knows are very personal to me. "Then I'll revise my statement," I say. "The most important responsibility a journalist has is to report as judiciously as possible, including only information they believe to be true after verifying first the legitimacy of their information to the best of their ability. Journalists who choose to sensationalize the news for their own ratings, people who scavenge over the truth like it's a goddamned buffet and they can take and leave whatever they decide without a thought or care for how their words affect people, that's the kind of journalism that should be avoided at all costs."

The room is silent. Lang considers this for a moment, his lips pursed. "I agree. But it's not always that easy, is it? Emotions often get in the way regardless of how hard a person may try to remain impartial." He breaks his focus, a reprieve from the intensity of his stare, and takes a look at the rest of the student body. "I have an assignment for you, class, and you can thank Miss Patterson for the extra workload. I want each and every one of you to tell me the truth. Tell me a greater truth about an event that has shaped and formed you into who you are today. And I don't want to hear anyone telling me such an event in their past does not exist, because that would be … wait for it … a *lie*. There's always something. We all have *one*. But—" he breaks off when the class starts groaning. "*But!* I want you to tell that greater truth from someone else's perspective, someone else who knows that terrible incident inside and out. This is where the problems begin, class. We hit brick walls when we start to borrow other people's truths. Our experiences, our prejudices, our own personal beliefs all color the way we choose to pick over the buffet of truth, as Miss Patterson so eloquently worded it. So, in short, be creative. Be bold. Be subjective. Be whatever you need to be, but most importantly, be honest. I'll expect all of your Pulitzer-worthy, vainglorious pieces to be turned in by the end of the week."

The lecture theater erupts into conversation and complaints as Lang begins packing his laptop and papers away, and I sit there trying to become invisible again. But I can't. He's asking me to do something, to put myself out there—but not only that. He's asking me to involve someone else in the process, look at my situation through their eyes and report it back in stark black and white without allowing my tormented past to affect the work. It's just not possible. It's cruel, is what it is.

I pack up my laptop, my desire to escape becoming more and more pressing by the second. I bolt before Noah has a chance to catch up with me. I don't escape without him noticing, of course. My cell phone's buzzing before I can clear the building.

Noah: Everything okay? You just took off like a

shot.

Me: Yeah, sorry. I just don't want to leave Morgan on her own for too long.

Noah: Will I see you later?

Me: Sure. I'll let you know what's happening.

I'm almost at Margo's when my phone vibrates again. I feel like shit, expecting the message to be from Noah again, wondering why I'm being so standoffish, but then I see Luke Reid's name flashing up on my screen.

Luke: Didn't have time to look through our homework I'm afraid. Something came up, so no news. Will call later if I have anything.

Me: No problem. Hope everything's okay.

I feel like an idiot as soon as I hit send. *Hope everything's okay?* That's bordering on the personal, essentially asking him what's up. I don't get to ask him what's up. Not when I've been pushing him away at every available opportunity.

I head inside Margo's diner and order two extra-large coffees for me and Morgan. My hands are in heaven the whole journey back to 125th Street thanks to the scalding takeaway cups, but the rest of me is a frigid ice block. Worse still, it starts snowing halfway home and my hair is damp and ratty, running melted water down the back of my neck by the time Morgan lets me into her apartment.

"Sheesh, you look like crap, Patterson."

"Thanks. You look terrific, yourself." She actually does look pretty good, aside from the shadows under her eyes and the way she seems to flinch whenever she moves, like every joint in her body aches.

"That for me?" She relieves me of one of the coffees. The wrong one. I snatch it back and thrust the other one out to her.

"Trust me, you don't want that one."

"Surprised you've got any teeth left, my friend."

"Your concern over my teeth is touching, Morgan, but you have more important things to worry about." I'm referring to her future appointments at Seabrook, but my friend isn't worried about that. She's worried about a certain missing person.

"I can't handle it. I just know something bad's happened to him, Avery. Tate and me, we didn't exactly live in each other's pockets but I know he would have called me by now."

"I know, babe. But I'm sure he's fine. He will show up, y'know."

"But that's the thing. We *can't* know that."

"Luke said he was gonna ask around, find out if the police have learned anything about where he might be."

"Luke?" Morgan's eyes widen, shining slightly. She looks like she might cry. "You spoke to Luke? I really need … I really need to thank him, Ave. God, he must think I'm a total fuck up. He came right away, you know. As soon as he knew I was sick—"

She cuts herself off, apparently not knowing how to continue. Her words hit me like a fist in the gut. Of course Luke rushed to her. I can picture him getting the call. I can equally imagine him dropping absolutely everything he was doing because someone he faintly knew was asking for his help. He's just that kind of person.

"He doesn't think you're a fuck up, Morgan," I tell her. "He's just glad you're okay."

"You're crazy, you realize?" Morgan takes a deep drink from her coffee cup, shoulders rounded in. She's still not her confident, loud self. I don't think that Morgan's gone forever, but she'll certainly be on hiatus for a while. "He's not the kind of guy you pass up, Avery. Not for any reason."

There's a truth to that statement, but I don't want to admit it. I don't want to own up to the fact that I may have passed Luke up. And I sure as hell don't want to admit that I may have missed whatever chance there may have been between us.

"Have you forgotten about a certain Irishman you pushed me into hanging out with?"

"Correct me if I'm wrong, but it's not like you've sworn your undying love for the guy yet, right?"

"No."

"Then it doesn't matter. You and him, you don't have anything. You don't owe him anything."

"I think Noah would probably disagree with you on that one." And I really do believe that. He's been sweet. He's been kind. He's been patient. And I have been picturing myself with another man nearly every time we've been together. What kind of person does that make me?

"You just need to tell him. He'll understand." Morgan sits herself down on her bed—I can see her hands are shaking. I want to wrap her up in cotton wool and make everything better for her, and here she is trying to fix my life. "Because you know, right, Ave? You know how Luke feels about you?"

I just blink at her, not too sure how to proceed. I wasn't ready to hear those words.

"Avery, come on. You can't—"

My cell phone starts ringing, preventing her from telling me what it is I can't do, though I know it in the pit of my stomach. I can't ignore this forever. I can't run and hide from absolutely everything in my life. I pull my cell phone from my bag, cringing when I see Noah's name. His ears must be burning or something.

"Is it him?" I don't know which him Morgan's referring to, but I think she figures it out pretty quickly from the look on my face. "Just tell him," she says. "I promise you he'll understand."

I take a deep breath, actually considering it. It's not fair to keep letting him think something could happen between us.

"Hey, Noah. I'm sorry, I—"

"Is it true?"

Guilt floods me, like I've been caught cheating or something. "Is what true?" I ask carefully.

"Was your father a serial killer?"

I taste blood.

"Avery, did your dad murder a whole bunch of people in Wyoming? Is your name … is your name really *Iris*?"

I can hear my heartbeat pounding relentlessly behind my eardrums. I don't think I can breathe. "What?" My phone buzzes in my hand, a text message alert.

"Look at the picture I've just sent you," Noah says. "Look at it and tell me that's some sick joke."

I look down at the phone, pulling up the message he's just sent me, and my whole world ends. It's me. Really me. *Iris Breslin*. The photo is of a crude, photocopied poster that bears my high school yearbook picture, under which my real name is printed in neat italics. Along the top of the poster, the words, *"Way Out Of Wyoming killer's daughter among you. Columbia's very own murder spawn."*

Sa-mO'BradyJeffersonKyleAdamBrightSamO'BradyJeffersonKyleAdamBright.

I drop my cell phone. Morgan's moving then, picking up the phone, talking into it, touching me on the shoulder, saying something to me, but it all flows over me. I can't … I can't …

"Someone knows," I mutter.

The world comes rushing back at me then, too loud, too bright, too overwhelming. Morgan's talking into my cell phone. "…handled that better, asshole. No, she doesn't want to speak to you. Just … no, just give her some time." She hangs up, worry etched into her features. "I'm so sorry, Avery. I didn't tell anyone, I swear."

"I know. I know. I think … I need …" I don't know what I need. I don't know what to do.

Morgan hurries to the bag she brought home with her from the hospital and finds her own cell phone. "Oh god, Ave. I've got the same picture. It looks like there were people handing out flyers."

People were handing out flyers? *People were handing out flyers.* They'd done that at high school before the teachers put a stop to it, but the damage was already done. And now it's happening here, too. I stagger to my feet and race across the room to bend over Morgan's trashcan, reaching it just before I throw up. It takes a long time for my stomach muscles to cease clenching.

"I'm going to find out who those bitches are and destroy them," Morgan growls as she rubs her hand up and down my back. "Hang in there, okay? This will all get sorted out. Melissa, hey, where are these people?" I look up to find that she's talking into her phone.

I groan and rock back onto my heels. Morgan's nodding her head while pulling on her shoes. This—a confrontation—is unlikely to score her any points with the administration after her recent absence. "Morgan, don't make a scene."

"It's about time someone made a fucking scene. This isn't your fault. They don't have the right to do this to you, Avery. This is five years past due." She storms out of the apartment and leaves me there bowed over the trashcan, shaking so violently I can hardly keep myself upright. My phone starts ringing while she's gone but I ignore it. Morgan comes back twenty minutes later shaking out her hand. She's too furious to speak at first. Eventually her rage dissipates.

"They were in our building. Two girls in our fucking building! They've been kicked out now, don't worry. I can't believe they'd go to all this effort just to make your life miserable."

I can totally believe it. "What did they look like?" My voice is monotone, betraying how hollow I feel.

"Both prissy, stuck-up bitches. One of them was called Casey. I didn't catch the other one's name. She had short blonde hair."

"Maggie," I say. "Maggie Bright. Her father was one of the men who …" *my dad killed.* God, I can't bring myself to say it. Maggie was president of the *Let's make Iris's life hell* club back in high school; it can only be her. She's a hundred different kinds of vindictive. Storming the building where I now live totally fits her M.O. But Casey? Why the hell has she gotten involved? "I know them both. The blonde went to my high school. And Casey … Casey is Luke's ex. I ran into her outside his apartment the other week. He called me Avery. That must be how she figured out I was here."

Morgan raises her eyebrows. "The one with the black hair is Luke's ex? She was a super bitch. Should have seen her face when I knocked her on her ass."

"You knocked her … ugh, Morgan, hand me my phone."

She passes it to me and I prop myself up against the wall. It takes ten seconds to dial Luke's cell. He doesn't pick up. He isn't at work. He said on Friday he has three days off. My mind instantly goes blank. I'd had one natural reaction as soon as I heard Noah ask me those things, and that was to run. And the only person I feel comfortable running to isn't picking up his phone. I slip it back into my pocket and look up at Morgan.

"Can I borrow the Jeep? I have to get out of here."

"Where are you going?"

"I don't know, I just … I have to get away."

A troubled frown pushes Morgan's brows together. "There's quite a crowd out there. It's probably not a good idea. I could go and get the car and drive around. You wouldn't have to walk through them all that way."

I nod, climbing shakily to my feet. "I'll need some stuff from my place. I can't stay here tonight."

"Forget that, babe. I'll come back and grab some stuff for you later. Let's just get you someplace else first." She snatches up her keys and dodges out of the apartment, and I hover by the window, trying to work out if the gathering on the street has anything to do with me. The people, hunched over against the cold, all wrapped in hats and scarves, beeline for Morgan as soon as she appears, answering that question for me. Of course they're there because of me. They're either there to demand answers or hurl abuse. From past experience I'm leaning towards abuse. It takes a while for Morgan to collect the Jeep from the parking garage. I see her turn onto the street and decide it's time to make a run for it.

No people in the hallways. That's a blessed relief, but when I get to the bottom of the stairs, my heart hammering in my chest, I realize they aren't loitering inside like usual because everyone is outside on the street. And Casey and Maggie are waiting there for me, too. Everyone's gaze follows the Jeep as Morgan pulls up out front, but not Casey. Oh no, she spots me as soon as I step foot out of the security door. Her cheeks are flushed from the cold and her eyes are bright, excited. It takes me a second to figure out why her lips are so red, but then I see that the bottom one is split and swollen. Morgan's handiwork. I jog forward just as she starts walking over, twenty other people hot on her heels.

"Iris! Hey, Iris!" Her arms pump back and forth as she hurries to reach me before I can climb in the passenger seat of the Jeep. "They say schizophrenia's hereditary, y'know. Your dad had to have been out of his mind to butcher those girls the way he did." She gets to the car before me, stepping in front of the door. The rest of the crowd isn't far behind her. They circle around me so I have nowhere to go.

"Just let me by, Casey."

She sneers in a way that makes her instantly hideous. "No way. The people here have a right to know who's living amongst them."

"She's right." Maggie appears at Casey's side. When I left Breakwater, I'd tricked myself into believing I'd never have to tolerate her hate-filled expression burning into me again. I was wrong. The pure aggression on her face is breathtaking.

"Good to see you again, Breslin. Tell me, have you started hearing the voices yet? How long will it be before you follow in Daddy's footsteps? How long before you start killing people?"

A rumble of murmured chatter ripples around the people standing behind me. They're listening to her—Maggie Bright is insinuating that I'm going to become a murderer and they're *believing* her.

Morgan revs the Jeep's engine and people scatter from in front of the car. A string of cars are forming behind Morgan's parked vehicle, all leaning on their horns, growing angrier and angrier by the second. I step forward but Maggie mirrors me, blocking my way. "You're sick, you know that? You'd have to be with a father who'd kill indiscriminately like your dad did. *My* dad was about to get married again. He was happy for the first time since I could remember, and your dad killed him. Just shot him in the back of the head."

"Let me by, Maggie."

She steps forward and shoves me by the shoulders, making me stumble back away from the car. "No! I won't let you by. I'm going to be there whenever you try and build something good for yourself. I'm going to be there to tear it all down and make sure people know who you really are."

"I'm not my father," I mutter, trying to dodge around her. Her hand whips out and slaps me, hard. I stagger back and clutch both hands to my cheek, not quite believing that she's struck me in front of everyone. This is hardly the first time Maggie has raised her hand to hurt me, but we were always alone when she did it in high school. I gasp in a shocked breath and focus, just in time to see Morgan flying around the car.

"You did *not* just slap my friend!" she yells.

"Back off, psycho. This has nothing to do with you."

It's not until Maggie's on the ground that I realize what has happened. Morgan kicks out at the back of Maggie's legs, causing her to crumple, and then she proceeds to pound her fist into the blonde girl's face.

"Morgan, stop! It's not worth it!"

Casey starts yelling and launches herself at Morgan, and then the next thing I know I have my arm locked around her throat, pulling her backwards. I've never fought back before. Some sick part of me always felt like I deserved everything I got back at Breakwater, but this is different. There's no way I'm going to let anyone hurt Morgan.

A scandalized cheer goes up from the people gathered around watching, passers-by all stopping to rubberneck the throw down on an Upper Manhattan street. I tumble backwards onto the dirty concrete, dragging Casey with me. Her legs flail as she thrusts back with her elbows trying to dig me in the ribs. A winded rasp rattles out of me when she finally contacts, forcing the air from my lungs. My grip around her neck slackens and gives her time to wriggle free, but not before lashing backwards one more time. Pain explodes in my head. I grasp my hands to my face, not sure if my right eye or my nose hurts more. The bright red color pouring between my fingers clues me into the fact that she's broken my nose.

Morgan lets out an enraged shriek and starts swearing like a banshee, and I hear Casey start crying. She sounds pitiful, completely different to the vitriol that was fueling her two seconds ago. "Oh, thank god you're here. She just went mad. She's an animal, Luke."

Luke?

My eyes fly open to see him standing between me and Casey. He's actually there in his uniform, the muscles in his neck working overtime. He shoots me a hard look where I'm lying on the concrete and steps towards Casey. For a long, awful second I think he's going to take her into his arms.

"I saw what happened, Case. Don't even think about lying. And you ..." He thrusts a finger in Maggie's face, causing her to shrink back. "You've earned yourself the pleasure of a ride back to the station. In fact, both of you have. Come on." Maggie's jaw falls open, but her shocked expression has nothing on Casey's look of horror.

"You can't be serious?" she whispers.

"As a heart attack." Luke narrows his eyes and grabs hold of her arm. She's too dazed to protest as he efficiently cuffs her and reads her the Miranda rights. A tall Indian officer I haven't seen before deals with Maggie, making sure she responds when he asks her if she understands the script he rattles off to her. She's glowering at me, bleeding from her temple as she spits out a hard yes. Both the girls are ushered into the back of the cruiser blocking Morgan's Jeep in, and then Luke is in front of me.

"Need some help?" he asks quietly. I stare at the gloved hand he's offering me and shake my head, pushing off the floor to get to my feet.

"I can manage." I dust the snow off my butt, feeling humiliated and pathetic as I say, "Why are you working?"

"I got called in this morning. You need to go to the hospital. Do you want me to come?"

"No." I wince when he reaches out and carefully touches the bridge of my nose.

"I'll go with her," Morgan says, threading her arm through mine. She's drenched down one side from scrabbling in the rotten snow with Maggie, and a deep gash marks her forehead. The sight of her blood makes me feel terrible. She's hurt because of me.

Luke purses his lips and lifts my face with his hand. "Here." He produces something from his pocket and presses it into my hands. "You'll need to come down to the station to give a statement, but I'll schedule that for another day. I'll be finished in two hours. Don't go anywhere. I want to talk to you."

I look down at the keys to his apartment and slip them into my coat pocket, not even bothering to argue with him. "I tried calling you," I whisper.

"I know. I was already on my way." He casts a disgusted glance at the back seat of his cruiser, where Casey's pale face stares out of the window. She looks wild. "She texted me and told me she was coming here. I knew there'd be trouble." He carefully reaches out and tucks a piece of my hair behind my ear. "I'm always gonna come running, Avery. Whenever you need me. Don't doubt it."

The traffic build-up has reached epic proportions, people in taxis and sedans leaning out of their windows to scream obscenities down the road. The Indian officer accompanying Luke gives a low whistle. "Hey, man, we should go."

"'Kay."

As his partner opens the cruiser door, Casey leans forward and shouts through the grill, setting my teeth on edge. "You're welcome to him, Breslin. He's as fucked up as you are, anyway. Just ask him. Ask him just how fucked up he is!" Her voice rises into hysteria at the end, and the other officer cuts her off by slamming his door closed.

"Sorry. I'm so sorry," Luke mutters, pulling me against his chest. For one brief moment, everything is right with the world. His smell floods my senses and I feel safe. Protected. He lets go all too quickly and hurries to the cruiser, turning back to look at me as he folds himself to get into the passenger seat. His eyes are locked with mine, blazing, until the car swerves out onto the road and burns away.

"Come on." Morgan catches hold of my hand and pulls me towards the now abandoned Jeep. She starts muttering about how there's going to be blood on her leather upholstery but I'm not really listening. I'm retreating inside myself, burying myself, hiding myself. I let my forehead press against the cold glass of the window as Morgan starts the engine and puts it into gear. I only snap my head up when she inhales sharply. I don't know what I was expecting: a crowd of people blocking our escape; a huge billboard with my name and face plastered all over it; the Dean, waiting to tell me not to bother coming back to college.

Instead, it's Noah running up 125th towards us.

"Do you want me to stop?" Morgan asks.

I register the panicked look on his face, the fact that he's actually come outside without his precious beanie. His eyes meet mine for a second, the same way Luke's did, and I remember the horror in his voice when he asked me those questions. I turn and slump so that my forehead presses against the glass once more. Morgan takes that as my answer and keeps on driving.

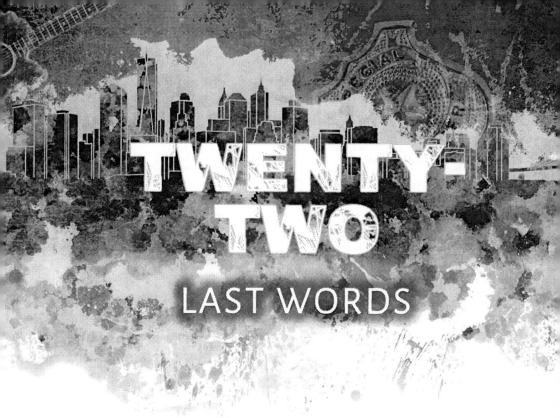

TWENTY-TWO

LAST WORDS

BY SOME miracle my nose isn't broken, after all. Casey's elbow just made it bleed like hell and bruised me up pretty badly, but the bone is intact. I'm not going to end up looking like a boxer. Morgan drives me across the city from the hospital. I silently take in the steam rising from the sidewalks and the thousands of yellow cabs, the people buried inside their layers, the food vendors, the buskers, the city an endless machine, feeling nothing. My phone doesn't stop ringing for a full hour after Morgan drops me off at Luke's. She offered to take it with her when she left me after I'd insisted I wanted to be alone, but I'd declined. I'd planned on calling Brandon as soon as I was by myself but then Noah had started texting and I was too numb to do anything but stare at the screen.

> **Noah**: Avery, please pick up. I'm so sorry. I'm not kidding, I thought it was all a joke!

A joke. He'd thought girls starting a hate campaign against me on campus was a joke. And the posters calling me that name? On what planet was any of that funny? I slip the phone down the side of Luke's leather sofa and go rifling for the blankets he used to make up a bed for himself the last few times I stayed here. They're folded neatly in a cupboard at the end of the hallway opposite his bedroom door, along with stacks of white towels and fresh bedding. I've never seen a cupboard so organized. I drag the blankets back to the sofa and curl up, determined to get my crying done before Luke comes home so I won't embarrass myself any further. No tears come, though. I'm still dry-eyed and hollow when the door knocks. I freeze, wondering if I'm supposed to answer it. Then I remember Luke gave me his keys and won't be able to let himself in. I go and open the door, and there he is, back in his jeans and a leather jacket looking as exhausted as I feel.

"Hey." He cups his hand over the back of his neck. I give him a tight smile and go back to the sofa. He comes and sits next to me, and we remain there in silence for a drawn-out moment. He's brought the smell of winter with him, fresh and bright, and I just sit there and breathe it in. Eventually he takes a deep breath and says, "Casey and Maggie were given warnings and released. If you want to get a restraining order against them, I can help you with that."

"Are they going to come back to campus?"

He shakes his head. "I don't think so. Casey's mom came to get her. Reamed her out in front of everyone. That's just about the most embarrassing thing that could ever happen to her. Plus there's the fact that her mom threatened to cut her off if she disgraced herself again."

"And what about Maggie?"

Luke lets out a sigh and slumps back against the sofa, stacking his hands on his stomach. "I don't think she'll come back. She's studying in Florida. She came all the way up here to …" He pauses and puffs out his cheeks. "I have no idea why she

172

came up here. I have a sneaking suspicion she might be slightly unbalanced."

"Your father being murdered will have that effect," I mumble, pulling the blankets up over me. Luke turns his head to look at me, frowning.

"Don't defend her actions. You don't deserve this." I look away and study my fingernails. Luke reaches over and hooks a finger under my chin. He lifts it so that our eyes meet again. "Listen to me, you've done nothing wrong. We're going to prove your dad didn't either, and then all this is going to go away."

The absolute belief on his face is what finally tips me over the edge. I clench my jaw, furious at the tears that are welling in my eyes. "We might be able to prove he didn't kill those girls, Luke, but he still killed Maggie's dad. That's not going to change."

"I don't think he did," Luke says softly.

"What?" I tense, my eyes roving from his, rimmed with those long, dark lashes, to his high cheekbones and full lips. His facial features are blank, his shoulders drawn up an inch like he's holding his breath.

"I don't think he killed *anyone*," he whispers. My heart is thudding when he says, "I've never believed he did. This whole time I've always believed he was innocent."

"That's ridiculous," I snap. I recoil so he's no longer touching me. Luke reacts and pulls back, too, flinching. I twist in my seat to face him and tuck my knees up under my chin, wanting to put a barrier between us. "Why would you say that?"

"Because it's true. There are things you don't know about me. Things ..." He trails off and swallows hard, sitting forward to rest his elbows on his knees. "That doesn't matter, though. I think your dad took the fall for something he didn't do."

"The room was locked from the inside, Luke. You told me that yourself five years ago. No one could have gotten in or out. Those men were bound, and my dad had the gun that killed them in his hand. Hell, it was the gun he killed himself with, too!" My voice cracks, my throat dangerously close to closing up. Why is he doing this? Why would he tempt me with the hope that my dad is innocent? It's cruel and unbearable, especially after everything that has happened today. I bury my face into my knees, focusing on my breathing.

"Avery. *Avery* ..." Luke takes hold of one of my hands and I try to pull it back, but he grips on tighter. "I'm not letting you go," he says. "I'm not trying to hurt you. This is just what I believe. There's something you weren't told before. There were certain things the police kept back from the press." I look up to find him biting his lip. "Max wasn't dead when we found him, Avery. He was dying but ... he was still conscious."

Luke slides across the sofa and grabs hold of the tops of my arms at the same time I lose it, like he knows exactly how I will react. I kick out at him, trying to push him away, but he's too close for me to get any leverage. A broken wail echoes around the room—mine—and I start hyperventilating.

"Calm down," he growls, drawing me to him so that my face is pressed into his chest. I can't. I can't. I can't. I shove against him, struggling to breathe through my sobbing, but he's holding me too tight. I try again and again but it's useless; he has me. Without thinking I let my body take control. I sink my teeth into his chest, biting down hard. Luke grunts and lets go, and suddenly he's standing up, clenching his fists.

He looks furious. I edge into the corner of the sofa and glare at him, choking on my tears. Luke sinks into a crouch in front of me and laces his hands behind his head, his anger turning to pain, written into the planes of his face. "For fuck's sake, let me hold you," he grinds out.

"You should have told me! You shouldn't have kept that from me!"

"I know. I'm sorry, I am, but I didn't have any choice. Please—"

I clench my eyes shut and put my hands over my ears. "No.

No, you said he died quickly."

I sense his movement again. Luke's hands take hold of my wrists, gently this time, trying to get me to lower them. I kick out and strike him square in the chest, but he just grunts and leans closer. "I'm not letting you go," he repeats. He manages to pull my hands down and climbs up onto the sofa again, kneeling over me. I open my eyes, trying to fill them with as much anger and hatred as I can. He doesn't back off; he grabs hold of my hips and yanks me towards him so that I slide onto my back, and then he straddles me and pins my wrists above my head.

"You can be mad at me, Iris. You can hate me and that's fine. I should have told you. I wanted to. Every time I asked you to meet me back in Break, it was because I told myself you needed to know. But you were still so broken. I didn't want to hurt you any more." He clenches his jaw and stares down at me, every single angle of him a study in determination. I buck and writhe, trying to unseat him.

"Get the fuck off me, Luke."

"No. Not until you hear this. Your dad didn't die quick, okay? He died slow and I held his hand while he went. His throat was torn to shreds. He could barely speak, but he did, okay? He *did* speak. Look at me, Iris. Look at me!" I turn away, resolved on not listening. Not strong enough to hear what he's saying. He gathers my wrists together and holds them in one of his hands, sliding the other palm underneath my cheek so I can't look away. "He said two things before he died. He said, '*the trade*'. Do you know what he meant by that? Does that mean anything to you?"

I struggle against him but it's no use. He is far stronger than me, and I don't have a hope in hell of getting out from underneath him while he's sitting on top of me. "No," I growl. "Now get off."

"Breathe, Beautiful. Come on, breathe."

"Don't you fucking call me that!"

He ignores me. "Breathe." He focuses his steady gaze on me and the power behind it is devastating. He blows out a sharp breath of his own. "Think about it. Just stop fighting and *think about it* for two seconds. Does 'the trade' mean anything to you?"

My cries hitch in my throat. I still a little.

"That's it. Just breathe. *Think.*"

I can barely see past the fact that he's holding me down and I need to be free, but Luke's words finally penetrate my panic. I inhale, long and deep, and try to make my muscles go limp. I am trembling with adrenalin and grief when I say, "No. It doesn't mean anything."

Luke's head slumps forward, his disappointment evident. "I'm going to let you up, okay? Don't freak out." His hand loosens around my wrists and he carefully lets go, sitting back on his heels. He's still straddling me but he leans back to give me some space. I flex my hands and then prop myself up on my elbows, trying to calm my frantic heartbeat.

"You said there was something else. That he spoke twice," I say, refusing to look at him, instead focusing on his scuffed metal belt buckle at my eye level.

"He did." Luke shifts back when he realizes I'm not going to try kicking him again. He swings his leg over me and sinks back onto the sofa, sighing raggedly. "It doesn't make any sense, though. He was barely alive by that point. I've played it over a thousand times in my head, trying to figure out if I heard him wrong."

"Just tell me," I whisper, bracing myself.

He bows his head into his chest and purses his lips. I don't fight him when he takes my hand again. He stares down at it in his lap, tracing small circles across the tender skin where he restrained me, apologizing with his fingertips. A ball of pent-up anticipation threatens to explode in my chest when he turns those deep brown eyes on me and says it.

"*Fly high, Icarus.*"

TWENTY-THREE

NEED

MY HEART stops beating. Luke squeezes my hand and inches closer. "What is it? You know what that means?"

I can't speak. My throat is burning so badly that I struggle to swallow. I just nod and let my tears slide free down my face. He makes a distressed noise and tugs on my arm. "Let me hold you. Please?"

His pain looks as real as mine. It seems to swamp him, makes him look lost. I sit up and crawl to him, climbing into his lap. He wraps his arms around me and presses his forehead against my temple, whispering soft, soothing things into my hair while I cry. We sit like that for a long time before I have the strength to pull myself together. Those words—*Fly high, Icarus*—they are a message. A message for me. They have to be. I can't tell Luke that, though. I'm too screwed up to talk about it, so instead I do something I know I'll regret. I bury my face into his shoulder and let myself cry for one more minute. And then I draw back a little and kiss his jaw, just below his ear. He stops whispering, his hands stilling where they were stroking gently up and down my back. I freeze, trapped in my indecision. Part of me wants to do it again, but part of me wants to scramble out of his lap and run for the door. Then I think about sitting on the subway all the way back to Columbia, and the posters, and Noah, and Tate still missing, and I need him. I need Luke so badly I can't breathe. I push down the desperate urge inside me to start tearing at his clothes and carefully press my lips to his skin again.

He makes a guttural sound in the back of his throat, like he's trying to form words. His hand travels up my back and he slowly gathers my hair in his fist, drawing it back out of my face. He slouches just a little, searching for my eyes. I hide from him, reaching up to the back of his neck, threading my fingers cautiously into *his* hair.

"Avery," he whispers.

I don't say anything. I can't. I just shift my body and twist my leg around so that I'm straddling *him* now. I dig my fingers into the skin at the back of his neck and whimper when he places his hands on my hips.

"Avery," he groans, his voice catching in his throat. "What are we doing?"

At least he didn't say, *"What the hell are you doing?"* I shift in his lap and press up against him, feeling his chest rise and fall quickly against mine.

"Avery."

I dip and press my mouth against his throat and his head tips back. "Please, Luke …" I cry softly. "I just need … I need …"

His hands tighten on my waist and then they're fumbling through my hair. He pulls me back, cupping my face in his hands. His eyes are on fire, searching mine. There's frustration in his voice when he speaks. "We shouldn't. You're upset. This isn't a good idea."

"Please, Luke!" I cover his hands with mine, finally daring to look at him. "Everything hurts. Just make it go away. *Please,* make it go away."

The moment he gives in is like a wall crumbling between us. A fierce intensity changes the way he looks at me. Concern and uncertainty transform into hunger. He growls and sits up to crush his mouth to mine. My head spins as he wrestles with the bottom of my shirt; he rips it clean off and presses his powerful hands into my back so that I fall forward against him. His fingers work quickly at the clasp on my bra, and I claw the straps over my shoulders in my hurry to get it off.

"This is such a bad fucking idea," he says, his voice hoarse. "I don't want you to hate me."

"I'm not going to hate you, Luke. I need you. I need you right now."

A fleeting moment of doubt passes over his face, and I act. I grab hold of his hand and cover my bare breast with it, and that's when I know he won't push me away. His need is visible; I can see it in the way he reverently strokes his finger across my sensitive skin. I shiver and he looks up at me in a way that makes my lips tingle. I lick them, imagining his mouth on mine again, and Luke watches me, fascinated. He tips his head forward to take my nipple into his mouth, turning my breathing ragged. A warm rush floods through my body, and I rock down against him, trying to tighten my thighs around his waist.

Luke reaches up behind me and holds onto me, scooting forward on the sofa so that he's sitting on the very edge, and I wrap my legs around him, groaning when he bites down on my nipple. I arch my back against his hands and push down, wanting to feel him between my legs.

If I'd doubted whether he wanted me before, that fear is cast out and blown to tiny pieces when I feel how hard he is. I rock my hips, grinding into his lap, and he groans, breathing heavily against my breasts.

"Fuck, I ..." he murmurs, "I don't know what to do." He sounds pained. I lace my fingers into his hair and tug his head back. I stare down at him, unwilling to look away as I fist his t-shirt and yank it up over his head. I throw it on the ground and press myself to him again.

"I need to feel your skin on mine," I pant. A low, animalistic growl rumbles out of Luke's mouth and he slips his hands in between us, stroking the material of my jeans between my legs. I cry out, clenching my thighs around him, pushing against the pressure of his fingers.

"Hold onto me," he orders. I wrap my arms around his neck as he hooks his hands underneath my legs, standing up in one swift, fluid movement, as though I weigh nothing at all. Our lips meet and he pushes his tongue into my mouth, stroking over mine, hot and impatient, as he carries me to his bedroom. He puts me down on the bed and leans back to unzip my jeans as I kick off my shoes, and then he falls on me again. I grip hold of his arms where they support him on either side of my head and bite down on his bicep, making him suck in a sharp breath.

"Oh god," he groans. "I want you, Ave. I want you so bad."

Hearing him say it makes my heart pound in my chest. I kick out of my jeans and gasp when he reaches down and drags them off my body. His hands are rough and hurried. When he lets his body press down on top of mine, I hitch my legs around him and squeeze him to me. I tilt my head up and gently lick my tongue across the sharp black lines of the tattoo sweeping over his shoulder. The severity of his expression makes me panic for a second, but when he shudders and his eyes close, I realize he's enjoying the attention. I run my tongue up and over his neck, tasting the salt on his skin, the smell of him filling my head. He smells, tastes, feels so damn good. I moan, and that's when he snaps.

He rips my panties down with one frantic tug and pushes his way in between my legs. I've thought about his hands finding me, about how it would feel and how I'd lose myself in the sensation of his fingers sliding inside me. I never imagined his tongue, though.

"Ahh!" I grip hold of the bed sheets and pull, the muscles in my legs contracting. I kick helplessly against the waves of pleasure coursing through my body with every languorous sweep he makes. He moans into me, his tongue still lapping persistently at the very center of me, causing my back to arch off the bed. Reaching up, Luke finds my hips and pulls me down hard against his mouth.

"Shit, Luke, please … please …" I beg, not sure what I'm begging for. What I need. My desperation seems to drive him crazy. He lets go of my hips and does what I'd imagined, slowly pushing a finger inside me, gently rolling his thumb over my sensitive clit.

"Fuck, you're so wet, Avery," he breathes. Our eyes lock down the length of my body. I buck against him, unable to stop myself from reacting to the searing heat that surges through my body with every thrust of his fingers.

"Please … please … ah, Luke!"

"I'm gonna make you come," he whispers, removing his thumb so he can replace it with his tongue again. My body is fire and ice as I shamelessly rock against his mouth. His tongue is unbearably hot, his movements torturously slow. I reach down and bury my hands in his hair, surprising myself with the weak, helpless noises I'm making. "Luke?" I pant, feeling the burning between my legs increase with every gentle lap.

"Yeah?" His voice is broken as mine.

"I need you inside me. Please …"

"I am inside you."

"Not … not your fingers …" I stammer. I don't know how to ask for what I want, but he already knows.

"I'm going to make you come first. I want to taste you."

It doesn't take long. The muscles in my legs start to cramp as the pressure builds inside me. Hot. I'm too hot. Every part of me burns. Just as I'm ready to start begging again, Luke slips another finger inside me and groans, and I lose the ability to speak. I can only moan and pant and twitch under him as he slowly pumps me with his fingers. "Come on, baby," he growls.

"Come for me."

I want him to go faster but he doesn't; he slows so that I feel every single inch of his fingers as he pushes them inside me, feel each teasing draw of his tongue as he strokes and sucks on me. I'm vibrating by the time the pressure explodes, stealing the air out of my lungs so I can't even cry out. I tremble under him and contort as he carries on, ignoring my thrashing legs.

"Stop, stop!" I gasp, clawing at my own thighs each time he licks. He lets out a savage groan and finally stops, climbing up my body, leaving a trail of burning kisses on my hip, my stomach, my breasts as he rises. He looks up at me from under heavy eyelids and another shiver runs through my body, the heat in his gaze too scorching to bear.

"You're amazing," he whispers. He goes to brush my hair, plastered to my skin with my own sweat, out of my eyes, but I catch hold of his wrist. Slowly, I lick at his fingers and watch his mouth fall open. I carefully wrap my lips around his index and middle finger and slide them into my mouth, running my tongue over them and sucking, tasting myself all over him. Luke's body judders and an agonized sigh stutters out of his mouth.

"Holy fuck."

Suddenly aware of the fact that I'm naked and he's still half dressed, I go about rectifying the matter. My hand is on his belt when he places his other hand over mine.

"Avery, I don't know if ... I don't think I'm gonna be able to stop myself if you do that."

I make sure he's looking at me when I say the words, not wanting him to doubt me. "I don't want you to stop."

I unzip his jeans and push him back so I can inch them over his hips. He grunts as he works them off with his feet. Not wanting to give him time to overanalyze anything, I slide my hand down the rock solid planes of his stomach and tease at the waistband of his boxer briefs. His eyes grow wide as I slip inside, and when I wrap my fingers around his hard erection his body tenses dramatically.

"Oh fuck. Fuck!" he growls, biting his lip and closing his eyes. "That feels so good."

I tease him the way he teased me, incredibly gentle with my contact, until he is quivering in my hand. His shoulders hitch up and down erratically and he struggles to keep his cool. I increase the pressure, adrenalin rushing like liquid fire through my veins every time he groans. "You're going to make me beg, aren't you?" he whispers.

I refuse to answer. I inch down his body and pull his boxers off, studying the sculpted lines of his torso and legs as I go. He stops breathing when I tentatively lick the tip of his cock, his body jerking.

"I can't. I need to be inside you," he rasps, digging his hands into my hair. "I won't last."

"Maybe I want to taste you, too," I whisper.

Luke's hands suddenly tighten around my waist, and he picks me up and throws me onto my back again. "I want to be inside you. I need to feel you around me, Avery. You're so fucking tight. I have to. Please. Please let me." He kisses me fiercely, forcing his tongue into mouth, and my body reacts, curving into him. I wrap my legs around his waist once more, but this time there's nothing between us. No jeans. No underwear. His cock presses up against me, deep between my legs, scaring and thrilling me at the same time.

Luke shakes his head, as though trying to clear it, and nuzzles into my breasts. "God, I know this is *not* right, but so help me I want you. Say it. Please say yes," he groans.

I push up against him, feeling him slide down so that he is on the verge of entering me, and I whimper, "Yes. Yes. *Please.*"

He quickly sits back. I think he's finally freaking out, but he isn't. He pulls at the drawer on his nightstand so hard it flies off the runners and slams to the floor with a crash. Doesn't seem to bother him; he rummages around for two seconds and comes back holding a small metallic blue square in his hands. He rips it open and I watch as he slips the condom into place, faintly aware of the fact that I'm staring. When he's done, he pushes back on top of me and braces himself over me.

"You're sure?" he whispers.

"I'm sure." I hitch my knees up and dig my fingernails into his ass, letting him know I can't wait any longer. When he rocks forward, pushing into me, we both freeze for a moment, overcome by the intensity of how it feels. He's bigger than anyone I've ever slept with before. The borderline pain of having him inside me is incredible.

"Oh shit, you're so tight. Don't move!" he begs. I still underneath him and watch his face as he struggles to even out his breathing. His eyes lock onto mine as he carefully draws out of me; staring the whole time he slowly inches back. I can't help it when he thrusts inside again; I buck and push upwards, desperate to feel him deeper. He lets out a pained groan.

"Fuck it." He grabs hold of my wrists the way he did before, except now I'm more than willing to have him pin them over my head. He kisses my throat as he thrusts into me again, delicious darts of pain firing between my legs as he sinks deeper and deeper.

That crippling heat is building like an unstoppable inferno when Luke starts to shake. "Oh, ffff ... I'm gonna ... I can't ..."

My legs lock, drawing him in as deep as he can go. I push up so that my breasts brush against his chest with each thrust, and suddenly we're both coming. He stiffens, letting out a panting cry, and I ride into him, my synapses firing blindly as I come apart piece by piece.

My hands are tingling when Luke lets me go. I brush my fingers up and down his spine, enjoying the way the muscles in his back twitch under my touch. He settles over me and starts whispering quiet, pretty things into my hair. After a couple of minutes I feel him tensing and know he's about to get up.

"Don't," I say softly. "Stay inside me."

Knowing it's exactly what I need, Luke gathers me in his

arms and cradles me to him. We stay like that until the very last of the daylight fades and we fall asleep as one.

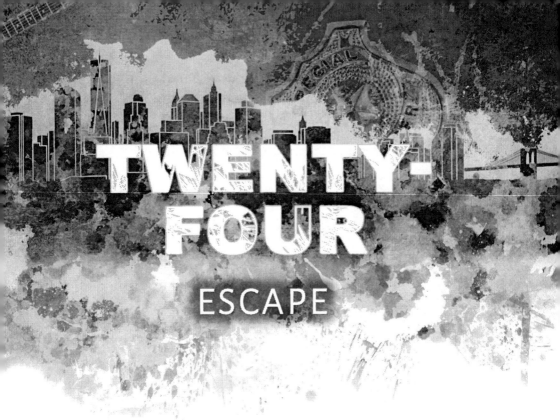

TWENTY-FOUR

ESCAPE

THE SUNLIGHT is a cold, desolate color when I wake. It reminds me of snow and Wyoming mountains and a silent world. New York City will never be silent irrespective of the weather, though. It will steam and smoke and teem regardless, and I have to make my way across it. Luke's sleeping on his front, his arms thrown up above his head, tucked under his pillow. The white bed sheet is twisted around his waist. I don't disturb him when I get up. I'm quieter than I ever thought I could be as I gather up my abandoned clothes and go in search of my shirt and bra in the lounge.

A war rages in my head as I debate whether or not I should hang around to make myself a coffee, but my cowardice eventually wins out. I've wanted this for the past few weeks. I have, and yet now that we're here I'm petrified. I leave as quietly as I can and run down the building's three flights of stairs, feeling more desolate with every step. I know what I'm going to have to do, but going to my mother's brownstone in Manhattan is almost as frightening as the prospect of heading back to Columbia. I should be able to turn to my mother in times like this. She should be a shoulder to cry on. In reality, she'd rather go to work than deal with my problems, no matter how upset I am.

I pull my coat around myself and step out of the building, immediately seeing that I was right about the snow. It's everywhere. Huge banks push up against the sidewalk where the roads have been cleared, and all the gray and black and in between is capped off with a seven-inch layer of white. Bodies already fill the sidewalk, steaming cups of coffee in hand, cigarettes in mouths, cell phones pressed to ears. No one bats an eyelid as I slip in amongst them. I let their anonymity engulf me.

A block away I enter the very first diner I come across and order a coffee. I'm taking a tentative sip, cupping the piping hot polystyrene in my frozen hands as I walk out of the door, when his voice startles me.

"I take it by the single takeaway you weren't planning on coming back, then?"

Luke's hair is ruffled and dusted with flecks of white where the snow has started up again while I was inside. He's wearing nothing but a t-shirt and sweat pants and he's out of breath.

"What ... *what the hell are you doing?*"

"No." He takes a step toward me and stuffs his hands in his pockets. "What are *you* doing?"

"I have class."

"Avery, you don't have class. It's six in the morning. And I seriously doubt you're planning on going back there today, either. You're running away from me."

"I'm not!"

"Then why didn't you wake me up before you left?"

"Because ..." I scan up and down the street, not wanting to look at him.

"You really know how to make a guy feel like crap, you know that?" He steps towards me. "I freaked the fuck out. We

... last night, I knew it was a bad idea. I know we shouldn't have done it but I kinda hoped you wouldn't hold it against me."

I stare down at our feet, noticing he's wearing thin sneakers he's barely pulled onto his feet properly. "Don't be stupid! I'm not holding it against you. I thought you'd prefer it this way."

"Prefer ..." He doesn't appear capable of finishing that sentence. He laces his fingers together behind his head, pulling his elbows in to his ears, the same way he did last night when he'd tried to hold me. His shoulders pull up as he takes a deep breath. "You can be so damn selfish sometimes, you know that?"

"Look, it's just ... it's better this way."

He narrows his eyes and closes the gap between us, drawing me to the side of the building out of the way of the pedestrians trying to shove their way past us. "*How* is it fucking better this way?"

"Open your eyes, Luke. You only slept with me last night to make me feel better. And now I feel better. So thank you."

"Thank you?" He shakes his head, like he can't understand the words. "*Thank you?*" He clenches his fists and for a second I think he's going to punch the wall. Instead, he takes hold of my hand and bites down on his jaw. "I didn't sleep with you last night as a favor, you idiot. Man, how can you not know that I care about you?"

I do know that he cares about me, and maybe that's what makes this worse. Because, if he cares about me, this is real. And something like this ... I have no idea how to cope with this. I say the first thing that comes into my head, and it's the shittiest thing I've ever said to anyone. "You don't care about me. You just feel sorry for me because my dad died."

"Seriously? You think that!" His cheeks have turned red. Those soulful dark eyes of his are shining a little too brightly. "You're so wrong."

"Then why are you always asking to meet up? Asking me to

go out for coffee with you?"

Luke angles his body back down the street but keeps his gaze locked on me. Anger spills like ink across his beautiful face. "I used to ask you because you reminded me of your dad. I wanted to make sure you were okay. That changed pretty quickly, though. I was ... I developed feelings for you. You were sixteen by then and broken, and so fucking beautiful, and I couldn't stop it no matter how hard I tried. These days it seems as though I can't remember a time when I haven't wanted to be the person you come to when you need someone. When you aren't the first thing I think about when I woke up in the morning."

"Now *you're* the one being ridiculous," I say, stepping away from him. "You were with Casey that whole time. I was a kid."

"You were never just a kid! And I was with Casey for the wrong reasons. I realized that as soon as I moved here with her. I stopped fucking sleeping with her because I didn't fucking love her! I stopped sleeping with her 'cause I couldn't get *you* out of my fucking head!" He's shouting. Businessmen in their expensive tailored suits scowl at us as they pass. I can't bear it.

"Please, Luke."

He flares his nostrils and stares at the lapel on my coat, too angry to look at me. "So, what?" he murmurs. "You're just going to go back to that guy at Columbia? He's gonna make you happy?"

I never told Luke about the decision I came to with Morgan—that I wasn't going to see Noah anymore. Right now, he's a convenient excuse. "Noah doesn't make me happy. We're just ... we're nothing. It doesn't mean anything."

Pain flashes across Luke's face. "If you're just using him for sex, if you're just taking your mind off everything, then do that with me. I'd prefer that."

"I can't."

"*WHY?*" he yells.

I stare at him, fighting back my tears. "Because I'm terrified of you, Luke."

He reels back like I've slapped him across the face. *"You're afraid of me?"*

I've hurt him. God, I can see it in his eyes. I've hurt him so much. I feel like I want to die. "I'm afraid of how you make me feel," I whisper.

He steps closer, exhaling hard down his nose. "How? How do I make you feel?"

"Like I'm falling. Like I'm out of control. Like I'm lost and I'm never going to find myself again, Luke. I can't afford to feel like that." I turn and run. I don't know if he's following me or not, but I doubt it. The snow comes down harder and I drop my coffee on the road. I run from the one, single good thing in my life.

TWENTY-FIVE

TOXIC

AMANDA ST. French, formally known as Mom, is leaving home when I finally reach Manhattan. I catch the flash of her bright blonde hair, brilliant gold against the drab grays of the overcast day, as she pauses on the doorstep, probably hunting for her keys. I tip the cab driver way too much, not hanging around for my change, and run down the street to reach her before she climbs into her Lexus. I nearly don't make it. She's opening the passenger door when I skid to a halt in front of her. An awkward moment follows where I see her, she sees me, and the woman she is holding hands with sees me, too. How did I not notice she wasn't alone? How did I not notice she was holding hands with *a woman?*

Her eyes flash, wider than I've ever seen them go before. I didn't think it was possible. Usually they're narrowed into slits. "Avery?" She shoots an embarrassed look at her … at her friend? The woman's in her early thirties—far too young to be one of Mom's staple lawyer friends. Her dark brown hair is pulled back into French braids that just brush the tops of her shoulders. She's wearing a Led Zeppelin t-shirt that's obviously brand new. I distrust her instantly. People who buy retro rock t-shirts in order to look hip rarely ever are. In the three-second gap where my mom stands silently opening and closing her mouth like a fish out of water, I've categorized the stranger (freckly) and also my mom (horrified).

"What are you doing here? Didn't you get my email?" she hisses. She angles herself so that the hand she's holding with the other woman is hidden between their bodies.

"Which email?" Maybe she's sent me a message that explains whatever is going on here. I furrow my brow, trying to work it out myself. I only come up with one conclusion, and it's too weird to be true.

"About your allowance. *Christmas*," she says through gritted teeth.

"Christmas?" My brain takes a little longer than it should to piece together what she means. Then I get it. If I've received my allowance and I know she isn't going to be available to spend any time with me, ever, then she really can't foresee any reason for us to interact.

It's truly shocking that, after the past twenty-four hours, I could possibly feel any worse than I already did. But here I am, feeling like utter shit.

"Mom, Maggie Bright was on campus. She ..." I glance at the woman, not sure if I'm going to get torn apart for breathing a word of what happened in front of her. The brunette gawps back at me like I have three heads. Her astounded gaze travels from me to my mom, who's adopted her trademark scowl. Except this time she looks even madder than usual.

"Mom?" the woman asks, raising an eyebrow.

"I was getting around to telling you," she says crisply. It is her lawyer voice—the one she uses to distance emotion from words, like she's presenting cold, hard facts.

"I see."

"We can talk about it later. Why don't you go on ahead? I'll meet up with you for lunch." Mom's used the same clipped dismissal with me a hundred times before, but the brunette clearly isn't used to it. She shakes her hand free from my mom's and holds it out to me.

"I'm Brit. It was lovely to meet you … Avery, was it?"

I shake her hand and nod. "Avery."

Brit gives me a warm smile that makes her somehow seem even more freckly and walks off down the street, making sure to throw a pissed-off glower over her shoulder at my mom as she goes.

"What the hell?" Mom grabs hold of my arm and pulls me up the steps to the house, rooting for her keys again in the trench coat she has slung over her arm.

"Ditto!" I snap. "Brit, Mom? *Brit?* Are you a lesbian now?" She casts a wary look about us as she fumbles to get the door open and then shoves me inside.

"Yes, I'm a lesbian now, Avery. I've been a lesbian the past three years."

"*What?*" I raise my eyebrows and blink, trying to force the words she just said to make sense. They won't.

"This is why I didn't tell you," she announces. She points at my boots. "Take them off. I just had the boards waxed."

I pull my boots off angrily, throwing them on the floor as hard as I can. "What do you mean by that—*this is why I didn't tell you?*"

Her mouth turns down at the corners, an expression that adds to her severity. "I knew you'd judge me."

"Judge you? What the fuck, Mom? Do you think I'm a homophobe or something?"

"That's an ugly word," she says. I note, in horror, that she doesn't deny it. I shake my head, completely confounded. Where on earth did she ever get the idea that I would react badly to her being with another woman? I search back through the handful of conversations we've shared about relationships and sexuality and can't think of a single thing that would have led her to believe anything so preposterous.

"I'm *not* a homophobe! I can't believe you'd think that!"

"Well, what was that face for, then?" she argues, stalking off towards the kitchen. I follow her, at a complete loss.

"The face? You mean *my confusion*? Maybe because you just announced that you're gay and you have been for three years, and you didn't think to tell me!"

"Oh, grow up, Avery." She turns her back on me and pushes her shirtsleeves up to her elbows, an indicator that she's ramping up for a fight. An even bigger fight. "Just tell me what Maggie Bright's been up to. I have a ten o'clock I can't miss and traffic's going to be hell."

"Great, I wouldn't want you to miss an appointment on account of your hysterical daughter. Don't worry, I'll make it quick. Everyone at Columbia knows about Dad. They know I lied about who I am. There are posters *everywhere* with my name and face all over them. They're calling me—"

"Avery, stop!" The look on my mom's face is classic. *Denial.* She leans forward and braces against the marbled counter top of her twenty-thousand-dollar kitchen island and yells, "This is so typical!"

"Sorry, Mom. There's not much I can do about it." I am under no illusions that she is upset on my behalf. She's undoubtedly panicked that people might figure out she is connected to me. "How long have you been seeing Brit?" I mutter, suddenly needing to know.

"Nine months," she grunts.

A manic laugh itches at the back of my throat, begging to be released. I manage to keep it at bay, but Mom still sees my lips twitch. "Why is that so entertaining to you?"

"You were *getting around* to telling her you had a daughter? She's never going to forgive you."

"Whatever, Avery." She pushes back and runs her hands over her perfectly neat ponytail, not a hair out of place. "What do you want me to do about Maggie?"

"I don't know."

"I can file for a restraining order, but that could take some time."

"Luke offered to do that already but I don't know if the offer still stands, so, yeah, I guess so."

Mom's face twists into disbelief. "Luke Reid?"

"Yeah."

She looks horrified. Disgusted, in fact. "You've been seeing him? When? Why?"

Her reaction is completely unexpected. "He's been helping me. He's always kept in touch. What's the big—"

She stalks across the kitchen and jabs her index finger into my chest, hard. "You're not to see him again, you understand me? I don't want you anywhere near that boy!" She moves over to the sideboard and pulls open a drawer, from which she produces a silver key. She doesn't give it to me; she puts it down on the marble and stares at it resentfully.

"You can stay here for the night, I suppose. I'm going to fix things at Columbia."

I'm so stunned from her outburst over Luke that I can't breathe a word. I know my mom well enough to know she means she'll fix things right here and now. She isn't one to put something off. Unless it involves telling her daughter or her girlfriend about the other's respective existences, of course.

I pace nervously around her kitchen, trying to find something even vaguely familiar or homely about it, while she rants for a full twenty minutes to the Dean of Columbia. She paid a small fortune to ensure my entry into Columbia—even though my grades were good enough to do that all on their own—and she isn't afraid of reminding the administration of her "charitable donations." By the end of her one-sided conversation, she has obtained a guarantee that the posters will be down by the end of the day and anyone found to be harassing me will be dealt with accordingly.

Just like back in high school, my mother thinks a sharp phone call with someone who has absolutely no contact with the student body will solve all my problems. Or solve them adequately enough that I can't say she hasn't done anything about it.

"I'm going out to dinner tonight. I probably won't come back after work. If you decide to stay here I won't see you until tomorrow at some point. Don't worry about making a mess. Consuela comes in the morning."

She flies by me in a cloud of vanilla perfume and then she's gone. The front door slams behind her, and I'm left standing in the cold, unfriendly kitchen, still staring down at the key she's finally given me to her house.

Noah: Avery, pick up your phone. I need to talk to you.

The message says the same thing every time I read it, but I still can't convince myself to call Noah. After sleeping with Luke … well, he's all I can think about, and there is just too much swirling around in my head to figure out how the hell I'm going to tell Noah I don't want to see him again. My blown secret identity is off-the-charts bad, and everything else just seems to be crashing down around my ears. Worst of all, I'm trapped in my mother's freaking sterile house with zero photos of me anywhere. Therapists all over the world would probably recommend I talk to someone about how I'm feeling before I go nuclear and take out half the neighborhood in my impending meltdown. But I can't. I just want to sit in silence and have someone else there with me, just to be with me. The person I want with me most of all is dead. The only other person capable of filling that void … I've royally screwed things up with *him*. Royally.

I run my fingers over the touch screen of my phone, jumping out of my skin when it starts to ring. Another unknown number. No way in hell. I can see it all happening again, all unraveling, leading me down the same road. I throw my cell on the couch and march to the kitchen, bracing myself against the counter. The slim handset on the bench starts ringing straight away.

"Damn it!" I glare at it malevolently. I won't get away with smashing things in my mother's house, which almost makes it impossible to resist. Instead I focus on the bright blue screen, narrowing my eyes at it until the answer machine kicks in.

"You've reached Amanda St. French's personal residence. Please redirect all business matters to my office. Thank you."

No, *leave a message after the beep*. No, *if you aren't calling about business, please feel free to try again later*. I know why; no one ever calls my mom unless it's work-related.

"Avery?" The sound of Brandon's voice emanating from the tinny speakers scares the crap out of me. "Ave? You there? My phone hasn't stopped ringing all morning. Pick up, kiddo."

My hands are shaking when I pluck the handset out of its cradle. "How d'you know I was here?" I croak. My throat is burning. Hearing the worried note in Brandon's voice is enough to tip me over the edge again.

"Luke called me, sweetheart. He's worried about you. You wanna tell me what's been going on?"

"*Luke?*" What the hell is he doing calling Brandon? "It's nothing, I ..." I can't really lie to my uncle. He'd know in a heartbeat, anyway. No matter how hard I fought to keep my tone level, he'd be able to tell. I let out a mighty sigh. "Didn't *he* tell you what happened?"

"He explained some. I want you to tell me, though."

Typical Brandon. He knows I'll only tell half a story if I can avoid rehashing all of it. "Just ..." I dig my knuckles into my forehead, gathering myself. "One of the girls from Break showed up with Luke's ex-girlfriend and outed me to Colum-

197

bia."

"And?"

"*And?* That's the very last thing I wanted to happen!"

"And I'm sure finally sleeping with a girl you're head over heels for, only to have her ditch before you woke up, is the very last thing Luke wanted to happen, too."

"What the fuck?! He *told* you that?" I close my eyes, sinking down onto a stool at the breakfast bar, considering thumping my head against the wall. Brandon only laughs.

"No, actually. He called me at seven in the morning, going out of his mind. That was the only conclusion I could come to. He didn't deny it when I asked him outright. Don't be mad at him. He's just looking out for you."

"Did he tell you that he lied to us all about Dad's death?" I snap. The line goes silent for a minute.

"No, he didn't tell me that. What do you mean, *he lied*?"

"The police kept things from us. Kept things from the public. Luke told us Dad was already dead when they found him, but he wasn't. Luke spoke to him. Luke held his hand when he died. He—"

"What did he say, Avery?"

"—said it took him a while to die after he found him, that he was in pain. All these years—"

"FUCK, AVERY, WHAT DID MAX SAY?!"

I freeze mid-sentence and blink, my eyes suddenly filling with tears. Brandon curses down the phone. "Shit, I'm sorry, kiddo. Just … what did he say? Did Max say anything about what he'd done? Why he'd done it? Did he say if there was anyone else involved?"

His voice is piqued with anger. I'm so surprised by his urgency that it takes me a second to respond. To even think straight. "No. It wasn't like that. He said … he said, '*the trade,*' and then he said, '*Fly high, Icarus.*'"

Brandon's breath rushes out, distorting the line. "Your father, that's the name he used to call—"

"I know." And there it is. Someone else realizing my father's last words are a message to me. It hurts like hell to have it confirmed.

"What about 'the trade', kiddo? Does that mean anything to you?"

"No."

"Are you sure? Think about it really hard."

"I have thought about it! I've thought about nothing else for the past eight hours. Maybe you should call Luke and talk to him about it. Sounds as though he and my dad had a pretty developed relationship, from what he was telling me last night."

I can hear Brandon sucking his teeth; he only ever does that when he's frustrated or worried. "You should cut Luke some slack, y'know."

"Why? He lied to us. He's still keeping secrets, too. Did you know my dad mentored him when he was a kid? He must have something pretty dark in his past for him to have needed help. Who knows what kind of a person he is. If we're honest, we barely know anything about the guy. He could be dangerous."

"Is that why you hopped into bed with him last night?"

I clench my jaw. That stings. More than I care to admit. "I made a mistake, Brand. One I won't be making again."

"He's a police officer, Avery. How in hell could he be dangerous? And, yes, I did know Max mentored him. Your father told me a few things about Luke that I wish he hadn't, to be perfectly honest. Makes it hard for me to look the kid in the eye when I see him, I feel so bad for him. If you gave him a chance then maybe he'd spill all the nasty, dark shit from his past and you'd see how wrong you are right now. As for lying to us, if the cops kept information from the public, then Luke did what he was supposed to. He could have lost his job if he'd leaked information they wanted to remain out of the papers. Worse, he probably could have gone to jail."

Brandon's diatribe is far from expected. He's usually so easy going and yet it's like I have touched a raw nerve. "Sorry, I …

my head is just totally screwed right now. I'm being a complete bitch."

"Yes. You are. Listen, just get out of your mother's house, okay? The air in that place is probably toxic."

"I can't. There's no way I'm going back to Columbia yet. And if you even dream of telling me to go to Luke's, so help me I'll scream."

"You can't go to Luke's. He's on his way here. Said something about going up to the house to look for your father's journal. Apparently you volunteered my services when he spoke to you about it?"

I slap my hand on the counter, feeling the beginnings of a headache start to come on. "I said that before! Why the hell is he doing this?"

"I dunno. Perhaps you hit the nail on the head. Maybe he *was* buried in a damned dark place when he was a kid, and maybe your dad was the only person who cared enough to dig him out. Maybe Luke feels what Max did saved him. Maybe he's *grateful*."

I chew on the inside of my cheek, knowing that despite his soft tone, Brandon is still reaming me out. "I'm sorry, okay? I guess I'm just a little thrown by everything that's happened over the past twenty-four hours."

"I know, kiddo. You've got your own dark places you need digging out of, too. You need to stop playing the victim, though. Get your ass back to school."

"Speaking of school, I need your help with something, Brand."

"What?"

I bite my lip, figuring out how to ask him. "I ... uh, I need to interview you about what happened."

Brandon breathes in deeply on the other end of the phone. "What do you mean, interview me about what happened?"

"About what happened ... Dad dying. What happened to me afterwards."

"Why on earth do you wanna do that?"

"I don't want to. I *have* to. It's for my Media Law and Ethics class. My professor's evil incarnate. He wants us to dredge up our most painful memories. Plus he wants us to get someone else's version of the events. Failing this class is the last thing I need right now."

"Why don't you just pick something else, Avery? Something that doesn't hurt so bad?"

I press my fingertips into my forehead, asking myself the same thing. I already know the answer, though. "Because he cornered me. I told him honesty was the most important part of being a journalist so now if I lie, I'll be a massive hypocrite."

"Well, okay, if you really want me to, then fine, Avery. But just so you know ... I think there's someone a whole lot closer to you geographically who would probably be a more sensible choice." Surely he can't mean my mother? He can't be that cruel. The sound of a car engine revs in the background. "I have a customer, kiddo. I gotta go. Just think about it, okay?"

He hangs up, and I am left standing by the sink with a sour taste in my mouth. I grab my coat, purposefully leaving Mom's apartment key untouched on the counter, and I leave.

TWENTY-SIX

THREATS

"**I WAS** wondering if you were going to come back. Were you going to call?"

I make it safely back to my building before I'm spotted. Noah sits on the low steps up to the entryway with his hands shoved in his jacket pockets. My shoulders sag at the sharp look in his eyes.

"So you're waiting for me outside buildings now?" I press the teeth of my keys into my palm.

"It's the only way I get to see you, love." His casual usage of the word "love" makes me cringe. He lets out a tight laugh. "Don't worry, Avery, it's just a term of endearment."

"I know that." My voice is small, despite how hard I try to sound irritated. I flick the keys over in my hand and motion towards the door. "I don't wanna stand out here for everyone to see. Would you like to come inside?"

Noah stands stiffly, hunching his shoulders a little in his coat. "There's no one here, Avery. Everyone's in class."

"Where you should be."

"Where we *both* should be."

I run my tongue over my teeth. "I'm going in. You can come if you want." I let myself into the building and hold the door for a second, waiting to see if he's following. He is. We make our way to my apartment in silence. Somehow, I've forgotten all about Leslie. She looks like a ghost when the door opens, her eyes round with surprise. "Hey, guys!"

"Sorry, Leslie. We'll uh … we'll go to the library," I say.

"God, no, I was just leaving." She leaps off the sofa and shoves her feet into some Ugg boots, slamming her laptop closed as she dashes out of the room. She wasn't just leaving; she's wearing sweats and her hair is a tangled knot on the top of her head. She doesn't even grab a coat. The sound of the door slamming closed rattles around the living room. I automatically head to my room, my heart sinking in my chest.

"Shit." I sink down onto my bed and stare at my hands, not really paying attention when Noah joins me.

"What's wrong?" The smell of his cologne is familiar yet far too strong. His arm wraps around my shoulders and he tries to pull me in, but I remain stiffly upright.

"Leslie probably thought I was never coming back. She's freaking out about sharing a room with a serial killer's daughter."

Noah sighs. "You're overanalyzing this."

"Oh, yeah? You didn't take the news very well."

He hangs his head, sighing deeply. "It came as a bit of a shock, is all. I was pissed that you didn't think you could tell me."

"I barely know you, Noah. It took me months to tell Morgan, and even then it was by accident."

"I know. You're right, I'm really sorry. But now that it's out in the open, you can trust me, okay? I don't want to give up on the beginnings of whatever it is we have here. We just need—"

"Noah, I don't … I can't see you anymore."

He pivots, frowning at me. "What? Why?"

"It's just too complicated. All of it."

He's silent for a moment and then takes hold of my hand. I open my eyes to find him staring determinedly at me. "You don't grow up where I did, when I did, but more importantly *around* the people I did, Avery, without knowing a few killers. Some of my friends' fathers are still in Portlaoise with no hope of ever being free men again. It doesn't matter how many times your parents fuck up in this life—their mistakes are their own. Whatever he did, love, *he* did. I'm only concerned about what you do. What you're going to do next." He squeezes my hand and slowly stands. He tugs me gently so I'll sit up. I do, hanging my head so my hair hides my face. "Look at me?" His voice is soft. It makes my eyes prick. I do as he asks, flinching when he picks apart the expression on my face. "I want you to come with me."

"What?"

"Come with me on my internship to Sierra Leone. It'll give us a chance to get to know each other better. All you'd need to do is talk to Professor Lang. He'd work out the small print so you could still apply for the journalism program later on in the year. I've already spoken with the people in Africa and they're more than happy to have another pair of hands helping out. It would look great on your—"

"*Noah.*"

"What? Tell me you wouldn't love some time away from this place. You'd only need to get through the next week and then Columbia closes for Christmas. By the time we get back, everyone will have forgotten about—"

"Noah, I slept with Luke."

He stops talking. For a second I can't believe the words have escaped my lips. Can't understand why I've said them out loud. Confusion flickers over Noah's face. "Luke? The guy from the bar? But ... but you said he was just your friend?" His voice is strangled. My stomach twists at the look of hurt on his face.

"He is. I mean, I ... he *was* my friend. I don't even think we're that anymore."

"And you slept with him?"

I nod, not trusting myself to make any sense if I speak. I scoot away so that my back rests against the wall, drawing my knees up under my chin. Noah crouches down by the bed and puts his head in his hands. For two whole minutes he just breathes deeply in silence. Eventually he drags his hands over his face and looks up at me.

"It doesn't matter." The hell it doesn't. I'm about to say as much when he holds up his hand, cutting me off. "It's not like you cheated on me. You were distraught over your Da. You probably only did it so you could stop thinking about everything, right?" The hope in his tone is painful. I'm a hideous, hideous person.

"No. No, I didn't do it because of that, Noah. I did it because ... I did it because I care about him."

"Do you care about me?"

"I do, but not—"

"Then you're coming to Africa with me."

"Noah—"

"No!" He stands quickly, rubbing the back of his neck. "None of that matters, okay? Look, I'm not saying I'm happy about the idea of you sleeping with another guy. You caring about him—I'm not saying that doesn't sting a little." His face has gone sheet-white. "But you just said it yourself. You care about me, too. That's exactly the reason why I can't let you go. I'm feeling like utter shit right now, and that's because I'm wishing it had been me. I want you, Avery. I don't want to share you. I want you all for myself. So you have to come to Africa."

He isn't hearing me. He's choosing not to. This is madness. Absolute madness. How he thinks I could possibly just up and leave with him after confessing that I just slept with another guy is beyond crazy. "Look, I'm really sorry, Noah. I know this is really unfair to you. I am so, so sorry for wasting your time, but—"

"You're so, so sorry for wasting my time?" Noah's eyes are alight when he snaps his gaze to mine. I should have seen how his eyes have the capacity to look wild like this, like he's seconds from jumping off the deep end. He rakes his hands through his hair, pacing up and down the length of my bed. *"Wasting my time?* You really are a silly little bitch, Avery. Do you have any idea how many girls have been trying to screw me the past few weeks, huh? I'm so—" He looks like he's physically lost the words he's searching for. I am still reeling from him calling me a silly little bitch when he clambers back up onto my bed, crawling up over me so that his legs bracket mine, his palms pressing against the wall on either side of my head.

"I am so fucking stupid," he breathes. His whole body is trembling. Every ounce of him screams, *Rage!* I should be afraid, especially when he leans in close and jabs an index into my face, but I just can't manage it. I stare blankly at him, calmly wondering if he is about to hit me, which seems to enrage him even further.

"You're coming to Africa with me, Avery." His voice shakes as he tries to control himself. "Don't you even fucking think about telling me no. I'm not taking no for an answer, you hear?"

"YOU'RE NOT going to fucking Africa with that psychopath!"

Morgan's boots make a creaking noise as we walk through the campus buildings towards home. We went for coffee, and I'd told her about Noah's meltdown. I just haven't told her what provoked it. She doesn't need to know about what happened with Luke. "Journalists die in Sierra Leone, Avery. They go out there trying to be good Samaritans and they get their heads blown off by child soldiers. You don't want that. *No one* wants that. Plus, correct me if I'm wrong, but it sounds like Noah threatened you."

"He did. He was furious."

"But he didn't hurt you?" Morgan glances at me out the corner of her eye. This is the fifteenth time she's asked me that. It appears she still needs some convincing.

"He didn't touch me. I told him to leave and he left. End of story." Yeah, end of story if you don't count him purposely knocking over the camera Uncle Brandon bought me at Thanksgiving. Noah also punched the wall on his way out, but from his hiss of pain and the complete lack of damage to the paintwork, I suspect he did more harm to himself than anything else. I didn't even switch the camera on to see if it was still working; I did the smart thing and left to find Morgan in case he came back.

As we approach our building, Morgan tugs on my jacket sleeve. "I'm glad that's over with, Ave. I don't trust him. Have you told Luke?"

"No, I have not told Luke. And I'm not going to, either."

Morgan looks like she's ready to throttle me. "You have to. Or you have to at least tell another member of the NYPD. He could come back. He could really try and hurt you."

"He won't."

"You don't know that!" Morgan grabs hold of me, stopping me in my tracks. "Look, I'm not saying Noah's a psycho killer or anything, but you never know. I don't want to be that friend on late night TV, crying over how … how if only I'd forced my best friend to report the dangerous behavior of some guy, then she'd be alive today." She gives me a pleading look. "I won't be able to sleep at night if you don't."

"All right, fine. I'll call the cops and report it. But honestly, it was nothing."

We head inside the building and start making our way up to my room. Morgan throws an arm around me as we climb the stairs, leaning her head against mine. "Thank you. My mind is now at ease."

"How about you put mine at ease and tell me how your meeting with the Dean went, huh?" Columbia doesn't exactly look too kindly upon its students missing classes because of their undisclosed drug habit. The meeting Morgan had with the school board this afternoon wasn't just to ascertain whether she could finish out her freshman year or whether she would have to start over. It was to ascertain whether she was going to get kicked out for good.

Morgan scowls. "You're supposed to be on my side. The Dean was pissed but I managed to convince him it would never happen again."

"So that's it? You're not getting the boot?"

Morgan rolls her eyes and tugs on the over-sized red sweater she's wearing. Red really isn't her color. She still looks like death warmed up. "There was mention of a two-year judiciary suspension but they decided on probation instead."

Probation is doable. Probation is a hell of a lot better than a permanent black mark on her academic record. "Just make sure this is the right thing for you, okay? Your mom was right about that. A college education is going to be useless to you if you're dead."

A tight smile pulls at Morgan's mouth; I can see what an effort it is for her not to snap at me. She looks tired. More than tired—washed out and exhausted. Delicate purple shadows linger under her eyes, and her cheekbones protrude more than usual.

"Are you eating?" I let us into my apartment, wracking my brain, trying to remember what I have in the fridge to feed her. Morgan shakes her head.

"I can't. Tate Rhodes has ruined my appetite for life. I finally managed to reach his mother in Bali. She said she hadn't heard from him. She didn't even sound that worried. She was more concerned about the media discovering he's missing. She said, and I quote, "He does this sometimes, sweet girl. He'll turn up when it suits him and I'll have to bail him out of trouble, yet

208

again. Just let the police look for him and keep quiet about the whole thing."

I sit down at my desk, chewing on the inside of my lip. "I'm so sorry. I said I'd get Luke to find out whether the police know anything more about Tate, but..." *I majorly fucked things up and now I can't speak to the guy.*

Morgan turns a pale shade of green. "That's okay. His mom said she also knew he was okay because she checked his credit card statement. Turns out his cards keep getting used in strip bars. She thinks he's just out partying."

"Has he done that before?"

"Sounds like it," she says, her voice hushed. "I'm so done worrying over him, Ave. We're over. I've left him four voice messages telling him so. Now he can go out and perve on as many strippers as he wants to, guilt free. Not that I imagine he's been feeling very guilty."

Poor Morgan. Tate is a fucking asshole. He has to know she's been sick by now and to not have even picked up the phone? I just can't believe he'd be such a bastard. "I'm sorry, Morgan. You know what? Fuck that guy. We're gonna rent a movie tonight and commiserate. Then, starting tomorrow, we're going to find you a smoking hot gentleman who'll take proper care of you. Deal?"

"Okay. Deal."

"I'll order some Chinese as well," I say. Morgan needs to get a proper meal in her. But as soon as I think about dialing for Chinese food, I remember Luke ordering for us in his apartment. The stack of *Spiderman* comics, the mountains of sheet music, the guitars, the neatly folded blankets in his cupboard. His ocean of books, and his endless supply of Jack. "Scratch that. We're having Indian instead."

TWENTY-SEVEN

DON'T LET THE BASTARDS GET YOU DOWN

I WAKE with the stale taste of Korma in my mouth, even though I brushed my teeth twice before bed. The taste isn't as bad as the ringing in my ears. I reach out to slam my palm down on my alarm clock, but then realize it isn't going off. Perhaps the high-pitched buzzing has more to do with the five beers I drank last night and less to do with the fact that it's time to get up. In fact, when I warily crack my eyes, it isn't even daylight yet. The only light in the room is bright blue, cast off by my cell phone as it vibrates noisily on my bedside table.

I snatch the phone up, wincing when I see it's six a.m. The wince develops into a flat-out frown when I see Luke's name on the screen. I hit answer, loud-whispering, "Why the hell are you calling me at six a.m?" For a second I hope he's pocket dialed me and I'm going to be able to hang up without speaking to him. When he starts talking, I realize it isn't so much as a pocket dial as a *drunk* dial.

"Wyoming's actually two hours behind New York, so it's … four here. Your uncle said I had to wait until sun up to speak to you, but he didn't say where the sun had to be coming up, so … is it up? It must be by now. Can you check?"

"No! No, the sun is *not* up! You need to go to sleep, Luke."

"I can't sleep."

"Why not?"

"You know why not," he says softly.

I pinch the bridge of my nose, trying to remember how to breathe. "Yeah. I do know."

"Brandon said to tell you that you had to let me dig you out," Luke tells me. The edges of his words are fuzzy. Not quite slurred, but not quite those of a sober person, either. "I have no idea what he means, but if you need help digging then you know I'm your man."

Jeez. Brandon and his massive mouth. "I don't need any help with digging, but thank you. You should go to sleep, Luke."

"Am I going to see you when I come home?" he whispers.

I pull my comforter over my head, screwing my eyes shut. My heart feels like it's breaking. "Do you *want* to? After the last time I saw you—"

"You told me you were falling."

I can still feel those words burning on the tip of my tongue. "I did. I'm sorry."

"Don't be sorry," he says, his voice still soft and low. "Just stop pushing me away. I may not know exactly what you mean when you say that you're falling. The way you said it sounded like it was a bad thing. But you have to know that I'll catch you. Whatever happens, I'll catch you."

I suddenly feel like the stupidest person on the face of the planet. My eyes sting, tears threatening to force their way past my eyelids. "Luke?"

"Yeah?"

"I fucked up. I fucked up really bad. You must hate me."

He goes quiet for a moment. I can hear his breathing on the other end of the line. Eventually, he says, "You know I don't

211

hate you. I feel exactly the opposite. That's the problem we're having here."

I dig my fingernails into my palm as hard as I can. "Do you feel like forgiving me? For leaving? Would it be really bad if I asked you for that?"

"No. But it would be really bad if you ever run from me again. I really did *not* enjoy that."

"I won't. I promise I won't."

"I don't want there to be any more secrets between us. Brandon says I should tell you … about what happened to me when I was a kid. I don't think I can, though. Not yet. Can you wait?" The words come out quickly, rushing together, the alcohol making him sound so young. Kind of adorable.

I press my fingertips to my mouth, trying to decide whether I'm about to cry or smile. "I can wait."

I don't go back to sleep. My head is spinning too fast for that. I feel like curling into a ball and sobbing, not because I'm upset, but because I'm happy. I never, ever once allowed myself to believe I could be with him. Not even for a second. Even when he was screaming at me in the street that he cared about me, had done since I was sixteen, did I really allow myself to believe it. I didn't want to risk the hurt, didn't want to risk any kind of hurt whatsoever, but now … I don't know. Now, maybe it will be okay.

HEADING BACK to Columbia is one of the hardest things I've ever had to do. If this were five years ago and I'd had a choice, I would never have gone back to high school. I'd have dropped out. I'd have been home schooled. I'd have moved counties and gone somewhere new. Basically, I'd have run away. Back then, my mother had control over my life and she didn't give me the option. I was forced to face the music, and it was awful. But now that I'm in control of what happens to me, I don't ever want to look back and realize that I chose to be outcast. That I chose to be bullied or judged. The time for running away is over.

I'm gawked at from the moment I enter the lecture theater to the moment I leave. The posters around the college have been taken down as requested by Amanda St. French, who always gets what she wants, but my mother can't make people stop staring. I am kind of used to it, but not on this scale. Columbia University is a hell of a lot bigger than Breakwater High, with a hell of a lot more people. Unfortunately they all know who I am now.

The time I've spent living as someone else here has been wonderful, but I passed every second worrying about what was going to happen when everyone finally discovered the truth. Now that I don't have to hide anything anymore, it's almost a relief. A sick and twisted kind of relief, but there all the same.

Class flies by without disturbance. I almost manage to block out the gesturing and whispered conversations. What I can't block out is Noah's intense gaze, fixed directly on me. Every time I look over he's watching me with a severe, angry look on his face. I know if I don't get it out of the way he'll be staring at me through the whole class, and I don't want to deal with that. I return his glare, eyes steady but my heart beating in my mouth, until he finally looks away. I make sure not to look at him for the rest of the class.

Ten minutes before the lecture ends my phone buzzes. It's Luke.

Luke: Sorry for the early morning wake up call. If it's any consolation, I have a raging hangover this morning. Forgive me?

I hit reply and type,

Me: Maybe. Depends.

Luke: On?

Me: On whether you think we can survive a week without talking. I'd like some time to work a few things out.

This is something I think we need. *I* need. I'm a mess over the nightmare with Noah, and I still don't know how I'm going to handle everything at Columbia. Dad. So many things piling one on top of the other. When I see Luke, I want to be able to put all of that worry out of my head. I want to be able to concentrate on him and him alone. He deserves that.

Luke: Whatever you need, Avery. I'm not going anywhere. X .

The X looks like an afterthought. Like something he wrestled over—*should I, shouldn't I?* It's kind of adorable that he's put a single kiss on the end of his message. He texts again.

Luke: And I really am sorry about calling you while I was drunk. Not cool.

Me: Seriously, it's fine. Never thought I'd hear it, though. I thought I was the one who hit the bottle when things got hard.

His response makes my heart contract.

Luke: Maybe not normally. But this is different. This is you.

Noah's at my side before the crush of bodies has filed out of the theater. He's hatless, and a few of the girls are staring. He brushes his hand back through his wavy hair and draws a tight smile. "You have another class after this?"

"I don't want to talk to you, Noah."

"Well, I think we need to. Don't you think there should be some sort of conversation about this?"

I shake my head, pulling my file closer to my chest. "We don't owe each other anything. We should just leave things as they are."

"But we had something—"

"We never had anything, Noah!" I stop walking, turning to face him.

He moves before I can register what he's doing. I have no time to avoid what comes next. He steps into me, pushing me back against the wall, crushing himself up against me. His mouth covers mine, lips pressing down so hard I can taste blood. Someone in the corridor cheers loudly, as though this kiss is a romantic, public display of affection. The cheer dies down when I struggle to push him the hell off me. I manage to rip my head away, turning to the side, panting, still trying to push him off me.

"Noah! What the fuck?" Anger laces my voice, along with a tinge of panic. Three girls have stopped in the hallway and are watching on with furrowed brows, clearly trying to discern if this is just a lover's spat or something more serious.

Noah takes a step back, but he has hold of my arm, fingers digging into my skin. "You act so fucking holier than thou, Avery, but you're just a slut. Plain and simple," he growls. "You shouldn't have been hanging around with me at all if you didn't want to commit."

My jaw hangs open. Some words are a red flag, can be heard over a chattering crowd. Slut is one of them. Alongside the anxious-looking girls, two guys pause in the hallway. The tallest, a dark-haired guy with full sleeve tattoos, steps closer and smiles. "Hey, Avery!" The smile says we know each other, but we don't. He continues, ignoring my look of confusion. "You know those notes you mentioned last week? You got time to go over them now?" He eyes Noah's hand gripped around my arm and his steely glare contains a clear message—*get your hands off her or I'm gonna fuck you up.*

Noah scowls but lets go. I rub my arm and step away from him, thanking the stranger silently with my eyes. "Yeah, sure. Now would be perfect."

The stranger shoots me a smile—no judgment, nothing—and gives me a nod. "Okay, then. Let's go."

I start walking, clinging onto my file for dear life. I don't look back. I can feel Noah's gaze burning into me all the way down the corridor, until the door slams closed behind us and I find myself stranded on the street with a guy I've never spoken to before.

"Thank you. That was a little …"

"Fucked up," the tattooed guy says.

I try hard to smile, to keep things light. I don't want this guy to know that Noah really scared me for a second there. "Yeah. That. I'm sorry, I … do we know each other?" I don't recognize the tattoos. His face is unfamiliar—not surprising given that the student populous clocks in at close to six thousand people and I generally keep to myself.

"No, we don't." Tattoo guy holds out his hand. "I'm Alex."

I shake his hand, though a seed of doubt is creeping up on me. "And you already know my name, right?"

He presses his lips into a tight line, tipping his head to one side. "I do. Can't blame me. Your picture was all over campus until, well, until last night, actually."

"Oh. Right." I pull my hand back, waiting for the ground to open up and swallow me whole. Alex just shrugs.

"I wouldn't worry about it. There's a new scandal every other day around here. You'll be forgotten by this time next week." He starts walking backward. "Don't let anyone here make you feel like you don't belong. You do. Just as much as they do."

I feel like laughing at that idea. "Easier said than done."

He shrugs. "Get out there. Be seen. Don't let the bastards

bring you down, right?"

I glance down at my boots, the leather mottled in dark patches from the snow. "Also easier said than done."

"Not true. Here." Alex pulls something from his pocket—a folded piece of paper. "I do a little club promotion to earn some extra cash under the table. You should come to one of these gigs. Have a beer. Dance with your girlfriends. You'll feel better about things, I promise." Alex hands me the paper—black, with white, blocky writing all over it. It's a list of upcoming music events. He starts to walk backward, hitching his bag up onto his shoulder. "And if you want any more of my hack advice, for what it's worth? You really need to report that guy to campus security. He looked a little crazy." He smiles, turns, and walks away. No questions about the posters, about whether they're true or if I'm a freak just like my dad. Nothing.

I watch him disappear into the crowds of people all headed to their next classes, and it hits me: maybe he's right. Maybe this time it won't be so bad. Maybe this time next week I will be forgotten.

There's one person who definitely won't have forgotten me, though.

I may have told Morgan I was going to report what Noah did to the police yesterday, but the honest truth is that I was just going to leave it. He was angry, and I felt guilty. But now … now I'm *worried*. Noah's had time to cool off and think things through, but it seems he's spent that time getting angrier and more aggressive instead. Hearing a complete stranger tell me the same thing as Morgan has opened my eyes a little. And besides that, I don't ever want to feel as vulnerable as Noah Richards just made me feel.

Never again.

As I walk home, I take a look at the flyer Alex gave me and I see a band name on the list that I immediately recognize.

D.M.F.

Luke's band.

I stuff the flyer in my pocket, and I head straight to the police station like I should have done first thing this morning. A young female police officer takes down my statement regarding Noah's behavior, though she doesn't seem all that interested. I guess working so near a college with so many young people getting drunk each weekend and causing all kinds of trouble can desensitize a person. She assures me that they take "this kind of thing" seriously, though. I don't mention Luke. It would look really bad for him if there were girls reporting romance drama, involving him, all over the city where he has to work.

I'm still running my fingers over the flyer in my pocket as I walk home.

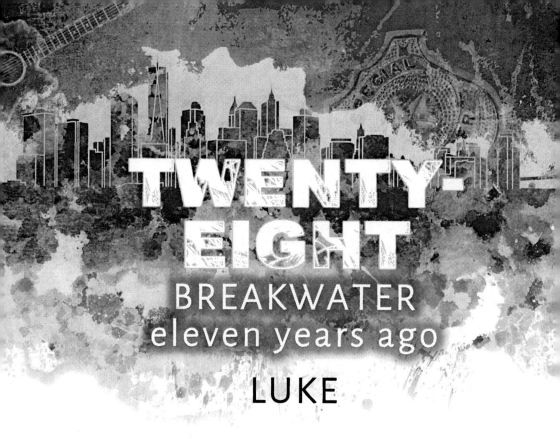

TWENTY-EIGHT

BREAKWATER
eleven years ago

LUKE

I CAN hear the gas oven struggling to light. Click, click, click. *My eyes are closed, but I know when it catches—there's a* whoompf *sound, followed by the whispered roar of the fire establishing itself. I crack my eyes, hoping that he's gone, but he hasn't, of course.*

He slides the silver thing—Mom uses it to fry eggs, can't remember its name—from the kitchen counter and holds it up for me to see. He looks dopey, a little stoned, like the pictures they've shown us of drug addicts in class. He's not high, though. He's drunk, which is worse. At least if he were high, he wouldn't be so angry. He nearly drops her—the small girl he's holding in his free arm.

"I mean it, Lucas. You hear me?"

I step back, hiding my hands behind my back, as though doing so will mean I can't do what he's told me to do.

"You want me to hurt her?" he slurs.

"I don't … I can't," I tell him.

"Fucking pussy. Fucking faggot pussy. Do as you're fucking told!"

I skitter back another step, ducking around the kitchen table, feeling safer now that there's an obstacle between us. My heart beats out an irregular tattoo against my ribcage. What will he do now? What will he do? What will he do now? *He scowls, face contorting into a confusing arrangement of features, all warring to get away from one another.* "All right," he growls. "Then you know what's going to happen." He lurches back to the oven, and he holds the silver thing over the flames.

He holds it there until the metal glows red.

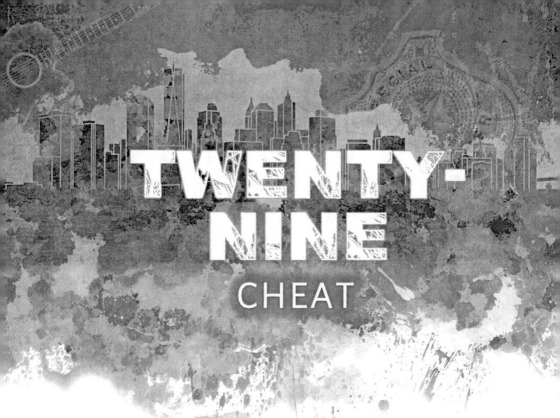

TWENTY-NINE
CHEAT

"THE SICK thing is, Glen, this guy was a part of the community. He had contact with troubled teenagers who were in vulnerable positions. Who knows what he could have done to any of them." The woman with the overly backcombed hair on the late-night news runs her tongue over her teeth as though she's used to getting lipstick on them. Her co-presenter focuses on her mouth for a second and I find myself absently wondering whether they're sleeping together. The guy takes a sip of water from his glass and nods.

"I think that's what the people of Wyoming are asking themselves right now, Kathy. We're only discovering the extent of this man's sickness now, years after the events took place. Max Breslin was not only a charismatic man, but he was incredibly intelligent, too. Good at hiding his dark alter ego. Who knows what else is going to come out of the—"

I switch off the TV and stare at the blank screen. Seriously? *Seriously?* A dark alter ego? My dad could be a dick sometimes, especially to Mrs. Harlow when she let her Bijon Frise crap on

our driveway, but come on. The extent of his malicious capabil-
ities was a strongly worded Post-it note stuck on her letterbox. I
tip my head back. Let out a loud sigh. There's no point trying to
bury my head in the sand by avoiding stuff like this. It's everywhere, and besides, I don't feel half as hideous as I thought I
would. Maybe that has something to do with how ridiculous the
lies are.

Leslie's out for the evening, and Morgan's parents are driving her to Seabrook for her first therapy session since "the incident." They're returning to Charlestown straight afterwards, so
no doubt Morgan is going to be in better spirits over the coming
days.

There was a *Way Out of Wyoming* movie poster stuck to my
apartment door when I got back from class, with my father's
face tacked over that of the hooded murderer's. I did the only
thing I could think of and I left it there. The only piece of advice
Amanda St. French has ever given me that seems to work: if you
don't react, people get bored. And if they are bored, they soon
forget about you and your baggage.

The knowledge the poster's probably still there is driving me
nuts, but I leave it there, a practice in will power. I want to be
ignored again. If I have to put up with a couple of weeks of this,
then I am damn well going to learn how.

I keep glancing down at my cell phone, holding my breath
like any minute it's going to ring. It's not going to ring, though.
A week. I told Luke I wanted a week to get my head straight,
and so far it's only been three days. He will, without a doubt,
honor that. I have to make sure I'm not the one who caves. In
the end, I decide to call Brandon instead of Luke. He's breathless when he picks up. "Tell me you were exercising and not
involved in some kinky sex game with Monica Simpson.
Please."

He makes a mildly disgusted sound on the other end of the
phone. "You're sick, you know that?" Brandon laughs. "I was
just outside. Had to run for the phone. Monica and I have de-

cided not to pursue our torrid affair."

"Just too hot to handle, Uncle B?"

"Exactly. Truth be told, those boobs were just too—"

"BRANDON!" I shake my head, trying to dislodge the mental image. "I'm already scarred enough. Please don't damage me further."

More laughter. "Okay, kiddo. I hope that unfinished sentence haunts you. What's up? Did you and Luke get things ironed out? I told him to call you."

"Yeah. *Thanks for that.*"

"Just doing my civic duty as a responsible uncle."

"Shouldn't you be warning him to stay the hell away from me or something? Where is he anyway? Is he … is he still with you?" I am such a cheater.

"He left this morning. Probably needed about five more hours sleep, but I couldn't stop him. Said he needed to get back for some music thing."

Some music thing? That rings bells. I press the phone to my ear as I walk across the apartment. My jacket's where I left it on the coat rack. I start rifling through the pockets. "So what time was he flying?"

"Why don't you ask *him*?" Brandon asks. He's teasing me. I can even hear the amusement in his smug voice.

"Because I'm asking *you*, jerk." I find what I'm looking for— the flyer that tattooed guy, Alex, gave me. D.M.F's halfway down the list of band names. The date: tomorrow night.

"He left early. Kid was green around the gills. I don't envy him, that's for sure. That's what he gets for trying to outpace the big dogs," Brandon says, laughing,

"Shit, Brand, you took him out drinking with your buddies? No wonder he was wasted."

"S'not my fault. Drinking yourself into oblivion is a rite of passage into this family, kiddo. You'll be pleased to know he acquitted himself with honor."

"Oh my god, do not say things like that. *Please.*" Brandon

just laughs like the evil bastard he is. "I'm assuming you told him a whole bunch of stuff about me that I probably wouldn't want him to know?" I ask.

"Of course."

"Why am I not surprised?"

"Avery?"

I close my eyes. "Yes, Brandon?"

"He's in love with you. Don't fuck it up."

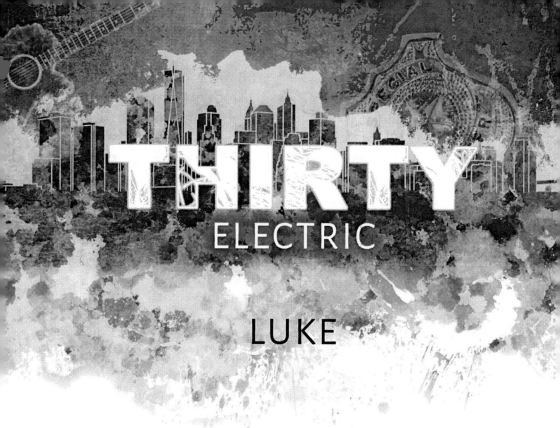

THIRTY

ELECTRIC

LUKE

SO FAR I've made it three days without calling her. It's a miracle of epic proportions. Not being at work hasn't helped. Being up at her old house, hunting through those closed-up rooms, made me think of her constantly. There were boy band posters on her bedroom walls. Weird, gangly looking blond teenaged boys that I'd always been convinced were girls. I took photos in case I need bribery material at some later date.

I didn't find a diary, which fucking sucks. If there had been a diary, it would have been a simple matter of looking up what Max was doing on the dates of the Ripper killings. If he was working, had appointments, etc., he would have had an alibi. Ipso Facto, Max couldn't be the killer.

But no diary means no alibi. I've come back empty handed, feeling like the whole trip was a massive waste of time. I needed to get out of New York, though. I needed to clear my head. A little time back home, despite the ghosts and the bad memories, has helped.

I'm passed out on the couch, still feeling like I've been chewed up and spat out by a wood chipper, when Cole calls. "Where are you, fucker? We need to practice for tomorrow. It's nearly four."

I check my watch—he's right. Four twenty-two p.m. I should have been over at the warehouse by three. "Shit, sorry, man. I am *not* feeling great," I groan, burying my face in a couch cushion.

"You'll be feeling worse if I have to come over there and kick your ass," Cole tells me cheerfully.

"All right, all right. I'm fucking coming."

"Bring food." Cole rings off without another word.

I take a shower, washing the hangover and this morning's plane journey from my skin; I feel a little more human by the time I'm dressed, but still not great. On the way over to Cole's, I grab a couple of pizzas from Rosito's, the place where I took Avery the night I told her about Colby Bright's book. I want to drive over to her building, instead. I want to talk to her. I can't, though. She asked me for this one thing, and I can give it to her. It sucks, but what's four more days?

Alt-J are blasting out of the warehouse when I arrive. I fucking love Alt-J. Cole throws a drum stick at me as I walk through the door. "Took your fucking time, asshole."

I shrug. "You wanted food."

Gus and Pete fall on the pizzas like half-starved piranhas. I manage to grab a slice before every scrap of pepperoni and mushroom has disappeared. Cole doesn't touch the food, though. He jerks his head toward the back patio, signaling me to follow him.

It's started to snow. The large, fat flakes have already settled onto the misappropriated garden furniture that just turned up one day over the summer, when me and Cole would sit out here and write the bare bones of new tracks together. "So," he says. "You thought about it? The contract?"

I've been waiting for him to bring this up for a while now. I brush the snow off of the closest garden chair and take a seat, stuffing my hands into my jacket pockets. "I have."

Cole doesn't sit down. He hugs his arms around his body, staring at me intently. "And?"

"And I need more time."

"MVP want to know by the end of December, Luke."

"The end of December's still two weeks away. Can you give me 'til then?"

Cole looks down at his boots, nodding his head slowly. "I can." He smiles then, shooting me a sideways glance. "Just figured you might not wanna leave your friend hanging is all."

"Ahh, you know me. I take pleasure in making your life hell."

"Don't I fucking know it. You'd better say yes, Reid. I've already told this chick I'm screwing that we're gonna be famous. You don't wanna make me look like a liar now, do you?"

"You *are* a liar," I laugh. "You'll say anything to get a woman into bed, right?"

He grins. "Something like that. Come on, man, it's fucking freezing out here." We head back inside. I only warm up once we've made it through the first part of the set we're playing tomorrow night. I'm dripping sweat, stripped down to a singlet by the time we're finished.

I drive home, my body humming like there's an electric current flowing through me. Whatever else he might say, Cole's right about one thing. I love playing. It's a part of me, inside me, taking me over whenever I have that guitar in my hands.

I'm still hyped when I climb into the shower. When I get out, drying myself, I see that I have a missed call and a voicemail waiting for me on my phone. They're both from Chloe Mathers. I have to play her message twice to make sure I've heard it right.

"Hey, Reid, it's me. Are you still in Break? Call me when you get this. Something's happened with the case. Something big. Something that could prove once and for all that Max Bres-

lin was innocent man."

THIRTY-ONE

D.M.F.

IM GOING to the D.M.F gig.

I shouldn't be going to the gig. I should be studying. I should be watching *The Price is Right*. I should be doing a thousand ab crunches or listening to Morgan extol the benefits of coffee enemas. Basically, I should be doing anything but going to see Luke Reid play in his band.

"Can't you text him to let him know we're coming? He could put us on a list or something, I bet. There's probably free booze backstage." Morgan shivers beside me as we make our way through the city, toward the club where D.M.F are playing.

"Dude! You're not allowed alcohol. Your body is recovering from an overdose, remember? Or have you forgotten all about your recent stint in hospital? I'm not letting you out of my sight. And as for trying to get on a door list, that kinda ruins the whole idea of me not wanting him to know I'm there. So, no, I'm not texting Luke."

Morgan grumbles into her scarf, shooting daggers at me.

"It's freezing cold, Ave. I *am* still recovering from a drug overdose and you're going to make me queue on the side of the street in Hell's Kitchen to preserve your weird sense of pride."

I resist rolling my eyes. "Papa Joe's is a dive bar. I strongly doubt there's ever been a queue to get in. And if there is, you can share my body heat. It's either that or we go home."

"Fine," Morgan pouts. "But just so you know, it sucks that I have to stand at the back of a dingy bar, lurking in the fricken' shadows like the phantom of the opera so you can get your stalker-gal rocks off without a damn beer in my hand. I still don't get why you don't just fuck this guy and get it over with. Luke is just so …"

Luke is just *Luke*. If only she knew what that really meant—how amazing and beautiful and hot the guy was in bed—she would die a death. I'm not ready to tell her that I've already slept with him. I try not to even think about that as I drag her reluctantly down the street. We take the third left and then a neon yellow and blue sign—*Papa Joe's! Papa Joe's! Papa Joe's!*—blinks on and off, lighting up the street no more than twenty feet away.

No queue. I pull a face at Morgan. "Told you."

"Yeah, yeah. Just get me through the door or I'm going to seize up. It's like, minus ten out here."

It really is about minus ten and I don't need telling twice. We head for the unmanned door, shivering even harder against each other as we hurry. On the other side of the door, the overwhelming sound of chatter, laughter, and grinding bass music hits us immediately. A long, narrow stairway descends into shady darkness, momentarily brightened by stabs of red and green and blue lights. It's busy down there. A crackle of static and a high-pitch squeal cuts through the hubbub below as I swallow and take the first step down, assisted by a pointy elbow in my back.

"Are you ready, ladies? Are you ready for the special gift your Papa Joe has been saving for you?" A deep, gravely voice calls out. A chorus of *whoo*-ing and *omigodomigodomigod!* answers the mystery voice. It sounds like bedlam down there. By the time we arrive at the bottom of the stairs, surveying the packed basement bar, we see it really is. The place is madness. A sea of people stand between me and Morgan and a large, raised stage at the far end of the bar. It's more of a club actually, with a service bar running the length of the right-hand wall. A portly guy in a fedora—Papa Joe, I'm guessing—stands on the stage, grinning and sweating as he takes in the horde of excited women, all of whom have glasses in their hands. Right now, I'm seeing a bobbing mass of women; I'm pretty sure Papa Joe is seeing dollar signs.

"Ladies, I hope you brought a spare pair of panties 'cause tonight we got some boys who wanna get you all wild and wet. Papa Joe thinks it's time to welcome on stage your favorite rockers…D…M…F!" He hollers out the letters, punching his fist into the air with each one, and the girls go nuts. It's kind of pathetic that they're losing their shit over a band in a basement, considering most of them look pretty respectable. Some of them even look sober. Morgan raises her eyebrows at me.

"D.M.F? That your boy?"

I don't say a word. I'm grinning on the inside though, because Luke Reid might now actually be my boy and that feels fucking amazing. I wrestle my way out of my jacket, heading over to the bored-looking coat check attendant. I slap the jacket down onto the counter and unwind the scarf from around my neck, ignoring the fact that Morgan is gawping at me—at the sheer silk green dress I've been hiding under my coat.

"What the hell is *that*?" she demands.

"It's called a dress, Morgan. I know you've got one on under that fugly fur thing you're wrapped up in too, so you might as well ditch it."

She pokes her tongue out at me. She loses her fake fur coat to reveal a little black number that clings in all the right places but has edgy rips and tears everywhere else. She looks like a rock goddess with her teased-out hair and killer outfit. Especially with the leather biker boots she's chosen to wear. I mean, yes, my Chucks do kind of clash with my dress, but whatever. It's a look I'm comfortable with.

The cheering rips higher over the sound of the thumping music. I know from the prickling on the back of my neck and the stupefied look on Morgan's face that Luke and his bandmates have just walked on stage. I lace my fingers through Morgan's and pull her backwards through the ever-growing crowd towards the bar.

"You're not having any alcohol," I tell her.

"But we're going to hang out by the bar?"

I nod. "We're hanging out by the bar."

She pulls a face, but it's only half-hearted. "Good job I love you, Patterson. And it's a really good job I can still witness *that* from back here, too," she points at the stage behind me, "otherwise you'd be lurking in the dark on your own." She licks her lips, tracing her fingertips over the base of her neck, and I feel like slapping her. Instead, I order two bottles of soda and thrust hers at her, resisting the urge to look over my shoulder. It's as though she can read my mind.

"How can you not be looking at this right now, Ave?"

"I just came to hear what they sound like. I can do that without drooling all over myself like a depraved hussy."

"Depraved hussy?" Morgan chokes back laughter. "Okay, I may be drooling. But damn, girl! All four of them are smoking hot! That bass player—his tattoos are just … they're … they're *everywhere*. I need to lick them."

I've never seen Luke's bandmates, but Morgan's fussy. If she says they're hot, they're hot. Given half a chance, she *would* lick a stranger's ink if he was sexy. I shake my head and drink my soda, tapping my foot nervously against the rail at the foot of the bar.

"Hi, guys! How's everyone feelin' this evening?" My heart leaps into my throat as the microphone echoes around the club.

It's Luke's voice. He's nowhere near as cheesy an MC as Papa Joe was; he's just talking to us, welcoming us, saying hello. The fact that he doesn't talk about himself in the third person also really helps. Morgan whoops, clapping her hands together, already sucked in by the atmosphere. I feel like I'm standing in a furnace. God, this was such a bad idea. I should have stuck to the plan. *My* plan. *It's okay. You're only here to listen, he's never even going to know you were here.* And yet, it feels like his eyes are already traveling across my skin.

"Thanks for coming out on such a cold night. We'd like to repay your kindness by sharing some of our music with you. How'd you feel about that?"

A thunderous roar lights up around us. Morgan's cheering and screaming along with everyone else while I drink my soda, staring straight at myself in the mirror behind the bar. I can also see a weaving tangle of bodies reflected in it, but thankfully not the stage. Luke starts laughing.

"In that case, we'll hit things off with a song that'll hopefully help warm you guys up. Don't be fooled by the title, okay? This one's called 'Cold Hands, Cold Heart.'"

A light, fast intro rips out of the speakers, and the audience literally goes wild. A heavy drumbeat follows and a few bars later and Luke is singing. It's nothing like his performance at O'Flanagan's, however. This is fire and arrogance all rolled into one. And it's pouring straight out of him like liquid sex.

Luke tears through the song, whipping the audience into a frenzy.

The coolest girl
thought I'd ever seen.
Eighteen
And still, a kid that haunts my dreams.
Hard as glass, quick to bite
ice queen
heart as black as night

but you and me,
we'll be okay
'cause when you're with me,
you melt away.

Got cold hands, got cold heart
woulda never kissed you
If I'd 'a' known from the start,
You've frozen me cold,
You've frozen me dead,
Now I'm leaving you here,
Unfinished in my bed.

The lyrics confuse the crap out of me. The song ends and Morgan's voice is already hoarse from screaming so loud. Her hands look red raw from all of her enthusiastic clapping. "Holy shit, Ave, they're amazing!"

"Yeah," I say quietly. "They are."

D.M.F plays three more songs and I refuse to turn around the whole time. Luke's voice sends thrills through my body and turns my blood ice cold in equal turns, making me wonder if I'm an ice queen, too. I know it's not me he sang about in that first song, though, because he sure as hell didn't leave me unfinished in his bed. No, that would be Casey, surely? The woman he refused to sleep with for so long? And yet he gave himself up to me in one evening. All I had to do was lose my father and have a nervous breakdown.

The bar area empties as close to every single patron of the club joins the crowd in front of the stage to watch D.M.F play. Before long it's just Morgan and me propping up the bar with Papa Joe talking to the bartender. Papa looks pissed. Probably because he just realized that none of his club goers are ordering drinks now that the music is playing, and he's not making any money after all.

Morgan finally picks up her soda and starts to down it, her

eyes still locked on the stage. They round out as a commotion kicks up behind us. She nearly spits her drink out altogether when the screaming suddenly gets louder. "Holy shit, Ave! He just jumped off the stage. He's walking right over here."

"Who?" I hiss. Stupid question, though. I know exactly who she's talking about. My body heats up like the fucking surface of the sun as Luke gets closer, closer, closer. I'm surprised there isn't steam coming out of my ears by the time I hear him clear his throat behind me.

"S'cuse me. You mind turning round a second?"

Oh, shit. This was not part of the plan. My mind starts racing. How the hell did he even see me all the way back here? I take a deep breath and turn around ...

Holy. Mother. Of. Mary.

Luke Reid is standing right in front of me with an electric guitar strapped over his chest, wearing a worn singlet that exposes the black ink spiraling all over his biceps and shoulders. His hair is all over the place, disheveled and dripping with sweat. In fact, his face and his arms are covered with a sheen of sweat that reminds me of one thing and one thing only: him on top of me, him inside me. My legs start trembling the moment a smile develops on his face.

"Ahhh, I knew it was my beautiful girl," he growls. The way he says that is so possessive, I'm instantly turned on. "It's very distracting playing to the one turned back in the room, y'know, Ms. Patterson ..."

The hundred or so girls standing behind him, all gawking, shoot me evil looks as the man of their dreams gives me his best *fuck me* grin. Not that he knows he's doing it, though, right? That's not Luke's style. Or at least not a Luke I've ever met before, anyway. This guy is an entirely different person. And he's so intimidating, I can't even speak.

"I need your undivided attention please, Ms. Patterson." Luke takes another step forward. "Give it to me."

The oxygen won't travel into my lungs quick enough. I clasp

hold of my empty soda bottle with both hands, my body tensing. The whole room has gone silent. I can tell Morgan's watching the exchange with an open mouth, as are a few other girls in the audience. Luke smirks, closing the remaining gap between us. He extends a hand and takes the bottle from me, leaning close enough to brush up against me as he places it on the bar to my right.

"What happened to seven days, huh?" he whispers.

"Math never was my strong suit."

He grins, and my stomach literally backflips. "Well, I'm glad you can't count." He looks away briefly to make eye contact with the bartender as he says, "Two," holding up his index and his middle finger. I hold my breath, a mixture of panic, chagrin and extreme arousal warring within me while Luke accepts the two shot glasses from the bartender and throws him a twenty. Luke holds out a glass to me. The amber liquid is filled right to the brim, and I can already smell that it's Jack.

"I'm not drinking that," I whisper.

"Why not?" His ruinous smile spreads even further. "I thought you liked Jack?"

"Only when I want to black the fuck out."

Luke shakes his head, still smirking. "I don't want you to black the fuck out, Ms. Patterson. I want you to remember this." Luke turns and grins over his shoulder, finally acknowledging that we have a crowd of mildly put-out, horny college girls watching us. "You guys think she should drink?"

"Hell yes!!"

"Yeah!"

"Drink it, bitch!"

"I'll take it!"

The response is deafening. Back on the stage, Luke's bandmates all start booing. A guy with a shaved head and tattoos everywhere—must be the bass player Morgan was eyeing up—leans over and talks into the mic Luke left behind. "Better do it, mystery girl. We'll be here all night otherwise. I wouldn't mind finishing our set so I can grab a shot of Jack myself."

"I'll buy you as much Jack as you want, sweetheart," Morgan calls. The guy winks at her, and I know we're all in trouble now. Looks like she's well and truly over Tate abandoning her and hitting all those strip clubs. Luke raises an eyebrow at me.

"Come on, Ave. One shot."

Morgan elbows me in the ribs. "Drink the fucking shot, girl. Jeez! Just 'cause I'm T-total doesn't mean you have to be."

I glare at her but then reach out and take the glass from Luke. "Fine." I can't seem to make myself look up at Luke. I'm too nervous to make eye contact, completely thrown by this new attitude of his. Instead I begin to lift the glass to my lips. Luke's hand shoots out to stop me.

"Not like that, Patterson." Confusion swamps me. I give in, then, and look up at him. Mischief, arrogance and lust all bear down on me from his gaze, and my tongue sticks to the roof of my mouth. Who the hell is this guy? Luke slowly guides my wrist so that I lift up the shot glass to *his* lips, and I suddenly understand what he wants me to do. He wants me to tip the Jack straight into his mouth. My fingertips brush the rough stubble on his jaw as he presses his full, lower lip to the glass, daring me to finish the job with his eyes. Fine. I can do this. It's not that big a deal. I tip the glass, the amber liquid flowing into Luke's mouth. He never takes his eyes off me. I snatch my hand back as soon as the glass is empty, but Luke doesn't swallow it. He leans forward and buries his hands into my hair, pulling me to him. He shoves his guitar behind him as his body slams into me, and then Luke is pressing his lips firmly onto mine.

The crowd starts whooping like crazy, and I freeze. For a moment I just stand there trying to figure out what the heck is happening. Luke's fingers entwine themselves even further into my hair as his kiss deepens. I'm reluctant at first, not sure I want a room full of people watching me when I kiss him, but then Luke's tongue brushes against my lips, his body curving towards me, and everything changes. My mouth wants Luke more than my head wants this to be private. He manages to tease my lips apart with his tongue and then fire is passing between us, burning and warm and so freaking hot. He's sharing the Jack I just gave him.

Somehow, I don't choke on the warmed alcohol. I swallow it, and Luke groans into my mouth, pressing even closer up against me. He doesn't pull away. I doubt in that moment that I'd let him. I kiss him back.

Understatement of the century.

I kiss him like this is my first kiss and I'm minutes away from dying a virgin. I kiss him like he's just been called up to war and I may never see him again. I kiss him like he's cared for me, looked out for me the past five years, shared his heart with me and given me everything he thinks I need. Because he kind of has. Applause fills the club. When Luke finally pulls away, his arrogance has slipped a little. He tilts my chin up towards him with his fingertips, studying my face intensely, before he smiles again. It's like sunshine breaking through clouds.

"Fuck, Reid, you're giving us hard-ons up here. Get your ass back on the stage, damn it!" the drummer yells. Luke backs away, still grinning, until the crowd swallows him and he makes his way back to the stage. They're only halfway through their set. Now that Luke knows I'm here, I let Morgan pull me into the crowd so we can watch a little closer. The band are on fire. They tear through another four songs before Morgan tells me she doesn't feel very well.

She's ashen and her skin feels clammy. "Sorry to ruin your buzz but I think I need to lie down," she says,

As we leave Papa Joe's, Luke's head is tipped back, muscles in his neck straining as he sings. He is fucking beautiful.

LESLIE'S OUT at her sister's again, so my apartment is empty when I finally make it home. I go to bed feeling exhausted but strangely wired at the same time. It's the early hours of the morning when my phone buzzes. On silent, it shouldn't have woken me, but the vibration on the nightstand has my eyes snapping open immediately. The lit screen shows a text from Luke.

Luke: You awake?

I shunt myself upright in bed, tucking my hair behind my ears.

Me: Yeah. You at an after party or something?

Luke: I'm outside.

Outside? Like, *here* outside? I fling back the covers and push the blinds aside, flinching at the cold when I rub the back of my hand over the frigid glass so I can see out. I spy Luke's Fastback parked illegally under a street lamp straight away. He is out of the car and leaning with his back against the passenger door, looking up at the window. Great clouds rise up as he breathes, highlighted by the yellowed sodium burn of a street lamp. His hands light up blue as he focuses on his phone.

Luke: Are you busy?

I let the blinds fall back. I didn't think I'd see him again to-night, but now my heart's pounding like a trip hammer in my chest.

Me: No. You want to come up?

A minute passes by and I hear nothing. What is he doing? I press my back into the wall and clench my eyes shut, waiting for the phone to buzz in my hand. It doesn't. *Shit.* I draw back the blinds again and he's still standing by his car. His head's tipped down, though, and for a moment I can't figure out what he's doing. When his back straightens I see that he's on the phone. I curse and throw my cell down on the bed, running my hands through my hair. What the hell is happening to me? Why am I so jittery?

I growl at myself and storm to the wardrobe, tugging out a folded pair of jeans and a light gray sweater. Shoving my arms forcefully into the sleeves of my coat, I gather my hat and gloves and go out to meet him. As I close the apartment door, I notice that the *Way Out of Wyoming* poster is still there. Someone's drawn a Hitler moustache on the serial killer's face. I ignore it, running quickly down the stairwell. My phone buzzes as I exit the building.

> **Luke**: Sorry if I woke you, Ave. This is probably a bad idea. I can call you tomorrow. Go back to sleep.

"Little late for that," I say. Luke, already half in his Fastback, starts. The snow muffled my approach and he obviously didn't hear me. His cheeks are blushed red, eyes incredibly bright in the dark. He smiles, the very corners of his mouth lifting ever so slightly.

"I came to apologize."

"For kissing me in front of a bar full of people?"

He scuffs at the snow with the toe of his boot. "Yeah, I guess. I get a little carried away when I'm in that environment."

"So you share Jack with a girl every time you perform, then, huh?" That thought makes me feel wretched. I immediately regret thinking it.

Luke laughs softly. "No. Never. Only with you."

A heavy silence steeps between us as I take that on board. Eventually he says, "Since our seven-day ban was kind of null and void, I also wanted to come and tell you that I found something when I was in Break. Well, someone else found something. I thought you'd want to know."

"At my parents' house?"

"No." His eyes are distant for a second. "There was nothing there. Only … memories."

"You remember the place?"

Luke's smile is sad. "I remember throwing up in your garden. And, of course, you smashing the window."

"Oh. Yeah." That probably wasn't something you forgot in a hurry. I was hysterical. "I just thought maybe my dad … maybe he'd taken you there or something."

A small shake of Luke's head. "No. We always met at the diner. Your dad knew I loved the milkshakes there."

"Yeah, he used to take me there for shakes, too." Why had he never taken us together? Had Luke been that messed up as a kid? I try to shake off the awkward feeling, but it lingers. Luke looks awkward, too.

"Listen, a video was handed into the station in Breakwater. It's big, Avery. It looks like there was someone else there with your dad and the others the day he died."

"A *video?*"

Luke nods and for a moment he looks like he's going to smile again. "Yeah. They won't tell me what's on it yet, but they did say there was a fifth person."

"Someone else?" The ground rocks beneath me. There was someone else there in that warehouse the day my dad died? Another person, a person who is still alive? There were only four bodies. They'd carried four dead people out of that place, and now Luke is telling me someone else witnessed what happened? My mouth works, trying to find something to say, but I remain mute.

"I know this is a lot to take in." Luke steps forward, and I am torn in half. What I really want to do is turn and run indoors so I can lock myself in my room and pace the floor, trying to figure out what this means. I clench my fists inside my gloves instead, knowing the only way I'll find out anything is if I concentrate and kept calm. "Tell me everything."

"It's freezing, Avery. D'you wanna sit in the car?"

"Okay, sure." We get in, and he starts talking; he seems excited, his eyes quick and dangerously bright. I don't know if that's from the gig he just performed or if this new information really is big. "Chloe, my ex-partner? She called me when I was back in Break. She told me an anonymous caller informed the duty officer of a package outside the station in Breakwater. They thought it was a parcel bomb at first. After they decided it wasn't going to explode, they opened it. That's when the fun and games started. The FBI have seized the tape for their private investigation."

"The *FBI*?"

"Yeah, they're looking into Bright's accusations against your dad."

Fantastic news. The feds didn't bother with the case the first time around, probably because it looked so cut and dried. Throw the deaths of fifteen teenaged girls in the mix and suddenly there are G-men all over the place. "And what are the suits saying?"

Luke places his hands on the steering wheel, grinning. "Nothing."

"Nothing?" Why does he look so damned happy if nothing is being said? It makes no sense. He reaches out and takes my hand, squeezing it hard.

"That's the best outcome right now. It means they're actually investigating the possibility that someone else might be responsible, Avery. Think about it. If there was someone else there and they were an innocent party, why the hell wouldn't they come to the police once they'd escaped? If it had been someone your dad had kidnapped and was going to kill like Adam and the others, why wouldn't that person report it immediately?"

"Well, they would have," I say slowly.

"Exactly. So it stands to reason that if there was someone

else there, they could have been responsible for the whole thing. It's not easy to force someone to shoot themselves in the head. Your dad's gunshot wound was to the throat—a complete mess. It could easily have been the result of him fighting as an assailant tried to pull the trigger."

My head is swimming, and Luke's rushed words aren't making it any better. "But the pathologist said suicides often turn out that way when people attempt to shoot themselves. They hesitate."

"That does happen, sure. But imagine just for a second … what if it's true? This could clear your dad of everything. The killings in the warehouse, the murders of those girls. It could all be over."

My hand is shaking in Luke's. I'm having trouble seeing. It's only when a hot streak runs down my cheek that I realize I am crying. "I can't imagine something like that, Luke. It's too dangerous. We have no idea what's on that tape. It could come to nothing."

His energy seems to flag a little when I pull my hand out of his. "I know. I guess I just like choosing to believe in the best outcome."

"And in your experience as a police officer, how often is the best outcome the most realistic one?" I can't afford to be as optimistic as Luke. It will destroy me to start believing things like that, only to have my hopes crushed when my dad isn't vindicated.

"Not very often," Luke concedes. A sad look forms on his face. "But that's not going to change my optimism. Or what I know about Max. What I know he would or wouldn't do."

What the hell is that supposed to mean? All of my excitement over seeing him vanishes like smoke. He thinks he knows my dad better than I do? I can't even begin to swallow that. "Screw you, Luke." I scrabble with the door handle, trying to get the hell away from him. He leans across me and puts his hands over mine as I struggle. I try to shrug him off and get out

243

but he grabs hold of my shoulders and pins me back. He isn't rough, but there's no way I'm going anywhere.

"Let me go!"

"No."

"You don't know my father better than me, Luke! You don't get to accuse me of not believing in him."

"I'm not saying that," he hisses, exasperation coloring his voice. I lash out with my elbow, trying to get free, but it's useless. "I'm just saying that I've never believed Max was a killer. Not like that. I knew he wouldn't have touched those guys. Stop fighting me, Avery! Fuck! Can't you just calm down for one minute? Why does it always have to be all-out war with you?"

I fall back into the passenger seat, totally and utterly slack. My chest heaves as I fight not to sob. "I know I said I'd wait, Luke, but you have to tell me. I'm never going to understand what he meant to you until you tell me why you were so close." A heavy silence fills the car. Muted light washes in through Luke's window, making his skin ghostly pale. His eyes are large and round, staring straight at me. His jaw clenches and I think he's going to speak, but then he turns away to stare out the window. "You're not going to tell me, are you?"

"I can't. Not yet."

"That's such crap, Luke. You know all my dark secrets. I didn't even know you played in a band until I ran into you on campus."

"Me being in a band is hardly a big deal, Avery."

"Of course it is! I watched you play tonight. You were in love with what you were doing up there. And yet here you are still working as a cop, when you could be making a career for yourself from your music."

Anger chases away Luke's sadness. "You think the music's important to me? Compared to *this*? I have to help people, prevent them from getting hurt like you and like … like me. I *have* to. Music's an escape, Avery, something I do so I don't have to be *me* all the time. It wouldn't be the same if I quit being a cop and started living out of a tour bus six months out of the year. As for my dark secrets, some things are just so black and fucking awful that a person never wants to air them out in the light of day. If you knew ... if I told you ..."

"If you told me, then what?!"

"Then you'd run, Avery! You'd fucking run away from me, and it would be the smartest thing you ever did."

I can't believe that's what he thinks. "You don't know me half as well as you think you do if you believe that."

Luke drops his head into his hands, sighing deeply. "You say that now."

"Maybe you should just give me some credit and try trusting me."

Luke turns his head to look at me, still slumped over in his seat. He looks heartbroken when he shakes his head.

That is all I need. I climb out of the car, and I leave.

⁂

As of Tuesday, the killer's wife, Amanda Breslin, is known to have relocated to New York City, leading many to ask the question: did she know what her husband was up to? Close friends of the Breslin family intimated that Iris, the only child to come from the Breslin marriage, has entered a fugue state and does not respond to outside stimulus. Doctors have given statements declaring that this is not uncommon. Many of them have witnessed such reactions when victims of abuse are freed from their captors. The psychological trauma the child could have undergone is apparently significant.

The library is quiet. Students sit with headphones plugged into the music players, heads bent over their work, while I stare at the crumpled piece of newspaper I keep in my bag. The paper is so thin from where I've folded and unfolded it repeatedly over the years that it's worn through entirely over some of the creases. The Wyoming press had a field day with my dad's story. At the time I was so wracked with grief that I hadn't been able to defend him. Everyone took my silence, my inability to breathe without hurting, as a sign that he'd done something to me. He'd never done anything but love me. I trace my fingers lightly over the folded, yellowed newspaper and tuck it back in between the pages of my text book, wondering. Wondering when I'll be able to move on. If it will ever happen at all.

Fly high, Icarus. He used to say that to me all the time. Right now there's no chance of me even getting up off the ground. It doesn't bear thinking about what my dad would say to all this. How I am behaving and letting everyone else get to me. How I'm treating people. And by people, I mean Luke. I'm in love with the guy—a scary thing to admit—and yet every time he brings up my father, I become this shitty, awful person that I hate. I shove my books angrily into my satchel just as I catch sight of Morgan bursting through the doors. Her hair has fallen out of a loose ponytail, and her short-sleeved t-shirt is crumpled and twisted around her body.

"No running!" the clerk calls, but Morgan's not listening. She charges straight for me, a wild look in her eyes. I stand automatically, registering that she's crying.

"What is it? What's up?" I ask, grabbing hold of her shoulders as she slams into me. With her face buried into my jacket, I can't make out what she's saying. "Morgan?"

She leans back and sobs silently. "Tate. It's Tate." She breaks down into uncontrollable fits of tears and collapses into my arms again. I struggle to hold her up, but her body is deadweight. Through the hollow ache inside me, and that small voice in my head asking, *is this really happening? Is this seriously happening?* I know. I know that Tate is dead.

"OVERDOSE?"

"Yeah." Morgan swats tears from her cheeks, trying to keep

it together. In the three days since the library, there haven't been many times when she's been able to accomplish that. We've been waiting for the coroner's report for days. Eventually we read it in the newspapers, just like everyone else. Like we hadn't been part of Tate's life and didn't deserve to know. Morgan swallows thickly. "The people in the neighboring buildings didn't see his body on the roof, because …" her voice wobbles, "because of the snow. They probably wouldn't have found him for weeks if the janitor hadn't gone up there for a smoke. He spotted one of his shoes."

I reach out and take her hand. She's cold, but more worryingly she's shaking. She just hasn't stopped shaking. "Have Tate's parents talked to you yet?"

She shakes her head. "They told the Dean to make me stop calling. They think I know how he got up there, but I don't. I'd tell them if I did. I've told them everything I know. I blacked out. The last thing I remember is some guy shouting at Tate because he was throwing up in the bathtub, and then … nothing. I only took one pill. He …" she sobs, "he took three!"

"Shhh, it's okay. I got you." I pull Morgan to me. She's barely left my apartment since we all found out, and I have no intentions of making her go. She is a wreck. "Tate's parents have no idea what went on, the same as the rest of us. How they think you're withholding information is a mystery. Don't freak out, though. We'll get it all sorted out this afternoon."

This afternoon I'm Morgan's ride to the police station, where she's required for questioning. Her parents don't know anything about Tate's death. She doesn't want them coming back to the city after they've only just left her in peace.

Morgan slumps down on my bed, her spine curved as she hugs herself tightly. "They're going to ask me where we got the drugs from," she whispers.

"Of course they will. You have to tell them, Morgan. It's important. This guy could be out there selling the same stuff to other students. People need to know."

Morgan's eyes, a watery gray from her constant crying, focus on me. It's perhaps the first time since the news that she's looked at me and really seen me.

"You don't understand, Avery."

"I would if you told me," I say quietly. No matter how many times I've asked, she point-blank refuses to give up the name of the dealer. Today is no exception.

"I can't. I'm sorry … I … it's someone you know."

Someone I know. *It's someone I know?* My mind races a million miles an hour. And it keeps racing, lightning speeds compared to the twenty-mile-an-hour traffic we find ourselves in as we crawl across the city later. When we finally reach our destination we enter the building together but Morgan is immediately whisked away. I'm abandoned to my own company in the thankfully empty waiting room, until a buzzing sound disturbs the silence and Noah emerges from inside the station. Our eyes meet and my stomach falls through the floor.

It's someone you know.

Surely not Noah? "What are you doing here?" I ask, my voice a sub-zero level of cold. Noah winces. He approaches me slowly, his hands shoved deep into his pockets. He gestures to the chair beside me and I'm too confused and concerned over everything and everyone to object. He slumps down into it, sighing heavily.

"I had to give a statement about when I last saw Tate," he says quietly.

"Right." *It's someone you know.* Somehow the possibility that Noah could be the one responsible for Tate's death and for Morgan's time in hospital hurts way more than the secrets he kept from me. It's all I can think about—*is this all his fault?* Memories of Noah meeting Tate and Morgan in the library that day, them swapping a huge amount of money for some textbooks, come flooding back to me. Oh, Lord, no. Dealers do that, don't they? Put their stashes inside books or CD cases or whatever they have handy to disguise them. I glance at Noah cautiously out of the corner of my eye, only to find him staring at me.

"Avery, I really would like to talk to you, please? If that's okay? I … I know you went to the cops. You didn't need to do that." He reaches out to touch my knee. I go stiff, and he sees it. He doesn't withdraw his hand, though. He tightens his grip, squeezing so hard his fingertips go white. "Listen, I'm really sorry about what happened in your place. And in the hallway, too. I get a little hot headed sometimes, but I would never hurt you. There's no reason to freak out."

"Well, I *am* freaking out," I tell him. I shift my leg, but he doesn't let go. I swallow down my panic and turn fully to face him, wanting to look him in the eye when I ask him. "This isn't just about that, though. I have something I need to know. That day … when we met Tate and Morgan in the library?"

Noah goes totally still. "Yeah …"

"Well, those books. Were they just books, or—"

I can't finish my sentence. I can't finish my sentence because one second Noah is gripping tightly onto my leg, a cold blankness in his eyes, and the next he is sprawled across the police station floor. A fury of black and gold rushes forward, and Luke—*Luke!*—grabs a fistful of Noah's shirt, practically lifting him off the ground.

"Get your fucking hands off her!"

"I wasn't doing nothin' wrong!" Noah cries, hands held high. "She's my girlfriend."

"She is *not* your fucking girlfriend." Luke raises a fist back. The cold realization that he's about to hit Noah and end his career shoots through me. I leap up and launch myself at him, grabbing hold of his wrist from behind. The second my hand touches his skin, Luke's fist uncurls. He blows out a sharp blast of air through his nose, growling at the back of his throat, and then lets Noah go. Noah slumps to the floor, eyes round and filled with fear.

"Get the fuck out of here, right now," Luke snaps. "If I ever so much as hear you've whispered her fucking name, I will break every bone in your goddamn body."

Noah struggles to his feet and hightails for the door. Luke pivots slowly, his dark eyes almost black with anger.

I swallow, trying to keep my back straight. I'm flooded with relief and gratitude that he showed up when he did, but I'm too worried to tell him that. Instead, I say, "What are you doing here, Luke? This isn't your station."

Luke's eyes narrow. "Prisoner transfer. Why are *you* here?"

"It turns out our friend Tate died the same night Morgan got sick. She's in there giving a statement right now."

Luke's anger falters. "The guy on the roof?"

"Yeah."

He nods once, clenching his fists by his sides. This really isn't good. I've never seen him like this before. "You need to come see me later. I have some more news about your dad. I tried calling."

He *has* tried calling, but frankly I've been too upset about our conversation in his car—the way I reacted—and I've been avoiding him. "I can't, I have to take care of—"

"Just come."

He turns and stabs a code into the keypad by the door that leads into the station proper and disappears without looking back once. On any other day, I'd ignore a demand like that. But not today. Not after what just happened. And Luke hardly seemed happy about the prospect of my company. Whatever he needs to tell me probably has something to do with the feds' investigation. I wait alone for another awkward hour, tensing when the door buzzes open, hoping and praying in equal measure that it is and isn't Luke each time. Finally the door opens and it's Morgan that walks through. She cries the whole way home, refusing to tell me anything besides the fact that she admitted to who provided the pills.

THIRTY-TWO

BREAKWATER
eleven years ago

LUKE

"HES COMING. I can hear him. Don't let him find me. Please, Luke."

"Shhh!" I hug the girl closer to my body, feeling her bones through the material of her summer dress. She's always been so thin, so frail, small, like a mouse. She buries her face against my chest, which can't be comfortable, because I'm still wearing my laser tag sensor. Mom bought the game for my birthday. My birthday, which is today. We've been playing in the woods, me and my friends, electronic shooting sounds zipping through the air, until now, when it's dark and he *is* out there looking for us.

"Lucas!" he bellows. "Lucas, you little fuck!" He's out there somewhere, reeling from tree to tree, barely able to stand up as he searches. The hairs on my arms stand up.

"Can you see him?" the girl beside me asks. I shake my head.

"Stay quiet, Rosie. He won't find us if we stay quiet." So the *girl stays quiet, stays so quiet I can hardly hear her breathe. Her silence doesn't matter in the end, though.*

Because I was wrong.

He does *find us.*

THIRTY-THREE

ADMISSIONS

"WHAT MAKES you think you can just tell me what to do?" The door isn't even open before I start speaking. At least I *am* speaking, not shouting. Luke stands in his doorway with a towel wrapped around his waist, dripping wet. I'm silently congratulating myself on the fact that I'm not staring at his ridiculously toned body when he grabs my hand and yanks me into his apartment.

"Shut up," he snaps.

"What the—"

"Stop talking!" He slams the door and storms through his apartment towards his bedroom, the muscles in his back tense. "I'm sick to death of this. Come with me."

"... *hell*?" I finish. Stunned, I follow after him, pausing in the doorway to his bedroom. I look away as he drops the towel and angrily kicks his way into a pair of jeans. He pulls a t-shirt over his head next and pads barefoot over to me. I've never seen him so wound up before. Well, I hadn't until this afternoon, anyway. He takes a firm hold of my wrist and pulls me into the room, sitting me down on the end of his bed.

"Luke, what the hell?"

"Wait here." He storms out of the room, and then returns a minute later with a stool from his breakfast bar in one hand and my Super Eight camera attached to a tripod in the other. Wait, *my Super Eight camera?*

"What the hell are you doing with that?"

"I borrowed it."

"From my apartment?"

"Yeah, from your apartment." He places the camera, attached to the tripod, directly in front of me and then turns it on. Once he's done that, he sets the bar stool down a couple of feet in front of me and sits on it. "Let's do this," he tells me.

"Do what? What the fuck's going on, Luke? You broke into my place?"

"I've done a lot worse. Now come on," he grinds out.

"Come on, what, Luke? What's this supposed to be?!"

Luke grasps his hands together in his lap, apparently trying to stop himself from snapping. He presses his lips together in a white line and stares away from me, out of his bedroom window. "Your college assignment. You have to hand it in tomorrow, right?"

"What?" How on earth does he know about that? And then it hits me: Brandon. He didn't mean I should ask my mom to do the interview with me. He meant Luke. And he told him all about it. Seriously? "Oh, we are *so* not doing this, Luke. You're the last person I want to interview about what happened back then."

Luke's shoulders slump but his face remains hard. He's still not looking at me, still staring out of the window, the cold wintery light casting his face into a contrast of light and dark. "Why not?"

"Because you won't be honest and that's the whole point of the exercise."

He finally turns and meets my gaze. "If you think you're fucking bulletproof, Avery, I'll tell you every single gory detail of what happened that day."

"It's not just that, though! It's not … it's not that you didn't tell me my father's dying words until years later. It's everything. It's why he was mentoring you. It's why you were so fucking close to him, and all the other secrets that you won't fucking tell me!"

I hate myself. I hate that I'm crying and screaming and swearing and I can't get my words out properly. Luke tucks his hands underneath his thighs, literally sitting on them. If I didn't know him better I'd think he was being a cold son of a bitch, refusing to look at me and glaring at the floor. But I do know him better. I know that if he doesn't sit on his hands, if he doesn't keep his eyes off me melting down, then he will be standing over me, trying to comfort me in two seconds flat. That makes my crying worse. I let my head fall forward, my hair obscuring my view of him, and that's when he starts to talk.

"The first thing you should know is that I'm in love with you, Avery. You *know* I am."

He loves me.

The world stops turning. I stop breathing. Everything just … stops. I should look up at him, should meet his eye. Should take in the look that he's wearing on his face, but I can't. Because if it matches the tone of his voice right now, it will set my very soul on fire and there will be no saving me. Luke sits quietly while I struggle to try and remember how to breathe. He loves me? Oh my god. How do I survive this?

"The second thing you should know is this …" Luke's chair creaks. "You were fourteen. You hadn't spoken in five days. The doctors were getting worried and your mom wouldn't even go into your bedroom to check on you. My partner and I came to the house to get a further statement from your mom, but I was feeling … I couldn't even step foot through your front door. Chloe left me outside, said she'd handle it. I sat in your front yard, right there on the front lawn, alone and crying. It was pathetic. But then you … you came down and sat with me. I was so embarrassed."

I don't remember any of that. I stifle back a sob and shunt myself back on his bed, hugging my knees to my chest. Luke continues, unfazed that I'm paralyzed and his words are hitting me with the force of a sledgehammer.

"You spoke. Your first words after five days were to *me*. You asked me why I was sad." Luke looks up, straight at me, straight through the camera, straight into my soul. "And I told you why. I told you exactly why I was sad and why your dad dying was the worst thing that had ever happened to me."

I shake my head, my eyes blurring. "That didn't happen. I don't remember."

"It did happen."

"Then what did you tell me?"

Luke just shakes his head. "You were quiet for a long time, but after a while you collapsed into my arms and started sobbing. You kept saying the same thing over and over: 'It hurts, it hurts, it hurts'. I couldn't bear that, Avery. I swore to you that it would stop hurting one day, I promised you it would. I carried you into the house and put you to bed. After that, Chloe came to get me and we left. But I made you that promise, Ave, and I wanted to keep it. That's why I kept coming back to see you all those years."

"And that's what this is now? You're still trying to make it stop hurting?"

Luke's eyes harden as he shakes his head again. "No, I told you. Everything changed when I came back to Break and saw you with that Justin guy. I wanted to kill him. You weren't a kid anymore, you were a woman, and I was blindsided by how strongly I felt for you. How …" he looks up at the ceiling, clenching his jaw, "how *insanely* jealous I was. I had to leave. I

256

didn't even speak to you that time. I just fucking left."

He remains quiet for a moment, a moment where I search my memory, scour it trying to find a snippet of recollection, anything that correlates with what he's telling me. But I can't. There's nothing.

"I was catatonic for eleven days after my father died, Luke. I couldn't have spoken to you after five." Luke doesn't argue with me. He just looks at me, brown eyes wide, t-shirt a little damp over his chest where he didn't dry his skin properly before putting it on. His shoulders are still slumped like he's resigned himself to something awful. I can see how much pain he's in. I can see how badly he needs me to believe him. And, for some reason, I do. "Why were you so angry with me at the station?" I whisper.

Luke sucks his bottom lip into his mouth. "You really don't know, do you?" he says, running his hand through his hair. "I was mad at you because you just sat there like it was completely normal, and the whole time ... the whole time ..."

"The whole time what?"

He can't do it anymore. He stands up, but he doesn't come to me. He prowls across his bedroom, looking up at me from underneath his brow—a dark, predatory, wild look. "That guy's hand was on your leg, Ave."

"What? Luke, I didn't want him touching me. I reported him to the cops last week. He pinned me up against a wall at school. I haven't seen or spoken to him in a while."

Luke stops pacing. He pivots so slowly on the balls of his feet until he's facing me, his limbs locked into place, his eyes unblinking. "He did what?"

"He ... he shoved me against a wall. He wouldn't let go of my arm."

A wall of color rises on Luke's face, first pink and then scarlet. "I'm going to fucking kill him."

"I thought you knew. I thought that's why you went crazy at the station."

"I went crazy because he was fucking touching you, Avery. He is not allowed to touch you. You're *mine*."

"We haven't even had that conversation yet, Luke."

"Well, we're going to. By the time you leave this apartment, you're gonna have promised me that you're mine, okay?" I open my mouth and just stare at him. He's totally lost it. "Tell me you haven't been thinking about me," he demands.

I let out an exasperated sigh. "Of course I've been thinking about you. You make it almost impossible not to. You call me, you turn up at my apartment, you kiss me in public, you tell me you don't think my dad—"

He cuts me off as he rushes towards me, grabbing hold of my head with both hands. With his chest pressed up against me, he crashes his lips down on mine and kisses me so hard I can do nothing but let him. For a heartbeat, a teeny tiny heartbeat, I let myself go. He straightens up, lifting me to my feet as he stands, and then he pulls back, breathing hard, staring at me fiercely.

"Tell me that kiss at the club didn't kill you. Tell me you haven't been thinking about me like this," he says, his voice rough, full of gravel. *Holy shit.*

"I didn't. I haven't." I'm still too scared to own this.

The corner of his mouth twitches. "Liar."

Damn. He pulls me to him again, and this time I don't resist. I've tried not to, haven't wanted to, but I've needed him. Missed him sorely. I meet him with just as much force. He tangles his hands in my hair and is stripping my clothes from my body before I can even sigh. Gone is the Luke who was so conflicted the last time we were alone in this room together. Now he's frantic, demanding, and frighteningly sexy.

"I'm fighting for you, Avery. I'm not letting you go. It doesn't matter what you say. I know you care about me just as much as I care about you."

"I don't. You're wrong," I lie, but I'm still tearing at his clothes like a woman possessed. In one hurried movement Luke

258

yanks down my pants and drags them off my feet, then lifts me so I can wrap my legs around his hips. He takes a step forward, narrowly avoiding knocking over the tripod and my camera, and then he throws me back down onto the bed, where he holds himself over me. Another deep kiss, his tongue parting my lips and playing over mine, has me panting, my hands clinging onto his arms. He kisses my jaw line, and then moves down until he's grazing his teeth across my neck. I've never told anyone about that secret spot, the one that has me melting and screaming inside all at once, yet Luke hits it straight away. He and my weak spot are best friends, apparently.

"Luke!" I gasp.

"Tell me," he growls. "Admit it."

"No." I am breathless, totally boneless underneath him as he reaches down and slips his fingers underneath my panties. A feeble moan works its way past my lips as he finds another spot that sends me just as crazy. He starts teasing me, running his fingers so softly against me so that my body begins to quake. "Please ..."

"Tell me," he repeats.

"I can't."

Luke freezes, his fingers still. He leans back and looks down at me, searching my face. "Then we need to stop," he murmurs.

The guy is trying to kill me. I can feel him pressed up against me, completely naked, his erection harder than granite between my legs, and I know this has to be killing him, too. "No," I whimper. At any other time, it would be humiliating that I'm so breathless and weak, but I need him. "Please ..."

"I can't have sex with you again until you admit it," he says softly, his eyes pinning me to the bed. I tremble when his fingers start moving again, just missing the small spot that will drive me over the edge. He found it no problem two seconds ago so I know he's doing it on purpose.

"Luke, don't tease me. *Please.*"

"You're doing this to yourself. All you have to do is admit

it."

"Admit *what*?" I grab hold of the sheets and screw them up in my hands. That's the only way I'm stopping myself from punching him in his face for making my body burn the way it is.

"You *know* what." His brown eyes are calm when I look in-to them. How can he not be losing it right now? *Two can play this game, buddy.* Reaching down between our bodies, I gently take hold of his erection and squeeze. His eyes flicker but they never leave mine. Even when I start stroking him, feeling him grow harder in my hand with every repetition, he doesn't look away.

"I want you, Iris," he whispers. "I know that. You know that. I'm not the problem here. I'm not the one afraid to admit my feelings. I love you, okay? And I know you love me."

I carry on stroking him, trying to push a smile onto my face. A hard one that will tell him what I think of his foolish declara-tion. Of what he thinks he knows about me. But it never mate-rializes. Luke reaches up and strokes a hand down my face, tracing his lips across mine gently. I stare back at him the whole time, wondering what the hell is happening. Why am I not leaping off the bed and running for the hills? Luke bites his lip and tenses a second before he finally gives in and slips a finger inside me. A rush of pleasure charges through my body, and I can't stop the embarrassing groan from escaping my lips.

"Say it," he whispers.

I close my eyes and I melt as he pushes another finger inside me.

"Say it, Avery."

Shake your head. Shake your head, damn it! But I don't. I rock up with my hips instead, begging for more of him to be inside me. "I need you," I moan.

"That's not it," he replies, drawing his fingers out. I cry out and he pushes back a little. He's so hard in my hand, and his muscles are twitching erratically. There's no way he isn't on the verge of coming.

"Please, Luke."

"Still not it," he says gruffly, his breath unbearably hot against my neck. I shiver and press my body harder against his. Luke leans away, making me whimper again. I'm frustratingly close to tears when he sits back completely, kneeling over me. He continues pushing his fingers inside me, but he puts his hand over mine on his erection. "You don't get to make me come."

"Are you ... bribing me?" I pant.

Luke shakes his head, his eyes intense. "Sex is important to me, Avery. That's why I stopped sleeping with Casey. It's okay for me to love you and do this, but I can't be with you like that if you don't admit what you're feeling."

My head starts spiraling in that crazy seeing-stars kind of way. He takes my hand off him and just about blows my mind when he starts stroking himself. I've never seen anything so hot in my entire life. I want to watch some more but he shimmies down the bed and pushes my legs apart roughly, pulling my panties out of the way. I know what's coming but that doesn't stop me from crying out when his tongue touches me.

"Shit! Luke, please!" I groan.

He doesn't stop. If anything my begging only seems to make him draw it out even more; his tongue sweeps across the very center of me, slower and slower until it feels like my whole body is vibrating. I can't take it anymore. I sit up and grab his arms, pulling him up the bed. He lands on top of me, still so incredibly serious.

"Just do it, Luke. Please just do it. I need you."

He is so close to being inside me, unbearably so, but no matter how much I wriggle he keeps moving away. Eventually he puts a stop to my ideas by grabbing my hands over my head and pinning me.

"I'm not some jerk who sleeps around, Avery. You've got to be honest. Tell me!"

I buck underneath him, fighting to get free. "You're insane," I hiss.

"And you're lying to me and to yourself," he says. "Now just do it." He presses down on top of me and the tip of his erection pushes into me, making my skin burn. I'm on fire.

"I ... I can't!"

"DAMN IT, AVERY, TELL ME THE TRUTH!"

And that's when I snap. When everything snaps. The wall I so carefully constructed and have been hiding behind for so long crumbles and I'm left naked in more ways than one. "Fine! I love you, Luke. I love you so much I think I might die sometimes!Are you happy now?" With my eyes finally open, I stare up into his face, feeling ridiculous when they start to burn.

"Do you mean it?" he whispers.

I can't answer. Tears streak down my cheeks as I nod my head yes, my heart breaking, suddenly feeling like a frightened little girl. This is the most exposed I have ever been in my life. There's no turning back. I don't know what I expect to see on Luke's face—triumph, maybe?—but it isn't pain. Yet there it is.

"Thank god," he says softly. And then he pushes inside me. I suck in a sharp breath and hold it, not wanting to make a sound. "Don't leave me out here on my own," he says, as though he knows exactly what's happening inside me: sheer, uncontrollable panic. I told him. *I told him!* "Look at me, baby." Luke draws me back with his soft voice, and I do as he asks. He pushes into me again, and my body shudders.

"Oh, god." I can't stop what is building. Nothing can. Luke's intensity only grows as he thrusts again, his shoulders starting to tremble.

"You're mine. Say it!" he growls.

I manage to say it as I come apart in his hands, my body disintegrating into blindly firing nerve endings. "I'm yours, Luke! I'm yours." And I really am.

Damn it.

IT'S STILL dark when the phone starts screaming in Luke's apartment. If I'm honest, I've been watching him like some creepy yet very confused stalker, and he totally busts me when his eyes snap open. He gives me a small smile when he comes to. He rubs at one eye sleepily before stretching and grabbing hold of the handset beside his bed. The blue glow from the screen lights up his face as he answers.

"Cole, if this is you, I'm going to cause you severe fucking pain. It's four a.m.," he groans into the receiver.

Four a.m., I'm naked in Luke Reid's bed, and I'm not planning my escape. That's a first. Then again I've never told anyone I love them before either, so tonight is clearly a night for firsts.

Luke goes still as he listens to the muffled voice on the end of the phone; he seems to be holding his breath. The voice on the other end of the phone stops talking. Luke just stares up at the ceiling for a second before he closes his eyes, pinching the bridge of his nose with his fingertips. "Wait, *what?* Say that again."

He's quiet for a few seconds, unblinking, as he stares blankly ahead of him. I study his face, wondering, fearing, panicking over whatever has made him turn to stone.

"And why the hell do they think that?" he asks, sitting up slowly. His free hand goes to the back of his neck, where he rubs back and forth anxiously. The tone in his voice is strained—not a good sign. "Yeah. She's here. Her phone's probably ... it must be in the other room." My stomach bottoms out. I sit forward, clasping my hands together, holding them to my mouth. Luke blinks, the look of a stunned man. "Yeah. Yes, I'll be there." He hangs up and leans forward, pressing the phone into his forehead.

"What is it, Luke?"

"Breakwater PD," he whispers.

Oh. God. My heart starts slamming in my chest. Whatever it was they just told Luke was worth calling for at four a.m. in the morning. And by the sounds of things they've been trying to call me, too. I scoot back in the bed, clutching the sheet to my chest, trying to work out how on earth I'm going to escape whatever it is I'm about to find out. "Just tell me." The words fly out, unbidden, in a whisper. I want to snatch them out of the air and cram them straight back into my mouth.

"That was the duty officer at my old station. He said ..." He trails off, shaking his head blankly.

"He said what?"

Luke's eyes are dark pools in the half light. "He said they just brought your uncle in for questioning."

THIRTY-FOUR

BREAKWATER

"IM GONNA need your keys, cell phone, jewelry, loose change, everything in your pockets, basically. That includes your lint. Place the items in the tray and wait until we call you." I don't know the young female officer behind the counter of Breakwater police station and she doesn't know me, but we've come to an instant mutual agreement: we don't like one another. She seems fine with Luke, though. "You can go through if you like, hon. Chloe's expecting you."

"That's okay. I'll wait out here," he tells her, slipping his hand into mine. We sit in the station for an hour before Chloe Mathers, Luke's old partner, comes to find us. I recognize her as soon as she walks through the door. She was with Luke the day they came to tell us about my dad. She made my mom a cup of tea, like that was going to fix everything.

"Iris," she says, nodding towards me. "Good to see you again. How you goin', Luke?" She bypasses his outstretched hand and pulls him in for a hug. "Not the most ideal circumstances to be seeing you again, but still a pleasure all the same."

Luke hugs her back awkwardly. "Yeah, good to see you, too, Chloe."

She nods her head through the open door behind her into the police station. "Come on. He's already been interviewed, I'm not supposed to do this but it can't really hurt. You can see him for five minutes."

My heart fumbles in my chest. I still have no idea why they pulled my uncle in, what they can possibly have discovered to make them think he had anything to do with this. They have to be wrong. We follow Chloe into the station and make our way to the holding cells. The place reminds me of a hospital, all bleach and blank faces and flickering fluorescent lighting. Chloe stops in front of a door, opens it, and gestures us inside. Through the door, there's a single peeling veneer table, three chairs, and my Uncle Brandon. He looks startled when his head shoots up, catching sight of me immediately.

"What are you doing here, kiddo? You didn't need to come." He looks like hell. He's always a little scruffy, but his unshaven face and the bags under his eyes make him look flat-out ill.

"You look like shit, Uncle B." I take a seat across the table from him and turn—Luke is hovering in the doorway.

"I can give you guys a minute, if you like?"

I shake my head. "It's fine. Stay. Please." There's no way I can handle doing this on my own. Besides, Luke will know better than anyone if they have grounds to keep holding Brandon. Luke nods, slipping into the seat beside me.

"I'll be back in five," Officer Mathers tells us. She pulls a tight smile and closes the door, leaving us alone.

"What the hell's going on, Brandon? No one will tell us anything."

Brandon closes his eyes, his shoulders slumping. He looks exhausted. "They say they think I was there the day your dad and those other men died. They think I had something to do with it."

My knee sets to bouncing up and down under the table. Just hearing him say those words makes bile rise up in my throat. "Why the hell would they think that?"

"Something about an old camera of mine. They had a video handed in at the station a week ago. It was apparently shot using a specific kind of film. A rare one that I used to use."

"That's ridiculous! I mean, anyone could have a camera that uses a certain type of film, Brand. Right?"

My uncle goes quiet for a moment, chewing on his lip. "Yeah, but there's a fault on this particular camera I own, a light leak. It allows light into the housing. It corrupts the video in a very specific way. Apparently, the film that was handed in bore a leak that could only have been created by my camera."

I process this for a second. "So, it was definitely your camera. Does that mean they can prove it was you who shot the thing?" My heart is beating like crazy. A small, terrified part of my brain is causing chaos, screaming, *Did he do it? Did he do it?* Of course he didn't, I know that, but still. That nasty little suspicion is making my whole body tremble. Luke puts his hand on my knee under the table, shoots me a reassuring look.

"I keep telling them that I loaned that camera to your dad, Iris, but they don't seem to be listening. He borrowed it months before he died. I never got it back. They seized it among his possessions, but they say someone was holding the camera when your dad was in that room with the other men … it wasn't on a tripod, it was following him around the room." A pained expression flutters across Brandon's face. He looks sick to his stomach. "You know I would never hurt anyone, right, Iris? You know I would never hurt your dad?"

I nod my head immediately. I can't get the words out, though. It isn't that I don't believe him. My throat is just closing up, refusing to let me speak. This is such a mess. Everything. My whole life, Brandon's life, Luke's …

"Brandon, I'm going to go see if I can get you a coffee," Luke murmurs. He squeezes my hand one last time and then plants a soft kiss on top of my head. "I'll be right back."

Brandon scratches at his stubble, his eyes searching my face. "I knew you were a smart girl," is all he says. His gaze drops to his hands, and it's then that I notice they're handcuffed together at the wrists.

"Oh my god, they've *cuffed you*?"

"I'm under arrest, kiddo. Generally means you get the five-star treatment."

"This is such bullshit. We're going to work this out, okay? Do you even know what's on the tape?"

Brandon sighs, heavy and worn down. "They're not sharing. I think they're trying to get me to slip up, waiting for *me* to tell *them* what's on the tape. I'm pretty sure they think they're gonna get me to accidentally admit to something that way."

"Will they tell Luke what—" My sentence remains unfinished. The door to the interview room slams open, and a tall woman in a pantsuit stands there, gaping at us. Her red hair is pulled back into a tight bun, so tight, in fact, that I wonder whether she's cut the circulation off to her scalp.

"What the hell are you doing in here?" The woman places one arm up on the doorjamb, the other on her hip. She glares straight at me, pissed.

"I—I was told this was okay?"

"Well, it's *not* okay. Who are you?"

"Iris Breslin. She's my niece," Brandon answers. I return the woman's steely gaze, getting the distinct feeling that she's pulling it off a lot more convincingly than I am.

"I'm FBI Agent Cosgrove, and this is a federal investigation. You can't be in here." She motions me to stand with a casual flick of her wrist. *Up.*

I rise, shooting Brandon a quick glance. "I'll call a lawyer, okay? You'll be out of here by tomorrow."

I have to leave then, under the watchful eye of Agent Cosgrove. She shoots daggers at me as she slams the door, blocking out my uncle and her unsmiling face as she does so. Luke appears down the abandoned corridor with a polystyrene cup in either hand, the coffee steaming.

"What's going on?"

"Some FBI bitch just booted me out. She was a real bulldog."

Luke bites his lip, staring at the closed investigation room door in front of us. He hands me a coffee. I take it, my hands still shaking. "We can't leave him in here, Luke. I know he's got nothing to do with this. We have to get him a lawyer."

A crease forms in between Luke's brows. Something's up. He looks … anxious. "I got that covered. I just made a call."

"Okay." I don't say anything else. I know there's more coming, something he doesn't want to tell me. "I contacted the legal firm on file as Brandon's representation."

"Right. When are they getting here? Which agency is it?"

Luke visibly blanches. "They'll be here first thing in the morning. And the agency is … it's Harrod, Whitt, St. French," he rushes out.

Those three names are like individual explosions in my ears. Harrod. Whitt. St. French.

Shit.

"You've got to be kidding me."

Luke flinches. "Yeah, I'm sorry, Avery. Your mom is on her way."

THIRTY-FIVE

MARLENA

SURPRISINGLY, THERE aren't any rules about lawyers representing family members. The phrase, *conflict of interest* is bandied around inside the station as Luke and I depart, but there's nothing the cops or the FBI can do about it. I leave with a ten-ton weight sitting in my gut. My mom is on her way from New York to defend Brandon. I feel sick just thinking about seeing her back in Break. I have no idea what Luke had to say to even get her to agree. She cares for Brandon about as much as she cares for me, as far as I can tell. And that isn't very much.

Night is closing in by the time we step outside. We hopped on the first plane out of the city when we were woken up, and as such we didn't even have a car when we arrived. It is freezing cold, snowing, and we're using one of Brandon's old beaters from his auto mechanics shop to get us around. Luke opens my door for me, his manners still somehow functioning amidst all the madness of the last twelve hours. "My mom—" he starts, then shakes his head.

"What? Your mom what?"

"Ahh, she said we should go by there for dinner tonight." He grimaces, like he suspects how badly I just want to be alone. There's a faintly hopeful glimmer in his eye, too, though. It suddenly hits me how good he's been since this morning when we heard about my uncle. He booked our flights; he called into work and told them he couldn't make his shifts for a couple of days; he drove me across New York in the mid-morning traffic so I could pick up clothes and toiletries from Columbia. He's basically held me together the whole day, when I was on the verge of falling apart. The least I can do is go eat with his mother.

"It's okay," I say softly. "We can go."

Surprise, then happiness forms on his face. "We don't need to hang around. We can leave straight afterwards."

I shake my head. "It's all right. You didn't see her at Thanksgiving. You should spend some time with her."

We make our way across Break, my stomach churning the whole time. I've only been gone five months but it feels like an eternity. Like the place should have changed dramatically in the time I've been gone, because heaven knows I have. And yet the bowling lane, the shooting club where both Luke's dad and mine had been members, the convenience store, the diner with its infamous thick shakes … everything still stands where it did half a year ago. Luke drives the long way from the police station to his mom's house, and I know exactly why. The quickest route takes us past Breakwater High, the sprawling institution where I spent four of the worst years of my life. Luke's smart enough to know I will probably burst into tears if I have to see it again. I grip hold of his hand as we pull up outside a ranch-style home that I've driven past many times, knowing that it's where he grew up, but never having been inside.

"Does …" I draw in a deep breath. "Does your mom know about …" Ugh, why can't I just say it? This is strangely awkward.

271

Luke smiles softly. "About us? I don't think so, no."

I don't know if that is a relief or just something else to worry about. Are we expected to go in there and explain our complicated relationship to Luke's mom now, too, on top of how my uncle has been arrested?

"Hey, don't look so freaked out. My mom's a sweetheart. She won't ask questions if you don't want her to." Luke crooks a finger under my chin, turning my head so I have to look at him. He's wearing a tense expression, worry all over his face. His deep brown eyes are studiously scouring me, searching to see if I am okay. He has a six o'clock shadow after not shaving this morning in our rush to get to the airport on time, and it makes him look older. How I can still feel small next to him, silly and girlish, with everything that is going on is a mystery. But I do. He's seriously hot. Not to mention loving and patient and kind. I feel myself welling up just looking at him.

"Hey. Hey, what's up?" he whispers.

"I just … I do *not* deserve you. I've been a complete bitch to you, Luke. I've been ungrateful and selfish and a massive pain in the ass, and you didn't deserve any of it."

"You have been a massive pain in the ass, yes." He smirks casually, and two fat tears roll down my face. He brushes them away tenderly, making me want to cry even harder. "But we're both a little broken, you and I. I see you, Avery. I really see *you*, the places you're wounded, and I want to be the person to put you back together. I know you still need some time to disassociate me with everything that's happened here, but I'm willing to wait. I want that so bad."

I can't control it any longer. Luke saying those words, it's like a levy breaking inside me. Tears slip freely down my face, burning my eyes. "You're right. I am broken, and somehow you *do* see me. I want to see you, too, Luke. I want to be the person to hold you together, too. I don't just associate you with what happened here anymore."

He sucks in a deep breath and it catches in his throat. His

eyes swim with emotion. "That's good." It's like a huge pressure has been released from his body. A small smile tugs at the corner of his mouth. It's adorably sexy.

"Yeah, now I associate you with alcohol and really hot sex, too."

Luke barks out laughter, but turns to look away from me. He covers his mouth, leaning against the car window, while staring at his family home. A heaviness lays over him that I feel like a tangible force. Somehow I've said the wrong thing. He stabs his fingers through his hair, pulling himself upright before I can ask if he is okay.

"All right," he says. "Time to go meet my mom."

I'VE MET Mrs. Reid a million times before, of course. Breakwater is small and she's on the PTA, plus she owns a bakery in town that everyone buys their baked goods from. The front door opens before Luke can insert his key, and all five foot nothing of the tiny woman rushes out to meet us.

"Thank god you're here! There's a huge snowstorm on its way in. I was worried you were gonna get stuck." She grabs a fistful of Luke's shirt and tugs him down to hug her slim frame before he can even open his mouth. Locked in her embrace, he groans, but it's all for show. His mom fixes eyes with me over his shoulder and smiles. "Iris Breslin, you look more like your father every day. Come here." She pulls me into a tight hug, too, startling me.

No one, *no one*, in Break ever speaks to me about my father, let alone tells me I look like him. A lump bobs in my throat. They feel to me like the kindest words she could possibly have said.

"Good to see you, Mrs. Reid," I wheeze. The little woman has a strong grip on her. She draws back, holding me at arm's length, studying me. Her brown eyes are the same color as

Luke's. Just as warm.

"Don't be silly. You're not in school anymore. You can call me Marlena. Come on, come in before you two catch pneumonia."

The house smells like cinnamon and fresh pine, two aromas that probably shouldn't go together but do. There's a stack of mail by the front door, unopened, and an ironing board propped against a closet in the entryway. Marlena leads us into the kitchen where she's obviously been folding laundry. There's a neat stack of clothes on the kitchen table, a huge pine thing that dominates the room. You can tell that this is the hub of the house, as any baker's kitchen should be. The place is lived in. Welcoming. A home. My mind instantly flickers to my mom's sterile brownstone, and I can't help but make the comparison. Her place reflects how cold and empty my mom is, whereas Luke's family home is a reflection of Marlena: loving and warm.

"Dinner will be ready in an hour. Why don't you two grab a beer and keep me company while I finish up?" She points at the basket of unfolded clothing at her feet. Luke glances at me—*is this okay?*— before I nod and sit myself down at the kitchen table. He smiles a little, slings his coat over the back of a chair opposite and makes his way over to the fridge.

"Why don't you grab me one, too, son?" Marlena hands me an armful of washing, winking, including me in her chore. The gesture is small, but it's a kind thing to do. She is giving me a purpose, telling me I am welcome, accepting me. Even if she doesn't realize I'm having sex with her son. I pick up a t-shirt and start folding.

Luke raises an eyebrow when he sees me. He sets down three beers and then proceeds to smack the caps off on the edge of the worn table. Marlena doesn't seem to mind. My mom would freak if I put down a bottle without a coaster, let alone tried to open it on the countertop. "I see you're putting your guests to good use, Mom. What did your other slave die of? Where is my little sister, anyway?"

"Staying with friends tonight. She didn't know you were coming back. You'll see her in the morning, though." Marlena sips on her beer between folding, taking a surprisingly big draught. Luke makes an awkward face.

"Ah, actually, I was gonna stay up at Brandon's place with Avery. Just to make sure she's not snowed in in the morning."

Marlena puts down her beer bottle, looking from her son to me and back again. "*Neither* of you are staying up at that place. What if *I'm* snowed in in the morning?"

"Uhhh. Well ..." Luke is a little lost for words.

I don't know why but I find myself telling her, "That's okay, I'd love to stay."

Marlena nods, like it was already a foregone conclusion. "Good. I've made up the bed in your room, Luke. You can both go dump your stuff in a moment before I serve dinner."

Luke and I exchange glances but don't say a word. When Marlena's done with the laundry, we do as she suggested and go to drop our overnight bags in Luke's room. And there it is: his double bed, freshly made, two towels folded neatly on top of it, a spare toothbrush still in the packaging on top of the pink one. Clearly meant for me.

"I thought you said you hadn't told her anything," I hiss, whacking his arm. Luke shakes his head.

"I swear I didn't. She just knows things. She's like freaking Yoda. I got away with nothing as a kid."

Dinner is surprisingly easy to get through, considering. Marlena talks endlessly about Luke's sister, Emma, and that is another kindness on her part. She knows without being told that I don't want to talk about Brandon sitting in a jail cell as we enjoy our beer and homemade lasagna. She also somehow knows the topic of my fragile relationship with Luke is off the table, too. He was right; the woman really does just know things. The only sore topic she brings up is my mother.

"I hear Amanda's on her way, then." She makes the announcement casually, but I'd have to be blind to miss the curious look in her eye. She's watching me, waiting to see how I will react. It is public record that my mom up and abandoned me to move to the city as soon as humanly possible after my dad died. No one really asked me whether her actions bothered me, though. That's what Marlena is doing when she watches me now. She is asking to see if my mom's presence is okay, if I am okay with her showing up.

"Uh, yeah. She's catching a red eye first thing." I take a long drink from my beer. "I didn't even know she was my uncle's lawyer, to be honest."

"Yes, well. I'm pretty sure your mother would jump through a burning ring of fire for Brandon, sweetheart."

That comment catches me off guard. "What do you mean?"

"Oh, nothing. They were close in high school is all. Insepa-rable, in fact. I always thought your mom had a bit of a thing for Brandon. Mind you, your mom and dad, plus Melanie and Brandon, all four of them were thick as thieves. We could never really work out who was with who half the time."

"Mom!" Luke looks horrified. The casual way she imparts the information that my mom might have had a thing with Brandon once upon a time makes it sound completely obvious. The look on her face says so, too. She puts down her fork and grins at Luke.

"Son, I didn't raise you to be a prude. In fact, I know you're not, so you just calm yourself. I'm not speaking ill of the dead. Melanie and Max were good people. I think they just married wrong, is all."

I pick up a forkful of lasagna, my eyes on my plate. "I'm not sure Brandon and my mom are as close as you remember them, Marlena. I don't think she speaks to him unless it's about me. And that's not very often." The email she sent me and copied Brandon into was testimony to that. She couldn't even be both-ered to write him a separate message.

"Pain does strange things to people, sweetheart. Just be-cause Amanda distances herself from people doesn't mean she doesn't care about them." The hidden message in that statement is barely hidden at all. I almost choke on my food; I want to laugh so badly. I manage to hold it in, though. Marlena's just trying to be nice, and I don't want to offend her. Or scandalize her with the news that my mother now prefers women over men. We eat our meal, and then Luke and I wash the dishes while Marlena watches *The Voice*. Every minute or so Luke brushes a hand across my back, tucks my hair back out of my eyes, touches me in some way to let me know he's there and everything is normal.

And it *is* normal. It's how life should be, doing domesticated things as part of a family. It's nice, and almost takes my mind off Brandon and my dad and the nightmare waiting for me when I get back to Columbia. I mean, shit. I have Tate's funeral to attend, Morgan to comfort, and Noah to deal with. Oh god, Noah. I haven't even had time to think about the drugs.

Even my worry over that can't keep me awake, though. I last twenty minutes on the sofa before my eyelids start to grow heavy. The next thing I know, Luke is laying me down carefully on his bed, his tongue poking out in concentration as he tries to put me down without disturbing me.

"Sorry. I carried you through. I didn't think you'd wake up."

"It's okay, I need to get changed out of these clothes anyway." Groggily, I get up and rifle through my bag until I realize that in my rush I didn't pack anything to sleep in.

"You need a t-shirt or something?" Luke is right behind me, incredibly close.

"I, uh—yeah that would be good, thanks." Instead of racing away, my heart thumps hard in my chest, making my head swim a little. Everything is so different with him, now. I'm hyper aware of him. Whenever he's in the room, my skin prickles with the knowledge that he's close by.

His eyes pick me apart as I wait for him to grab me something to wear. A small smile ticks at the corner of his mouth.

"What?"

"Nothing." His smile transforms into a full-on smirk. "Here, wear this one." He tugs the t-shirt he is wearing right off his back and tosses it at me. I catch it out of the air, mouth hanging open a little. The black fabric is warm and smells deliciously of him.

"Really?" I laugh.

He nods. "Really." I try not to gawp at him, his bare chest, packed muscle over his stomach and rippling over his tattooed shoulders as he walks slowly towards me. The way he moves is predatory, like I'm a frightened deer likely to bolt before he reaches me. Maybe in some ways I am. It's still so strange to be with him like this.

"Are you gonna put that on?" A wicked look glints in his eye.

"Maybe. If I can get some privacy."

I'm totally playing and he knows it, which is why he pretends to pout as he says, "Don't worry, I won't look. Your modesty will be entirely preserved."

I unbutton my jeans and shimmy them down, never breaking eye contact with him. He's good, I'll give him that. I know for a fact I'm wearing my nice underwear today, the lacy stuff. Miracle upon miracles, I'm wearing a matching bra, too. That never usually happens. As I pull my top off over my head, I sense him watching my every move. Sure enough, his dark eyes are burning into my skin. I thread my arms into his t-shirt and pull it on, enjoying the smell of him as I do so. I barely have time to gather my hair out of the shirt before he lunges for me, grabbing hold of my waist.

"I'm sorry, that just has to be the sexiest thing I've ever seen."

"What, a girl in your clothes?"

"*You* in my clothes," he whispers back. His mouth is on mine before I can say another word. I might have been sleepy twenty seconds ago, but now I'm suddenly very awake. I tangle my hands into Luke's hair and he lets out a low growl. That small sound sends a bolt of heat shooting through my body and pooling somewhere a couple of degrees south of my waistline. I melt into him. He catches me up, lifting his shirt that I now wear so he can palm my butt cheeks. I never knew someone grabbing my ass could turn me on so damn much. My breathing is ridiculously fast, matching his. Luke reaches up and grabs my hair, winding it around his fist. He tips my head back and starts kissing my neck, his other hand sliding up underneath the t-shirt. I gasp when his fingers begin tracing the cup of my bra.

"Luke! Luke, your mom!" He stops long enough to meet my eyes, and I know there's no point protesting any further. Desire, animalistic and undeniable, gazes back at me. This is happening, and I want it to. Badly. "Fuck it."

A scandalous grin spreads across Luke's face. He reaches down and hooks his hands beneath my thighs, lifting me up in one smooth movement so that I'm wrapped around his waist.

"I'm sorry. No matter how much this turns me on, the shirt has gotta go," he groans. I have just enough time to lift my arms before he rips his shirt off my body, making me squeak a little. Not sexy at all, but Luke doesn't seem to notice. He's too busy devouring my cleavage with his eyes. His pure lust makes me uncharacteristically brave. I hook my thumbs under my bra straps and tug them forward, biting my bottom lip.

"Want me to lose this, too?" I run my hands down over the front of my bra, and Luke's whole body shakes. His erection presses insistently into my stomach, even more evident when he takes three large steps and slams me roughly up against the wall.

"You're asking for trouble, y'know that?"

I do know. And I'm not asking. I'm begging. "Please, Luke. Tell me what you want." I reach around and unclasp my bra, sliding the straps off my shoulders. Luke sucks in another deep breath. Urgent. Desperate.

"Ave, you're so beautiful. I can't wait ..." He dips his head and sucks one of my nipples into his mouth, running his tongue over and over the hardened tip. I arch my back, curving into him, just as desperate myself. I fumble between us, struggling with his belt. Takes me two attempts before I have it undone and yanked out of his jeans entirely. After that I make short work of his pants, pushing them down over his hips.

"I want you inside me, Luke. Now."

Those must be the magic words. Luke doesn't even bother pulling my panties down. He rips them off me like they're made out of tissue paper, not incredibly expensive lace, and then they're gone. He slides a hand down the front of his boxers and then I feel him against me. Holy shit, he's going to …

My mind goes blank. He pushes inside me, and in this position I'm so stretched and completely full. My nerve endings fire delicious darts of heat through me, scattering any hope I might have of coherent thought. Luke makes a pained noise in the back of his throat and stills his body.

"Are you okay?" he whispers. My whole body has gone stiff. Then I realize—he thinks he's hurting me. I can't answer him. I wrap my arms around the back of his neck again and smash my lips to his, breathing heavily into his mouth instead. I can't help it; I have to move. I start rocking up and down on him, using the wall as leverage.

"Avery! Fuck!"

This is all I need to hear. It hasn't escaped me that Luke hasn't put a condom on, but at this exact second in time I couldn't care less. So reckless, but he feels incredible. I tighten my legs around him, riding him harder.

"Come inside me, Luke. I want to feel you come."

Luke pulls back to look at me, fixes me with his eyes. "Are you sure?"

I nod, clinging to him, forcing him inside me as hard as I can. "I want you. I want to feel everything."

And he so does.

THIRTY-SIX

SUCKER PUNCH

THE SOFT *whoomf* of snow sliding from the roof wakes me. I'm tangled in Luke's arms. The gentle sounds of his breathing sends an alien jolt of happiness through me. I shouldn't be happy. I should be stressed out and terrified. I'm back in Breakwater, for crying out loud. I'm seeing my mother today, because Brandon is *in jail*. Okay, so maybe I am freaking out a little bit, but in this tiny second, with the silence of the outside world and Luke holding me so close—I really am happy. How is that even possible?

A tap at the door finally wakes Luke. My peaceful moment is gone the second he jumps out of his skin, but I've already stored it away, ready to call on it when I need a moment of sanity.

"You two awake in there?" Marlena calls through the door. Luke makes a non-committal groaning noise. Apparently that means yes in the Reid household because Marlena comes right on in. I nearly elbow Luke in the face trying to make sure I'm covered up.

Luke does some scrambling of his own. "Jeez, mom! What the hell?"

I peer over the top of the comforter, grimacing when I see my bra and torn—torn!—underwear lying on the floor. *Oh, dear God in Heaven, please let the ground swallow me up now.* Marlena grins at us. She's brandishing two cups of coffee.

"Well, now, you two kept me up most of the night. Figured you might need something to give you a bit of energy this morning."

Luke slumps back against the pillows, closing his eyes. "Just get out, Mom." Marlena shrugs, still grinning. She starts to leave but he stops her. "Hey. Leave the coffee."

She set the cups down and *winks* at me, then leaves. We can hear her laughing across the other side of the house.

"YOU LOOK like you've been sleeping rough, Avery. Don't you own a hair brush anymore?" I've been in my mother's presence for all of thirty minutes and she's already criticized my jacket, my teeth and now my hair. She also said my flushed cheeks are unladylike. It's minus twelve degrees, so I don't know what she expects me to do about my rosy cheeks. Or why they are unladylike in the first place.

She is also disapproving of my hand-holding with Luke, although that disapproval is of the silent variety. Pursed lips, narrowed eyes, sharp as razor blades, whenever he isn't looking. I already want to slap her. Marlena offered to let her sleep in their spare room but my mother none-too-politely declined, saying that she needed room to spread out her work and the Reid's place just wasn't big enough. As a result, she is spending two hundred and eighty dollars a night at the Cliffson's bed and breakfast, paying for all five bedrooms, because she refuses to have anyone else stay there while she is.

She's never really liked Breakwater, wanted to escape as soon as she and my dad were done with college, but my grandparents on my dad's side both fell sick at the same time, and naturally my dad wanted to stick around. Mom always held it against him. Dad was nursemaid, cook and cleaner to my grandparents for four years while they slowly deteriorated, until Mom insisted they go into assisted living. Gran died two weeks later of a heart attack, and then Pops six months after her from pneumonia. My dad hadn't been present to say goodbye to either of them. And all my mother could say was, "It's for the best, Max. At least now you can get full-time work and use that teaching degree of yours." She'd said teaching degree like it was a dirty word. Like my dad's job hadn't carried them for years while she was studying law and putting in crazy hours, never at home. My dad had just smiled and taken it. He was a saint like that.

"I'm not staying in that police station any longer than I have to. I'm going to choke down the swill the diner tries to pass off as coffee and read over these notes."

Luke shoots daggers at my mom as he parks up Brandon's beater in the diner's parking lot. He doesn't even need telling; Amanda St. French does not open her own car doors. He gets out and opens her door, gesturing grandly for her as she climbs out and teeters on her ridiculously impractical, tall heels.

"Avery, give me your cell phone. Mine doesn't get reception here. Tell whoever's on the front desk at the station to call when they're ready for me," she says through the window. Since she's technically paying for it, it is kind of her cell phone. I buzz down my window and hand it over. "You and I need to have a little chat later," she says under her breath. Her blonde, immaculate hair, down to her mid-back, swings from side to side as she manages to power walk through the snow into Jerry's Diner. Luke turns and looks at me, hands held out. *What the hell?*

I get out of the back seat where I was relegated and clamber into the front. Luke climbs in, too, still shaking his head. "She's a real piece of work. I don't remember her being like that when I was a kid."

"Yeah, well, she was a lot nicer to people she thought she could get something from. Maybe your mom's position on the PTA bought her some brownie points or something."

"Yeah. Or something."

We check in at the police station but they won't let us see Brandon. Apparently Chloe was given hell for letting us see him yesterday.

"That Cosgrove bitch chewed my ear off for twenty minutes," she laughs. "I'll be copping traffic duty for the fore-seeable future."

"Sorry, Chlo." Luke looks beyond contrite; traffic duty must really suck. Chloe shrugs it off. "Ahh, it's okay. Anything for you kids." She reaches out and plucks something from my jack-et. "Stray hair," she says, shrugging. "You guys are welcome to come over to my place for dinner tomorrow night, if you like? The place certainly isn't New York standards, but it's warm and I really know how to fry a steak. What d'you think?"

Dinner's the last thing on my mind. Luke accepts, saying we'll confirm once we know what's happening with Brandon. On the way out of the station, Agent Cosgrove passes us in the hallway. She locks eyes with me and I swear icicles form on my breath. Back at Luke's house, his sister's home; she squeals like a banshee when we walk through the door. Launches herself at him, she's grinning from ear to ear. They share so many familiar features—same dark hair, dark eyes, quirky way of smiling. It's impossible to ignore that they're siblings. Even though she's Luke's younger sister, Emma was still two years above me in high school. She was popular, a cheerleader, but always a lot kinder than the other girls. She grins when she sees me, draw-ing me in for a big hug. "Good to see you, Iris," she says, giving me a genuine smile. "I trust my brother's been taking good care of you?"

I give him a look, screwing up my nose, pretending to think about that. Luke is mock-offended until I say, "You know what, he *has* been taking good care of me. The best." The curve of his smile seems to promise an extra special taking care of later, which makes my cheeks burn.

The telephone call from my mother comes at midday, only three hours after we dropped her off. Luke holds out the Reid's old-school Bakelite corded handset like my mom is liable to bite him down the phone.

"Hello?" I answer.

"They've got no grounds to keep him." She dives straight in. No hello. Nothing. "He'll be out this time tomorrow. They've got a warrant to search his house but they're not going to find anything. I've advised Brandon he might have grounds to sue, but the bull-headed man won't listen to—"

I hold my hand up, like she can actually see me. "Wait, so he's not going to prison? They can't pin anything on him?"

Mom's frustrated sigh rattles down the phone. "That's what I just said, isn't it?"

Relief surges through me, powerful and overwhelming. "So what does that mean? Do they still think Dad was responsible?"

"I don't know, Avery. That's not why I'm here. I came as counsel to your Uncle Brandon and I've done my job. Any other elements pertaining to this case are not my concern."

I've been calm about my mother's overblown hatred for my father for so long now that I almost accept this statement from her. But my clenched jaw and my bubbling fury won't let it slide this time. She's unbelievable. "How the hell can you say that? You know they've got evidence that could prove Dad is innocent, right? Shouldn't you want to try and take a look at that evidence? You're a terrible mother but you're an excellent lawyer. You just got this thing with Brandon pretty much ironed out in less than three hours. Don't you think you might be able to work the same magic?"

My mother snorts. "You're not a kid anymore, Avery.

There's no such thing as magic. There's black and there's white. Guilty and innocent. Your Uncle Brandon is innocent, which is why I can 'iron out' his problems in under three hours. No amount of poring over federal files is going to make your father any less guilty."

"You're unbelievable!" I grip hold of the phone so hard it creaks, like it might shatter any second.

"No, I'm a realist. I know what your father was like. And I also know what that new boyfriend of yours is like, too. I told you to stay away from him, didn't I? Has he explained why your father used to mentor him yet?" I'm trembling with rage, so angry I can't speak. My mother ignores my silence. "I'm sure he hasn't. Let me just say this—if he had been two years older when he did what he did, he sure as hell wouldn't be a cop right now. He'd be on the sex offenders register and he wouldn't even be able to get a job bagging groceries. Now you listen to me, Avery, you stay away from him!"

"*JUST SHUT THE HELL UP!*" The outburst rings through the Reid's residence. Everyone falls silent. Luke stands and walks across the kitchen, concern written all over his face. Pure terror washes through me as my mother's words ring out loud and clear in my ears. *Sex offenders register.* What the hell did he do? For once, my mother is quiet on the other end of the phone. I draw in a deep breath and say what I should have said a long time ago. "You can't control my life when you want nothing to do with it, Amanda. When all you want to do is throw money at me like I'm a problem you can buy off and make disappear. I'm glad that you're here, that you've helped Brandon, but from here on out, I don't want to see you. I don't want your money, and I certainly don't need you interfering in my love life when you can't even be honest enough with your own partner to admit that I damn well exist!"

I slam the handset down so hard that the phone falls off the wall and bounces off the counter, cracking open and spilling wires everywhere like guts. That's how I feel right now: raw, torn open, exposed. My insides on the outside.

Luke stares at the broken phone, his hands twitching at his sides. He looks nervous. "What was that about?"

I can't think. I'm wound too tight to say anything but those three words—the words threatening to take the one good thing in my life and destroy it forever. "Sex offenders register?"

Marlena shoots to her feet, her hand covering her mouth. Luke reels back, his face draining of all color. "What?" he says breathlessly.

"My mom ... she said you should be on the sex offenders register. She said that's why my dad was mentoring you. Was she telling the truth?"

Pain, an awful, gut-wrenching pain, flashes across Luke's face. He doesn't need to answer me, but he does. "Yes."

The single word is like a punch to my gut. I stumble back, hands reaching out for the tabletop to support myself. "What ..." I can't even finish. I want to ask him what happened, what he did. But the knowledge will destroy me, I'm sure of it.

"Avery, wait. It's really not what you think. I swear, if you'll just listen—"

I pull myself together and rush past him, straight into his bedroom. I can't, I just can't. I'm throwing my few items of clothing into my bag when Marlena enters in after me.

"It's not as simple as any of that," she says quietly, wringing her hands. "He was twelve years old. His father ..."

Oh god. *Twelve years old.* Who *is* he? Who is this guy I've grown up around my whole life? The guy who watched over me from afar for so long. The guy who I slept with. Who I stupidly let myself fall in love with. My stomach twists violently. Suddenly I'm shoving past Luke's mom and running for the bathroom. My knees explode with pain as I fall to the floor and bring up everything I've eaten today. I throw up until my eyes are streaming tears.

I don't go back into Luke's room. I walk straight back into the kitchen and pick up my keys, ignoring Luke. He's still frozen to the spot, staring blindly at the shattered telephone on the floor. I bite back a sob when I see the endless sorrow in his eyes. He looks up at me finally—*pain, regret, anger, fear*—and that's my breaking point. I race out of the kitchen, out of the front door, fumbling with my keys before I eventually manage to get into Brandon's borrowed car and tear away.

THIRTY-SEVEN

HOME

I'VE NEVER been good at driving in snow. Ben, Brandon's employee at the auto mechanics, mentioned that he would put chains on the tires of our borrowed car if we brought it back in today, but we didn't get around to it. The wheels spin each time I slide through a corner at breakneck speeds. Through my tears I'm only vaguely aware of how close I come to rolling the vehicle.

My eyes are red raw by the time I reach Brandon's house. I park the truck and jump out, determined to lock myself in the one place I'm likely to feel safe in this godforsaken town: my old bedroom. But when I reach the front door, a police officer, a fresh-faced guy with the beginnings of a fuzzy mustache, blocks the way.

"Whoa, missy! You can't go in there."

"What?"

"Police investigation. We're carrying out a search warrant right now. You can't go in." He tucks his thumbs into his belt and rocks back on his heels, looking me up and down. "Hey, aren't you Maxwell Breslin's girl?"

I breathe through the urge to punch him square in the mouth and peer through the door past him, where more officers are tearing Brandon's house apart. "How long will you be?"

The young officer shrugs. "We just started, ma'am. Could take hours. Even then, you ain't gonna be allowed inside. Not until them federal agents have given the final say so."

Chloe Mathers emerges from Brandon's kitchen into the hallway and stops dead when she sees me. She holds spools of unraveled film in her latex gloved hands. It twists and curls down to the floor in eight-millimeter tentacles. She thrusts her hands out at another young officer fumbling to pull equipment from what looks like a fancy fishing tackle box. "Bag this. Label it *kitchen*." The young officer takes it and Chloe makes her way down the hallway towards me, her expression stoic. "Can't be here, Iris," she says stiffly. All of her warmth from earlier has vanished. However, the stern pull of her eyebrows softens a little when she looks at me properly. "Everything okay?"

Fighting back even more tears, I watch the police officer winding the film around and around, trying to tidy it up enough to get it into an evidence bag. "What is that?"

Chloe looks over her shoulder, tucking her cropped mousey brown hair behind her ear. "There's a lot of film here, darlin'. I'm sure there's nothing untoward on it, but we're finding it in the strangest of places. Gotta check it out. Where's Luke?"

A body-wide shiver slams through my body at the mention of his name. If I lose concentration, if I let it slip just for a second, I'm going to be a sobbing mess all over again. I can't do that in front of strangers. "He's at home."

"Don't you think you should get back there, sweetie? The roads are going to be impassable soon. Snow's coming down hard and fast." And it really is. The clouds overhead are loaded, pregnant-looking things, dirty gray and filled to bursting.

"I'm not staying there tonight," I tell Chloe. "I'm staying ..."

And I realize I only have one place left to go. One place I know my mother won't bother me, where I'll be able to lock myself away and not have to deal with Luke, the secrets, the uniforms pulling Brandon's life apart. "I'm staying up at the old place." Every single muscle in my body tightens at the prospect.

IT TAKES twenty-five minutes to drive out to my old family home. Despite being off the beaten track, tucked away down hair-pinning, twisting roads set back from the main town, it should normally only take half that time, but with the snow coming down thicker than ever, I have to take it slow. The beater's engine starts making a strange whistling, grinding sound about halfway there. I spend the latter half of the journey praying angrily that the thing holds out until I make it to the house. It does hold out, but only just. Steam billows from the hood as I park up outside the house where I grew up—it's difficult to tell whether the steam's just because the engine is hot or if there is something more sinister going on underneath the hood.

I glare hatefully at the rundown truck and then turn to the house. My chest squeezes painfully as a flood of memories surge over me—my dad clearing out the gutters; him shooting hoops with me around the side of the house where the steel ring is still bolted to the side of the building; my dad and I sitting in his old station wagon as he showed me how to operate a car for the first time. He'd promised to teach me properly when I was old enough, but of course that never happened. He'd died a horrible death, and a stranger in a Lexus had been paid to teach me how to drive. I pull out an all-too-familiar key, one I haven't used in over five years, suck in a deep breath, and walk up the driveway. The front door opens easily. I hurry inside, not wanting to loiter there. That single spot carries perhaps the most painful memory of all—Luke standing there in his uniform,

Chloe Mathers at his side, as he told my mother that my dad was dead.

Inside, the house is warm, and the upstairs landing is lit by a yellowing light. My throat swells so badly it feels like it's going to close off altogether. I know Brandon maintains the place well, keeps it clean and heated. The lights must be to deter would-be burglars, but I'm caught off guard by how *right* it feels here. Lived in. Like my dad is still sitting in his study, his old records hissing and scratching out sounds of old sixties music while he grades papers for school. I wander around the ground floor, a little stunned by the fact that everything is as it used to be. Caricature drawings of me and Dad are still pinned to the fridge; there's even one of Mom tacked up there, too, a huge shit-eating grin on her comically too-big mouth. Cooking utensils still hang from hooks over the oven, like someone still prepares food here. The TV remote still sits on the arm rest of Dad's favorite chair.

I trace my fingers over the buttons, not wanting to disturb it in case Dad was the last person to touch it. I know he probably wasn't. The police came through here and jacked everything up the same way they are doing over at Brandon's, but I can't help myself. The house is full of small reminders, each one bringing me back to him, bringing me closer to the ghost of my father.

Upstairs is even worse. My bedroom is still the bedroom of a fourteen-year-old girl. Band posters hang from the walls. Everything seems far too pink. I can't remember ever liking pink this much. I pull the comforter from my old four-poster bed and drag it down the hallway towards my dad's study.

The smell of old leather and musty books hits me with the force of freight train when I enter the room. Mom had removers pack up all her stuff when she left the house, but she clearly never had them pack up Dad's belongings. His study is a little jumbled, books out of place, papers strewn across his old mahogany desk, but other than that it's how I remember it. The battered old La-Z-Boy that he refused to throw out still sits in the corner by the window. The archaic projector he used to love watching home movies on remains hooked up, pointed at the blank, white wall at the far end of the room that he kept bare specifically for that purpose.

I dump my comforter onto the La-Z-Boy and pace the room, running my hands over the shelves and knick-knacks, the clay disasters I constructed in kindergarten that Dad clung to with such fierce price, the photos of him and my mother back when she used to smile and they seemed deliriously happy. I have no idea what changed to make that happiness disappear, but the looks on their young faces as they hold onto one another like nothing will ever tear them apart makes me unbelievably sad.

I desperately want to call Morgan then, just to have someone to talk to, to fill the silence in this empty, lonely house. My mother still has my cell phone, though. I pick up the phone on my dad's desk and I'm surprised when I hear a dial tone. Surprised and relieved. I punch in Morgan's number and sit down in my dad's old desk chair, pivoting from side to side as the line rings.

I'm terrible at sharing my problems. I have no experience with it all, no matter how hard Brandon tried to draw me out of my shell and discuss my issues when I went to live with him. I'm so lost in trying to figure out how I'm going to talk to Morgan about everything that's happened, is happening right now, that I don't realize how long the phone has been ringing out for. And then I get it. She's not going to pick up. I place the handset back in its cradle, staring at the grain of my dad's desk, numb and lost.

I'm alone.

I've never needed my dad more than I do right now. Just a hug, the sound of his voice, the smile on his face would be enough to fix everything. Then the idea hits me, and I grab hold of it with two hands. His projector.

I leap up from the chair and drop to my knees, focusing on the drawers to his desk. I know he kept his old reels in the larger bottom drawer, ordered neatly in rows with handwritten labels describing each one's contents. It was always locked unless he was in there. I used to sneak in here when I was small to try and watch them, but I could never find where he kept the key. Thankfully, when I pull on it, the drawer slides open noiselessly. But all the films are gone.

I feel hollow, like I've lost him all over again. Slumping back against the wall, my knees drawn up to my chin, I let a few tears slide down my face. Anger takes a hold in the pit of my stomach as I consider what could have happened to the films. The only conclusion I can come to is that Amanda must have thrown them away. I give her the benefit of the doubt for a moment, the judicious thing to do, but I know she wouldn't have thought twice about trashing them. In fact, she probably had a bonfire in the back yard and watched on with grim satisfaction, arms crossed, as the flames ate my childhood and all evidence of how wonderful and loving my father had been towards me. Most of the films featured Dad and me alone, after all. She was gone most of the time, fighting battles in court that kept her from participating in the role-plays and games she considered juvenile. Which they were, of course, but I *was* juvenile. I was a little girl, who wanted both of her parents to be around. To love her.

If Amanda really did burn those films, then I don't know what I'll do. I'm reckless enough at this point to fantasize about burning down her pristine brownstone, a justice in symmetry, but just as the flames are establishing themselves in my mind, another image comes to me. It's the young officer at Brandon's, winding those Super Eight films and placing them in the evidence bags. Of course. They would have taken my dad's films, too. They must have done. But they hadn't found anything on them, otherwise I would have heard about it. So where are they now? Where would they have put them?

I scramble to my feet and charge from room to room until I've exhausted every avenue. They're not in the kitchen, in the lounge, nor any of the bedrooms or the storage closets. I'm beginning to lose hope when I spot the door leading from the kitchen down into the basement, the basement where the indoor pool is located.

I was never supposed to go down there without an adult. It's funny how I still feel like I'm breaking the rules as I twist the round brass doorknob and jog down the stairs, my dad's voice warning me in the back of my head: *It's not safe to be down here without me or your mom, little monster.*

I throw the light switch; only the floor lights in each corner of the room flicker to life, casting a cold blue hue over the tiles, the walls, the ceiling. Another jolt of surprise relays though me when I see that the pool is still filled. I'd expected it to be empty, but instead a dark blue pool cover gently bobs on top of the water. At the far end of the room, in front of a wooden rack still complete with folded towels, are cardboard boxes stacked high. A spark of hope—have I found what I'm looking for? That spark of hope transforms into relief when I rush over and find that, yes, they're exactly what I'm looking for. I open the flaps on the box and my dad's blocky, neat writing greets me, taped to canister upon canister of film. I could literally cry tears of happiness right now.

I waste no time in lugging the first box back up the stairs, leaving the place lit in case I need to come back down for more. I have the projector switched on, prepped in under thirty seconds, and a random canister opened, the film threaded up just like my dad showed me when I was a kid. The old thing sputters into life, making a familiar, comforting, whirring sound as the film flies through the feeder. Images, stilted at first, develop on the far wall. My heart rises up into my throat.

My dad's smiling face grins out at me, laughing as he swats the camera away from him, the camera I'm holding. He reaches out and takes it from me.

"I'm not the star of the show, Monster. That's you. Come on, tell me the story again." The camera spins and suddenly I'm on the wall, eight or maybe nine years old me, missing two front teeth, hair tied into braids on either side of my head.

"Well," I say, tipping my head to one side. "It's about Icarus. He lived in a prison with his daddy."

"A prison?" my father asks, off screen.

"Yes, a prison." I screw up my face in concentration. "Kind of a maze, actually, a maze his daddy built, but they couldn't get out so it was a prison, too."

"Uhuh. And what happened in the maze?"

"Well, Icarus's daddy wanted to escape the prison, but he couldn't. There was water all around." I gesture wide with skinny arms, making my dad chuckle, the sound close to the camera. "And so one day, Icarus's daddy realized the only way to escape would be to fly away. He collected all the feathers he could find, and he made two pairs of wings."

"And how did he stick all the feathers together?"

"With wax! He used candle wax," I say.

"And what then?"

"He gave a pair to Icarus and kept a pair for himself. He flew away, but before he left he told Icarus to follow him. He said, "Don't fly too close to the sun, otherwise the wax will melt and all the feathers will fall off the wings!""

My dad laughs at me shaking my finger, pretending to be Daedalus, Icarus's father, warning him. "And what did Icarus do?"

"He flew too close to the sun, Papa!"

"Oh no!" he gasps. "Did the wax melt?"

I nod sagely. "Yep. He fell out of the sky. But he was okay in the end."

More laughter. The image shakes as my dad puts the camera down, and then it becomes stable again. He walks into frame and sits down beside me. He pulls me onto his lap, and I lay my head against his shoulder, the camera recording us now completely forgotten. "What do you think the story means, Iris?" he says softly.

"It means to always listen to your daddy," I reply confidently. This earns me a smile from my father, who gives me half a nod.

"Yeah, you should always do that, I guess. But what else?"

I frown, thinking hard. "That if you go too high, you have a long way to fall?"

"Uhuh. But I like to think of it like this. Icarus couldn't help flying so high. He was trapped in such a bad place for a very long time, and he was so happy when he was free that he just had to go up and up and up. He dreamed of big things, of touching the sky. He wanted to reach his goals so badly that he forgot what his daddy said."

"So I shouldn't have big dreams, Daddy?" My heartbeat thumps in my throat, my eyes furiously burning as I listen. The tender look in my father's eyes breaks me, breaks me so badly I don't think I'll ever be whole again.

"No, baby girl. I'm saying the exact opposite. You should always reach for your dreams."

"But won't I fall?"

He shakes his head. "That doesn't matter. Fly high, little Icarus. I'll always be there to catch you, I promise."

I'm sobbing by the time the film blisters and cuts out, the projector still chugging through the reel. I hurt so bad inside that I want to crawl into a ball and cry until I can't feel anything anymore. I know from experience that's not how this works, though. I'll still feel everything, all the pain and sorrow and misery, regardless of how many tears I shed.

I'll always be there to catch you, I promise. Except he's not here to catch me. Why would he say those words as he died? *Fly high, Icarus.* Why would that be his last message to me? The only thing I've been able to think of is that he wanted to tell me that he wasn't going to break his promise. That he was never going to leave me. Not really. And in some ways, he hasn't.

The opening chords of a song startles me from my tears. My head whips up. A new image that has taken shape on the wall.

It seems the film wasn't done, after all.

Luke. Luke with a much-too-big guitar balanced in his lap. He can't be more than eleven or twelve, I'm guessing. His hair is longer than I remember it, and there's a heavy, haunted look in his eyes. My dad walks around the camera and sits next to him, smiling. "Are you ready?" he says.

Luke looks up at him hesitantly, hands hovering over the guitar like he's worried to handle it. "I ... I don't know."

"Yeah, you do. Come on, I know you can do it. You've played it for me already." My dad's smile grows. "It doesn't matter if you make a mistake or two, Lucas. Making mistakes is part of learning. And I'm right here. I can help you."

My hands fly to my mouth. Luke cautiously peers down at the neck of the guitar, carefully placing his fingers over the frets. After one more hesitant look to my dad, he strums his other hand across the strings, pauses, reforms the shape of his fingers over the frets, and begins to play.

"Blackbird."

My dad taps out the rhythm with his foot, humming gently as Luke stumbles, then finds where he needs to be. Luke and my dad sing the lyrics together, and what was left of my heart fractures into tiny pieces.

I should have listened to Luke, heard what he wanted to tell me earlier in the kitchen, no matter how awful it was. I look at the twelve-year-old before me, and all I see is how much pain he's in. No matter what my mother says, I can never imagine that this poor, broken boy did anything malicious to anyone, sexually or otherwise. It doesn't matter that he didn't deny it. I just simply can't believe it. The scared little boy on the screen in front of me was learning to live again, and my father was trying to help him. My father was trying to help both of us—to give us both wings so that we could learn to fly. The wings he built for me, and the ones he wanted to fix for Luke. I turn the projector off and wrap myself up in the comforter in my dad's La-Z-Boy, and I cry myself to sleep.

THIRTY-EIGHT

ESCAPE, PART II

MY HEART slams against my ribcage with a fierce thud. It takes a moment for my head to clear, to figure out why I'm panicked. A sound, the sound that woke me, comes again, loud and clear: breaking glass. I scramble forward in the chair, kicking off the comforter, my ears straining to hear what's happening downstairs. More shattering. The sound of a heavy boot kicking against wood. My first thought is that it's Luke, come to try and talk to me, but the logical part of my brain is working faster than the conscious part. Why would he be smashing a window to get in?

Another heavy *thunk* from downstairs has me out of the chair and fumbling in my pockets for my phone. But I don't have it. Damn. I run three paces across the room and snatch up the landline, my heart racing even faster now. I dial Luke's cell phone and hurry to the window. There's a huge black SUV with tinted windows parked up behind the beater, blocking it in. In my sleep I didn't hear it approach.

The phone rings.

Rings.

Rings.

He doesn't pick up. "Come on, Luke. *Come on!*"

A strange whirring sound downstairs makes me freeze, statue-still, and my thumb hits the *end call* button. *Holy hell, what is that?* I tiptoe out into the hallway and lean over the handrail, holding my breath. The whirring grows louder, and I suddenly place the sound. It's the garbage disposal unit on the sink, churning, churning, churning.

Every single horror movie I've ever seen plays out in about ten seconds flat. I know with every part of me that I should *not* go downstairs. Instead, I clutch the cordless phone to my chest and soundlessly make my way down the hallway, creeping into the spare room. The walk-in closet beckons, but I don't make that mistake. I'll have nowhere to go if I shut myself away, and it's probably the first place someone would look. No, the reason I picked this room glints in the darkness behind the door, right where my dad left it. A baseball bat, for this specific purpose.

I wait behind the door, the handle of the bat growing slick from sweat in my hands, trying hard not to breathe too loud. Eventually I hear the sound I've been waiting for over the grunting and groaning of the garbage disposal: a creak in the stairs. Whoever's in the house is coming. *Shit, shit, shit.* I peer through the slim gap where the open door to the room meets the frame, squinting into the dim lighting to see if I can make out who it is.

A black head emerges like a specter, followed by black shoulders and a black torso—a person dressed entirely from head to toe in black, a ski mask covering their face. I bite down on my bottom lip, desperately trying to keep from breaking down into tears. The figure reaches the top of the stairs and pauses, head swiveling up and down the hallway, clearly trying to pick which room to enter. I see a flash of silver in the tall person's hand. I have to rail against the urge to make a dash for it when I realize it's a knife. A five-inch long, curved, wicked blade made for hunting, skinning, gutting. I hold my hand over my mouth, counting to five. Count to five and calm down, that's all I can think.

The figure moves stealthily to Dad's study, where light still pools out into the hallway. He disappears inside. I panic then; should I run down the stairs? Try and make it for the door? My legs are trembling, half ready to bolt of their own accord, when the cordless phone I'm still gripping hold of starts to ring.

"Shit!"

I drop the phone like it's stung me. I recoil into the corner of the room, fear taking hold, locking every single one of my joints frozen. The phone keeps ringing, echoing around the house from the other handsets dotted throughout the different rooms. But there's only one handset up here on the first floor. *And it's in here with me.* I clench hold of the baseball bat with both hands, holding it out in front of me.

Just breathe, Iris. Just breathe. It's going to be okay so long as you stay calm. My dad's voice is strong and confident inside my head. It's precisely what he would say. It's enough to help me edge forward so that I'm back behind the door again. The ringing is cut off by a loud beep downstairs. The answer machine.

"Ave? You there?" Morgan's voice fills the deadly silent house. "Ave? I'm assuming this is you given the Wyoming number and all. Anyway, I hope everything's okay with your uncle. I'm seriously hoping you're gonna be back by Thursday. I don't think I can handle the funeral without you. Sorry, I know that's really selfish, but still … Let me know how you're getting on. Love you."

The answer machine clicks off.

And a gloved black hand grasps hold of the door.

I'M LASHING out before I can even think properly. The baseball bat connects with wood and then with something softer. A loud "*uffff*" comes out of the figure as he staggers sideways, holding his arm, knife still gripped firmly in his hand, which gives me enough time to raise the bat over my shoulder and swing with all my might.

The white ash contacts with the side of the intruder's head. He drops to his knees, one hand on the floor supporting himself. I run, then. Run past the person who smashed their way into my house, heading for the stairs. A hand reaches out and grabs hold of my ankle, though, firm fingers digging into my skin, and I shriek.

I kick out, my shoe landing a solid hit against his shoulder. He spins and falls onto his back, letting me go. Bat still in hand, I charge down the stairs, racing for the kitchen. Broken glass carpets the floor. The back door hangs off one hinge. The thunder of footsteps behind me has me running again, and I don't think. I react, barreling out of the doorway into the night.

My breath blows in and out, in, out, short, sharp blasts of air over my teeth as I run faster than I've ever run before. Past the beater and the black SUV. Past Mrs. Harlow's abandoned house. My arms pump furiously, bat still in my right hand. I know it's stupid to look over my shoulder, but I can't help it. I have to know. I throw a glance behind me. My attacker is charging out of the house, barely twenty feet away. And he can run.

The snow that's been falling heavily all day coats everything—the driveway, the trees that surround the house, the road beyond, everything. The world is white and gray and black as I run blindly, veering left and then right, hoping to gain some cover in the trees. They're spindly and bare, however, and do nothing but get in the way. I have to get back onto the road. I have to make my way down on the highway that leads back into Breakwater proper. I'll be safe if I can do that. I dodge more trees and lift my knees up as the snow gets deeper. It sets like concrete around my lower body every time I try to push forward.

The bat is just getting in the way now. I let it go, praying to god that I'll be okay without it. That I won't need it again. That I can get away from this crazy person and make it back to civilization before I'm stabbed to death. I reach the small roadway leading away from the house. My lungs are on fire. Luke. I have to get to Luke. I run faster, an agonizing burn surging through my legs each time I force them forward.

And then suddenly my legs are no longer beneath me. Fire sings through my nerve endings, a high-pitched chatter of pain that blinds me. I'm falling, crumpling in a heap into the snow. I can't stop shaking. My back contorts, my body balking against the alien, frightening, painful sensation coursing through it. A low and fast *tick, tick, tick, tick, tick* sound fills my ears. After that, all I hear is the creaking and crunching of boots slowly approaching through the snow. And then blackness.

THIRTY-NINE

PLEASE TRY AGAIN LATER

LUKE

MY MOM won't stop crying. She won't stop crying, and I can't fucking think straight. "This isn't fair. I have half a mind to call Amanda St. French and ask her what the hell she thinks she's doing, still spreading rumors about you after all these damn years. The police cleared you. *She has no right.*"

I've never seen her this mad. "Calm down, okay. This is my fault. I should have told Avery sooner."

My mom's shaking her head before I can finish speaking. She throws the plate she's washing into the sink, water and soap suds erupting everywhere. "Do *not* say that this is your fault, Luke. It is not your fault. You did nothing wrong."

I bury my face in my hands, breathing deeply. "Yeah. Well. Avery's mom is a prosecutor. She's programmed to believe everyone's guilty, no matter what. I could ace a lie detector test and she'd still think I'm lying."

Mom turns to face me, one hand on her hip. Her facial expression is slack; she looks like she's in shock. Eleven years on, and she still can't deal with this. Neither can I. "You need to go after her, baby. She doesn't have the full story. I can't bear to think she's out there, thinking ill of you."

"I won't be able to change that, Mom. Even if I do tell her the truth, what's to say she's going to believe me? She might be like her mom."

"You really think that poor girl is anything like her mother?"

When it's put like that, the answer is obvious. No. No, of course she's not. Avery and Amanda couldn't be any more different. "She just needs time. Maybe I ought to give her some space."

"Time is the last thing she needs, Luke!"

"And the last thing *I* need is you shouting at me."

She leans against the counter, her shoulders curving in on her body. She starts crying again. "Oh, lord. I'm so sorry, baby. This just … I'm your mother. I'm supposed to protect you, and there's nothing I can do about this."

I get up and hug her. She's shaking in my arms, so distraught that she doesn't notice when Emma walks into the kitchen. My sister takes in the scene, cheeks flushed from the cold outside, jacket still zipped up underneath her chin. "What's going on?"

Mom jumps, wiping her face with the backs of her hands. "Nothing, sweetheart. Avery and Luke just had a little misunderstanding. I'm trying to convince him to go look for her."

Emma walks straight up to me and punches me on the arm. "First girl you bring home since the super bitch and you've already managed to screw things up? What's wrong with you?"

"I know. I'm a jerk." I don't feel like telling her what this is really about. Emma hates talking about what happened with me as much as I do. She scowls at me, throwing her purse down onto the kitchen table.

"Well, you'd better fix it, okay? I like Avery. And Mom's right. You have to go look for her."

When the Reid women gang up on you, you know about it. "All right, all right. I'll … I'll head on over to Brandon's place. She must be there."

Emma shakes her head. "Can't be. I just drove by there on the way back from the hospital and there's a police cordon around the whole place. They're conducting a search or something. I had to take the long way around Bleeker."

My mom places a hand on her chest, looking worried. "Then where can she have gone? It's not as though she's got friends here or anything." I give her a dirty look. It's true, but she doesn't need to put it so bluntly.

"Wouldn't she have just gone back to her parents' old place?" Emma asks.

The possibility of that happening is pretty low. "I doubt it. She hates it up there."

"Just call up to the house. You never know, right?" Mom's handing me her cell phone—she has the number stored. When I was up there recently, searching for Max's diary, she called me a couple of times to the Breslin's landline. Cell reception up there is patchy at best; it was the only way she could get hold of me.

The phone is silent as I hold it to my ear. I can hear my heart bang, bang, banging in my chest as I wait for the line to start buzzing. It doesn't, though. *"We're sorry, but the number you're trying to reach is currently out of service. Please try again later."*

"Weird."

"What is it?" My mom looks like she's ready to have a nervous breakdown. I'm only a few seconds behind her.

"The line's down. It can't have been canceled. You used it only a week ago, right?"

Mom nods. "Perhaps the snow's causing problems?"

"Maybe." I have this awful, sinking feeling in my gut, though. Something's not right. Even if it is the snow causing havoc with the lines, that means Avery's probably snowed in.

306

"Mom, give me your keys. I'm going up there." Avery took the car Brandon's assistant loaned us, and besides, the family Jeep is a four-wheel drive. Mom hands the keys over, her forehead wrinkled into countless lines.

"Be careful, okay, baby? I have a bad feeling about all of this. Drive carefully. And bring her home with you, you hear?"

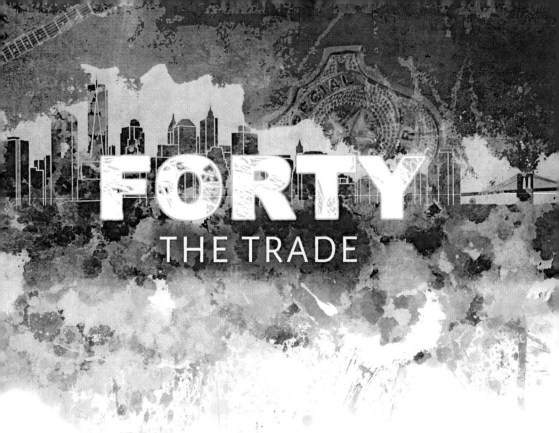

FORTY
THE TRADE

HUMMING.

The sound of lapping water.

A familiar whirring.

My head is killing me. I struggle to open my eyes, instinct telling me that I need more than my sense of hearing right now. Burning pain sears through my head as I manage to crack my eyelids, the light flaring into blinding brightness and then dulling a little. Not enough for the pain throbbing behind my eyes to dissipate, but enough to allow me to see.

I'm strapped to a chair. And I'm in the basement. The pool cover has been removed and the water throws marbling reflections of light up onto the ceiling and the walls. My father's projector sits on top of a wooden chair—one of the breakfast bar stools from the kitchen. The projector's switched on, but there's no film loaded. A solid plain white square is the only thing displayed on the wall at the opposite end of the room.

I spin around, but I'm alone.

Terror rips through me then. Whoever tied me to the chair has left me down here, with god knows what in mind, and I have no means of getting away. The bindings tying me to the chair are strong and tight. I tug against them but the effort is wasted.

"I'd save my energy if I were you," a low voice echoes off the walls. It's twisted at first, strange in my ears, until I work out that it's being distorted somehow. Leather boots complain as someone, my attacker, makes their way down the stairs into the basement. My body seizes as they walk slowly towards me, face and body still entirely covered.

"What are you doing?" I hiss, paralyzed by panic.

The figure holds a small black box to his mouth and presses a button. "Is this where we cue the stupid questions?"

I don't answer. The figure doesn't say anything else. He paces carefully to the projector where he opens up an old film canister, not one of my dad's, and threads the film into the feeder. He works in silence, cueing everything up until the job is complete.

"I have a video of your father that you probably haven't seen yet," he tells me, speaking into the voice distorter. "I thought we could watch together."

I yank on the restraints pinning my hands behind my back, locking them to the chair. It feels like a zip tie, the plastic cutting into my skin. The figure stalks towards me and strikes me across the face with his gloved hand.

My cheek stings with the force of the slap. Tears spring to my eyes. I've always thought I would be more defiant in a situation like this, but the reality of being held captive, fearing for your life, is terrifying. I can do nothing but whimper. The man in black returns to the projector and picks up his voice distorter again. "I told you not to bother, didn't I?" He doesn't say anything else. He sets the film rolling, and suddenly my father's face is on the back wall of the basement. His eyes are filled with tears, and his lower lip is bleeding. A sinking stone of dread pulls at my insides.

"What … what is this?"

The man in black strides toward me quickly and grabs a handful of my hair, forcing me to look up at my dad. "Watch," he growls into the voice distorter. And I have to. Dad's eyes are bright, like someone's shining a light into them. A male voice off screen begins to speak.

"You're a very lucky man, Max. Do you consider yourself a lucky man?"

My father swallows. "Most of the time." His voice shakes.

"Only most of the time? You have a beautiful wife, a beautiful daughter. A good job. You're respected in the community. You're a goddamned saint, in fact. Isn't that so?"

"I suppose so," he says softly. He sounds uncertain, like he doesn't know if he's saying the wrong thing.

"So what makes you think you're lucky only most of the time?"

"Well, I wouldn't be *here* if I were lucky all the time," he breathes out, his voice hitching.

A person off screen huffs out a burst of laughter. "Your presence here today is very lucky, Max. You just don't understand why yet." The sound of boots grinding on concrete fills the basement. Dad's eyes flicker to the left. Someone is moving around him. "Do you want me to explain why I say that, Max?"

"Ye—yes."

"Okay, then. I will. Here's how it is. A hand appears on screen in front of my father's face. In it is a rectangular piece of paper. I can't see what's on it, but my father does. He lets out a pained cry, his face crumpling into tears.

"No! No, don't. Please! *Please!*" he begs. The hand spins the piece of paper over and I see that it's not a piece of paper but a photograph. Of me. Fourteen-year-old me, smiling out of the glossy image. My stomach rolls.

"You see, Max. One of our own wanted your little girl to be sitting where you're sitting right now. But you're a special case.

Your holier-than-thou, virtuous personality has rubbed quite a few of us up the wrong way, see. We voted on it, and we decided that you should be given an opportunity here."

"Adam, please," my father whispers. "Please don't do this."

Adam? *Adam?* Like the movement of an old pocket watch, the gears and cogs of my mind begin to turn. He's talking to Adam Bright. Mayor Bright's brother, Breakwater High's basketball coach, Maggie's father ... he is the person threatening my dad? The man in black pinches hold of the back of my neck, digging his fingers deeper into my skin. I wince, staring at the video unfolding before my eyes. Adam moves into the shot fully as he leans forward and punches my dad in the jaw, hard. Dad rocks back with such force that I cry out. Adam remains on screen now, a familiar face, a man I'd known since I was born.

"So, this is your opportunity, Maxwell Breslin. You're being given a choice. You can take your daughter's place. You can remain a sanctimonious asshole and kill yourself with this," he produces a gun from the back of his waistband, shoving it into Dad's face so he can see every gleaming black inch of it, "or you can let your daughter be our sacrifice. What d'you say, Max? Are you willing to make the trade?"

Oh, god.

Oh please god no.

The trade.

"*NO!*" I scream so loud it feels like my vocal chords are tearing in half. No. No, no, no! This is what my father had meant—this is the trade he made. My life for his. He died to save me. Bile burns the back of my throat, my eyes filling with tears. My father's shoulders sag. He exhales heavily, and then leans forward and spits blood onto the floor.

"I'll do it. I'll kill myself."

Adam turns to the camera, a hundred-watt smile grinning right out at me, a specter from the past. "You heard the man, Jeff. He's making the trade." Adam seems over the moon that my father has agreed to his sick ultimatum. Jefferson Kyle, one of the other men my father was accused of killing, speaks, his body out of sight.

"Wouldn't gloat too much, Adam," he snaps. "You know Chloe's gonna be pissed about this. She has her heart set on the Breslin girl."

It takes a solid three seconds for the words to compute. The name that Jeff says so casually. *Chloe.*

Icy cold fingers of alarm grip hold of me. No. No, how can that be? But sure enough, when I jerk my head back to look at the person digging their fingertips into the back of my neck, the ski mask has been removed and Chloe Mathers is staring down at me.

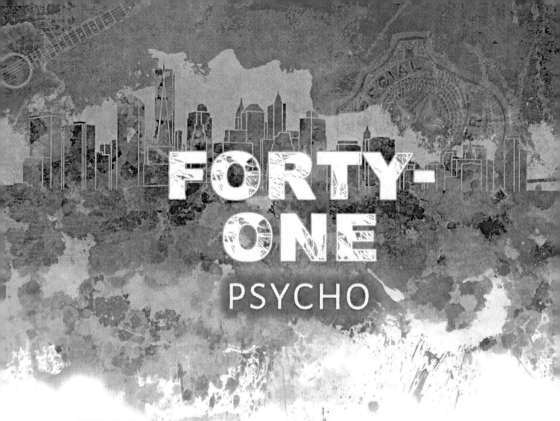

FORTY-ONE
PSYCHO

CHLOE HOLDS a Taser in her hand, pressing the trigger so that an arc of electricity fires between the two conductors. The expression on her face is deadpan, completely flat.

"The boys had no right to make that deal," she says evenly. "It was my turn. I was supposed to get to pick who and how, but no. They switched everything out, picked your dad up while I was working. That wasn't fair. That wasn't how it was supposed to work." I'm too stunned by the news that Chloe is involved in this, *is a killer*, to say anything. She seems content enough that her captive audience is listening, anyway. "I only got to plan two. Jeff planned three. Sam planned three. Adam got to do *seven*. Psychopath," she spits. "He chased those girls around with a blunt machete. What was so smart about that? He thought he was fucking Picasso." She drags her hands back through her cropped hair, inhaling a huge breath. She seems to calm down a little.

"There's nothing clever or beautiful about drowning some-one or setting them on fire, either. That just makes a mess. Everything should be neat and tidy. Yes, that's right, neat and tidy. You can appreciate that, I know you do." She paces up and down along the edge of the pool, scratching at the same spot on her head over and over. Suddenly she turns and pins me under a fierce gaze. "You have to treat them kindly. Make them look pretty. Brush their hair." She stands directly in front of me and reaches out, her hand trembling. She brushes a lock of my hair out of my face. The reverence behind the action betrays a disturbing darkness. "You have such pretty hair," she whispers.

I immediately start strategizing, trying to figure out how I'm going to get myself out of this situation. Because this situation is grade A fucked. Chloe crouches down, staring straight at me. I get the feeling she's not really seeing me, though. "You looked just like her back then. Now, well, your coloring's a bit darker, yes, but I think that's okay. It'll still count. She would have looked like you now, just like you looked like her then. Does that make sense?"

Horror is my new best friend. I shiver, kicking myself when I remember Chloe plucking the hair from my jacket back at the station when she invited us for dinner yesterday. Such an innocent gesture then that is creepy as hell now. Chloe stands up, rocking back on her heels, looking me over.

"I'll let you watch the rest of the video, and then we can get on with it."

"No! I don't want to see!" I scream. I lash out with my feet, trying to kick her, but she's out of reach. My shouting flicks a switch in Chloe's demeanor. She lunges towards me, brandishing the Taser, and presses it into my neck. I see stars for the second time—this is how she brought me down outside. I'm retching when she removes the conductors from my skin.

"Shut your mouth, you silly little bitch." Chloe leans forward so that her face is inches from mine. "You're ruining everything. This is all your fault, you know. Your dad would still be alive and I wouldn't have gotten angry and killed the others, either, if it wasn't for you. Everything got so messy." She shifts, coming even closer. "All your fault," she spits. Her furious expression vanishes, a sudden void taking over. She straightens up. "But maybe you're right, though. We don't want to see all that mess again. And we've waited long enough."

Chloe goes into her pocket and draws out a slim, black box. My heart starts hammering again. She mentioned Adam's machete, and then drowning and fire, so that means ... that means her method of killing was poisoning. *Is* poisoning. *Strychnine. It's a convulsant. Both girls asphyxiated. These were the two last killings before they stopped altogether, and they were also the only ones with the fourth symbol on their palms.* Luke's words come back to me, unwelcome and terrifying. Chloe opens up the box in her hands; a syringe lies within, alongside a small vial of clear liquid. She removes both items from the foam protector and pops the cap off the syringe.

"If you're a good girl, I'll make you look pretty afterwards, okay?" She sinks the needle into the small vial, adept and practiced, and I let rip. No sense in holding back now.

"HELP! SOMEBODY HELP ME!"

Chloe looks unimpressed. My shouting wouldn't bother her at all if it weren't for the sudden rumbling overhead. I know that sound well, used to listen for it nearly every weeknight when I was waiting for Dad to come home from work. A car has just pulled up outside the house. There's someone here, someone who might actually hear me hollering.

"HELP!"

"What the hell?" Chloe sets the syringe down and rushes to the stairs, staring up them into the kitchen above. The kitchen door must still be off its hinges, and there are lights blaring out into the darkness. Whoever is up there will definitely know something's up if they take the time to walk around the back of the house. A car door slams above us. Chloe runs back to the stool that the projector sits on, snatching up the sharp hunting knife she was carrying earlier.

"Be quiet," she snaps, pointing the knife at me. "If you make a sound, I'll kill whoever's up there. Don't think I won't." I don't doubt that she's mad enough to follow through with her threat. It takes every scrap of will power I own to keep my mouth closed. I sit, listening intensely and praying. I've never prayed so hard or so much in my entire life.

I'm holding my breath again, when I hear a voice upstairs. "Ave? Avery, are you here?" It's Luke. I let my head fall forward, my chin pressing into my chest, and I start crying.

Chloe tugs off her loose black shirt to reveal her police uniform underneath. She tucks the knife into her waistband and shoots me a warning glare. "I'll kill him," she hisses, and then she's off up the stairs. "Luke!" she calls. "It's Chloe! We got a break-in call 'bout half an hour ago, but there's no one here!"

Clever bitch.

"Chloe? Avery tried calling me, too. When I rang back, the line was dead."

Chloe cut the line? Relief and horror races through me. If she hadn't done that, Luke probably wouldn't have come. But now that he's here, he's in very grave danger. I need to see up the stairs into the kitchen. I need to see what the hell is going on. I shuffle my feet as far forward as I can, a mere two inches from the chair legs, and shunt myself forward. The chair makes a scraping against the tiles, and my heart explodes in my chest. She said not to make a sound, and that definitely qualified. I sure as shit don't want to die, but my need to keep Luke safe outweighs my own desire for self-preservation. I don't try it again. Instead, I lean as far forward as I can, bending double at the waist. From that position, I can see a bolt of yellow light up in the kitchen—along with a pair of black police issue boots and a pair of scruffy Chuck Taylors with the bottom of wet jeans cuffed up around them.

"Was the door like that when you got here?" Luke asks. He sounds perplexed, worried. Panic tinges his voice, although I can tell he's trying to rein it in.

"Yeah, there were footprints in the snow. Signs of a struggle.

Did anyone know she was up here alone?" Chloe asks.

Only you, you crazy bitch! I pull on the zip ties binding my hands behind my back but there's barely any point. Chloe has had years of practice in making sure people don't escape from these things. I'm not going anywhere.

"No. No, *I* didn't even know until she called from here," Luke says softly. "We … we had a fight."

Silence fills the kitchen. And then, "She find out about your dad?"

"No." Luke lets out a long, heavy sigh. His feet turn around and then turn back again. I can picture the look on his face as he anxiously surveys the kitchen. "I was going to tell her, but …"

"S'okay, I understand. No sense in adding another body to the list, right?"

"It's not that. I just—" he breaks off abruptly. "The dead should stay dead." He pauses. One breath. Two. There's an edge to his voice when he asks, "Why were you in the basement?"

Chloe takes a step backward. A pulse of adrenalin floods through my body. This is it. He's figured something out. He knows. Is she going to kill him? The world tips sideways.

"Lights were on down there. Don't think anyone's been down there, though."

More silence. *Oh, come on, Luke! Work it out, work it out!* I screw my eyes shut, holding my breath, waiting, praying, hoping that everything snaps together inside his head and he rushes down the stairs. But he doesn't.

"Okay, I'll run a sweep upstairs. You take the downstairs?" Luke says, his voice firm. Determined. Like his confidence has been bolstered now that he thinks he's got help. That Chloe is his backup and not the psychotic bitch who orchestrated this whole thing. My hopes plummet when Chloe agrees.

"Sure thing. Holler if you find anything."

Luke's Chucks squeak as he turns and leaves the kitchen. I

hear him racing up the stairs, calling out my name. I want to scream out for him, but by the time he reaches me, even if he hears me two floors down, Chloe will have charged down here and slit my throat. I keep quiet. I've bitten my lip so hard, my mouth is now full of blood. Chloe's boots pause at the top of the stairs before she hurries back down into the basement, the knife back in her hand. She looks crazy. Crazier than before.

"We don't have time for pleasantries anymore, Miss Breslin. I'm afraid we're going to have to rush through procedures. I hope you don't mind."

"You can't be serious? You can't honestly think you're going to be able to kill me and get away with it when Luke's upstairs?"

A twisted smile develops on Chloe's face. She calmly walks to the small stool where she left her syringe and the poison and carefully withdraws the needle again. "Luke isn't the brightest of boys, Iris. He's been spending more time singing in bars than he has concentrating on his work recently, or so I hear. And this will only take a second. Besides, it's about time I received some recognition for my work."

Bile bubbles in my throat. Recognition for her work? Luke's words replay in my mind, and I finally realize that I'm doomed. *Serial killers usually want to get caught. Typically they're proud of their handiwork. They want to claim responsibility in the end.*

"You left that video at the station, didn't you? The one the FBI were looking into?" I rasp.

"Of course I did. I had to. Fucking Mayor Bright and his fucking book. The great Breakwater tell-all, the grand exposé on what really happened to all those poor, murdered girls. It's all bullshit. That was *me*. Me and the boys. Why should I let Max take the credit?"

"But you let my father take the blame for *them*. You let him take the blame for Jeff and Adam and Sam's deaths."

Chloe shrugs one shoulder, staring blankly at me. "Well, that was just too tidy to overlook. And I was still pissed at the time. Now, things are different. And I have to finish what we started." Chloe paces forward, a small smirk playing over her lips, and goose bumps burst out over my skin. There's no point in keeping quiet now. I tug with all my might against the zip ties, the narrow plastic biting angrily into my skin, and I scream.

"Luke! In the basement! *LUKE!*"

Chloe tuts, standing right in front of me. "Pathetic. Really pathetic." She roughly pulls up the sleeve on my shirt, exposing my arm. I try to shy away from her touch but there is nowhere for me to go. She brings the tip of the needle to my arm, bending in concentration as she searches for a vein. And that's when I notice Luke running down the stairs behind her.

"Chloe, what the fuck! Chloe, no!" My eyes meet his—the emotions pouring out of him are overwhelming. Fear. Panic. Anger. His terror hits me hard. The situation looks bad. He doesn't think he's going to reach me in time. And he doesn't.

The sharp burn of the needle tears through me, forcing its way upwards, cold and unstoppable. The pain that follows is worse. Far, far worse. It's instant, like a bomb going off inside my head. The crippling sensation spreads through me, polluting me. An uncontrollable trembling follows behind it. Luke crashes into Chloe, sending her sideways and ripping at the needle, tearing my skin. Their bodies hit the ground hard, but the needle remains hanging out of my arm. I watch as Luke reaches back and swings, punching Chloe in the face as hard as he can. The utter despair on his face destroys me. I'm not worrying about his despair for long, though. I'm worrying about my own. My head snaps back as every single muscle in my body tightens. I start convulsing. The spasms wracking through my body are so strong I can hardly breathe. The force pushing down on my body refuses to let my diaphragm contract enough to pull in a single draw of oxygen.

My eyes roll back into my head. Another kind of pain lances through my body as something hits my thigh. Instead of a spiraling, deep pain, this new pain is a bright stinging, burning pain, radiating up my leg. A terrifying scream builds inside me, but I have no means of letting it out. My body is now convulsing so hard that I can feel where the zip ties have cut all the way through my skin, the wet sensation of my blood running over my hands and dripping from my fingers.

A loud, echoing bang fills the basement, alongside Luke's desperate shouts. The chair I'm sitting on takes a heavy impact. I want to open my eyes to see what's going on, but I can't. My body is no longer my own; it won't respond to my will. A pressure starts to build in my chest, my heart laboring, beating way too fast. The pressure builds, builds, builds until my heart pauses and then hiccups in my ribcage, beating once really hard and then racing away again. The pressure starts rising again. I know the poison is doing its work, tightening its chokehold around my vital organs so they can no longer function. I don't have long left.

Another huge impact rocks the chair beneath me, more shouts and screams ringing off the tiled walls of the basement, and the world starts to tip all over again. But this time it's real. The sickening sensation of the ground reaching up for me floods my stomach, and suddenly I'm back in my room in my apartment. I'm falling backwards onto my bed, and Luke is standing over me. He's laughing as I squeal, and I'm laughing, too. I'm safe, I'm warm, I'm protected. My bed cushions my fall, softening my landing, and for a moment everything is normal as Luke looks down on me, smiling, warmth and adoration in his eyes.

"Love you," he whispers.

I smile back. When I open my mouth, words forming on my lips, water fills my mouth. Cold, rushing, persistent. I can't figure out why water would be rushing into my mouth, but I make sure I finish telling him how I feel. Somehow, I know this is the last time I'll be able to.

"I love you, too, Luke. I really do. And I'm so sorry."

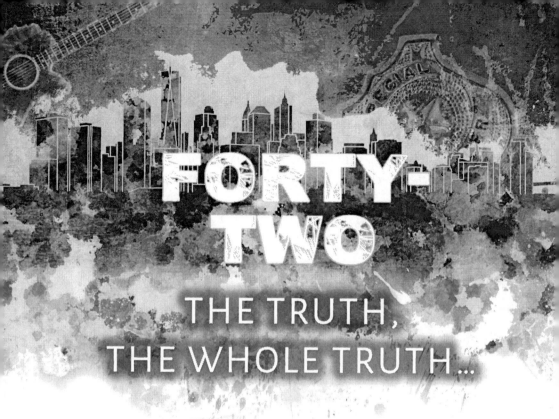

FORTY-TWO

THE TRUTH, THE WHOLE TRUTH...

MY EXISTENCE is a dream. Time has no real meaning. I drift and fade from a world where everything is too bright, too loud, into something less tangible, something less painful, until I can't really tell the difference between what's real and what isn't anymore. The beeping sound at my head is the only means of counting time. Eventually, I don't even notice the beeping. Sometimes a rough hand in mine brings me back to the soft bed I lie in. Sometimes it's gentle words from familiar voices that tempt me back into my body. For a long time, the pain of returning is just too much to bear and so I flee from it, preferring the abyssal peace of the dark places inside my mind. It's comforting there.

But I can only hide for so long. My body wants me back, wants me to move, to confront the pain so I can heal. No matter how hard I try to ignore it, it becomes more persistent each day. And then, one day, I don't have a choice anymore.

I wake up.

"Avery? Look, she's waking up. Somebody get a nurse."

A throbbing ache punches through my head as I open my eyes. Everything is white for a second as my eyes struggle to focus, remembering how to process colors and shapes. And then Morgan is sitting on the edge of my bed, brushing her hand slowly up and down my arm. Her lip is wobbling like crazy as tears race down her face.

"Morgan?" My throat feels like someone took a sandblaster to it. I wheeze painfully, and Morgan reaches forward to help me sip some water out of a white ridged, plastic cup. I choke on most of it, but the water feels good running down my skin, pooling at the hollow of my throat.

"Oh my god, Ave. I never thought you'd come back. I never thought—" Her voice catches and she can't speak anymore. Her face crumples into a half smile, half grimace. She leans forward and buries her face into my hair, hugging me tight. The pressure of her skin against mine hurts like crazy.

"Morgan? Morgan, I can't ... breathe."

She lets go immediately. "Oh, sorry. I just ... I can't ..." She starts crying and shaking her head, holding her hands up to hide her face. I reach up and brush my fingers against the back of her hand, and the effort of the movement nearly kills me. She pulls in a deep breath. "I'm sorry." She sniffs, wiping her face with the sleeve of her black shirt. "Your uncle's here." Her voice is still wobbly. "He ran to get the nurse. He's gonna be right back, Ave. We've all been so worried."

I finally take a look around and notice my surroundings. Light pours in through a huge window, revealing mountains beyond. To my left, an IV bag drips at regular intervals, while a heart monitor maps out the fragile perseverance of my heart. Everything smells of bleach. The sheets on the bed I'm lying in are starched within an inch of their lives. I'm in hospital, in Wyoming by the looks of things.

"What ... what happened?"

A torn look flashes across Morgan's face. "I'm not supposed

to tell you anything until you remember, but fuck that. Are you sure you want to know?" The last thing I recall is a sinking, falling feeling, and then an unbearable pain pulling me into a forever darkness. I nod my head.

"I need to hear it."

"You were drugged by that insane police woman. Luke found you. He attacked her. Both he and you got shot in the process. You fell into the pool, but Luke managed to knock that bitch out. He jumped in to save you. He gave you CPR for forty-three minutes until the ambulance could get to you through the snow. He nearly bled out and died, Ave."

Tears blind me halfway through Morgan's brief description of what I'd believed were going to be the last minutes of my life. So I'd fallen into the pool. That explains why it had felt like my mouth was filling with water—because it actually had been.

Luke had been shot trying to save me. He nearly died defending me, giving me CPR while his own life blood seeped out of him. I suddenly feel sick.

"Where was he shot?" I whisper.

Morgan's smile fades a little. "In the chest. The bullet punctured his lung and shattered. Three different pieces of shrapnel lodged inside his chest cavity. He had two operations, one to remove the shrapnel and then another when he coded later on. They didn't know what was wrong until they went back in and realized they'd missed a piece and it was pressing down on his aorta. He nearly died all over again, but he pulled through. You're so alike, Ave. You're both fighters."

My first reaction is to try and sit up. It hurts like hell, though. The room spins.

"Whoa, girl, where d'you think you're going?"

"I need to see him, Morgan. I need to see with my own two eyes that he's okay. What room is he in?"

She shakes her head, pressing her palm against my shoulder, forcing me back into the bed. "He's not in any of the rooms, Ave. He was checked out of hospital three weeks ago. He's still recovering, but he's up and walking around just fine now."

"Three weeks?" That information just won't compute. Won't make any sense inside my head. "How long have I been out for?"

Morgan pulls up one shoulder, looking a little sheepish. "Not long, babe. Only seven weeks."

My mouth hangs open. I've been unconscious for seven weeks? I'm no doctor but even I know this is a miracle. I should never have woken up after such a long time. I should be dead. I stare down at my bed sheet, feeling awful. "I missed Tate's funeral."

"Yeah," Morgan smiles at me sadly. "It's okay, though. I'm sure he knows you would have been there if you could have been." I squeeze her hand, hating that she's trying to comfort me when I should have been there to support her.

"I'm sorry, Morgan. You had to go through that on your own—"

She shushes me, squeezing my hand back. "It's okay. My mom actually came with me. She's … she's been surprisingly good." That's unexpected news. Maybe bridges are starting to be built there. "The cops actually arrested the person responsible for the drugs." Morgan continues cautiously. "Leslie's been remanded until her court date later on in the month. They're trying to charge her with manslaughter."

"*Leslie?* My *roommate* Leslie?"

"I know. I didn't want to tell you. I just didn't want to have to deal with it at the time. I'm sorry."

I had been way off base about Noah, then. "So she's a *drug dealer?*"

Morgan nods, yes. "She wanted to show her parents she was capable of earning her own way. She wanted to leave college with more money than when she started. Figured selling pills was an easy, lucrative way to do that. She knowingly bought pills that were cut with goodness knows what."

"My god. I had absolutely no idea."

324

Morgan just shrugs. "You were shot in the leg in case you were wondering. And the quacks thought you'd suffered major brain damage from lack of oxygen to the brain. They told your uncle that the kindest thing to do would be to take you off life support, that you weren't going to come back and if you did you were gonna be a vegetable. But Luke wouldn't even let them talk about it. He punched a doctor and got banned from the hospital for a week. He groveled until they eventually let him back in."

I trace my fingertips over the bump in the sheets that is my right thigh, feeling a twinge of discomfort when I try to flex my toes. Shot in the leg. That's what that secondary pain had been. I close my eyes, taking a deep breath. I feel like I'm on the brink of losing it. "I need to see him, Morgan. Right now. Where is he?"

"I'm right here," a soft voice answers me. I open my eyes and Luke is standing in the doorway, his left arm bound against his body in a sling. As always he's wearing a black t-shirt and faded-out jeans, but there are dark shadows under his eyes. They tell stories of countless nights of lost sleep, of anxiety and worry. He looks like the broken little boy my father had taught to play "Blackbird." My heart breaks a little for the lost, haunted look he wears. "You woke up," he states. His voice is flat, expressionless. I nod my head.

"Been a while, I hear."

Luke doesn't say anything. He just stares at me. Morgan clears her throat. "I think I'm going to go see where Brandon's got to. A girl wakes up from a coma, you expect the nurses to come running, right? Sheesh." She stands and ducks past Luke, who doesn't move an inch when she sidles past him through the doorway.

"Are you okay?" I whisper. It's a dumb question; I can tell just from looking at him that he's far from okay. He blinks, and the action seems to wake him from his trance. He steps into the room and pauses, looking behind him before he closes the door softly. He paces towards the bed and stares down at my hands clasped in my lap.

"I would have killed her. I wanted to, but I couldn't leave you. If I stopped pressing down on your chest, you would have been gone forever. I kept going, Ave. I kept going." His eyes are filled with tears. I reach out and take his right hand, hanging limply at his side, and pull it to my cheek. He is so cold. I can smell cigarettes on him, and I know he's been smoking.

"I'm so sorry. I'm so sorry I ran out on you." I promised him I wouldn't. He told me twice that I would hightail it the second I found out about his past, and after everything I'd said in return he'd been right. I'd done exactly that. I'm disgusted with myself as I press the back of his hand against my forehead. His fingers twitch, wanting to curl around mine, but they don't. I think he's too numb to do anything but stand there and let me touch him. "Will you forgive me, Luke? Please say you'll forgive me?"

A strangled sound comes out of his throat as he sinks down and sits on the edge of my bed. "You have nothing to be sorry for, Ave. You still don't know what happened back when I was a kid. I should have been honest with you when we started all of this. That would have been the right way to do things." He smiles a sad smile. "Why's the right way always the scariest, huh?"

I'm too overwhelmed to answer. I wait with bated breath to see what he'll say next. Whether he'll tell me that he's happy I'm okay, but he really should be getting back to New York. That I screwed everything up and it's too late for us. He clears his throat, and I prepare myself for the worst. He doesn't say what I expect him to, though.

"If anything, I'm the one who should be sorry."

"What?" I can't keep the surprise from my face. Luke holds a hand up to stop me before I can start speaking.

"I should have figured it all out. Chloe would never have been able to get close to you if I'd realized she was involved in this whole thing."

"You couldn't have known, Luke. How could you? She's a cop, for crying out loud. She knew exactly what to do and what not to do to stay under the radar."

"She bragged about that," Luke admits. A look of pure bewilderment crosses over his face. "She told us everything. They worked together, the four of them, each took it in turns to kill whoever they felt like killing. Chloe knew the four different signatures would throw us off. She fed the others information about our investigation. Made sure we never got too close."

The one question that has been bothering me since Chloe pulled the ski mask off her head and revealed herself back in the basement forces its way out of my mouth. "I just don't get it. Why? Why would she want to kill anyone in the first place?"

"Her twin sister died when she was eight. Their parents had strychnine traps all through the crawl space under their house to deal with a rodent problem. The two of them crawled under there one day during summer and Chloe dared Michelle to eat the stuff. She didn't realize it would kill her. Anyway, it changed Chloe. She became obsessed with her sister and the way she'd died. How it was all her fault. She wanted to relive it over and over again."

I shiver, the horror of the story sinking deep inside my bones. Luke sees my reaction. "It's okay," he whispers. "It's all over now. She's going to prison for the rest of her life. Let's not talk about that." He inches closer up the bed, a determined look forming. He slowly reaches out to stroke my hair back out of my face. I close my eyes and lean into his touch. My eyes are stinging again. Sadness weighs heavily on me, fear racing through me as I pluck up the courage to ask my next question.

"Luke, what happens now?"

His hand stills. "What do you mean?"

"Well." My voice hitches. "The stuff my mom told me about you—"

"A little girl used to live next door to my family when I was a kid," Luke says, interrupting me. "Rosie. She was three years younger than I was. She had all this crazy, curly dark hair." He goes quiet, eyes locked on the scuffed kick plate at the bottom of the door to my room. "She was Emma's friend, really. She used to come over and play with her after school. I'd tease them. Put dirt in Emma's doll's house. Chase them through the woods at the back of the elementary school, sometimes."

I've been awake for all of five minutes. I don't know whether I can handle hearing this, whatever he's about to tell me, but if I stop him now, there might never be another time. I hold my breath, bracing myself.

"I was eleven when it started. My dad was supposed to be watching me and Emma while Mom was at work. He went out in the early morning and told me to keep an eye on my sister. He did that a lot. Rosie came over to play with Em. About three in the afternoon, Dad rolled home, steaming drunk. He never used to drink, but then all of a sudden he just ... did. He got violent when he was like that. Emma and Rosie had fallen asleep in the living room. I was in the kitchen, making sandwiches for us because he hadn't come home to give us lunch. I was going to wake the girls up when the food was ready. Instead, Dad came and found me, and he was holding Rosie in his arms. She was still asleep. He told me to take my clothes off."

"*What?*" I want to pull my knees into my chest, somehow make myself small, but my thigh hurts too much. Luke doesn't look at me. I don't think he can. He closes his eyes. Swallows. "I was a funny kid. I thought I was a grown-up already. I didn't want him seeing me naked. Didn't want *anyone* seeing me naked. I told him I didn't want to take my clothes off. Dad, he staggered over to the oven and turned on the stove. Gas stove. The biggest ring. He turned it up as high as it would go, Rosie still asleep in his arms, her head on his shoulder, and he got the metal spatula Mom always used when she was making omelettes. He held the flat end of it in the flames until the metal was glowing red, and then he said to me, you take your fucking clothes off right now, or I'm gonna put this on her fucking skin." Luke stops again, clearly struggling. He blows out a deep breath. There are tears in his eyes.

"I knew he'd do it. He was fucking crazy when he was drunk. I didn't want Rosie to get hurt, so I … I took off my clothes. Dad shook Rosie awake then. She didn't understand what was happening. He told her we were gonna play a fucking game," he spits.

I feel like I'm choking on my own breath. I cover my mouth, hands cupped over my face, dreading what's coming. Suspecting it. Not wanting it to be true.

"And so Rosie says, what kind … kind of game are we playing? She was fucking … eight years old." His voice is so strangled, he can barely talk. "And my dad, he says, you and Luke are gonna play and me, I'm gonna watch. He gets Rosie to take her clothes off because she doesn't fucking understand what the hell is going on, and then—" Luke chokes on the last word, tears falling freely down his face now. He doubles over, shoulders shaking, body trembling uncontrollably.

"It's okay. It's okay. You don't need to say anymore." I shunt myself down in the bed, wrapping my arms around him, but he remains rigid.

"I didn't fuck her. I knew it was fucking wrong. I couldn't have even if I'd wanted to, anyway. I was too young." Luke's face hardens. "Made him furious that I wouldn't fucking try, though. Called me a fucking pussy. Told me I was gay. He picked up the spatula and told me if I didn't touch her the way he wanted me to he was gonna hurt Rosie, and then he was gonna go wake up Em and hurt her, too." Grief shakes him, shakes him hard enough that I think he's going to come apart at the seams. "He stripped himself naked and jerked off while he watched us, and then afterwards he just left us there, naked in the kitchen. He went upstairs and passed out, snoring so loud we could hear him downstairs. That was the first time it happened. The second time, it was my twelfth birthday. I had friends over at the house. Once again daddy dearest got wasted. Rosie hadn't been back to the house since the first time, she was scared, I think, but Mom had gone over and gotten her, said Em could have a friend over, too.

"Me and my friends watched movies at the house. Later on, when it was getting dark, we went out into the woods to play with the laser tag gear Mom had bought me. Ems and Rosie wanted to come too. Somehow, it all happened again. He found us, separated us from the group. I could hear my friends all around us in the dark, laughing and shouting at each other. They thought we were hiding, me and Rosie. When we didn't come out after a while, the other kids ran back to the house. Their parents were there to pick some of them up. They came back with their kids to look for us." He lets out a hard sob. "And they found us."

"Oh, god. Oh, god, no, Luke. Luke, it wasn't your fault. It wasn't your fault." He goes limp against me finally, collapsing as though under the weight of the confession. I press my face into his hair, crying with him. How? How could a boy's own father do something like that to him? How? It doesn't make any sense. "Where was he?" I ask, fighting to speak around the anger building in my chest. "Where was your dad?"

"He heard them coming. He left us there."

I want to smash something. I want to break something. I want to scream until my lungs bleed.

"The parents called the cops. Said I was sexually abusing Rosie. I denied it, of course, told them about my dad, but he said I was lying. That I was *always* lying. The police couldn't decide what was true so they did nothing. They let my dad go, and I had to start seeing your father. Community counselling, they called it."

"And you told him everything that happened?"

Luke nods. He breathes in deeply, sitting up straight, then scrubbing away his tears with the back of his hands. "I was a child. And so was Rosie. Her family moved away right after.

She … she died of leukemia when she was thirteen." Luke looks at me, and I can see the self-loathing in his eyes. It's heartbreaking.

"You're not to blame," I whisper. "My dad must have told you that?"

He looks away, screwing his eyes shut. "Yeah. Yeah, he did. He took care of me, Ave."

My heart feels like it's on the brink of shutting down altogether. All the times that I've felt cheated by the relationship Luke shared with my father feel extraordinarily petty now. Pathetic. I was awful to resent the kindness my dad showed to him. Luke needed him so much.

"I'm glad," I say. "I'm glad he was there for you." We sit together in silence, neither one of us moving, for a long time. Eventually, I lie back in the bed, exhaustion overcoming me. "We're both pretty fucked up, aren't we?" I ask. "But at least there are no secrets between us anymore. What happened, Luke … you were a victim of that as much as Rosie was. And it changes nothing about how I feel for you. I still … I still love you. I still want us to be together."

Luke buries his face in his hands. He's quiet for what seems like an age. When he turns his head, still resting it in his hands, to face me, he tries smiling. It's a twisted, sad smile. "I love you, too, Avery." He sighs. "There's just one more thing, though. One more thing before all of this is over."

"What? What is it?" Whatever it is, I can handle it. I know I can. After all of this, I think I can handle anything.

"Your dad," he says, the sad smile still there. "Max has been cleared of killing the girls. The men in that warehouse. But he did kill one person, Avery." I already know what he's going to say before he says it. "Your dad killed my dad. And I loved him for it."

EPILOGUE

three weeks later

A LOTS changed while I was sleeping. It turns out Luke's no longer a member of the New York Police Department. Well, he is, but he's on sabbatical, taken a year off to go record an album with his bandmates over in Los Angeles. He still doesn't seem sure about his decision, but there's no backing out for him now. He's packed up his belongings, and I've moved into his apartment. Since Leslie's currently serving out an eighteen-month prison sentence for the supply of a controlled substance, I was without a roommate. I didn't feel like waiting to see who Columbia sent to live with me, so Luke asked me to watch over his place while he's gone. It's an ideal set-up: rent free, and the apartment won't get ransacked because there's no one living there.

Luke grabs me from behind, wrapping his arms around my waist as I watch his bandmate and best friend, Cole, load up a rather fancy-looking tour bus that their record label has supplied. "Are you sure you don't wanna come live out the back of a bus filled with stinky boys for a while?" he whispers into my hair.

"Um, no thanks?"

"Ahh, come on. It'll be fun. You'll be well versed in all the rock classics by the time we arrive in L.A. Plus you'll know every single pick-up line ever created and used by man, too. Cole won't be able to help himself."

Cole hears this. He tosses a sleeping bag into the back of the bus, and then points an index finger at Luke. "It's not my fault that you chose to hook up with a hot woman, Reid. I can't help it if I notice her from time to time."

Cole's actually been a gentleman around me, which is apparently out of character. Luke grins at him. He does that a lot these days—grins, laughs, smiles. I notice myself doing it more and more, too. It seems as though the two of us are easing into ourselves a little more. With my father no longer held accountable for such unspeakable atrocities, I've come out of hiding. I've changed my name back to Iris—it was the name my father gave me, after all. When I was born, Amanda said she didn't really care what I was called so long as I slept through the night. It was Dad who'd agonized over what I should be known as for the rest of my life. I always felt a little shamed that I'd adopted a new name to go by; it felt like I was disrespecting him. Now that I'm Iris again, everything just feels … right. I am who I'm meant to be.

Luke's still Luke, but there are subtle differences to him now. Since I found out the awful things he went through when he was just a child, it's as though there's nothing holding him back anymore. He's come alive, and so have I. We're figuring out how to be alive together.

Does it matter that my father actually did murder someone? I don't know. When Luke dropped that bombshell, I was shocked for a long time. I spent days wondering if it still counted, if Dad was still a bad person. But Clive Reid was a drunk who sexually abused two children. And when a young boy confided in my father all the terrible things he'd been made to do, my father did the only thing he felt would keep that young boy safe from further harm. Because it would have happened again. Clive was just that sort of person.

"You're all set to start back at Columbia?" Luke asks. I nod, leaning back into him, enjoying the security of him pressed up against my back. The college administration decided that due to the mitigating circumstances of my absence from school, they would let me attempt to catch up on my own time. That way I wouldn't have to restart the whole year … or lose my spot on the Journalism program. Professor Lang recommended me highly for the placement. Said he was interested to see how many fires I would start.

"And you'll be coming out for the summer break?" Luke nuzzles into my neck, nipping lightly at my skin with his teeth. I feel like dragging him back upstairs to the apartment, but his bandmates are already pissed that he still can't lift anything because of his injury. If we vanish off to have sex—again—there'll probably be a full-blown riot.

"I've booked my flights and everything," I say.

Luke squeezes me harder. "Good. I wouldn't bother bringing many clothes. You're gonna be naked most of the time."

I don't doubt that. I don't object, either.

The time comes when they have to leave. I feel like I have a ten-ton weight on my chest as Luke kisses me and climbs up into the bus. "I'll call you later," he promises. "Don't go falling in love with any other guys while I'm gone."

"I won't."

"Pinky swear?" He holds up his pinkie, smirking like a fool. I loop my little finger around his, squeezing hard.

"Pinky swear."

Cole guns the engine on the bus, hollering at us from the driver's seat. "Come on, fucker! Let's get this show on the road!"

Luke kisses me one last time. His hair's so long now. Way

longer than he was ever allowed to wear it as a cop. With his six o'clock shadow and all of those outrageously sexy tattoos on display, he's beginning to look every part the highly sexed rock star.

"I love you," he mouths as the door closes between us.

"I love you, too," I mouth right back.

The D.M.F tour bus moves slowly off down the street. I stand on the sidewalk, watching it go, my heart breaking just a little. But despite how crappy being apart feels right now, this is something Luke has to do. I know that in my bones. And besides, summer's right around the corner. I feel that in my bones, too.

CPSIA information can be obtained at www.ICGtesting.com
Printed in the USA
LVOW07s0252180315

431008LV00025B/614/P